Reggie

A Stag At Bay

First published in Great Britain in October 2013
by
Wigmore Books Ltd.

ISBN 978-0-9569061-2-0

Wigmore Books Ltd
Wigmore Abbey
Leintwardine
SY7 0NB

Printed in Great Britain by CPI Group (UK)
Ltd, Croydon, CR0 4YY

Reggie

A Stag At Bay

A novel by John Challis

By the same author:

Being Boycie
Boycie & Beyond

Reggie - A Stag at Bay is a novel.
The characters and situations in this book are entirely
imaginary and bear no relation to any real person
or actual happeming.

Acknowledgements

I would like to thank the following people
for their support and encouragement throughout
this venture:
Peter Burden, Joyce Brisbane, Martin Ellis,
Steve Dawson, Jill Fieldhouse, Nina Burden,
Ben Stone and my wife, Carol.

I would also like to thank
Sue Macartney Snape for her wonderful
drawing of *Reggie*.

Chapter One

Reginald ffinch-Leigh walked out of the bank, through a pair of double doors on to the top of High Town in Ludlow. He was a tall man with fine silver hair, wearing a beige linen jacket and pale salmon cords. A yellow silk scarf was tied loosely around his neck, and on his feet were a pair of light brown brogues.

He blinked his lively blue eyes in the May morning sun which beamed over the Georgian rooftops as he paused for a moment on the top stone step. He sniffed the air like a wary fox and glanced up and down the street before stepping down on to the worn flagstones of the pavement to walk up the hill.

As he passed the town's old-fashioned draper's shop, he was hailed by a woman with a strong contralto voice which reminded him of the late Margaret Thatcher.

'Reggie, good morning!'

Reggie stiffened and closed his eyes a moment, before turning reluctantly to acknowledge a tall, spiky woman of about sixty in a green tweed skirt and a horsey Hermes scarf, and not unlike the 1950s plaster mannequins in the shop window behind her. Lady Watkins was chairman of the Marches Woodland Hunt and president of the town's literary festival. He squeezed out a smile for her.

'Mornin', Gwendoline,' he said, already on his guard.

'Now then, Reggie, you won't forget to let me have that cheque you pledged at the Festival Fund Dinner, will you? It was *so* generous of you.' Lady Watkins stretched her small mouth into an ingratiating smile.

Reggie tried to chuckle but managed only a short bark, like a smoker's cough.

'Would I forget?' He'd learned since he'd lived in the Welsh Marches never to forget a charity pledge. He nodded affably and carried on up the hill.

Passing below the arches of the town's honey stone Buttermarket, he pushed through the door of the *Castle*, an ancient pub in an alley on the far side.

1

A pimento-faced man behind the bar gave him a friendly smile. 'How are you, Mr Finchley? The usual?'

Although Reggie ffinch-Leigh was well-liked by most of the local people for his genial sense of humour, that morning he wasn't in the mood to exercise it. 'Thanks,' he murmured and waited while the barman poured a large gin and tonic.

He picked up a *Daily Telegraph* lying on the bar and took it with his drink to sit at a table in a dark, panelled corner.

He stared at the paper's front page for a while without reading a word, while barely registering the half-page photo of the Duchess of Cambridge standing with her husband beside an African elephant. After just a few minutes, he pushed the paper to one side; his eyes fell on the battered, blackened oak surface of the table. He felt himself staring into a dark, spinning vortex which threatened to suck him down into depths from which he would never return, for he had never, in sixty colourful and generally fruitful years, found himself in such a deep hole as he was in now.

He drew a long breath. But, however bad it was, he told himself, no one was ever going to know. He didn't mind so much for himself – he'd live – but he hated the thought of how it would disappoint his lovely Rosita – his own little Colombian rose and the light of his life.

He was hauled back to reality by the *diddle deedum, diddle deedum* of the old Nokia tone he'd never learned to change as it tinkled in the pocket of his linen jacket.

The text told him it was Rosita calling. He let it ring, until it stopped after just three chimes. Reggie sighed; Mrs ffinch-Leigh, although, in his eyes, a perfect expression of womanhood in almost every way, he had to admit, lacked patience.

He filled his lungs again, and held his breath; he would have to tell her, of course. He would never be able to hide the truth from her. But if he promised her that no one would ever know, she would trust him completely not to let her down.

Decisively, Reggie pushed the crisis from his head, gulped the last of his drink, stood up and made his way to the door, where the warm cheering sun outside almost lifted his spirits.

'Reggie! What ho?' It was Archie Pemberton, a tall, slender man in his early forties with a big house and a small brain, both inherited from his father. 'I hear you've taken a table for twelve for the Charity Race Day luncheon. Well done! And I dare say you've lined up a few big spenders for the auction, eh?'

Reggie clenched his teeth momentarily, but managed not to wince. He was going to have to get used to this. Somehow he'd have to inform every charity, good cause, and rustic pursuit looking for funds that he was no longer a reliable soft touch. And he'd have to do it without telling anyone he'd gone bust. *Chinless long streak of whatnot!* he thought as he looked at the languid young man in front of him. He would happily have done without the lunch but it was too late to get out of it now. He produced a big warm grin. ''Ello, Archie. Yes, of course. Lookin' forward to it,' he fibbed. 'See you there.' Reggie didn't want to talk to anyone just then; he nodded amiably before quickly walking across the busy street.

To avoid any more impromptu encounters, he kept his eyes on the pavement as he walked back down the hill towards a quietly gleaming dark green Bentley – a high-roofed, unashamedly opulent vehicle built to last and to impress at a time when Harold Macmillan was still Prime Minister and Bentleys were driven by toffs.

On the other side of the street, Emmet Rafferty was unloading from his dented Toyota pick-up. He took down an old cast iron umbrella stand he'd bought as scrap and had sold for a good price to one of the town's many antique shops. He watched with curiosity as Reggie, in an unexpected show of frustration, kicked the bottom of one of the Victorian lamp posts which Ludlow's Civic Society proudly maintained.

Reggie hadn't noticed Emmet. He looked down with irritation at the small dent he'd just made in the toe of his Jermyn Street shoe, unlocked the Bentley and stepped up into it.

Ten miles west of Ludlow, where the river snaked through a valley between two ranges of round, wooded hills, Emmet's nephew, Mickey Rafferty lifted his head over the high wall of mellow brick which enclosed the kitchen garden behind Mortimer Towers.

In his early twenties, baggy-jeaned, and half-stoned by mid-morning, Mickey tried to focus his bleary eyes on a large bronze statue of a naked classical maiden that stood in the middle of a newly created rose garden. She was, he thought, the most desirable thing he'd ever seen; he wanted her, and he was going to have her.

''Er's worth more'n a grand – just for the bronze,' his father, Charlie, had told him, adding, 'You'll never get 'er, though; you ain't got the bollocks!'

'Don't you bloody dare,' Emmet had growled at his nephew. 'Nor you, Charlie. There's no call to go nicking stuff from Reggie; there's nothin' wrong with him.'

Mickey was gazing at the bronze beauty now with a mixture of lust and avarice and woozily considered ways of removing her from her rocky plinth and transporting her from the formal garden where, permanently clutching folds of cloth about her shapely thighs, she gazed west across the valley towards the higher hills of Wales. He was jerked out of his daydream by a sharp clipping sound almost below him on the garden side of the wall.

He looked down. Gliding beneath him was a large circular dish of plaited straw, preceded by a slender brown hand holding a pair of secateurs, and another clutching a few long-stemmed irises.

His already dilated pupils grew wider with excitement. He knew that beneath the over-sized headgear was the object of another of his most cherished fantasies – Mrs ffinch-Leigh, a former burlesque dancer from Colombia, and wife of Reginald ffinch-Leigh, master of Mortimer Towers.

He feasted his eyes on the straw disc, content to imagine the dark, passionate features it hid from his gaze, when his thoughts were abruptly shattered by a shriek from beyond a yew hedge between the rose garden and the redbrick Victorian vastness of Mortimer Towers. Mickey recognised Sue Price's voice – fat saucy Sue from the village he'd known since he was born – who came up to clean at the Towers three days a week.

'Mezzis Finchlee?' she was shrilling, 'You there?'

The hat spun round like a straw flying saucer and started to glide back towards the house as the red-faced, over-fleshed Mrs Price rumbled into view around the pert perfection of the bronze beauty's behind.

'What is want?' Mrs ffinch-Leigh asked with Latino huskiness.

'There's two blokes, with a lorry; says they're bailiffs to see Mr Finchley,' she blurted between gasps. 'I told 'em he was out, but they says they'll stay till he's back – and just walked in, like.'

'They did, huh?' Rosita ffinch-Leigh spat out the words.

Mickey nodded his approval and grinned as she strode off towards the house.

He chortled a few moments later when he heard a lorry start up and crunch away from the house. (He and his uncle had applied a meagre layer of tar and gravel to the drive a few years before, when the ffinch-Leighs had turned up out of the blue to buy the great Victorian pile that had lain empty for half a dozen years before.)

With Rosita's magical presence gone, Mickey suddenly didn't feel like spending more time on his plans for the abduction of the bronze goddess. He slithered limply down the wall and slipped through a gap in the hedge from the meadow beside the garden wall. As he emerged, an old Bentley S1 in discreet dark green purred by.

The Bentley slowed to a crawl as it approached the elaborate brick piles surmounted by stone griffins, on which the curly wrought-iron gates to Mortimer Towers were hung. Reggie wasn't looking forward to arriving back home, or confronting his wife with the bald truth that, despite the wealth apparent in the massive house, the ten acres of garden, the Bentley and the hunks of jewellery with which he presented her from time to time, he was now, as an economic unit, a spent force; a busted flush. He was – he had to tell her – totally boracic lint.

The insurance and financial services salesman who these days passed for his bank manager had just told him that no further facility could be contemplated until current unauthorised borrowings had been sorted out.

Why, the little functionary had simpered, didn't Mr ffinch-Leigh take out a mortgage on Mortimer Towers? The bank could offer very competitive rates.

Reggie wasn't going to tell the pint-sized, capitalists' lick-spittle that in a moment of inspired caution he'd placed the house in his wife's name and that she would have potent views about putting it up as security.

At least, he thought, despite unpleasant images of creditors sending letters, final demands, county court judgements and – the ultimate humiliation – enforcers in the form of bailiffs, debt-collectors and, in certain cases, heavily-muscled men plastered with tattoos wishing to discuss his future health, he would always have a roof over his head. And although he would have nothing to live on, nothing to buy food or clothes or with which to pay his Ladbrokes' account, no money to fill the tank of the incurably thirsty Bentley (if it didn't get snatched), nothing to pay for the gents' country suitings, to which he'd become very attached since he settled in the deeply bucolic Welsh borders, he knew he would find some way to survive.

He wondered how Rosita, his little flower, would take it as he allowed the stately old car to crunch slowly up the drive to the oval sweep of gravel which the local travellers had laid for him, and drew to a halt in front of the ornate *porte cochere* commissioned by the Victorian glove-maker who'd built the great brick wedding cake to which it was attached.

He switched the motor off and stayed where he was, pondering the next few minutes, and how they might change his life, when his wife burst from the front door and stood outside the car with her hands on her hips.

He pressed a button to lower the passenger window. "Ello, my lovely little Spanish rose.'

Reggie's Spanish rose stood five feet six inches, plus five inches of Jimmy Choo heels. Full-breasted, slender-waisted and well

6

hipped, she was now in her mid-forties – a younger, smoother version of Nancy Dell'Olio.

'Hah!' she declared. 'I no Spanish; I no rose. I bloody furious.'

Reggie sighed and prepared himself for the onslaught as he let himself out of the car.

Half an hour later, having used all his patience and powers of persuasion to reassure his wife that the bailiffs were nothing to worry about, Reggie was sitting in a high-backed tapestry wing chair beneath the bogus gothic beams of his library. Here, to combat the chilly air that filled the place, even in spring, a log fire burned on a grate in a cavernous stone fireplace which the first owner of the house had hijacked from a crumbling mediæval castle just across the border.

Opposite him, in a similar chair, sat Rosita, his wife of half a dozen years, and his proudest possession. Between them, on a fine carved Jacobean oak table as genuine as the house was not, was an open bottle of *Chateau Latour* '76 and two full glasses.

'Might as well drink the stuff before the bleeding bailiffs get their mitts on it,' Reggie had reasoned. He had told her the whole truth about his finances, holding nothing back and, as he'd hoped, she'd risen to the challenge.

Mrs ffinch-Leigh leaned back in her chair. 'You leave those bailiffs to me. They take *nothing*! I tell them is my house, and all the innards.'

'Thank God Uncle Arthur taught me to be careful,' Reggie chuckled. 'He used to say, "Reggie, if you ever find a woman you can trust – and that's a long shot – you put the things you never want to lose into her name." I always trusted you, my little petal, but I 'ate to put you through this now.'

She shrugged. 'I don't give the monkey's, but why you such bloody fool to put all your money in interweb business? They all crooks hiding in islands you never heard of.'

Reggie sighed. 'That's not what you said when we were getting bloody great divvies from them, and the shares was worth ten times what I paid for 'em.'

'I didn't know they crooks then!' Rosita expostulated.

'Yeah, well, nor did I – slimy Eton gits. I'm not the only one they done. There's thousands of punters got taken in. I mean, it looked bloody brilliant. I never 'ad a clue they was running a sort of a Ponzi. They must have got away with a few hundred million, and they'll never get their collars felt.'

'Why you put everything in?'

'I didn't, did I, my little flower. I got this place, loads of lovely pictures and stuff, and a dungeon full of fantastic bloody claret.'

'You don't got it. *I* got it – remember?' She looked meaningfully at Reggie. 'So, now you buy the dust, you skint, what you are going to do for living? I no going to starve.'

'Perish the thought, my little senora. I'll think of something.'

'What? You haven't done no work for ten years. You can't go back to London – I won't let you. You can't run no strip joint or lap dance place in Ludlow. What else you know?'

Reggie had thought about little else since he'd realised he'd been comprehensively shafted by the company in which he'd invested.

'Gawd, who'd a thought I'd be kippered by a gang of lily-handed, pin-striped stiffs.' And now he was going to be bankrupted by the banks and other dodgy institutions he'd borrowed from to crank up his holdings in *GlobWebLink* – a greatly over-hyped international business networking site – when that particular bubble was still at the rapid growth stage.

'Before you knew me, before you came to the *Burlington Burlesque Club*, you know I was a trader – a market trader? I'd buy and sell *anything*, so long as I always bought it for a lot less than it was worth, and I wouldn't get my collar felt for selling it,' he added quickly. 'Uncle Arthur used to say, "Never buy anything for more than you know for certain you could job it out the next day."And I always had an eye for a bargain – didn't matter what it was – cars, army surplus, scaffold boards, gaffer tape, orange juice...'

'But Reggie, you no going to find that sorta stuff up here in the middle of no place.'

'Maybe, but people buy and sell other stuff all the time out here in the sticks too, you know – hay, straw, apples, logs,' Reggie paused, and licked his lips, '...and *horses!*'

'For God's sake Reggie, you don't know nothing about horses.'

'Now, my little Colombian jungle bird, that's where you're wrong. I've spent a good bit of time talking to the hunting types round here about horses. In fact, Ted Buckton has been teaching me how to ride, and I'm doing great. In the autumn I'm going out with his hunt – the Monty & West Salop, they call it.'

'You? Don't be bloody crazy, Reggie. You sixty one years old – that's old geezer!'

'Not so bloody old; just you wait. And I've talked to Emmet Rafferty– he's told me a bit about animals he's bought and sold, and he's the sharpest bloke in the village.'

'Why you hang around with that gaucho when you friends with all the big cheese round here?'

'I hang around with people I like,' Reggie huffed. 'That's my bleeding charm. Besides, Emmet may be a gypsy, but he's a good man; his brother Charlie's not, nor's his boy, but he is.'

'Look Reggie, you may be good dealer, but *horses*? Why? Is like dodgy car dealer. Why not antiques? Pictures? You got the good eye, and if you can buy cheap...?'

Reggie poured himself another glass of wine and stood up to survey the eclectic contents of his library. As well as the hundreds of leather-bound 19th century sermons and 18th century estate records he'd bought by the yard, he'd based his ideas for furnishing Mortimer Towers on illustrations of comparable country houses he'd found in a series of bound copies of *Country Life* from the '50s. He'd developed a bit of a mania for buying anything quirky or unusual, big or small, to cram into any available space. He realised he didn't need to match the furniture with the period of the house, which was, anyway, an anachronistic hotch-potch, and went for anything with age, patina and quality – even a little well-spotted shabby-chic (which his wife didn't understand). 'Yeah,' he nodded thoughtfully. 'You're right – antiques... *and* horses.'

'Oh Reggie...' Rosita shook her head. 'Just so long as *nobody* know you are a trader now…OK?' Her eyes sparkled like Roman candles to make her meaning clear; Reggie understood well enough. His precious Colombian burlesque dancer had as much pride in her dignity as any of the Jane Austen heroines she loved so much.

Not every person crammed onto the raked seating around the sale ring at the next monthly Hereford horse sale looked dishonest, but enough of them did to unsettle Rosita. She stood beside Reggie with her bright chocolate eyes darting, her nostril slightly raised and her shapely lips in a cynical moue. Reggie calmly surveyed the gathered farmers, breeders, tinkers, Irish dealers, riding school owners, hunting folk and knackers' men with curiosity. Although he'd lived out here on England's margins for over two years, this was his first horse sale and experience of the strange mix of countrymen it attracted. He knew or recognised several faces in the crowd although he had no idea which were buyers and which sellers.

He grinned at the adrenalin rush he'd always enjoyed in the old days before a game of poker or a horse race when he'd had a large bet, or at the car auctions, where he'd first learned how to turn a half-honest quid. He nodded cheerfully at an octogenarian ex-diplomat and his formidable wife who lived in his village and liked to drive along the local lanes in a trap drawn by one of several hairy ponies they owned.

'Morning, Sir Compton. Does one of the old ponies need replacing?'

'We're going competitive. Need something with a bit more dash. What on earth are you doing here, Reggie?'

Reggie had his cover worked out. 'I was thinking of taking up hunting next season.'

'Good God! I hope you can still bounce,' the old man chuckled.

'So do I,' Rosita said with a lift of her slender, arched brows.

On the other side of the ring, Lady Watkins, still in an Hermes scarf and tweed skirt, stood protected by a *cordon sanitaire* of horsey-looking girls. Nearby, Charlie Rafferty, Emmet's brother, lurked shiftily by the gap where the horses would come in, whispering from the side of his mouth with a couple of grimy, dreadlocked backwoodsmen. While Reggie had a lot of time for Emmet, who somehow managed to make his precarious living with surprising integrity, Charlie – who was short, skinny, with drainpipe jeans and sideburns half way down his chin – he didn't trust an inch.

There was, Reggie observed, quite a collection of other hobbit-like people drawn by the horse sale, presumably from the depths of the scrubby dank dingles that lay between the rangy hills of the Welsh Marches.

Despite the presence of vets and other knowledgeable horse folk, the buying and selling of horses at a country sale was not a scientific process. Most of the horses that arrived at the sale would have some kind of flaw – some minor and curable, others major and intractable. But often these flaws – or 'dodges' – weren't evident on the day of the sale.

Reggie had been to see his friend, Edward Buckton, a day earlier and casually sounded him out on what to look for. 'Honestly Reggie, you never know what might be wrong with a horse, just from looking at it. It could have any one of a number of dodges about it. It could be lame... and drugged up to the eyeballs with pain-killers. They might be crib-biters or wind-suckers; they could have terrible stable manners, splints in their shins, murmurs in their hearts, an abject terror of traffic on the open road, an abhorrence of farriers, a tendency to buck or leap sideways at every bit of flapping black plastic, and a hundred other beastly habits. Of course, their sellers will do anything to disguise these negative qualities.'

Reggie wasn't unfamiliar with the concept of inaccurate descriptions or disguising flaws in items for sale, but he'd been encouraged when Edward told him that the auctioneers allowed vendors to issue a strictly enforceable warranty that the horse they were selling had come to market free of specific vices. If a buyer took a horse home and found within three days that it possessed flaws which the seller had warranted against, they could send the animal back and the seller wouldn't get his money. It had become a reliable filtering system and, as a result, there were always plenty of genuine buyers.

Reggie had insisted on getting to the sale early and he'd dragged Rosita around the pens outside with the sale catalogue in his hand to see if any of the animals on offer were worth bidding for.

After hours of chatting with local hunting people, he'd worked out that there was always a shortage of 'weight-carriers' – conveyances for large, stout men which were sound, would keep going for a few hours, and could jump at least the lowest of the obstacles they came across.

He'd been looking for big strong animals with plenty of 'bone' – solid looking legs, not spindly racehorse pins. As a long-standing fan of jump racing, Reggie had learned that horses with well-developed backsides tended to do better on the long-distance steeplechases, and he reckoned the same characteristic would make a good hunter.

Most of the animals on offer seemed to be ratty little ponies of sour demeanour and evil eye. An unwarranted, elderly hack gazed dolefully at him, as if he knew the only bids he'd get would be from one of the knackers' men who lurked discreetly on the edge of the crowd, snapping up any lots who were past their sell-by date as riding horses and sending them on to be recycled into Ikea meatballs, cheap burgers and lasagne sauces. There were a few big hefty piebald horses, with hooves like small cart-wheels and voluminous shaggy fetlocks. Reggie knew that these gypsy draft horses were much prized among nervous hunters for their generally placid temperament, with the result that they were now fetching inflated prices. He marked three of them in the catalogue with a maximum bid and moved on.

It was only when he reached a very tall, broad-chested gelding with a gleaming chocolate brown coat and well-polished hooves that his pulse quickened. 'Bloody hell, Rosi! Look at him!'

Rosita sniffed, determined not to become involved in her husband's foolishness. 'He too shiny,' she said dismissively.

Reggie laughed. 'For gawd's sake – that's 'cos he's healthy and been looked after.' He looked at the lot's catalogue entry. 'And look at that – "warranted sound, good heart, no vices". That's brilliant. If I can get him for under three grand; I'll have him.'

'If he's so good, why not everyone else bid for him?'

'If they do, I won't get him, but you never bloody know. That's the whole point of auctions.'

The auctioneer, short with a wrinkled visage and a loud voice made almost incomprehensible by a crackly Tannoy, had sold the early batch of broken-down ponies and knackers' victims and had come to the first of the piebald horses.

'Now look what we have here. A wonderful opportunity to bid for a very sought after, sturdy coloured cob, up to weight and, I'm told, jumps like a gazelle. He'll make a lovely all round hunter. Now, who'll put me in at three thousand?' He gazed around at the surly uncommunicative faces of his silent audience for a few moments until he spotted a slight twitch just in front of his rostrum. 'All right, then, one thousand... twelve hundred... fourteen hundred...'

Reggie raised his hand and waggled it at the auctioneer, who acknowledged the appearance of an unknown bidder with a slight tilt of his head. 'Thank you, sir. Sixteen hundred.'

Many pairs of eyes turned to identify the new bidder, and lit up in those who recognised Reggie ffinch-Leigh, for, since moving into the area, he had established a reputation as a usefully big spender. But they were disappointed when two bids later, he dropped out and the piebald horse went on to sell for double Reggie's maximum.

The other coloured horses went for about the same as the first. Reggie turned to Rosita. 'I knew they'd fetch good money.'

'So, you not the only person thought they were good,' she shrugged.

'The big one's coming up next.' Reggie was already tense as he waited for "Lot no. 163: 8 y-o, brown gelding, 17 hands."

A small woman in a greasy, creased waxed jacket led the horse in. The animal stepped out around the ring with his ears pricked and his head held so high he almost lifted his little handler from the ground. Reggie sighed and whispered to Rosita. 'He looks too good to go cheap.'

The auctioneer cleared his throat 'Right. Lot number one six three. A lovely big gelding, lots of bone. Look at him – calm as a mill pond, and he'd carry plenty of weight. Now who'll give me four thousand for him?' Reggie found the auctioneer's gaze directly on him.

He raised his hand. 'Two grand!'

'All right, two thousand... two two... two four...'

Reggie scoured the crowd to spot the other bidder until he saw Charlie Rafferty, twitching discreetly on the other side of the ring. *Why the hell was a dodgy little clown like Charlie bidding for a big hunter?* he thought – sure there must be some nefarious reason.

Reggie made his final bid, three thousand, and watched Charlie twitch his shoulder at the auctioneer, who immediately turned his eyes back to Reggie.

Reggie didn't move, and glanced across at Charlie who was gazing at him with disappointment.

'If you want him, you'll have to bid,' the auctioneer urged. 'It's here by the entrance, three thousand, two hundred.'

Reggie, wondering if another bidder would emerge, shook his head firmly.

A few seconds later, someone behind him had nodded and the bidding went on up relentlessly, with Reggie listening ruefully, until it stuck at £5,800.

The auctioneer gazed around the ring mournfully. 'Come on, who'll give me six? This is a lot of quality horse?' He held on for another ten seconds until, evidently defeated, he coughed, 'Bought in.'

Reggie was almost relieved the animal hadn't reached his reserve. It meant that if the bidding had stopped where he'd wanted, he wouldn't have got the horse anyway. The vendor must have been hoping for a couple of private punters wanting the animal badly enough to go all the way.

Rosita was gazing at the retreating horse with a look of grim satisfaction.

Reggie forced a chuckle. 'That's the way it goes, my little ray of sunshine,' he said. 'If I'd got him at three, like I planned, I'd have got a hell of a bargain.'

'And if your auntie had *cojones*, she'd be your oncle.'

Nothing else had caught Reggie's eye, and after he'd watched a few more lots go through, he and Rosita clambered down the stand and pushed through the unsavoury crush towards the café, where he knew that a great deal of useful gossip was dispensed along with the thick, strong tea.

As they entered the pungent eatery, Charlie Rafferty sidled up to him. ''Ello, squire.'

Reggie looked up slowly and fixed on the man's eyes which were darting from side to side. ''Ello, Charlie. You were bidding against me for that big 'orse.'

'Why shouldn't I? That was a lovely animal. I could've turned him easy enough, but I couldn't go no higher. I 'eard you was looking for an 'unter for yerself.'

'Who from?'

'In the village,' Charlie answered vaguely. 'If you like I'll tell you the bloke that's selling that big 'orse. He might make a deal wi' you.'

Reggie perked up. 'Do you think he'd sell it for less than the reserve?'

''E might. That's him over there.' Charlie nodded at a tall lanky man carrying a cup of tea to a table. The man had straggly grey hair and was wearing a tweed jacket two sizes too big for him. Horse dealers, he knew, could come in any shape. 'Jack Sanders, he's called.'

'Thanks. Rosi, go and get yourself a cup of tea. I won't be long.'

Jack Sanders looked up blankly from his tea when Reggie introduced himself. 'What can I do you for?' he asked in a lilting Marches accent.

'I was biddin' for that 'orse o' yours.'

The dealer returned a surly gaze. 'Oh, yeah? That was you, was it? But you dropped out at three grand.'

Reggie was used to the local country people's resentment of his obvious London accent. He waved a hand at an empty chair and raised an eyebrow; Sanders nodded and Reggie sat down opposite him at a scruffy Formica table. 'You must have had a big reserve on the 'orse.'

The man shrugged. 'Six grand. He's a good 'oss; he's worth it.'

'But no one paid it.'

'No. Tight bastards! I was sure he'd go today, so I put a big price on him to kip that auctioneer on his toes. But seems like it backfired.'

'Do you still want to sell him today?'

'I don't want to take him home.'

'So,' Reggie said, warming up. 'I'll take him off your hands for two grand, cash, right now. Nothing for the auctioneer.'

Jack Sanders grinned, baring an untidy cluster of tobacco browned teeth. 'I'm not that fuckin' desperate.'

'How fuckin' desperate are you then? Two and a half?'

'Five.'

'Three, and that's my best bid.' Reggie looked him straight in the eye.

'Four. Not a penny less.'

Reggie screwed up his face and sucked a breath through the side of his mouth. 'Right. Three and a half, and that's yer lot.'

Jack Sanders looked at him a moment, before a small shrug of his left shoulder. 'Done.'

'And you drop him off at my place.'

'That'll be another fifty.'

Reggie sighed more than he felt. 'And you'll let me have that in luck money.' He held out his open hand.

The dealer spat on his own and slapped it down on Reggie's. 'No getting the vet in, mind, and fuckin' about on the price when I gets 'im there?'

'No, no. The warranty's good enough for me.'

'That's all right then. Now let's have the money.'

'You can have three now and the monkey when you bring the 'orse.'

The dealer thought about it for a moment. 'All right then. I've got a couple of things to see about. I'll be there at four.'

'And I'll be waiting with the rest of the dough,' Reggie said agreeably.

Chapter Two

Reggie was nearly back at Mortimer Towers with Rosita in the battered Landrover he liked to use for rustic activities when he remembered that Jack Sanders hadn't asked him where he lived – and he'd already given the greasy toe-rag three grand in cash, which had taken all his powers of persuasion to get Rosita to cough up from her own untainted account, along with the extra monkey they'd just picked up from her bank in Ludlow.

'Don't worry, my little treasure, the money'll be safe and sound, back inside your account inside of a week,' he had promised, 'and a nice little bit of Tom Foolery for you – to mark my first deal.'

Now he needed all his self-control not to blurt out his suspicion that he'd just been comprehensively shafted by a scruffy, potless bumpkin. He had no receipt for the cash; no idea where the man lived; nothing to record the deal they'd done – not even an outside witness, for all the help that would have been.

Gawd help us, Reggie thought, *I've completely lost my bloody touch.*

And even if, by some miracle, the horse did turn up, he hadn't thought about where he was going to put it. There were four or five Victorian stables behind the house, but, even after two years, they were still full of junk and he hadn't done anything about getting them cleaned out, or filled with straw for bedding. He'd thought vaguely that if he did buy a horse, he could turn it out into the paddock by the walled garden, but, although he'd asked Mickey Rafferty to check the fences, he had no idea if that had been done.

Jesus, he thought to himself, *it looks like I've lost my bloody marbles, as well as all my wonga.*

For the moment at least, Rosita was calm. She'd even been a little impressed that he'd got a horse that had been bid up to £5,800 in the ring for just £3,500 outside.

'I tol' Sue to sweep the horse room, what-you-say, stable, and get Mickey to bring some straw,' Rosita said cheerfully. 'It should be done while we are at sale.'

Reggie winced. He'd learned that, with his wife, it was safer to get the bad news delivered sooner rather than later. 'If the 'orse ever gets there.'

Rosita turned to him sharply. 'What you say? Why it no get there?'

Reggie gulped. 'He never asked where I live.'

'For Gossake, Reggie! You crazy ol' man. He just take your three gran' and walk away? You know where he lives? Let's go there now.'

'I don't know where he lives.' Reggie shut his eyes for a moment, allowing the vehicle to lurch onto the squishy verge towards the deep ditch at the side of the lane.

'Eh, Reggie. What the 'ell you do?' Rosita squealed and slid across the bench seat to grab the Landrover's large steering wheel and yank it back on course. 'Okay,' she said once they were back on the road, 'Who told you he was selling the horse?'

'Charlie Rafferty.'

'That slippy bugger! He probably tol' the bloke to try it on you.'

'No,' Reggie shook his head. 'I'm not saying he wouldn't but he didn't have a chance.'

They'd reached the gates of Mortimer Towers and Reggie slowly turned the Landrover through them to find the drive blocked by a large, battered old horsebox with the ramp down on the gravel. Jack Sanders was leaning against the side of the lorry puffing on a cigarette with his head in a cloud of smoke.

A wave of relief surged through Reggie.

The horse had arrived! The black cloud of paranoia and self-reproach that had been enveloping him rolled away in an instant.'Hey, look, Rosi. I'm not such an old fool. I knew I could trust him – my instincts told me.'

'Pooh – you instinks! You just bloody lucky.'

Reggie was already out of the car. ''Ello mate,' he yelled at the horse dealer. 'Glad you found the gaff all right. How d'you know where I lived?'

Jack Sanders heaved himself off the lorry, and walked a few

paces towards Reggie. 'You never told me... Charlie the tinker did.'

'Ah, good. Anyway I'm bloody glad you're here.'

'Course I'm here. What d'you expect? You got the money?'

Reggie turned to where his wife was following him from the Landrover. 'You got that monkey, my little rose?'

Walking towards the lorry, Rosita took an envelope from a large crocodile bag and pulled a wad of fifties from it, counted out ten and placed them in the dealer's outstretched hand.

He nodded. 'Thank you, missis. Now, where do you want this 'oss?'

'Stables round the back,' Reggie said.

'Want me to lead him?'

Reggie nodded. 'Probably best.'

'So I 'eard,' Sanders said quietly, walking up the ramp to get the horse.

Reggie watched him quizzically. 'Charlie Rafferty a friend of yours, is he?'

The dealer hooked a lead onto the horse's grubby head-collar and was leading him out of the lorry. 'No, I've known him too long for that.'

'So, you know him well, do you?'

'Oh, yes.'

'Okay, Reggie. So, you got a horse.' Rosita and her husband were gazing at his new purchase as it wandered around the stable looking for something to eat. 'But how you going to feed it?'

'Sue Price's old man's bringing some hay and a few bags of horse food.'

'And how you going to sell it?'

'I'll get Ted Buckton round to have a look and tell him I bought a hunter, but may have bitten off more than I can chew. He'll soon put the word round that there might be a good, big horse coming on the market.'

Rosita nodded. 'You sure it's okay? Nothing wrong with it?'

'It's fine, my little Latin rosebud. It was entered in the sale fully warranted – that means it's guaranteed against vices or other health problems.'

'I still think he too shiny,' his wife said, pulling back the bolt on the stable door and letting herself in. She tip-toed nervously across the bedding and piles of fresh dung which the new purchase had already produced and stroked the horse's flank.

'Bloody hell! Is all greasy, like 'air-cream.' She smelt her hand. 'Bloody Brylcreem!'

'Course it's not.' Reggie said disdainfully. 'It'll just be some kind of finish they put on, to sort of ponce it up a bit – you know, like T-Cut on a car. I expect they do it all the time in the horse shows and that sort of thing.'

Rosita was rubbing her hand vigorously across the animal's rump. 'Is soaked in it.'

Reggie let himself into the stable and gingerly approached the horse. He put his hand up to do the same as Rosita. 'Cor, bloody hell! That is greasy.' He sniffed his hand too. 'It's probably just what they do.'

'If they want the horse to look 'elfier than what he really is.'

'Well you can't blame the bloke for that. And of course they don't guarantee the animal's fit and ready to race – just what they call sound in wind, heart and limb – ticker, lungs and legs.'

'I wouldn't buy a plank of wood from that geezer,' Rosita scathed. 'To me he look like total crook.'

'Just 'cos he's got long hair and he's a bit grubby doesn't make him a crook. If he was a crook, he'd have just taken my money and we'd never have seen him again.'

'I hope you right, Reggie.'

Edward Buckton, with a sharp sense of humour and a drinker's ruddy features, was a gentleman farmer and fanatical hunter who genuinely liked Reggie. He didn't see him as just a flashy cockney parvenu who had no right to be living in one of the area's larger mansions. He thought Reggie had brought with him a good dash of naive frankness to the business of living in the country and he admired his whole-hearted, if untutored enthusiasm for country pursuits.

'Oh dear!' Edward was grasping the large bowl of a briar pipe stuffed with black shag and a dash of locally grown weed as he gazed mournfully at Reggie's new horse. The animal, whose documents had disclosed that he was named '*Gladstone*', was vigorously gnawing the top edge of his lower stable door. 'A crib-biter, *and* a bit of a wind-sucker, too, by the sound of it.' He looked closer. 'And his coat's a bit lacklustre. Have you had his wind and ticker checked?'

'No, he was fully warranted.'

Edward raised an eyebrow. 'Get him out of the box so we can have proper look at him.'

Reggie had some trouble strapping on the grimy head collar as Gladstone tossed his head up and down while backing into a corner of the stable. With an effort and his heart pounding, he managed to get it on and secure it. He clipped on the straggly rope lead Jack Sanders had grudgingly left, and led him out of the stable.

Edward looked doubtfully at the horse. 'Now just trot him across the yard.'

'Bloody hell, Ted! I'm not a bleeding stable lad!'

'Shall we ask Rosita, then?' Ted suggested with a mischievous grin.

'No, no. I'll do it.'

Reggie set of at a lope, dragging the horse behind him until, reluctantly, it broke into a trot.

'Bad news, Reggie,' Ted called behind him 'He's as lame as a ballerina with bunions!'

'But he wasn't when chummy led him off the lorry yesterday.'

'He was probably stuffed to the eyeballs with Bute – powerful painkiller, used all the time to hide the effects.'

'But I told you, he was guaranteed sound – look here in the catalogue.' Reggie pulled the dog-eared booklet from his pocket and showed Edward where he'd drawn a circle around Gladstone's entry.

'Well that's something. At least you'll be able to send him back.'

'Why can't I sell him on to someone else?'

'Reggie, Reggie... Why make extra work for yourself, with all those dodges to contend with. He's a big beast though; he'd make a goodish price just for the meat on him. You'd get a good few Tesco-burgers out of him.'

Watching Edward Buckton drive away in a muddy dented Volvo, Reggie tried to muster the strength to tell his wife about his new horse's shortcomings.

He decided it might be better to organise sending the animal back, so he could get the money before having to own up to his horrific cock-up.

He slipped quietly into his study, dialled the auctioneers in Hereford and asked to be put through to the horse sales department.

'Hello,' he said when the phone was answered by a bumptious-sounding young man. 'My name's Reginald ffinch-Leigh. I bought a horse at yesterday's sale, but I've got it home and there's everything wrong with it.'

'I see. Which lot number?'

'One six three,' Reggie said.

'One six three wasn't sold, sir.'

'Maybe not in the ring. But I bought it from the vendor afterwards.'

'That's against our rules, sir. And we would have no responsibility for any transaction that didn't go through us. After all, we made no commission on the sale.'

'No, I know that, but what about the warranty it was sold with?'

'That only applies if it's sold from the ring and we are holding the purchase money – which it wasn't and we aren't.'

'So the warranty doesn't stand up if I bought it direct?'

'Of course not... sir.'

'But why would the vendor warrant it if he knew there were all these things wrong and he'd have had it kicked back if he *had* sold it through the ring?'

'May I suggest, sir, that he was probably well aware that it wouldn't reach its reserve and therefore wouldn't sell through the ring.'

'But it almost did. The bloke told me he'd put a reserve of six grand.'

'We have to take the bids that are made, in the belief that they are genuine. In this case, it seems very likely they weren't.'

Reggie's stomach, already in turmoil, seemed to sink below his knees.

'You mean,' he groaned, 'he was just setting it up and I've been conned... kippered... totally filleted?'

'All of those, by the sound of it, sir, but I fear there's nothing I can do about it.'

'What? You can't do *nothing*?'

'We do recommend that purchasers peruse our terms and conditions before participating in a sale.'

The blood drained from Reggie's face as he put down the phone.

It wasn't just losing the wonga on his very first deal; it was telling Rosita about it. He loved his wife deeply, but he was under no illusions about the ferocity of her reaction to a fiasco like this, which was entirely his own fault. And she would expect the money she'd taken out of her account for the purchase to be back in it within the week, as Reggie had rashly promised.

He couldn't face her now. He stood up and walked across his snug, oak-panelled study where, normally, he liked to sit in front of a coal fire in a C19th cast iron fireplace and leaf through one of his bound copies of *Country Life* with a large glass of claret beside him.

Just then, he needed air. He opened the door quietly, stood listening for sounds of his wife for a moment, until, confident she was out of the way, he slipped along a short dark corridor to a garden door. He let himself out and walked round to the stable block which consisted of a cluster not just of cobbled stalls, but an old coach house, a fodder barn and a handsomely appointed tack room, which, though rainproof, had now fallen into some dilapidation. He'd seldom had reason to venture into the building, but he thought now it would be a good spot to smoke a cigar while he worked out what the hell he was going to do.

He let himself in and quietly closed the door behind him. He looked around and in the murky light of the high windows he saw a dusty but comfortable-looking old elm armchair. Pulling a large tartan silk handkerchief from his breast pocket he wiped the dust off the chair and lowered himself into its creaky seat. From an inside pocket, he pulled out one of the dark Costa Rican cigars which had replaced his beloved Cuban Monte Cristos since he'd realised he was incontrovertibly on the skids. He lit it, lost himself in a long, stress-relieving drag on the stout torpedo of black tobacco and tried to focus on the crisis he'd brought on himself. He had never run from danger, and he'd known a few crises in his life – personal and financial. But the mess he was in now was in a new league of direness. It worried him that he could have been so careless as to have been caught the way he had. He couldn't even think of seeking reparation from Sanders who'd sold him the horse. The man hadn't had to tell him a single porky to reel him in.

While he tried to get some solace from the musky, pungent smoke, he looked around at the contents of the tack room. It was full of junk – old rugs, cast iron lamps, iron bedsteads, a violin which at some time had had an axe through it, a small grand piano with a leg missing, several deer antlers, singly and in pairs, a brown saddle turned green with age and damp, and assorted furniture that was redundant, damaged or had simply fallen out of favour with the last owner of Mortimer Towers. The old man had gone off to live in Jamaica, left the stuff there and had never come back to reclaim it before he had died. In fact it was old Bertie Cheney-Longville's death that had triggered the sale of the house and the ten acres that remained of the once substantial park that had sprawled around it. While he was still alive, Bertie had turned down every offer for the place; his executors had been more than happy to accept Reggie's offer, which was only the second they'd had; the first being from some iffy-looking people who said they wanted to convert it into a home for 'difficult minors', a use that would have been highly unpopular among the vocal locals.

In the two years he'd lived at Mortimer Towers, Reggie had never taken the trouble to look closely at this stack of junk, but now, pushing to one side for a moment the fiasco of his first venture into horse-trading and thinking of Rosita's preference in his choice of new sales careers, he found himself concentrating on the jumble of objects he'd taken possession of, along with the house, now all piled on top of one another, almost up to the big oak crossbeams. He tried to see it through what he imagined were the eyes of a hard-nosed antiques dealer.

Gradually each item seemed to emerge from the tangle and take on its own identity. From among the clutter of legs, a couple of feet in from the front of the stack, Reggie's eye was caught by a slender, pale mahogany pair that made his heart quicken. They had, to his eye, an unmistakable quality as they narrowed to delicate tapered feet.

He remembered just such legs on a table in the Belgravia house where his mother had worked when he was a very small boy, before they'd gone off to live with Uncle Arthur; she had been allowed to bring him in with her, where the man whose house she cleaned had always indulged him with small treats. The table stood in the high, elegant hall of the house, ready to receive the morning's post. It was strictly not for playing on or around.

In a state of heady nostalgia, Reggie was intrigued by his familiarity with this particular style of leg. Now, happily putting his other hassles to one side, he was once again a hound on a fresh scent. He was sure those legs could only belong to a fine and potentially valuable piece of furniture. Resting his cigar on a prominent cobble, he stood and walked across a floor worn by many iron hooves and hobnailed boots, becoming aware of scents he hadn't smelled since he was a kid in his grandfather's old stable at the back of Berwick Street – moist horsehair stuffing, stale potpourri, dried bird droppings, the unmistakable odour of rodent and very old horse dung.

He moved a broken mahogany chair to one side and looked at the small table to which the elegant legs were attached. It turned out that they were the front legs of a demilune table with two plain, unblemished straight square legs at the back. He lifted an old damask cloth from the top, blew a light coating of dust from it, and smiled.

He lifted the table out carefully, pulled his tartan handkerchief from his breast pocket again, and rubbed the top all over, grinning with delight that he'd never bothered to look at any of this old stuff before. The top was inlaid with an elaborate marquetry shell in three paler shades of maple and satinwood and was still, remarkably, intact.

'Bloody 'ell!' he whispered in awe. 'Pure bloody Chippendale, or I'm Phil the Greek.'

In a daze, Reggie wandered back to pick up his cigar from where he'd left it and sat down again on the rickety elm chair. He sank back into it and glanced up at the cob-webbed beams high in the roof above him. 'Thank God!' he murmured with a long sigh. Suddenly he'd seen a possible way of getting Rosita's money back into her account before the week was up.

At two o'clock the next afternoon, Reggie strode into the Castle Tavern in Ludlow with his head high, feeling a good bit more buoyant than the last time he'd been there, just after the bank manager had told him bluntly that he was now, officially, as skint as a Trappist monk.

He looked around the bar for the man he'd phoned the evening before. Evan Pugh was a small Radnorshire man with a head the shape and hue of a turnip, flat-faced and narrow eyed. He was lurking in a dark corner of the bar, giving the impression that he didn't want to be seen by anyone. Reggie spotted him, walked between a clutter of battered tables and rickety chairs and sat down on a worn crimson velvet banquette beside the Welshman. He tried not wrinkle his nose at the mixed animal aromas that hung around the man's grimy clothing.

'Did you get the photo I sent?' he asked, knowing that Evan didn't do small talk. He held his phone so that the Welshman could clearly see the shot he'd taken and sent.

'No, didn't get it.' The little Welshman shook his head and squinted at the phone's screen. 'Call that a photo?' he grunted through his nose, with teeth clenched, as if opening his mouth would tempt someone to steal the air from it. He peered hard at the shot on Reggie's phone. Small as it was, it clearly showed the table Reggie had just found in the tack room. Reggie flicked on to the next two photos to show detail of the wonderful slender legs and the marquetry top. Taking care not to look too openly at Evan, Reggie was thrilled to see the man give an involuntary shiver and clear his throat.

'I can't tell nothing from that, can I?' Evan shook his head. 'Anyway, why would a rich man like you be selling little bits of furniture?'

'It's not just a 'little bit', though, is it Evan? That's pure Chippendale. And there wouldn't be many around.'

'Two a penny, they used to be; and it's not that good anyway.'

'Listen, d'you wanna see it?'

Evan shrugged. 'Don't mind.'

Reggie knew that meant 'yes', and that his instincts were right. 'Oh well, if you're not interested, I'll go and have a pint.'

As he turned to get up, Evan muttered, 'You get me one too.'

Reggie grinned to himself.

A few minutes later he sat down opposite the Welshman with two pint jars between them. 'How's the trotters?' he asked.

Evan's brow clouded irritably at the change of subject. 'Them's fine, we start training proper next week. But this...' he nodded at Reggie's phone and stopped himself.

'The table?'

'Yes. Where did you find it?'

'It's been standing in my study, but I need the space for something else.' He wasn't going to tell Evan there was a barn full of potential gems among the outhouses at Mortimer Towers.

'I'll have to see it proper.'

'Oh, well, if you're interested, you'll have to come round later today. I'm dropping it off at the auction first thing tomorrow.'

'I'll come now,' Evan grunted.

'No. Come in two hours,' Reggie said firmly. He needed time to clean up the table, and to explain to Rosita why the evil-smelling little dealer was coming round.

He drove up to the house, relieved to see Edward Buckton's mud-spattered Volvo standing outside the portico.

Rosita loved seeing Edward. 'He's proper English gen'leman,' she would always say after they'd seen him. Edward blatantly flirted with her, using his wicked humour and dancing blue eyes that beamed from a booze-russet face.

He was doing it when Reggie walked in and found them in the kitchen. Rosita was shrieking with laughter and battering Edward's upper arm with a small fist.

'You bad man!'

''Ere! What's going on?' Reggie boomed.

'E tell me when he fell in the river, huntin' yesterday, he get out like Mr Darcy, all dripping with water, looking for me to dry him.'

'Actually, I was just trying to seduce your lovely wife,' Ted added lightly.

'You'll be lucky, so long as I'm around,' Reggie chuckled confidently. 'What brings you over then?'

'I wanted to talk to you about that horse of yours,' Edward said.

Reggie was so focused on doing a deal with Evan Pugh that he'd almost forgotten the animal. 'Oh. What about it?' he asked, not daring to hope that Ted might have a solution. But he still hadn't told Rosita the horrible truth. 'Tell you what, Ted, I've got Evan Pugh coming round to look at a bit of furniture in a minute. Come and tell me about it while I tidy it up.'

Rosita's ears pricked up. 'Why you let that little rata round to our house?'

'Because he always knows where he can shift a nice bit of furniture.'

'Evan Pugh?' Ted asked with a lopsided mouth. 'Little fella with a flat face? Looks like a Neolithic wife-beater?'

Reggie nodded. 'That's him.'

Ted shook his head. 'I wouldn't trust him as far as I can pee – and that's not far these days.'

'I don't have to trust him, do I? I tell him what I want, he gives me the cash, I give him the table, he takes it away – that's all.'

The two men walked from the back of the house across the cobbled yard.

'What about the horse?' Reggie asked huskily.

'Have you met Jason de Chateauneuf?'

'Is that who the locals call 'Chatternerve – the Geordie geezer who's bought the Panty-hose estate?'

'Pant-y-Groes, Reggie,' Ted corrected him. 'Yes, the man who wants to put fifty wind turbines along four miles of boggy ridge.'

'Bloody hell! Is he going to do that?'

'If he gets permission.' Ted shook his head. 'He must be mad. He told me how he thinks he's getting on so well since he arrived here, but he just doesn't understand how much he's upset everyone. He's a nasty, self-centred bastard and everyone loathes him. It's the way he seems to think that, because he's turned up with a helluva lot of dough to throw around, everyone's just going to stand back and say, "Help yourself!" They're independent folk up here, and even the people who don't usually give a toss about the landscape are objecting.'

'He's bloody short on charm, that's for sure,' Reggie nodded.

'But he's so thick-skinned, he thinks he'll be able to buy support for his scheme – including from me, damn it! Last night he came to see me, as Master of the Montgomery & West Salop Hunt, and asked me if he could pick up all the losses we've accumulated over the last few years, and pour a pile more money into the hunt. I suppose he thinks that'll make us all love him and support his application for the wind farm. I said we could only accept that kind of support if it came from an active member.'

Reggie chuckled. 'So he's going to start hunting?'

Ted nodded with a grin. 'Maybe, though I should think the only hunting he's ever done was rat-hunting in the low-rent district of Newcastle where he was born. I'll tell you what, Reggie, to get you out of a hole, I'll flog that horse to him. You leave it up here, but I'll take it off you, and anything I get over the three and a half grand you gave for it, I'll keep. OK?'

'Yeah, course that's OK!' Reggie laughed. 'But d'you really think you'll sell it to him?'

Ted nodded confidently. 'Yes, I should think so – using a bit of sales psychology.'

'You mean bullshit?'

'Oh, no. I won't have to tell him any lies; I'll just be economical with the truth.'

As they were talking, they walked into the old tack room. Together they carried the table back to the house and into Reggie's study. With a couple of lint cloths, they gave it a thorough rubbing down with beeswax until it gleamed and the marquetry picture seemed to spring to life in rich 3-D.

Ted stood back and looked at it, impressed. 'That's a very handsome object. What do you hope to get for it?' he asked.

'Three or four grand, I should think. More than I paid for that bleeding 'orse, I hope. '

'Not bad for a bit of tat from the barn.'

They lifted the table carefully and placed it against a panelled wall, where it looked as if it had stood for the last hundred years.

'Thanks for that Ted,' Reggie said. 'What about a quick glug?'

'Have you still got any of that '48 malmsey you found in the cellar?' Ted asked hopefully.

'All right,' Reggie grinned. 'You deserve it.' He took a pair of small crystal glasses from a chunky Victorian cabinet beside the window and filled them from a decanter of the dark Madeira wine.

Ted sat in a deep leather club chair opposite his host and smiled happily. 'Thank God old Bertie Longville had a good taste for his wines, eh? Is there much left in the cellar?'

'Quite a bit, and I've added a ton of cases of claret since I've been up here.'

'But did all this stuff that was here just come with the house – the booze, the furniture, those pictures you found in the attic?'

Reggie shrugged. 'I dunno. I guess the trustees were so bloody glad to get shot of the place, they didn't look into it much. The agents said they'd had another offer from some geezer who wanted to turn it into a kind of delinquents' home, but the trustees were very worried about upsetting the locals and, anyway, half the lead was gone from the roof... you know; it was in a right ol' six & eight.'

Ted nodded. 'I remember it well. We sometimes strayed into what was left of the park when we were hunting. But didn't Bertie's heirs make a claim for the contents?'

'Never heard a word. So far as I know, he had just the two nephews I used to see when I was a kid and my mum worked for the family as a housemaid in their London place.'

'Is that how you came by this house?'

'Nah. Rosita was getting a bit restless in town; every time we went out to the sticks for something she'd be on about how she wanted to live in a gracious country mansion like in a Jane Austen book. Then I saw a bit in the *Sunday Times* about wrecks in the country, and there was this old dump.'

'Yes, it was well and truly on its uppers then.'

'I had to see a man about something in Brum, so I took a drive over here, saw the place, remembered it from when I was a kid – like it was yesterday – and made a bid. I had to up it a little to see off the borstal bloke, but I got it. I bought an old print of the place as it used to be from a shop in Ludlow and drove back to tell Rosi. I showed her the picture and she fell in love with it right away – she's got a bit of weakness for crumbling ol' wrecks – as you can see,' Reggie gestured towards himself and grinned. 'That was it. I bought it – and gave it to her. Best thing I ever did. She's been happy as a lark ever since.'

They'd just finished their malmsey, when the door opened, and Rosita disdainfully ushered Evan Pugh into the study.

'Good afternoon, Evan. Thanks for coming up. Not out of your way, I hope?'

Ted nodded at Evan and grinned with a quizzical sniff.

Evan ignored Reggie's civil greeting and looked around the room suspiciously. His eyes alighted on the table 'That it?'

'That's it,' Reggie agreed.

In a moment, Evan was on his knees, almost as if in adoration of the exquisite object. His eye was level with the top. He made a sucking noise through the side of his mouth. 'Some of the inlay's lifting.'

Reggie said nothing.

'There's a bit of a splinter off this leg,' Evan went on.

Reggie still remained silent. He could tell from the tension in Evan's small body that the man was happy with what he saw. After a couple of minutes, Evan straightened his legs and stood up. 'Where's the other one?' he asked, matter-of-factly.

'What other one?' Reggie asked.

'These console tables were always made in pairs. You need them both for them to be worth much.'

'There's just the one, Evan.'

The Welshman crunched up his face in apparent disappointment and started looking at other objects in Reggie's warm study, as if he'd lost interest in the purpose of his visit. His eyes settled on the cast iron fireplace. 'That's nice. How much do you want for that?'

'I don't want to sell my bloody fireplace, Evan. I was just giving you first shout on the console table, being as I like to support local business. If you don't want it, like I said, it goes to the saleroom in Shrewsbury tomorrow, or maybe down to London.

Evan's eyes took on the bleak look of a fisherman's as a fat salmon starts wriggling off the hook.

Reggie knew that Evan was giving himself time to come to the right offer.

Evan didn't know if Reggie knew what the table was worth, but he knew he'd soon get a pretty good idea if he took it down to a London auction. 'It's not a bad little piece,' he said. 'I'll give you nine hundred for it.'

Reggie was ready for a ridiculous bid. He'd seen Evan's eyes slide sideways, just for a second, as he'd said, 'nine hundred.'

He let out a huge, good-natured guffaw. 'Nine hundred?' he bellowed. 'Bloody 'ell, Evan. I know you blokes like to come in low, but d'you think I just got off the bus from the back of nowhere? I wouldn't be pissing about selling something for nine hundred quid, would I? Nine *grand* might be nearer the mark, but still not enough.'

It was Evan's turn to act indignant. 'Come off it, Reggie, I got to make a turn, or what's the point? We're bloody miles apart 'ere. You take it up to London.' The dealer shrugged his shoulders and turned for the door.

Reggie let him get half way out before he replied. 'Don't arse about Evan. Just give me your best offer.'

Evan stopped, but didn't turn around. 'Three grand.'

Reggie didn't say anything for a moment. He winked at Ted.

After a moment he let out a big sigh. 'All right. Seven grand.'

Evan turned his head slowly, then swivelled his whole body. He fixed his narrow black eyes on Reggie's. 'Four'

Reggie lifted his brow. 'Six.'

Evan shook his head slowly.

Reggie emitted a loud grunt.

'All right, Mr Pugh. Five and a half, and that's it.'

'Five. In cash. Today,' Evan replied.

Reggie looked steadily back at him, for a few long seconds, before sighing gently. 'OK, Evan – as it's you.'

Chapter Three

Ted Buckton drove his ancient Volvo slowly home from Mortimer Towers, across the tranquil water meadows by the Teme, and he chuckled to himself. He'd enjoyed seeing Reggie dispose of the table he'd found in his barn, and he loved the idea of selling his dud horse to the bumptious, narcissistic Jason de Chateauneuf. And if it worked, it seemed that would help to get Reggie out of a hole.

Although Reggie had told no one about the pecuniary mess he was in, Ted had become a friend and got to know him well in the two years since he'd been at Mortimer Towers, and he had recently detected a slight uneasiness in the man. Reggie's agitation at his disastrous horse purchase, when before he would have laughed it off, suggested to Ted that his apparently bottomless source of funds – whatever that might have been – had dried up, and the old fellow was going to have to go back to a bit of wheeling and dealing to make a living. If there was anything he could do to help, Ted thought, he'd happily do it.

He had liked Reggie since he'd first met him in a Ludlow pub, three years before, when Reggie was in the process of buying Mortimer Towers. Shortly after Reggie and Rosita had arrived to move into the great Victorian pile that they loved so much, Ted had asked them to join him and his wife, Belinda, at a big charity bash that was held every summer at Ludlow Castle.

He remembered it well...

The June sun was still shining strongly as it dropped towards the worn stone turrets of Ludlow Castle. A lone pigeon appeared from around the edge of the lofty keep and powered across the open space of the outer bailey, defecating carelessly as it flew over a multi-coloured 'mediæval' style tent, pitched beside half a dozen tall white poles where chivalric pennants fluttered in a gentle breeze. The evening song of the blackbirds perched in the oaks within the castle echoed between the curtain walls while, beneath them, a motley crowd of knights in baggy tights and tabards, and their ladies wearing long trailing dresses and pointed hats trailing flimsy veils, started to pour through the castle postern. With them came Robin Hoods and Friar Tucks, serving wenches in dyed sack-cloth, and a few guests dressed thriftily and unconvincingly as Saracen opponents of King Richard's crusader knights in Moroccan hippy wear, relics of a distant youth unearthed from attics of local country houses.

Reggie ffinch-Leigh and his wife Rosita climbed out of their gleaming green Bentley where it was parked below the castle by the banks of the River Teme. On the way to Ludlow they had picked up Ted and Belinda Buckton, and now they all walked up beneath the castle's soaring walls.

Ted couldn't take his eyes off Rosita. Without any concessions to the mediæval theme of the party, she was dressed in a voluminous French 18th century swagged and layered long blue dress with a tiny waist, and breasts pushed up like a pair of shimmering sapphire mangoes, while her own shiny black hair was gathered up in an eighteen inch pile above her head.

'Good heavens,' Ted gasped. 'You look like Marie Antoinette ready to go out and do real damage among the peasantry – completely the wrong period, but that doesn't matter a damn.'

Reggie regarded his wife proudly. 'That's what she says, innit, my little Columbian orchid?'

Rosita fluttered heavily shadowed eyes. 'I know is the wrong time,' she agreed happily in her heavy Spanish accent. 'But the *medival* stuff is so *ugly*.' She was careful not to let her eyes rest on the dull brown sackcloth garment Belinda was wearing, which made her look like a wandering friar. 'For woman, main thing is to look good as possible,' Rosita said emphatically, 'never mind wrong century.'

'Believe me, no one will complain,' Ted reassured her. He was wearing a pantomime mediæval tunic over an old pair of Belinda's purple tights and a diamante encrusted codpiece she had made for him in papier-mâché.

Reggie glanced at it. 'Great outfit, Ted, but you'd better watch out you don't spill any wine on that thing or it might collapse.'

'Wouldn't be the first time wine's had that effect on him,' Belinda remarked drily. 'But you look magnificent Reggie!'

Reggie was dressed in a full-length robe in maroon wool, trimmed with white rabbit fur and black stoats' tails – a rough approximation of ermine. On his head was a big squashy velvet hat adorned with a pair of peacock feathers. Tall, tanned, blue-eyed and silver haired, he cut an impressive figure as he strolled with his party through the castle gates.

'Does that thing bite?' Ted asked as a pair of pigeons swooping towards them checked and veered sharply.

'No, not any more,' Reggie answered, patting the brown feathered head of a large, beady-eyed goshawk perched on a leather gauntlet that covered his left hand and forearm. 'Not since he was stuffed.'

Most of the two hundred people who had come to support the local hospice by attending the annual Ludlow Castle Mediæval Ball already knew each other and were intrigued to know who the Bucktons' distinguished looking guest and his dramatically voluptuous wife were.

Ted nudged Reggie and nodded ahead at the gathering of ersatz mediævals already milling around the lawn. 'There's a good turnout tonight – most of the local *grandes fromages*, and they'll all want to meet the people who've taken on Mortimer Towers.'

'They must think we're barking mad,' Reggie chuckled.

Rosita's eyes sparked; she'd never really understood Reggie's sense of humour.

Ted mollified her. 'Don't worry, I'm sure they're all very grateful you bought it from under the noses of those chaps who wanted to turn it into a young offenders' stronghold – I know *we* are. Mortimer Towers may not be the most beautiful house...'

'What you say?' Rosita interrupted with flashing eyes. 'Is a *perfick* house – jus' like from Jane Austen.'

Ted laughed gently. 'I know Rosi; the locals love it too, really – it's got so much character.'

They strolled across the expanse of mown grass inside the castle walls, while everyone they passed warily eyed the large, angry-looking raptor perched on Reggie's forearm, before realising it was stuffed and glancing up to see who was carrying it.

Ted's party reached the cavernous coloured tent and went in through one of the open sides. At one end, a raggedy gang of musicians wearing grimy, laced leather jerkins, their sisters' tights and long, curly-toed shoes, were puffing and strumming, apparently randomly, at an assortment of ancient instruments, while the guests milled around looking for their places among the long plank tables and thick rustic benches.

'Good Lord!' a voice boomed softly from behind Reggie. 'It's Henry II!'

Reggie turned to find a tall, languid man in his early fifties, beaming at him affably, and impressively attired in a fur-trimmed robe of midnight blue damask, with long, bag sleeves and a stuffed torus hat, like a fabric doughnut with beads and bells dangling from it.

Ted turned too and nodded. 'Evening, Peregrine. Have you met Reggie ffinch-Leigh?'

'Finchley?' the man asked, 'like a former Prime Minister's constituency?'

'No. ffinch-Leigh, like the bird, but with two small effs, and Leigh like Vivien,' Reggie explained patiently.

Ted completed the introductions. 'Reggie, this is Peregrine Rokesay.'

Reggie held out a hand. 'How d'you do?'

The other man took Reggie's hand and shook it warmly. 'It's good to see an interesting new face around here,' he murmured. 'Tell me, where does your name come from?'

Reggie grinned. 'Out of the London telephone directory. My Dad's name was Sidney Bottoms; it needed changing.'

The lanky man's eyes sparkled at Reggie's unexpected origins and his resonant London street trader's voice. 'How wise! And it's a pleasure to meet you, Mr ffinch-Leigh. By the way, congratulations on your wonderful garb. I wish I'd thought of the goshawk.

Where *did* you find him?'

'He goes with the outfit – it all come from an old boozin' pal of mine from the Coach & Horses in Soho; he's a bit of an actor – Sir Bradford Peverell – he played some mediæval geezer at Stratford last year.'

'Indeed!' Peregrine said excitedly. 'I saw him playing it, and wearing this very hawk, I think.'

'Yeah, well,' Reggie went on. 'He liked the costume so much, he asked if he could take it home – for shindigs like this. I'm the same size as him, and he's lent it to me.'

'Is he really a friend of yours, Reggie?' Ted asked with a laugh.

'Yeah, a good friend. We used to get pissed together years ago, when I first started barking fruit and veg in Berwick Street and he was a young shaver carrying spears and that in the theatres down Shaftesbury Avenue. We reckoned we were both in the entertainment business.'

Peregrine was beaming at him. 'It's so good to meet a Londoner who's not ashamed of it. Most of them try to disguise their origins when they come out to this neck of the woods.'

'Not me – London and proud of it,' Reggie said emphatically. 'But that doesn't mean we can't appreciate the old rural idyll, though – eh Rosi?' Reggie cut himself short. 'By the way, this is my wife, Rosita – she's from Colombia.'

Peregrine lifted his eyebrows. 'My goodness, what a wonderful confection you're wearing Mrs ffinch-Leigh – like an eighteenth century Dame Edna.'

Rosita drew herself up, until the top of her head was level with Peregrine's nose. As her chocolate eyes sparkled angrily, Reggie caught her attention. 'It's aw'right, Rosi – it was meant as a compliment.'

'Of course!' Peregrine looked relieved. 'I'm a great fan of Dame Edna. And I'm sure you'll both be happy here. I can tell you're a real romantic Reggie; you'd have to be to take on old Tottering Towers – and you're going to love living in the Marches and the land of Camelot.'

He was interrupted by a serving wench carrying a tray of leathern mugs and a second mob-capped girl with a flagon of thick golden liquid which she poured into the mugs, handing them round to everyone, although Peregrine declined with a faint wave of his left hand.

'Enjoy!' the wench commanded like a Costa barista, though with a strong dash of irony.

Reggie took a short slug. 'Bloody hell; what's that?'

'That's mead,' Ted laughed. 'An acquired taste which I've never acquired.'

Peregrine raised a hand to Reggie. 'If that revolting stuff gets too much for you, just come and find me. I have a private supply of Chateau Lafitte '66.' He wandered off, beaming and nodding at everyone he passed, greeting those whose names he could remember.

Reggie watched him go with approval. 'Seems like a nice bloke. Is he local?'

Ted chuckled. 'He's the 20th Earl of Rokesay. His family has lived in Rokesay Castle up the road for the last six hundred years.'

Rosita's eyes popped and her small cupid's bow mouth became a perfect 'O'. 'He is a *Earl*? Like a *Lord*?' she gasped, much as a Jane Austen character might have greeted the information. 'But he is charming – like ordinary man!'

'Not that bleeding ordinary,' Reggie growled.

'Oh Reggie – and he liked you, too!' She turned to Ted's wife. 'Didn't he Belinda?'

'Yes, he did,' Belinda agreed. 'But Perry's a very easy going chap who generally likes everyone. That's what makes him unusual.'

At the far end of the tent Lord Rokesay joined his own party. A tall, angular woman in a pointed hat and veil who could have been his sister but was in fact his aunt Henrietta, caught his attention. 'Perry who were those extraordinary people you were talking to – she looks like a blue meringue and he has a stuffed falcon on his arm?'

'They are Mr and Mrs Reggie ffinch-Leigh,' Perry said. 'He's a splendid chap with a lot to offer, I suspect, and she's a wonderfully fiery character, from Colombia, I think. They've come from London and bought Tottering Towers.'

'Oh yes. I'd heard it had been bought by a market trader.'

'He may have been a market trader, but I would say he had a few other irons in the fire. Anyway, Aunt Henri, just you make sure you're nice to him and look after him – he's wonderfully unbogus – and we could do with some good down to earth characters around here to liven up this bunch of tweedy old flatulators.' He waved his hands around the crowd in the tent. 'And Rosita is heaven! You couldn't make her up. You must introduce her to the Tory Ladies' Group – that'd put a firecracker up their backsides!' Peregrine laughed.

While Peregrine and his aunt had been discussing him, Reggie was glancing around at the swirling crowd of mediæval characters, who were cautiously swilling mead and chewing on chunks of dark bread from baskets on the tables, while the fatty aroma of spit-roasted suckling pig wafted from a corner of the outer bailey.

He spotted Lord Rokesay standing with a haughty, handsome woman, looking across at him, while a lot of other people in the tent appeared to be inspecting him, his stuffed goshawk and Rosita.

He turned to his host. 'Here, Ted. Have we overcooked it, coming like this?'

'Far from it. It's great that you've made an effort – and especially Rosi – and the people here like to see a bit of commitment at a bash like this. We're really not very sophisticated out here and we don't think it's cool to be blasé.'

'We'd better be careful then – we can be very blasé, can't we Rosi? But we'll try and fight the urge,' Reggie chuckled. He already felt he was going to like living out here in the distant sticks.

They sat down to chew their way through a laborious dinner of greasy, overcooked piglet and soggy roast potatoes by the light of breeze-blown, guttering candles, while some musicians – two young men in short tunics and ballet dancers' tights which barely disguised their genitals – strolled around, lingering near any young female guests, while they sang *Hey-Nonny-No* and played endless variations of *Greensleeves* on badly tuned lutes.

Belinda caught Rosita's eye. 'Anyone for meat and two veg?' she asked mischievously.

'No!' Rosita protested. 'I already have enough little pig.'

As they wandered away after the meal was over, Reggie explained what Belinda had said.

Rosita gasped, for despite her natural earthiness and all the suggestiveness with which she had performed as a professional burlesque dancer, she could be unexpectedly decorous.

The air was still warm, and the stars were out in their thousands in the unpolluted midnight sky above them as they strolled around the castle purlieus to have a closer look at the ancient place. As they walked – he with his wife on one arm and the stuffed hawk on the other – people came up, introduced themselves and thanked them for saving Mortimer Towers from the young offenders.

'Let's get back and see if Ted and Belinda want to go home,' Reggie suggested later, as they gravitated back towards the tent.

Suddenly in front of them was a small, neatly turned-out jester in a quartered black and yellow tunic, long curly-toed shoes and a matching five-point hat with bells on. From beneath the cap, a few snow white curls escaped around a face as ruddy and grizzled as a mangle wurzel. Beside the jester stood a woman, a head taller than him, looking faintly bored and ready to go home, but more mediæval than any other woman in the castle.

The little man stuck out a hand. 'Mr ffinch-Leigh, I believe? Sir Compton Wynyates,' he introduced himself, taking Reggie's large paw in a tight grip. 'And Lady Wynyates.' He waved a hand at the woman beside him. 'She is a mediævalist and should be in her element. Sadly not, though. Studying the smelly little beggars at a distance of six hundred years is one thing; living like them is quite another, eh? She finds the mead makes her very flatulent, don't you, my dear?'

Sir Compton didn't wait for an answer. 'Cecilia and I live in

Teme Manor, a mile from the Towers, and we're delighted to welcome you to the village.' He turned to Rosita who was gazing at him with amazement. 'This delightful if anachronistically attired lady must be Senora ffinch-Leigh. My spies tell me you're from Colombia. *Usted e mucho buenvenida!*' he added in Spanish with much lisping and guttural vowel sounds, as he took her hand, bent his head and kissed her knuckles. '*Encantado!*'

'*Encantada,*' Rosita responded with glee. 'You are a *Knight*?'

'Kindly Call Me God,' Sir Compton nodded at a baffled Rosita. 'You know – KCMG?'

Rosita had no idea what the man was talking about.

Reggie, feeling he'd been a little left behind in the conversation, came to her rescue.

It means Sir Compton is – was a diplomat, don't it?' He turned to the jester, who nodded happily.

'Her Majesty's plenipotentiary in Guatemala, Uruguay and other former Spanish colonies,' Sir Compton replied.

'I never met a plenni-what's it before, but it's a pleasure to meet you,' Reggie said.

'Indeed,' the little man agreed. 'You must come and see us, and tell us all about what you're planning to do.'

'We thought we'd start with the roof,' Reggie said. 'Most of the lead's been robbed over the last twenty years.'

'I meant by way of recreation,' the diminutive diplomat went on. 'Are you going to hunt with the Marches Woodland Hunt or the Monty & West Salop? And where will you shoot? Have you got yourself down yet for a rod on the Wigmore Fishery? There are about ten people to fall off the perch before you'll get in there, but I'll put in a word for you.'

'That's very kind of you, but I've lived in London all my life until now; the only foxes I've ever seen were running through the back gardens of East Finchley; the only guns are nine mill shooters that the Soho brothel owners like to pull out when they're pissed, and all I know about trout is they've got lots of bones.'

Sir Compton gave a loud, appreciative guffaw. 'That's marvellous, Mr ffinch-Leigh; anything you need to know, come and ask me.'

'Thanks very much, but please call me Reggie.'

'And I'm Compton.' He pronounced it cum'ton. He turned to Rosita. 'It's been a great joy meeting you and if you ever want a good chinwag about your native land, I'm at your disposal.' He bowed, fixed Lady Wynyates' arm more firmly onto his and strode off with huge paces, which made his little legs look longer.

'What a fantastic man!' Rosita sighed.

'He's a bit of a charmer, that's for sure.'

'What ho, Reggie,' Ted Buckton boomed as he appeared beside them. 'I see you've met Our Former Man in Montevideo. If he likes you, he'll be showing you off as his latest discovery to everyone in the area.'

'He certainly liked Rosita,' Reggie grinned, feeling far easier than he had when they'd first walked through the castle gates.

'Have you enjoyed yourself, Rosi – on your first party in the Marches?' Belinda asked.

'Oh, *yes*. So much. Everyone is so *friendly*. They say nice things about my dress.'

'Except Perry Rokesay,' Ted laughed. 'But he meant well.'

Rosita had already forgiven Perry his Dame Edna comment. 'He very nice, handsome man; so *charming* – like *Mr Willoughby* in *Sense and Sensible*.'

'Now then Rosi, he's not a character from Austen. But they all liked you both,' Ted went on, 'except for a few of the other ex-Londoners who have been here a long time but still haven't managed to integrate.'

'Yeah, but little chummy, His Excellency, kept on about who I was going to hunt with, and where I'll shoot and fish!'

Ted put a hand on his arm, but withdrew it sharply as the goshawk lurched forward, beak poised. 'You just carry on being yourselves, and you'll be fine.'

The evening after Evan Pugh had come to Mortimer Towers to pick up the Chippendale table and, as promised, had handed over five thousand pounds in grubby twenties, Reggie tucked his cords into a pair of purple woollen socks, pulled on his thick-soled brown brogue walking boots, heaved himself into a long tweed coat, topped it off with a broad-brimmed, brown fedora and set off across the meadows to his favourite watering-hole, the Fox & Ferret. As he walked, he fondled the thick bundle of notes in his pocket. He would go into Ludlow next morning and pay three and a half thousand straight into Rosita's account. But first, he wanted a couple of pints and a bit of what the Paddies liked to call 'the craic'.

The Fox & Ferret was a long, low 15th century building, made from stone raided from the ruins of a nearby Cistercian abbey, and roofed with stone tiles covered in moss. It lay in the centre of the village on what had once been the M5 of Roman Britain. Ale and cider had been served there to the villagers' ancestors for over five hundred years and the plaster that flaked from the inside walls gave the feeling that, over the centuries, they'd soaked up tens of thousands of conversations, dodgy deals, obscene tales and woeful confessions.

A collection of old pine tables and rickety chairs stood on the flag-stoned floor beneath low beams, which were blackened with tobacco smoke and age. At one end of the bar, the younger punters were playing on fruit machines and watching football on a Sky screen which had been fixed incongruously to a timber-framed wall. Leaning on the bar at the far end of the murky room was a cluster of older regulars – short, for the most part, male, and clad in stained khaki waxed cotton with grimy tweed flat hats on their heads. Around them, blending with the indigenous smells of spilt beer and damp walls, hung an aroma of horse, fag-smoke and cattle dung.

Standing at the edge of the group, but firmly holding court, was Emmet Rafferty. Despite his Irish tinker ancestry, Emmet was liked by most of the working locals. They respected him more than they did the rest of his clan for his straight dealing. He was shrewd, clever and knew a lot about many things – from wood-craft to works of art – and when he gave his word, he kept it.

One of the villagers was glancing through the window. 'Here's your mate Reggie...' he said to Emmet, '...coming across the meadow, looking thirsty.'

The others nodded with a grin. 'He's a card, isn't he?' one said. 'Is that right he bought an 'orse last week?'

'Hell aye,' Emmet confirmed. 'My bloody brother had summat to do with it.'

'What's Reggie want with an 'orse?'

They couldn't really understand Reggie; there were too many anomalies about him.

'I 'eard it was a bad 'orse,' Emmet said, 'but you'd think old Reggie'd be a natural dealer, wouldn't you? He must have made his money somehow.'

'He won't have got an 'orse to go hunting,' one of the others mused. 'He's got a lotta dough, all right, and he lives like a toff – our Sue says – but there's nothing stuck-up about him.'

As the last man spoke, the door opened and Reggie walked into the bar like a craggy old John Wayne straight off the prairie. Inside he stamped some earth off his boots onto the stone floor, took off his hat and walked over to the beer-stained, cigarette-burned bar, aware that conversation had dwindled since he'd come in.

'Evenin' all,' he said in a way which didn't demand a specific response, and ordered a pint of Towncryer. He stood at the bar to drink it while the conversation picked up again.

Emmet Rafferty detached himself from the group at the dark end of the pub. Carrying the remains of a pint of Beamish, he came over to where Reggie stood and put his glass on the bar beside him.

''Ullo, Reggie. 'Ow're yer doin'?'

'Not so bad. Keeping busy. Can I get you another pint?'

Emmet nodded. 'Hell, aye.'

Reggie glanced at Crobin, the landlord, who nodded. 'OK, squire.'

'I 'eard as you been doin' a bit of tradin',' Emmet said, gazing at the thick, black pint as Crobin poured it for him.

'What trading?' Reggie asked lightly.

'Fine Chippendale table...'

'Evan told you?'

''Course. And you bought an 'orse at Tuesday's sale.' Emmet looked up at Reggie with half a smile.

Reggie grinned back. He'd expected Emmet to know about that. 'Yes – a bloody great horse, but a bit fresh for a novice like me, so I've sold it on to Ted Buckton.'

Emmet didn't even try to hide his surprise and, apparently, some relief.

'Mr Buckton bought that big 'orse?' he asked, still incredulous.

'Yeh, but not for him – if that's what you're thinking.' Reggie paused a moment. 'He's got it for Mr de Chatternerve.'

A big smile spread across Emmet's walnut shell face. 'Heh, heh,' he chuckled. 'That'll learn the little bugger. He's trying to chuck my cousins off of the long acre down by the mill – and they allus goes there, every May June for the last thirty years.'

Reggie had seen the bow top caravans with their horses down on the broad verge at the side of the lane the day before. He envied the travellers their freedom from the ridiculous sort of money troubles plaguing him. The travellers would never have been tucked up by a bunch of crooked pin-stripes, the way he had been.

He grinned back at Emmet. 'Yeah, well. Keep it to yourself for the moment, eh?'

'For sure,' Emmet chuckled. Are you going to do a bit more trading?'

Reggie leant closer to Emmet's ear. 'I'll tell you, OK? But don't tell the others. I've been getting a bit bored, with nothing to do, and I always used to do a bit of dealing. I've got some good contacts, down London, and up here, now.'

'What're you going to deal in?'

Reggie shrugged. 'Whatever'll turn a few quid – horses, pictures, antiques.'

'Oonts?'Emmet asked.

'Oonts?' Reggie took a step back. 'What the 'ell are oonts?'

'An oont is what they call a mole round 'ere.'

'Why would I want bloody moles – or oonts?'

'No, not to buy – to sell! I've got a punter wants four hundred moles – for a special job, like.'

'Four hundred moles!? What the hell for?'

'He didn't say, but he'll pay well. Fifty quid a head – that'll be twenty grand.'

'Fifty quid a head? But that must be way over the odds for killing a mole.'

Emmet tapped the side of his nose. 'That's the point Reggie. If it was killing 'em – no problem – all me cousins could do it. But he doesn't want 'em dead. He wants 'em alive and well. That's why he'll pay so much. All to be delivered to the Welsh coast in a few weeks.'

Reggie cocked an eye. 'I want to believe you, Emmet, but – I mean – you can't be serious. And, anyway, why don't you do it yourself?'

'I am. I'm doing two hundred of 'em, but it takes some skill, and a bit of money up front, and somewhere to keep 'em safe while you gets them all together. I reckon two hundred's about as many as I can handle. I'd rather give you half the job than take it all on and then screw it up. These punters are what you might call a bit moody.'

'For gawd's sake, Emmet. I do want to do a bit of dealing, but I want a comfortable life, too.'

'Come on, Reggie, of course it's not easy. If it was, every Tom, Dick and whassaname would be at it. The messier the job, the bigger the pay. You know that, I'm sure. And this one's got a lot of profit in it. Ten grand you'll get for 200 – and it shouldn't cost you no more'n a two or three to put it together.'

Reggie looked at Emmet, trying to guess where the catch was... and yet, he'd known Emmet since he'd first come back to buy the Towers; they'd often talked of many things, which had taught Reggie a lot about the realities of life in the country. Reggie's gut instinct was to trust him. This was a really wacky deal; he could have fun with it... And besides, ten grand was ten grand.

'Okay, Emmet, me old china. You're on.'

Emmet whose features generally gave away very little, looked relieved. 'That's great. Look I'll give you one steer, though never say I said so.'

'All right. What's that?'

'There's not a lot of fellas as knows how to catch live oonts, so to save a bit of time, you'll need pointing in the right direction. You needs to go and see a tricky little operator called Foxy Warren.'

'I know Foxy Warren,' Reggie said. 'He comes in here from time to time, and I know what he's like. I had a few big families of rats with their feet well under the table at my place when I first got there, and he came in and sorted them all right.'

'Fine then. Take my advice, though, don't tell him I said so, and ask him, casual like, if he knows anyone to supply live moles.'

'Fine by me.'

'OK, then. I'll be off. You tells me how yer gettin' on.'

With a quick farewell gesture to the others at the end of the bar, Emmet hooked up the grubby old khaki webbing bag he always carried and left the pub, while Reggie stayed on a little longer to laugh and joke with some of the others.

The smoking ban at the Fox & Ferret was accommodated by the use of a small, foul-smelling room at the back of the pub into which the smokers would go from time to time. Although it had no exit of its own, there was trapdoor into a cellar under the bar.

Reggie joined them that evening and helped to pollute the atmosphere with one of his new, tar-black Costa Rican cigars.

'Has Crobin ever had to evacuate this place,' he asked Guffer Griffiths who drove tractors on one of Peregrine Rokesay's farms and was now standing close up beside Reggie in the confined space.

'Hell, aye! He panicked once. He comes in and says there's a bloke in a suit with a briefcase walkin' up the lane. We had to get out of sight. He shoves us all through that little bloody trapdoor, down a broke ladder and we can hardly move, packed in like anchovies in a tin, and can 'ear them walkin' around the bar – seems like for hours, then Crobin opens up and says, "OK, you can come out now. It was just the new bloke from the accountants, but I didn't want him to know that I let you bloody lot smoke." Bloody 'ell, an' ol' Percy nearly died!'

Guffer laughed at the thought of it. 'Tell you what, though, Reggie, that thing you're smoking smells like some kind of wacky baccy. Last time I was in the Millennium Stadium, there was some blokes smokin' roll-ups that smelled like that. They passed it to me for a drag – bloody hell! I felt like I was going loony.'

'This baccy isn't wacky, I'm afraid. But what were you doing so far from home in the Millennium Stadium?'

'The rugby, of course. It was a good game, but oh, I hated it there.'

'Why was that?'

'Full of bloody Welsh.'

Reggie had often come across this raw prejudice on the English side of the Marches, and it puzzled him.

'What's wrong with that, Guffer?'

'I hate the bloody Welsh.'

'You? You hate the Welsh? But what do you think you are? All of you lot round here may live east of Offa's Dyke and say you hate the Welsh, but you've all got Welsh names, you look Welsh, and in some ways you sound Welsh. Do you think the old Anglo-Saxons just came and drew a line and said right – everyone on this side is English from now on. You're all Celts and should be proud of it.'

'Bloody 'ell, Reggie. You said about this before. Just cos you're a bloody cockney, what does that make you?'

'A right bloody mongrel I should think. Anyway I hope you lot are going to take part in the pageant of Ancient Britons at the fête this year, Lady Wynyates was very disappointed more people didn't show up last time, and most of you can call yourselves Ancient Brits.'

Back in the bar, Reggie swapped jokes and gossip for a while longer before strolling happily back across the cow pastures between the silver loops of the river, with the newly leaded tops of the towers of his house gleaming dully over the willows as the sun set behind him. There was a bounce in his stride which he hadn't felt for a long time. This mole deal, he felt, was like backing a horse at a longish price when you knew everyone in the race wanted it to win. He wondered who the punter was; and what the hell kind of project would need four hundred live moles. In the meantime, the first thing he had to do was to track down the elusive Foxy, renowned rat catcher and man of many rare talents, legitimate and otherwise, and, as Reggie had already found, a great source of information on who possessed tradable rustic skills.

Rosita, too, was happy and trilling like a Colombian lark as Reggie let himself in through the back door of his house.

'You sound chirpy, my little bird of paradise,' he called ahead to her.

'Oh yes, I am! Lara's coming!'

Reggie's spirits, high as they were, flagged only a little. Rosita would want to talk about nothing else until her friend – her most unlikely but best English friend – had arrived in Shropshire. That at least, Reggie thought, would prevent him from talking or giving too much away about the deal he'd now decided he was definitely going to consider. The idea of Reggie ffinch-Leigh, the 'Mole King', didn't sound glamorous, and certainly not plausible, which, maybe, was why the deal might work. The best deals were often done in the most unlikely commodities, he thought, but best not to discuss it with Rosita.

Eight years before, on the day of London's biggest summer party in Belgrave Square, Lara Lydbury had been at her hairdresser's, Carlo, in Knightsbridge.

The celebrity crimper had just got his scissors to her, when the chair beside her was taken by a curvy dark haired woman she'd never seen before. In no time, the woman was telling Manolo, the salon's most up-and-coming young stylist, how she wanted to look.

'You know Betty Rubble in the Flin'stones?'

'Who in the what, dear?'

'Betty Rubble... in the Flin'stones.'

'Thch... Oh dear; never heard of them. Are they a band?'

'OK. OK. You don' know. You heard of Doris Day?'

'Of course.'

'Then do it like her, like she had her hair in fifties.'

'I know just what you mean, sweetie – bit of back-combing with nice little flick-ups. Very retro... and it'll suit your little round face *perfectly*.'

Lara found herself grinning at the conversation between the woman and the stylist. But as the woman was transformed into a plausible likeness of *Betty Rubble*, Lara's own hair was finished and she was out before she found a chance to say anything beyond a faint smile and a nod.

Back then Lara did PR for a Mayfair art gallery and lived off the King's Road in her father's London pied-a-terre which she shared with a female drama student, Poo Ponsonby. At home that evening, Lara was getting herself ready for seven or eight hours of drink and dance and a whiff of weed. She found herself thinking about the woman in the hairdresser's. She had always enjoyed the warmth and craziness of the Latino women she'd met floating around Harvey Nicholls and she recognised in them a kind of kitsch, unselfconscious stylishness she loved.

'There was an amazing woman at Carlo's today,' she told Poo, who had wandered into her room, stark naked but for a pair of eyelashes as long as broom bristles. 'South American I guess,' she went on, 'who asked Manolo to cut her hair like Doris Day in the '50s – all back-combed and flick-ups. I wonder who she is?'

'Why,' her friend asked, 'What was so special about her?'

'It's hard to say, but she had tons of energy and pizzazz, and she was funny, too – maybe without meaning to be, I think, but a sort of Latino Ruby Wax.'

Lara didn't have long to wait for this mystery woman to reappear in her life. That evening as dinner came to an end in a marquee that looked – inside – like one of Saddam Hussein's palaces and filled half of Belgrave Square, she was already bored with the men on either side of her. Her friends always thought it funny to put the most outspoken woman they knew next to the dreariest men at a party. Tonight she was between a braying cavalry officer and a smug City trader, both of whom evidently thought a woman's place was in the bed, and she had taken ample opportunities to dig forks into the back of their groping hands.

She was just planning an escape when there was a commotion in the marquee, with people standing up, trying to get a glimpse of a table towards the middle of the tent. Lara climbed and tottered on a small gilt chair and, astonished, saw a woman dancing some kind of Latin American dance – a fandango, a Flamenco, a salsa? Whatever it was, it was electrifying! The dancer kicked up her legs while she flung her skirt around in a way that raised the temperature in the already hot and sweaty canvas palace.

Lara opened Poo's *Daily Mail* next morning, and found several photos of 'Belgravia's MegaBash'. The biggest one showed *'Rosita Salamanca, Prince Charles' favourite burlesque dancer, keeps her clothes on in a wild Fandango.'* It was the woman she'd seen the day before in Carlo's salon, complete with the Betty Rubble hair-cut. Lara googled Rosita Salamanca, and images of the small bombshell popped up by the hundred, and eventually, some of her with a handsome, older man, who stood a good foot taller than her, tagged 'Reggie ffinch-Leigh'. Whoever he was, she thought, he must be quite a man.

Chapter Four

Eight years after her first encounter with Rosita, Lara was driving through South Shropshire, not far from Mortimer Towers. She wore a vintage leather flying helmet with straps flapping as she swung her silver convertible DB5 along the empty roads, before turning between a pair of stately gate-posts and pulling up in front of her father's rambling Tudor manor house. She'd grown up in the Welsh Marches, ridden her horses across the hills, knew every inch of the country around her home, and always loved to come back. But she didn't often get the chance, now she wrote for the glossiest of social glossies which meant being out partying vigorously while unearthing details of fresh liaisons and personal misdemeanours among the rich, the famous and the aristocratic.

She strode through the ancient oak frame of the front door, shaking her short bob of blonde hair free of the flying hat.

In the drawing room, among the musty furniture and odours of wood smoke, her father glanced up from the *Spectator*. '*Who* did you say you were coming up to see?' he asked vaguely.

'Rosita. I've told you about her dozens of times – my best, wickedest friend. She came to live out here a few years ago – at Mortimer Towers.'

'Is she something to do with old Reggie Wassisname?'

'Yes,' Lara answered crisply. 'Wife.'

Lancelot Lydbury laughed. 'Yes, of course! I know her – a great little fireball. Wasn't she a stripper once?'

'No, Dad – a burlesque dancer. I met her at my hairdressers' years ago, and then she came into the gallery to buy some regency pictures – she's absolutely obsessed with Jane Austen – and we've been great mates ever since; she's wonderful; she doesn't give a dog's bollock what she says about anyone, and she's nearly always right. When she lived in London she was a fantastic source of gossip for my page – people seemed to feel that because she sounds so mad and Latino, they could tell her stuff they'd never tell anyone else.'

'She likes Jane Austen, eh? Frankly, there isn't much of the Mr

Darcy about old Reggie – though he's been a great addition to the local scene; he's splendidly frank, and he doesn't pretend to be anything other than an old market trader who got lucky.'

'Yes, dad, I know; I've known him for a long time.'

Her father carried on. 'And he seems to know a lot about all sorts of things. Of course, the pushier newcomers aren't so keen; while they're trying to set themselves up as local squires and lords of the manor they think it'll interfere with their credibility if they're spotted hanging around with an old Soho barrow boy. And some of the wrinklier women aren't so keen on *her* either; though why they think she'd be interested in their dreary old husbands I've no idea; she's obviously still besotted with Reggie.'

'So he gets on all right with all the stuffy old huntin' and shootin' types round here, does he?'

'Oh yes. Everyone was so relieved that Mortimer Towers didn't just fall down after old Bertie allowed all the lead to be taken off the roof, and even more relieved that it wasn't turned into a home for wayward children, which it bloody nearly was, just before Reggie turned up and outbid them.' He considered a moment. 'In fact, you must ask them back here some time.'

'Dad! To this mad house?' She waved a hand around towards the large timbered hall through which she'd entered. As well as some extravagant hunting murals, it also contained a few dozen stuffed animals, from a squirrel's tea-party to a giraffe whose neck stretched beyond the first-floor gallery that surrounded the space.

'Mad house?' her father repeated, puzzled.

'Lara,' Rosita fizzed as she filled her friend's glass with pink Bollinger. 'I love to live here, I very happy – like a pig in ship – but I want more to do, maybe do something with this great heap of house – what you think?'

Lara pondered a moment. 'There's loads of things you could do to keep you busy – weddings, film location – all the kind of things which mean you could get the place back to yourselves and chill between gigs – and have lot of fun dressing it up.'

'Weddings? That's fan*tastic* idea. Would be so romantic...'

'For some, yes. But you have to get caterers who won't poison the
punters, and be prepared to put up with high heels on your lawns,
sick on the borders and discarded knickers in the shrubbery.'

Rosita chuckled and looked around proudly at her gardens. The
two women were sitting on a terrace of broad flagstones, looking
south across the lawns that swept down to the walled garden on
one side and a small brook leading into a lake on the other, with
some wonderful borders which Reggie's loyal gardener, Harry
Huggins, had created with great care, in an attempt to reproduce
the garden which Huggins' own father, Albert, had tended before
and after the war.

'Fan*tas*tic!' Rosita's mind was already exploding with ideas of
how Mortimer Towers could become the perfect wedding venue,
featuring in every other issue of *Hello* and *OK!*

'The only trouble is,' Lara went on, knowing she was heading
for choppy waters, 'you'll need a website and Twitter and everything – which means you'll *have* to get a computer.'

Rosi's happy face fell. 'O, my God! I say to Reggie we never have
computer. And you know, Reggie lose money, loads of wonga – he
say – in computer scam.'

'Rosi, that doesn't mean you can't use one. You must!' Lara had
been trying to persuade her friend since she'd moved to Shropshire that she couldn't keep up with the world outside if she refused to submit to the attractions of the internet. 'You'll need a
website and email.'

Rosi was making a face when a man appeared from around the
side of the house, and walked on to the terrace where they sat. He
wasn't tall, about five foot eight, with a flop of fine brown hair, a
small nose and a mean mouth, wearing dark glasses and a Hack-
ett jacket in loud tweed checks with pristine beige breeches and
unmarked shiny brown riding boots.

'Hi, Rosita. I hope I'm not interruptin',' he said in a discernibly
Geordie accent.

'Jason! 'Course you itterrupting; this is two girls chatting. But
never mind. What you want?' Rosita asked. 'You OK?' she added
with a grin as she noticed that their neighbour, IT multi-million-

aire, Jason de Chateauneuf, was gazing with undisguised lust at Lara.

He closed his mouth and pulled himself together. 'Yes, yes. I'm okee. I arranged with Reggie to meet Edward Buckton here to look at an 'oss.'

Rosita turned to Lara with a grin. 'Lara, this is Jason de Chatternerve. He buy big, *big* estate where is that big hill.' She waved her hand towards the rising horizon in the west. Lara's dad is Lancelot Lydbury. She is my bes' friend from London.'

She leaned back and savoured for a moment Jason's reaction to her beautiful friend.

'De Chateauneuf? Are you French?'

'You're kiddin' me? I'm from the North East.'

'Newcastle?'

'Like my name. It sounds better in French, don't you think?'

'Yes. It's sweet,' Lara smiled.

'So,' Rosita said. 'You come to look at Gladstone? He such a beautiful horse! So big and strong. Too strong for you, I think?'

De Chateauneuf's jaw tightened at this slur on his masculinity. 'I don't think so. I'm in pretty good shape.' He flexed a sinewy dorsal muscle that rippled visibly beneath his shirt.

Lara already sensed an easy prey. She opened her eyes very wide. 'Gosh,' she said. 'What huge muscles!'

She'd gathered from Rosita's behaviour that here was a man who had turned up to engage in some kind of negotiation where well-placed flattery might well go some way to clinching a satisfactory deal for her hosts.

De Chateauneuf's eyes swung back to her, delighted at her reaction. 'I'm sure I won't have any trouble with this animal,' he said jauntily.

Lara already doubted that he'd sat on a horse in his life. 'It'll be great to see you handle it,' she murmured breathlessly.

'Jason, have some chappagne.' Rosita turned towards the house. 'Sooo!' she shrieked, and Sue from the village who had come in to help prepare lunch, walked from the house. 'Soo, darlin', can I have another glass for Mr Jason?'

Sue scuttled off and de Chateauneuf, feeling awkward, lowered himself to sit beside Rosita in a chair which she'd vaguely indicated.

'So, why you want this big 'orse?' Rosita asked him.

'Well, you know – a bit of hunting, in this fantastic country.' He waved a hand towards the hills in the distance.

'You want to hunt foxes?' Lara asked, incredulous.

'Well, yes.'

' "The unspeakable chasing the uneatable," Oscar Wilde used to call hunters,' Lara yawned and looked away.

'Well, you know – we must keep them under control.'

'You don't need a horde of tomato-faced oafs charging all over the place on horses to catch a few foxes.'

De Chateauneuf, wrong-footed by Lara's abrupt change of attitude towards him, tried to get a grip on the exchange. 'Look, I'm a fair-sized landowner around here, and I reckon it's my duty to be part of what goes on across my land and in the area generally. My neighbours hunt, and so should I.'

'Some of your neighbours do demonstration about willmills, too,' Rosita said. 'Will you do that with them, too?'

De Chateauneuf reddened. 'I feel strongly that we need to move towards renewable energy sources...'

'Especially if it brings in loads of filthy lucre?' Lara said, nodding an inclined head to show her reasonableness.

'Ah,' Rosita announced. 'Here's Reggie and Ted.'

The two men had strolled into view from behind the coach house, apparently in deep conversation.

Lara leaped to her feet and rushed to meet them. 'Reggie! How are you? You're looking great!' She flung her arms around him.

'And so are you, you little Desdemona,' he said, unwrapping himself from her before Rosita's eyebrows got any higher. He nodded as if he'd only just noticed de Chateauneuf, who was also somewhat reluctantly getting to his feet.

''Allo, Jason. Why are you looking like someone out of *Downton Abbey*?'

'Ted told me this 'oss of his is stabled here; I've come for a test drive.'

'You're looking a bit poncified for just trying out an 'orse, if you don't mind my saying so. But then you always like to do things right, I hear. It's OK – Ted told me you were coming.'

'If you're planning to try it, you should probably do that before you have any more to drink,' Ted added.

'No,' Reggie laughed. 'Let him have another to deaden the pain when he falls off.'

De Chateauneuf, with a visible effort, ignored the jibe. 'Thanks Reggie, I think I will.' He picked up the bottle of Bollinger and topped up his own glass.

Reggie turned to Ted Buckton and winked.

When Ted led Gladstone out of the stable, the horse looked like a dozy teenager on a Sunday morning; he was blinking and could hardly put one leg in front of the other. Ted had given him a good brushing to add a little lustre to his coat and had saddled him before he and Reggie had appeared on the terrace. Now de Chateauneuf stood in the yard grinning, and trying to hide his fear.

'He's a big strong horse,' Ted said, 'but you're obviously a fit man; you shouldn't have any trouble.'

He cupped his hands in front of his knees to give de Chateauneuf a leg up into the saddle. 'Stirrups OK?' he asked, having left them much too short.

'Yah, perfect,' the horseman replied.

Lara and Rosita had followed them into the yard.

'What are you talking about?'Lara asked. 'They're miles too short. You look like you're just about to ride the Derby.'

'Yah, but that's how I like to ride,' Jason said airily.

'Actually, I'd prefer it if we did take them down a little,' Ted said. He didn't want his punter to fall off just yet– not, at least, until he'd bought the horse.

He let down both leathers by half a dozen holes and stood back. Gladstone stayed standing where he was, steady as a rock.

'OK, Jason, that looks good; you've got an excellent seat, so now you can just take him out through the gates, turn left and follow the track up towards the ridge, that'll give you a good mile to try him, and get a bit of a gallop out of him. He's got a lovely soft mouth so you shouldn't have any trouble stopping him – not a man of your experience.'

Gladstone still wasn't going anywhere. Jason looked uncertainly at the back of the horse's head and tentatively jiggled his heels, like he'd seen Clint Eastwood do in spaghetti westerns and Gladstone moved off at a lethargic walk. De Chateauneuf turned to the watching group. 'All right folks,' he said, more jaunty now. 'See you later.'

The large horse lumbered on towards the gate, where his rider yanked the left rein, at which Gladstone stopped in his tracks. De Chateauneuf kicked again, and after a little thought, the horse moved off in the right direction, disappearing around the yard gatepost.

No one in the yard said anything for a few seconds, until the heavy hoof-falls had faded away.

Lara laughed first. 'What a bogus tosser. I bet that horse drops him at the first chance.'

'No way,' Ted said. 'He's half asleep, and fairly lame. Jason will be lucky to get him into a trot.'

'Nah,' Reggie shook his head. 'He won't even try.'

'Let's see how he's getting on,' Lara said and they all walked across the yard to peer around the gatepost. Gladstone's large backside was slowly moving up the green track with de Chateauneuf's trim figure perched on top, looking nervous – even at a hundred yards.

'Right,' said Reggie. 'Time for a top up.'

'Reggie – whas' happen to him?' Rosita asked, an hour or so after de Chateauneuf had set off on Gladstone.

'Gawd knows. He probably got lost, dopey git.'

The four of them had finished a fresh bottle of Bollinger while they waited for the rider to return.

'But Reggie, if he's come off and killed hisself, he won't buy your horse.'

'Not mine now – Ted's.'

Ted grinned. 'He hasn't fallen off. That horse wouldn't drop a baby – he's half asleep. Our friend has just walked the horse up to the ridge and is probably walking back, thinking he's in full control of the big strong animal, and feeling very pleased with himself.'

'He's clearly never been on a horse before,' Lara said disdainfully. 'What is he trying to prove?'

'Who knows?' Ted said. 'I'm unfamiliar with the petty anxieties of the super-rich.'

They looked up as the clump of heavy hooves falling on cobbles reached them from the yard.

They all went down to see Jason swing a stiff, awkward leg over the horse's rump and hop around with his other foot still wedged in the stirrup. Lara helpfully grabbed his calf and tugged the foot free of the iron. Jason, flushing, tried to straighten himself and looked around for someone to hand the reins to.

Ted took them and grinned at his potential punter. 'Well, what do you think?'

Jason nodded his head appreciatively. 'What a great horse! He was good as gold – didn't give me no trouble at all.'

'Well done. They always recognise a rider who knows what they're doing. With a fearful rider they can sense it through their arse.'

'Yah, right. Anyway I'll have 'im. Three and a half K, you said?'

'I did, but I've got another buyer who'll pay four. I'm giving you first bite, but you'll have to match that, I'm afraid.'

A quick wince passed across Jason's face. He may have sold half his company for £550m, but he still hated being bounced up in a deal. 'Three seven?'

Ted shook his head.

Jason looked sharply back at him, trying to gauge whether or not he was simply being tucked up.

'All right,' he agreed grumpily. 'But only because I can see this is a quality horse.'

Ted said nothing, but extended a hand, which Jason took and shook far more firmly than was necessary.

There was a big grin on Reggie's face. 'We must have another gargle to seal the deal,' he offered.

'No thanks. I've got people coming up from London who'll want to see over the place.'

He started flexing his aching muscles before moving off. 'I'll send a cheque down with my bloke when he comes to pick up the horse.'

'Let me know if you need a bit of tack, won't you?'

With a curt nod, Jason turned on his heel and strode stiffly from the yard.

Reggie and Ted grinned at each other, while Lara and Rosita squealed with laughter.

''Ere, let him get out of the gates before you start mocking him,' Reggie admonished her. 'At least – wait until the cheque's cleared.'

Reggie was feeling very pleased with himself as he drove the old Landrover across the hills towards Bishop's Castle to meet up with Foxy Warren, the rat catcher, one of the local characters he enjoyed. Foxy was a sharp little man, short in the leg with a long pointed face, rusty hair and a vicious sense of humour. His sideboards were trimmed long and stretched across to his cheek bones. They matched the moleskin waistcoats and green cord breeches he usually wore. Reggie liked seeing him because, although far from the most truthful man he'd ever known, he had a sharp sense of irony and told a good story.

There wasn't much he didn't know about ways to catch, trap and destroy rats, wasps, moles, starlings, even foxes, buzzards and badgers. When he wasn't destroying God's creatures, he was buying – or sometimes just being allowed to carry away – stuff that he found in the remote barns and outhouses his job required him to visit, where the owners were mostly unaware of the potential value of the junk their forebears had been chucking out for the past three or four generations. There were pitchforks, milk churns, butter churns, meat grinders, iron bedsteads – any number of household or agricultural objects long thought to be obsolete, though now eagerly sought after by vintage and brocante dealers from Hampstead to Harrogate. However, Foxy, for whom *Country Living* and even – when he could find discarded copies – *Interiors Magazine* were required professional reading, was well aware of the worth, or, at least, the retail price of such objects.

Reggie had already earmarked Foxy as a good source of obscure items to buy and sell, but on this occasion he wanted to talk about moles.

They met in a corner of the dark bar in Big Ben's *Five Bells*, where anything they said would be drowned out by the sound of drinkers of Big Ben's own brews. Foxy, in tune with the hippy outlook of the obscure Marches town and its former rock star inhabitants, wore an Indian silk scarf around his scrawny neck and a T-shirt proclaiming *LED ZEPPELIN WORLD TOUR 1983*. By way of openers, Reggie asked him if he had anything interesting to sell.

'As it 'appens, I've got a couple bits – I found a doorstop in an old farmhouse up Beguildy way which is a nice old stone corbel – probably from Abbeycwmhir – almost perfick. Must have been nicked and put away nigh on five hundred year ago – the head of a goblin with hardly no wear on him.'

'Bloody 'ell, Foxy, you've got all the sales pitch, ain't you? I'll have a look at that some time. What else you got?'

'A lovely little dog cart, still got some original paint on 'im – must be 1800, maybe earlier.'

'Sounds a bit Jane Austen. My missus'd like that.'

'Her would – it's bloody lovely. I could just see old Lady Wynyates driving it, with one of them little welsh ponies of hers.'

'Why not sell it to her then?'

'Her won't have me in the house – not since I bought a governess cart off 'er a bit cheap like, a few years ago. She has a go at me like a bloody game-cock every time I sees her. Last time I tried to buy summat off her she tried to charge some exuberant bloody price.'

'You leave it to me, Foxy, as long as there's a good something in it for me,' Reggie offered.

Foxy looked at him sharply. He hadn't previously seen Reggie in the role of intermediary dealer, just as end-user. 'You'd do that for I?'

'Yeh, of course. Between you and me Foxy, I miss a bit of dealing. In the old days I was at it the whole time. I've sold plenty of stuff in my time – orange juice by the lorry load, timber, bricks, cars – old nails I've had off the South London auctioneers – when I was a bit of youngster starting out.'

Foxy clearly saw this as a business opportunity. 'I'd always leave something in it for you, Reggie, like a bit of remission.'

'Yeah, I'm sure you would, Foxy, and I'll go and see Lady Wynyates about the dog cart, but that's not why I've come to see you. It's about moles – what you lot call 'oonts'.'

'Oh, got a few oonty-tumps popping up in the garden, have you, in the middle of your lovely lawns?'

'No – not a mole-hill in sight, thank God. No – I want some live ones.'

Foxy did a quick double-take and stared at him. 'You're looking for live oonts? What the hell for?'

Reggie smiled, and touched the side of his nose with his right index finger. 'Never you mind about that Foxy. But can you help me out?'

The ferret faced rat catcher regarded Reggie for a few moments. 'Maybe I can, but if there's money to be made – I'll want a sniff of it.'

'Of course,' Reggie replied without hesitation. 'If you can set me on the right path, there's a ton in readies for you.'

'Hundred quid?' Foxy's mouth turned down. 'And I thought you was a serious man.'

'All right – two hundred – but that's it, and I've got to have a result.'

'You will, Reggie. You will.' He dropped his voice. 'You needs to go and see Owen the Oont, as we calls him, up past Clun way and across into Wales. Nobody don't know much about him, apart from he can allus rid a field of moles, which sometimes has appeared out of nowhere, not long after he's called.'

'You mean he plants a place with live moles so's he can come back and be paid to catch them?'

'I'm jus' saying the oonts turns up, out of the blue, like, soon after he's called in to see if they need him.'

'How does he do that, with live moles?'

'If I knowed that, I'd be much richer than I am right now. And don't you tell him I told you.' He fixed Reggie with a hard, manic glare to emphasize his point.

Reggie noted the same reluctance to be named that Emmet had shown. He shrugged his shoulders. 'If that's what you want. But what's he like, this Owen?'

'He's a mysterified sort of bloke. Sharp, like, and knows all sorts. He's pretty long i'the tooth, but no one knows how old – and hard as a ground toad. Lives on his own in a wattle bothy, with a couple of ship-dogs for company; he makes the best cider, stills 'is own spirit. And he's got a lot more money than you might think, so don't you go thinkin' you can pull one over him.'

'As if I would,' Reggie answered indignantly.

Two mornings later, Reggie was heading further west into the hills of the old Radnor Forest, following the lead Foxy had confidently given him, on the strict condition that he didn't tell the man he'd sent him to, who had sent him.

With the sun glittering through the early, pale green leaves, and primroses and forget-me-nots glowing in the verges, Reggie had a feeling that luck was running his way. He'd had a fistful of grubby notes from Evan Pugh for his table, and been able to put back the money Rosita had got him to buy the horse, and first thing that morning, Edward had come round and had divvied up another £3,500 after completing the sale of *Gladstone* to Jason de Chateauneuf.

Rosita was happy, too; Lara had taken loads of shots of her sitting in the restored splendour of Mortimer Towers to illustrate her piece, *A Colombian Beauty in the Welsh Marches*. And Rosita was in full steam, turning the Towers into a leading venue which would specialise, she declared, in the perfect *Pride & Prejudice* wedding.

Now, on the advice of the cautious Foxy (who had demanded his two hundred up front for the intelligence), he was on his way to see Owen Preece, known as Owen the Oont or, these days, Owen the Mole, and famous from Bishop's Castle to Montgomery to Church Stoke for his skills in catching moles. In the small town of Clun, Reggie asked final directions to Owen's home, and was sent up along a deep dingle, until he spotted a tiny, timber-framed dwelling that clung to a steep bank amidst a coppice wood of birch and hazel. He drove on by slowly, passing a shiny new Landrover which stood in the rutted lane fifty yards below the cottage, and parked a little way up, out of sight of the cottage. As he walked back down the lane, Reggie marvelled that a calling as humble as a mole catcher's could stretch to a thirty grand vehicle, and, curious as always, he glanced in the back of it as he started the walk up. All he could see was a short, handy spade, a small square of plywood and a deep, very clean-looking enamelled bowl, such as a country woman might once have washed her smalls in. Beside the bowl, apparently fitting over the top of it, was a piece of light cloth, stretched over a kind of umbrella frame with a short straight handle that might have fitted into a small recess in the centre of the base of the bowl.

Reggie pondered the function of these objects as he strolled up the bank in an unhurried stride.

The front door was open. A sheep dog on a dirty rope uttered a token bark and wandered over, wagging his tail in a leisurely way, to sniff Reggie's legs as he tapped on the faded green planks.

A small man, not unlike a mole himself, peered from the darkness as he shuffled into view from the depths of the cottage, and for a moment looked alarmed to see anyone at the door. With his thick, itchy-looking trousers, he wore a waistcoat of glossy moleskin. 'Who be you?' he asked.

'I'm Reggie ffinch-Leigh. Are you Owen the Oont?' Reggie said carefully.

'I surely am,' he said with a Marches lilt. 'Wev you come from?'

'Mortimer Towers.'

'I knows it; big ol' pile. But you're not from hereabouts are you?'

Reggie chuckled. 'No, I'm up from the Smoke.'

'Lunnon, eh? But you looks like a right toff!' He appeared to be making an appraisal of his visitor, while Reggie didn't move. Evidently satisfied with what he saw, he beckoned his visitor in. 'You come on in, then. We'll have a chat first, afore you tells me why you're here,' he added, as if determined to get the most out of this unusual visitor.

He turned back into the front room which was cluttered with a century's accumulation of household ornaments and utensils. 'You'll have a sup of applejack?'

Reggie had heard of the local spirit – illegally distilled from cider like French Calvados – but he'd never drunk it. He'd also noticed among the clutter of Gaudy Welsh china on the top of the dresser, a small copper globe for distilling spirits. He nodded warily. 'I'll try anything once.'

Owen waved him into an old elm armchair and took a dusty bottle from a cluttered dresser, along with a pair of thick shot glasses which he filled with a liquid the colour of ripe hay.

Reggie took one and had a sip. 'Bloody 'ell!' he gasped, not without pleasure. 'That slips down well.'

'I 'ad this five year in the barrel, and five in the bottle; 't'would win prizes, if it were legal,' Owen nodded. 'So, how come you've got yourself up from Lunnon to this neck of the woods?'

'It's a long story. Sure you want to know?'

'Oh yes – I likes to know all there is.'

Reggie chuckled. 'I bet you do. Well, to begin about half way through the story, I met up with Rosita, my wife...'

Owen the Mole uttered a short cackle. 'I 'ear she's a bit of a cracker, your missus.'

'You can say that again.' Reggie had ceased to be amazed by the way knowledge of him and Rosita at Mortimer Towers seemed to have spread far and wide among the country people. However,

Owen looked like a good listener and Reggie thought there'd be a lot to gain in trusting the strange old man. He leaned back in his chair. 'Anyway, I met her about ten years ago when she come to do a show in the Burlington Burlesque Club, a place I used to own. And it was a *burlesque* show, not a load of common ol' strippers. It was really tasteful, and quite famous – what you might call a thinkin' man's strip show, with beautiful, elegant girls, and all the arty-farties from the Harpo Club round the corner coming to see it.'

Owen's chocolate eyes were gleaming at the pictures in his head. He picked up the bottle and poked it at Reggie. 'Have another,' he said. Reggie nodded while Owen filled their glasses to the brim, and he glanced around the ancient cottage, with a few framed sepia photos of wizened womenfolk on the walls, a couple of grimy old rosettes from the Royal Welsh Show for farmhouse cider pinned to a hefty oak beam, and a pair of grimy white Stafford-shire horsemen. Dangling from the stanchions were several pairs of dagging shears and beneath the window, a well-worn pig-bench that looked as if it was still used for its original job. He thought they couldn't have been further from the old Soho club.

He turned back to his host, and took another sip of cider brandy. 'Rosi was doing it because she loved to dance and she was fantastic at it. She didn't need the money. She'd been married a few times – to a bull-fighter from Malaga, then a Honduran banana king. Don't know what she saw in me after that lot,' Reggie mused. 'But it must have been something, 'cos the minute we first clapped eyes on each other, we knew it was going to happen. I was already over fifty, with quite a few women and one marriage behind me and a kid. But I'd never felt nothing like I did with Rosita.'

'She wouldn't be like some of the women round these parts,' Owen interjected with a hint of bitterness. 'They be 'ard – know the price of everything. Don't give their men summat for nothing. But before, where was you brung up?'

'My mum, Doris, was a housemaid in a big gaffe in Eaton Square, a very posh part of London. The place belonged to a family of grand old toffs – real ones, not counterfeit like me...' Owen saw the joke and cackled again. 'The head of the family was a cantankerous geezer, by all accounts, called Lord Ashdown, with a daughter called Clarissa, and two sons, the Honourable Piers and the Honourable Rupert Cheney-Longville...'

'Like what used to own Mortimer Towers?'

Reggie nodded. 'That's right – but that was Bertie Cheney-Longville, their cousin, and they used to come to visit up here. Sometimes my mum came up to help out. In fact, one of my earliest memories was at the Towers. I was about three, and I can remember her trying to scare off some bats that'd got into our bedroom, right up at the top of the house. She was terrified they'd get in her hair – or mine, I suppose. And I can still remember her hanging out washing on a beautiful sunny day out in the walled garden, about 60 years ago.'

Owen lifted his head and looked closer at Reggie. 'Who was your Dad?' he asked.

'Sidney Bottoms. Mum married him when she left Eaton Square, just before I was born. They lived in a flat on the top floor over my granddad's warehouse off Berwick Street. But I don't remember him at all. He had to go in the army; he went off to fight in Korea and was killed before my first birthday, so Mum went back to work for Lord Ashdown for a few more years, though she didn't live in any more. Sometimes I would go with her, and hang around in the kitchen in the basement with the cook and Lord A's old butler. But I didn't go there much again after I finished at the old secondary mod school when I was fourteen, then Mum gave up working at Eaton Square. I went round with her to say 'goodbye', and that was the last time I ever saw Lord Ashdown, or Piers or Rupert. My mum hardly ever spoke about them again after that. I went to work helping my Uncle Arthur, who'd taken over granddad's business.'

'What'd he do?'

'Market trader – bits and pieces, household goods, brushes, floor mops – anything for the house that he could sell cheap, even if it had a bit of quality. But never food. He always used to say, "At least if you've bought a stack of ironing boards or scrubbing brushes and you don't sell them for a few weeks, they don't go bad".'

Reggie, loosened more by the applejack, grinned at the memory; he'd loved his Uncle Arthur, looked on him as his dad until he too had died, soon after he'd met Rosita. 'Old Arthur had been caught once, a couple of years after the war, trying to sell ten thousand cans of US Army issue Florida Orange juice which was well and truly gone – turned into a nasty sort of solid soup, they say – and he'd ended up in court. But in his defence, he told the judge the orange juice had been bought and sold a dozen times by various wheeler-dealers across Europe over the last couple of years, and it was never meant for human consumption – it was just for trading.'

Owen grinned, showing his sense of humour and a total lack of front teeth. 'You still gets people out here trying that with sacks of maize cobs or 'taters or a flitch of bacon.'

'Mostly,' Reggie went on, 'Uncle Arthur was a straight dealer. I used to hang around the coffee bars in Soho, helping out a bit – I was a dab hand with the old Gaggia froth machines – and I knew Arthur Bottoms had a bloody good name.'

Owen looked at him shrewdly. 'Why did you change it, then?'

'Ah, well,' Reggie chuckled, 'that was my first wife, Betty. She had aspirations, as they say, and when I asked her to marry me she said, she'd never be called Betty Bottoms. Can't say I blame her, and I was in love. I was just twenty, so I said I'd get a new name.' Reggie shrugged. 'Me mum's family come from Finchley, and I thought if I have to change my name, I might as well make it something a bit different, so I had a thumb through the phone book, found ffinch-Leigh – and there it was.'

'Are you a straight-dealing man, too, then, like your uncle?' the old mole catcher asked.

Perhaps it was the booze that encouraged Reggie to confess to what he thought Owen might see as a weakness. 'Strange to say, Owen, despite my personal history, and what's been done to me from time to time, it's not in my nature to stitch people up deliberately. I do like to deal straight, and I always have. Sometimes it backfires, but at least I can live with my conscience. But...' Reggie indulged in big grin '...I admit that I was party to selling a man a dud horse the other day – but only because he deserved it.'

'And you needed to get out of it, I shouldn't wonder...' Owen murmured.

Reggie wondered if by chance he'd heard about Jason de Chateauneuf's purchase of Gladstone, or was he just being canny?

'Can I tell you why I've come to see you?' he asked.

'You want some oonts off your ground?'

'No, as a matter of fact I don't – just the opposite.'

Owen's normally undemonstrative features betrayed a quick flash of uncertainty. 'You want me to put some oonts down in someone's place? That'd be bitter revenge.'

'No, nothing like that. I've got a customer who wants to buy two hundred *live* moles.'

Owen the Oont looked back leerily.

'But I *kills* moles for a living,' he said quietly.

'But you could catch 'em live, couldn't you?'

Owen's small dark eyes narrowed to black slits. 'Who told you that?'

'I heard that sometimes you'll drop your calling card into a place where they haven't seen a mole for a few years, and a month or two later, suddenly they appear, and you get called in to get rid of them.'

'You gets lots of coincidences in life,' Owen grunted.

'And some people are better at coincidences than others, eh, Owen?' Reggie looked the little man straight in the eye with only a ghost of a grin. 'You needn't worry; I won't be telling anyone how you drum up business. And, by the way, I can pay you twice as much for a live mole than anyone would for dead 'un.'

Owen sniffed. 'What does they want 'em live for? Wouldn't they just want the pelts?'

'No, they wouldn't. All I'll tell you is they'll pay for healthy, live moles.'

Owen the Mole furrowed his rugged brow. 'Who's been talkin' to you 'bout me?'

Reggie firmly tapped the side of his nose with his right index finger, in a way which Owen understood. 'Can you get 'em?' he asked.

Saying nothing, Owen tipped the bottle and poured a little more applejack into Reggie's glass. He leaning back in his chair, he sniffed again. 'How much a head?' he asked.

Chapter Five

'Why you so'appy?' Mrs Reginald ffinch-Leigh cocked her small dark head at her husband, who sat opposite her at a table in the Speedy Snail, their favourite eating place. They'd met there after Reggie had returned from Owen the Oont's lair with a big, enigmatic smile on his tanned face.

'Aren't you just happy that I'm happy, my little rosebud?'

'Course I am; I just not used to it at the moment.'

'There's more where this came from,' Reggie chuckled loudly. 'Now I've got the bit between m'teeth,' he added inscrutably.

'Reggie!' Peregrine Rokesay's distinctive upper-crust voice boomed across the small cluttered dining room of the Snail, followed by his languid figure, clothed in a tweed suit of subtle cut and bright checks. 'Why have you got the bit between your teeth? And I hear you're going hunting, and buying and selling the odd horse – very odd, I'm told. And our local billionaire is going to take it hunting, too!'

'Let's hope so,' Reggie said with a wink, unsurprised by Lord Rokesay's keen grasp on local intrigue. 'Though I don't suppose he'll be up at the front much.'

Peregrine grinned. 'No, but I'm looking forward to seeing you all at the Monty & West Salop Hunt Ball; will you come on our table, then we can sneak off and watch the footer together? And you too, Mrs f...f...finchley, will you come and show us all how to dance?'

Rosita shrieked with laughter. 'Perry, I teach you the tango, proper – OK?'

'I can't wait,' he replied and, nodding genially, moved on to join his table on the other side of the room.

Rosita leaned across the table with a show of affection for her husband.

'Reggie, I very happy, too.'

'Delighted to hear it, but then you always are, that's what I love about you.'

'I had some good news today. My hairdresser, Samantha, I tol' you she's getting married.'

'Maybe you did, my flower, but I've forgotten.'

'Oh my God, Reggie. You getting dimension.'

'Dimension?' Reggie queried.

'Like old man, forget things.'

'Oh, yeah. Dementia. No, I'm not, but I can't remember every little bit of stuff you tell me, can I, my cherub?'

Rosita let out an exasperated sigh. 'This is important. Samantha's getting married and the place she was going to have her reception has been burned down last weekend, it was in the *Wassaname Carry-on?'*

'Ludlow Clarion?'

'Anyway, so she needs somewhere for the reception. I say she can have it at the Towers!'

'What?! That's a bit premature, isn't it?'

'You a bit premature. I have everything ready for it.'

'Already?' Reggie tried not to let his doubts show. 'You are a clever little senora, aren't you?'

'Lara gave me so many ideas,' Rosita started eagerly. 'We going to have a romantic bridge over the lake full of lilies and ecstatic gold fishes...'

'Ecstatic goldfish?' Reggie murmured.

'Erotic?' Rosita ventured.

'D'you mean exotic? Like carp?'

'Carps, that's it! And there'll be harbours in private places around the gardens, and big beautiful lawns where people can walk around in their naked feet. And the toilets will be like little log cabins.'

'I hope you don't think I'm going to do all this?'

'No, no. Harry Huggins is going to do it all with his father.'

'But old Albert Huggins must be over ninety. I thought he was old when I came up here as a boy.'

'Harry say he very strong for his age. And don't worry about money. I do it all – as business.'

'But Rosi, you're a dancer, not a businesswoman.'

'I got very good instinks for business; Ted Buckton say so.'

'Oh yeah?'

'And how did your business go today?' Rosita diverted the conversation.

'Didn't get much done in the end.' Reggie felt it unwise to tell his wife about his prospective deal with Emmet Rafferty, or his meeting with Owen the Oont that day.

'OK, then,' his wife went on. 'I got other news for you.'

Reggie sensed that she wasn't sure how enthusiastic he would be over this extra item. 'Oh yeah?' he said guardedly.

'When I was in the village this morning, posting a plane ticket to my sister, I saw Lady Wynyates, and she say to me - can we hold the fête in our garden?'

'Bloody hell, Rosi, that's only two weeks from now isn't it? What's wrong with where they usually have it?'

'They say the ground's too wet from the floods and it won't be dry in time, and will turn into like a swamp, with everyone tramping around on it.'

'So we're going to have them tramping all over our garden, instead – just when you want to be getting it nice for the wedding party.'

'Don't worry, Reggie,' Rosita said, putting a reassuring hand on his. 'Harry Huggins will be in charge. He say no problem.'

Between Rosita's announcement that they were to hold the village fête at the Towers and the day that major event on the village calendar was due to happen, the annual Charity Race Day was held at the local race-course. The old-fashioned steeplechase venue was surrounded by picturesque Shropshire Hills from which, on less sunny days, a brisk wind tended to descend and freeze the punters on the top of the cast iron Edwardian grandstand. In view of this, that day's event was being held in a monster marquee specially erected for it and now ready for lunch to be served to four hundred long-suffering donors who turned out every year for an indifferent lunch and six or seven undistinguished horse races. Reggie, having volunteered when times were better to host a table of ten, had not been able to wriggle out of this year's event.

The race day, despite its shortcomings as an entertainment, was a very popular social occasion, held to raise money for injured jockeys. Reggie was careful not to broadcast his scepticism about this cause, but as they stood by their table, muttered to his wife, 'Of course jockeys are going to get injured. They're bound to, if they choose to make a living pounding over large jumps on bloody great thick, mutinous animals.'

'Then why you so keen to do it yourself?'

Reggie had told her that Ted Buckton was trying to persuade him to get some useful experience by riding a horse in the Monty and West Salop Hunt Ride the following week.

'I was winding you up, my gullible little princess. I'm not bloody mad, am I?' he muttered to Rosita as they sat down at their table. 'But now I'd better decide who is going to sit where at this table.'

'I want Sir Wynyates next to me, so we can talk in Spanish.' Rosita loved Sir Compton Wynyates' extravagant flirtation.

'You have all the fun don't you? I'll have his missus on one side and Belinda Buckton on the other.'

'I hope they won't get you too excited,' Rosita said, aware that Lady Wynyates was well-known for her flirtatious advances.

Beneath the roof of the marquee, their guests were drifting across the sisal matting that covered the uneven turf, towards the ffinch-Leigh table. Once most of them were sitting down, an army of stout, clumsy teenagers were let loose into the tent and were soon serving up gobbets of overcooked, unidentifiable meat and a selection of tepid vegetables, while Reggie, trying to forget the bill he would get for it, sloshed wine into his guests' glasses to deaden the experience of eating.

As he chewed his way through the main course and a helping of cheesecake with the texture of cement, he kept up a healthy banter with Lady Wynyates, whose hand Reggie would find every so often lingering on his thigh with an almost imperceptible squeeze. He had no idea if she was stimulated by his status as the unlikely owner of Mortimer Towers, or if she had sexual designs on him.

'Have you heard about Terry Cotter the potter and the landlady of the Speedy Snail?' she asked him with a knowing look.

Lady Wynyates seemed often to have fresh stories to tell of marital indiscretions in the village and soon Reggie was chuckling loudly, while Rosita, who had often voiced the view that Lady W ''ad the 'ots' for Reggie, threw him a few warnings with her dark flashing eyes.

After lunch, Dennis Lennon, a local auctioneer with short legs, a purple face and a loud pompous voice stood up, grasping a microphone into which he boomed with loud popping and squealing.

'Now we've got a large number of fantastic lots to sell,' he announced grimly. 'And I hope you will all bid generously to support this excellent cause.'

His audience stifled a soft groan.

Reggie, who saw some value in participating in this aspect of the event, moved his chair round 90 degrees and, lowering it back onto the ground, put one of the rear legs into what might have been a rabbit hole under the sisal matting. He started gently to tip backwards, while the side of his chair got hooked onto his neighbour's, taking Lady Wynyates inexorably down with him so that they both found themselves on their backs– in Lady Wynyates' case, with her skirt spread out around her waist and her naked legs waving in the air, giving a clear view of her surprisingly brief and decorative lace underwear.

Reggie, even as he'd started to tumble was aware that his neighbour was coming with him, and that they would end up in a state of potential embarrassment. The same thought had occurred to the photographer from the *Shropshire Clarion*, on duty to catch some pictures of this high profile social event. He was handily close, as it happened, and started snapping in rapid time as soon as Lady Wynyates had hit the ground.

Most of the people on the nearby tables had witnessed the undignified fall, and the air was thick with part-stifled laughter, while Reggie wondered where the photographs would end up.

As the excitement over Reggie's and Lady Wynyates' debacle died down, Dennis Lennon coughed loudly into his mic.

'Now then, to start with, a wonderful painting by Lady Watkins, chairman of the Marches Woodland Hunt – an oil painting, apparently, called '*Gone to Ground*,' he intoned, doing his best to disguise any hint of his own views. He waved his arm towards the large canvas in a shiny gilt frame, now being held up by one of the hunt terrier men, a stocky man in a tweed suit. With a horrified start, he had his first view of the painting which showed a group of deformed fox-hounds crouching around a hole in the earth of a woodland dell, into which two thick-limbed, low-browed men were releasing their frantically barking terriers, while a number of Hogarthian men in red coats stood watching on the ground with mad, staring eyes, while others looked on from the backs of implausibly large horses.

Still smarting from the sight, the auctioneer turned back to face the gathering and challenged them not to bid.

It was Reggie's policy on these occasions to start the bidding with a noisy flourish then, having made his mark, to let others take up the running, and get lumbered with a day's shooting or fishing they didn't really want, or a week in a flat in South Kensington they would never use.

'Now what am I bid for this excellent piece of artwork?' Lennon the auctioneer bellowed, with eyes clearly averted from the picture he was selling. 'Must be worth a lot of money – an original painting by Lady Watkins. Who'll bid me a thousand pounds to get us going?'

There was a drop in the background buzz of conversation as everyone waited to see who would risk a bid. As the silence intensified, the auctioneer looked around resentfully. 'Come on now, this is a very worthy charity.' He evidently wouldn't go as far as commending the actual item on sale.

Reggie saw his chance. 'Five 'undred quid,' he said loudly.

The auctioneer perked up. 'Thank you, Mr Finchley – a man who knows quality when he sees it.'

His audience, aware of Lady Watkins' opinion of her own work, tittered anonymously, guessing that Reggie was bidding out of support for the charity, not out of any appreciation for the work.

'Now, who'll give me seven hundred?'

As no one responded, the volume of conversation began to rise again.

'Ladies and gentlemen, we cannot allow an important item like this to go for so little. Who'll give me six hundred?... Five hundred and fifty?'

Reggie glanced over at the next table where Gwendoline Watkins sat with other grandees of the Marches Woodland Hunt. He almost felt sorry for her although not as sorry he would feel for himself if he got stuck with the picture, which, as the seconds ticked by, was beginning to look likely.

The auctioneer was conscious that the longer he left it, the more embarrassing it would become. 'Well it looks as if Mr Reginald ffinch-Leigh has made all the running on this one. Going once, going twice...' he banged down his gavel. 'Sold! To Mr Reggie ffinch-Leigh!'

Reggie was ready for this. Whatever happened he would have to pay for the ghastly daub, but he was damned if he was going to take it home. 'Put it back in!' he called across the marquee.

'Mr ffinch-Leigh, having won this wonderful, atmospheric hunting picture, instead of taking it home with him...' Dennis Lennon was having trouble keeping the laughter from his voice, 'has very generously re-donated it for a second sale. So, for a second time, for this excellent picture, *Gone to Ground*, by Lady Watkins, what am I bid?'

The background murmur of conversation dwindled to nothing but as Dennis Lennon's eyes swept the room for bidders he was beginning to look uncomfortable, until a hand, reluctantly raised by a weary-looking man on the hunt grandees' table, signalled a bid. 'A thousand pounds!'

The auctioneer pounced. 'Thank you, Sir Harry Watkins...'

There was a ripple of stifled laughter, cut short only by a crisp counterbid, delivered in distinctive Geordie tones. 'Twelve 'oondrid!'

'New bidder, Mr de Chatternerve. Thank you. Who'll give me fifteen hundred... He gazed around the marquee. I'll take a bid of one thousand three hundred...'

He gazed expectantly at Sir Harry Watkins, but having done his duty by his wife, Sir Harry evidently wasn't prepared to take his generosity to absurd lengths. No doubt he considered that the unpopular new local multi-millionaire had some kind of duty to get him out of trouble. 'Thank you for your generosity, Mr de Chatternerve, it looks as if you'll be the lucky one who'll be taking this fine picture home, where I'm sure it will enjoy pride of place.'

The next day, Reggie was still laughing about Jason de Chateauneuf's misfortune, while he and Ted Buckton were sitting on hay bales in Ted's yard, drinking Floppidick, a viciously potent cider made by some renegade farmers in Radnorshire. They were already on their third pint.

'I s'pose he thought ol' Gwendoline Watkins would be all over 'im if he bought it. He'll learn,' Reggie laughed. 'She'll jus tell 'im how lucky he was to get it.'

'No, I heard him afterwards,' Ted said. 'He was telling someone he thought it was a great piece of naive art – dopey git! It's not naive, it's just plain incompetent. Although I agree – it seems he'll try anything to impress the local squirearchy. He's determined to win this bloody hunt ride on Gladstone. And do you know what? That horse has turned out to be not half as bad as I first thought. Whatever – I'm proud to say that after a few weeks' TLC and proper attention in my place, it's quite a decent horse. Maybe your eye didn't mislead you quite so much, after all.'

'Bollocks!' said Reggie, who was never shy to own up to his own mistakes. 'If it's turned out OK, that's just a bloody fluke, and I was shafted by that little Sanders bloke.'

'I don't know about that, but Chatternerve's definitely going to have a go and he's a very determined chap – that's how he's made so much dough. I'm sure he's been up to something because he's managed to improve his riding a hell of a lot in a pretty short order.'

Reggie nodded. 'I've heard these early starter tycoons usually get there by sheer bloody-minded determination.'

'Yes, well. There's a way you could put him in his place. You go in the hunt ride on my Bob the Cob, and I can give you a pretty good chance of winning, which will upset the little tit.'

Reggie took another slug of the Floppidick. 'That sounds like a very nice idea, but you know I can't do it.'

'Reggie, you can! You bloody well can!' Ted leaned over and gripped Reggie's large red hand in his own. 'You're a sportsman, I know it. I'll give you some more intensive schooling; it's not as if you have to jump anything – you just have to open one gate – and that can be made simpler. Listen,' Ted urged with the exuberance that three pints of rough Welsh cider could give, 'the horse you'll be on, Bob the Cob over there...' – Ted nodded at a short, stout docile beast gazing at them over his stable door – 'he may not look as if he has much racehorse in him, but he's got a surprising turn of speed if you know how to ask him.'

'And how am I going to do that?'

'Just do what I tell you and you'll be fine. And if you come in first, I'll make sure there's a nice little bonus in it for you...' He sensed that Reggie's apparent new state of impecuniousness might swing it. 'When Jason de Geordie told me he was going to come out on Gladstone, I told him to park the animal here in my yard, and I've been stuffing it with oats and other hard food to hot him up. There he is, over there,' he pointed at the big brown head, trying to waggle from side to side but constrained by an iron anti-weaving gate on the stable door. 'He's looking better every day. Of course, he still weaves and wind-sucks when he gets the chance, but he's not lame any more – I found a nasty little flint buried in his foot which his last owner had missed and I pulled it out like Daniel in the Lion's den.' Ted took another slug of the potent cider. 'He should be more than somewhat on his toes by the time of the ride. Actually he won't be a bad horse by then, and Jason won't know if he's coming or going.'

'Is it a race, then?' Reggie asked, trying not to show any anxiety.

'Not officially, but it is really, for most of the hunt. And Gladstone will think it is,' he added with a grin. 'I'd better tip off the St John's Ambulance to be on their marks.'

'What's the course like – are there jumps?'

'I told you – no jumps. And you needn't worry about the course.

It's never fixed until the night before and no one's allowed to walk it – it's a sort of hunt tradition. Just follow instructions and you'll be all right,' he said enigmatically, and took another gulp of Floppidick as he gazed thoughtfully into the middle distance. 'By the way, I was looking through the catalogue for Lennon's auction this evening and I saw a table that looked very much like the one you sold Evan the Pong. In fact, it's the star lot, and on the front cover.'

Reggie sat up a bit fast, and had to shake the effects of the cider from his head. 'Bloody hell! Do you think it could be the pair to it?'

'Looks close enough and the dimensions are right, I should say. Hang on, I've got the thing in my arse pocket,' he wheezed and lent forward to pull out the crumpled catalogue which he handed to Reggie.

Reggie opened it and tried to focus on the page Ted had dog-eared.

'Hey, you're right! It does look like it, maybe in slightly better nick even. Estimate: £10,000 – 12,000. Bloody hell, Evan reckoned a pair would be worth £25 grand. If by some miracle I could get this one for seven or eight – well, maybe I could sell it to Evan for a good few grand more – whadda you think?' He turned woozily to Ted Buckton.

'Too darned right, my friend.' Ted agreed.

'Right!' Reggie heaved himself unsteadily to his feet. 'It's lot number two hundred and three; if we get our skates on we can get there before it comes up.'

Ted was standing up too. 'I'm not sure we'll get there in time. We could phone a bid...'

'No, no. I'll have to see the thing first. We'll get there; the motor always goes faster when I've got a pint of cider in me.'

'Three pints,' Ted corrected, 'and the Three Tuns bitter you had in the pub on the way here.'

'Great – we'll go like the bloody Sirocco, then, won't we?'

Reggie had set out that morning in the Bentley, which, while comfortable at speed on a motorway, wasn't at its best on sinuous country lanes. Ted strapped himself into the passenger seat with a fixed, anxious grin on his face as Reggie hurled the lumbering vehicle round tight bends and within inches of passing tractors. Nevertheless they arrived at Lennon's sale rooms in Craven Arms while the early lots were still being sold – battered cardboard boxes containing bits and pieces of household objects – sets of fish knives, chipped Toby jugs, framed samplers, bed pans, albums of faded sepia family photos – a clutter of abandoned stuff that, very occasionally, if the auctioneers hadn't spotted them, might contain a gem like a rare book or a Japanese ivory figurine.

With his judgement askew, and his optimism lifted by the strangely potent Floppidick, Reggie had bid for and won five boxes of junk before he'd made his way through the crowd of punters to the more serious lots.

He soon spotted the inlaid side-table and went over to it. Rocking a little on his heels, he attempted to examine it properly. He turned to Ted, lurching beside him, and winked. 'It's the pair, all right. Apart from that little bit...' he nodded at a section of the marquetry which, on the one he'd sold to Evan, was slightly warped and twisted, '...it's pretty much identical!'

Ted was less sure. 'I don't know, Reggie, that bit's not the same as I remember. Surely they would have been identical, or at least a mirror whassaname?' Lurking beneath Ted's alcohol-induced high sprits was a vague worry about what he'd set in motion, and he didn't want to be responsible for any disasters that might occur. On the other hand, he didn't want an argument about it. 'Could be, though, it does look quite like it.'

Reggie put a hand over his own mouth, leaned towards Ted and whispered loudly, 'I'm going to go for it! Up to ten!'

Two dealers right behind him heard and grinned at each other. They didn't like amateurs barging in and screwing up their own buying. Ted saw them and made a face at Reggie, but Reggie was far too excited to register. He could barely contain his excitement when lot no. 203 came up for sale and, while he was waiting, bought a grand piano, a stuffed and mounted head of a Hereford bull, and two salmon in a glass case. Other dealers were beginning to notice him; some knew who he was and where he lived; they assumed he just wanted to fill up his cavernous house.

The auctioneer – a partner in the business with Dennis Lennon, who had conducted the auction at the Charity Race Day – had the appearance and demeanour of a good-natured tortoise. He was happy to see a new buyer who seemed fairly indiscriminate in his bidding. 'Now, lot two-o-three. A fine Chippendale table, in mahogany with fine marquetry inlay in maple and satinwood. An outstanding example of the type and period. What am I bid to start? Ten thousand?'

There was a pause before the auctioneer picked up a bid towards the back of the room. 'All right, then, five thousand, five two, five five....'

Reggie hadn't raised his hand yet; even in his inebriated state he knew it would be wiser to wait before entering the fray. The two dealers were waiting to see if he would start, and were poised to get in and make him pay for his bumbling amateurism.

Ted was eyeing him with concern.

The bidding had got stuck at seven thousand, two hundred. The auctioneer craned his wrinkly neck, gazing around slowly like a tortoise looking for its next leaf of lettuce.

'Seven thousand two hundred. Come on; that's not enough for a piece like this!' he admonished the punters as if they were lazy schoolchildren. It was a moment before he spotted Reggie's catalogue waving at the side of the room.

When he did catch sight of it, he sighed with audible relief. 'Ah, new bidder, seven five... seven seven, eight,' he said contentedly, acknowledging the arrival in the bidding of one of the dealers beside Reggie.

Reggie waved again and was instantly upped by someone he couldn't see on the other side of the room.

As the price rose, Reggie became mesmerised, as if what was happening wasn't real. And at the back of his befuddled mind were Evan's words, 'A good pair of them could fetch up to twenty-five K.'

At last, it was all over. 'Am I done then?' the man at the rostrum asked, looking around his audience with an air of satisfied smugness. 'For the last time then, twelve thousand, two hundred.' Bang! He smacked the gavel down. 'Sold. Mr Finchley.'

Someone must have identified Reggie and briefed him.

Reggie had successfully pushed to the back of his mind the inconvenient fact that if he won the table, he'd have to come up with the money; he continued to overlook this problem in his elation at getting the thing. Lit up with Floppidick, he wasn't in any doubt that he'd be able to pass it straight on for fifteen thousand to Evan Pugh, who would then have a pair he could sell for an easy five thousand pound profit.

Rosi would sort out the money – now that the Gladstone deal had worked out – and this time he'd make a quick two and half grand. He ambled through to the office to explain that he'd be back with the cash when he picked up his purchases.

The cashier raised an eyebrow, but said nothing as she handed Reggie a bill for the table for just under £15,000, and another bill for the bits and pieces. In his euphoria – and inexperience – he'd clean forgotten about the commission which, with VAT, would absorb almost all the profit he had planned to make.

Ted was waiting outside looking worried. 'Do you think you should have paid so much for it?'

'Yeah, well, I forgot about the commission, which means I'll have to get a bit more than I thought out of Evan for it, but he won't be able to refuse, not with a pair of that quality to sell.'

'Are you sure they're so good?'

'Yeh, 'course I am,' Reggie blustered. 'I've been doing my homework.'

'I sometimes think it's rather dangerous to go to casinos or auctions when you've had a few.'

'Don't be so soppy, Ted. Tell you what – we'll ring Evan right now.' He fumbled around in his trouser pocket for his mobile phone and notebook where he'd written Pugh's number. After four goes with fingers that wouldn't do as he wanted, he managed to key in the number.

''Ello?' Evan answered suspiciously.

'Evan? It's Reggie.'

'What do you want?'

'It's what you want, my little Welsh wheeler-dealer.'

'You're pissed,' Evan replied flatly.

'So what. Listen, you know that table you bought from me?'

'What about it?'

'I've just got the matching pair!'

''Ave you? So?' He didn't sound at all interested. Reggie took the phone from his ear and looked at it, shaking his head with exaggerated perplexity before returning it to his mouth and speaking with deliberate slowness, as if to a dim child. 'So... if you buy it from me, you'll have a pair to sell, like you said, worth maybe twenty-five grand.'

'But I haven't got the one I bought off you. I've sold it.'

Reggie shook his head in bewilderment. It hadn't occurred to him that Evan might already have moved the table on. 'Bloody hell, Evan, who to?'

'I don't know; I don't care. It just sold to some punter at Lennon's for twelve and a half grand.'

Reggie froze; the phone dropped from his hand to the tarmac in front of the sale room entrance, where, after a moment, Evan's voice could be heard squawking briefly from where it lay on the ground.

Reggie was gaping at Ted.

'What happened?' Ted asked anxiously.

Reggie stared back; all the merriment in his normally bright, and currently inebriated eyes had gone; his tanned, healthy complexion had turned *eau de nil*.

Two days later, a large gathering of people from the surrounding hills was clustered near the starting point of the Montgomery & West Salop Hunt Ride – an event that had been held over a four-mile course every year, even during two world wars, for more than a century. They had come for what could often be a rewarding sight in terms of dented egos, dramatic falls and unexpected changes of fortune over the wandering and confusing course which followed a different route every year, and which was, in all but name, an unregulated, out-and-out steeplechase.

A pair of opportunistic bookies from mid-Wales, knowing that there was always some heavy gambling by the locals on the outcome of the race, had set up their soapboxes and umbrellas on the edge of the crowd, although they had to compete with Crobin, the landlord of the Fox &Ferret, who had been taking bets on the outcome for several weeks. He was there to make sure nothing happened to upset his own interests. He was watching with detached and not unfriendly amusement as Reggie ffinch-Leigh appeared, apparently quite relaxed on the stout, weight-carrying cob he had been lent by Mr Buckton.

Crobin was suddenly conscious of a pungent aroma – a blend of horse dung and stale tobacco smoke – and felt Charlie Rafferty's presence at his side.

'A'right, boss. What price'll you give me for a ton on Reggie?'

Crobin who, though he liked Emmet, was always cagey about his brother, gave Charlie a quizzical look. 'You wants to back Reggie? Have you doped the rest of them, or what?'

'Just give me a price.'

'Fives.'

'What?!' Charlie exclaimed. 'Come on; that's no kind of price for a total outsider.'

'He ain't - not if you've got a ton on 'im.'

Charlie pulled a small wedge from the pocket of his jeans, and waved it under Crobin's nose. 'I've got plenty to put on.'

'Well you go and bet with one of those two Welsh gentlemen,' Crobin said, nodding at the two legitimate bookies on their stands.

'I bloody will, then.'

Crobin watched Charlie walk away as Charlie's son, Mickey Rafferty sidled up to him. 'Who did Dad back?' Mickey asked.

Crobin sniffed. He wasn't in the habit of divulging other punter's fancies but he didn't want to discourage the boy. 'He seems to fancy Reggie.'

'Chuffin muffin! Even if Bob the Cob had McCoy on board, he'd be lucky to come home half way down the field. I'll have a tenner on de Wassaname.'

'De Chatternerve – on Gladstone?' Crobin checked

'Yeh. I saw the 'oss gallop with Mr Buckton up on Ferney Ridge Tuesday marnin'. Looked pretty good.'

It wasn't Crobin's function to advise the young traveller that, last time he looked, Jason de Chateauneuf could barely sit the horse at a trot, let alone a gallop over four miles.

'Fine; you can have him at twelves.'

Although Crobin could remember every bet he took, he pulled out his notebook to jot this one down in case of later dispute. As he was scribbling with a stub of chewed pencil, Lord Rokesay appeared with an entourage of his extensive family. Following a long annual tradition, he had turned up to present the prizes at the end of the race.

'What ho, Crobin. Who do the great British public fancy for the Shropshire National?'

'There's a bit of scratch for Lady Nellie.'

Lady Nellie Slim was a gutsy rider, and Lord Rokesay's youngest daughter. 'Well she'll be trying, that's for sure, with the family honour to uphold. And the horse was bred to win the Derby – rather expensively as I recall – though, sadly, it never won a race on a real track. Ah well, I'd better have a tenner on her.'

Lord Rokesay didn't produce any cash. If he lost, the sum would be added to his tally, while in the rare event of a win it went to reduce his due. It was understood that he would settle up every year or so, when the landlord would present him with a fully itemised account of any costs he had incurred through him – anything from firkins of ale for the beaters' lunches, bets on the size of bags on the shoot on any given day, and bar services supplied at various functions up at the Castle.

Having placed his bet, Lord Rokesay wandered away towards the collecting ring.

From fifty yards away, Crobin heard him booming across at Reggie, who was circling quietly on his cob with half a dozen other early arrivals. 'Ah! Do I spy the sporting squire of Tottering Towers?'

Reggie's thoughts were miles away as he sat on the shaggy-legged cob that Ted had lent him; he registered Perry Rokesay's greeting with only a nod; there was too much else on his mind. Not least, the question of how he was going to explain to his wife why she was probably going to have to wait for the fifteen thousand quid she'd coughed up so he could pay for the table he'd bought at Lennon's auctions; although he'd had his disastrous news from Evan, he knew there was been no way he could back out of his purchase without fouling his reputation right at the start of his new career as an antiques trader.

The only glimmer of hope had come through Harry Huggins' doddering old dad, Albert.

Like most serious users of the Fox & Ferret, Albert had heard all about Reggie paying several thousand pounds more than he'd got from Evan Pugh for the table he'd sold him for five in the first place.

Albert had come up to the house the evening before, and found Reggie gloomily smoking one of his black cigars on chair outside the stable. He coughed gently to announce his presence and, with old fashioned deference, touched the peak of his stained, threadbare tweed cap. 'Evenin' squire,' he murmured. 'I 'eard 'bout the table, and I 'eard they ran you up a bit.' He shook his head sympathetically. 'It was the one you found in there, weren't it?' he nodded in the direction of the cluttered tack-room.

'Yeh,' Reggie agreed glumly.

'I put it there,' Albert said, significantly, 'after Mr Rupert's son Jonty come here and help himself to the other one.'

Reggie's thoughts snapped back into focus. 'Other one?'

'Yes. There was two of them – a pair, like. And after old Mr Bertram died, Mr Rupert's lad came down claiming he was due some furniture. I was living in the stable flat then, and they'd left me in charge, but I couldn't really stop him. He takes a few bits – along with that other table – and goes, but I thought I better keep him from taking more good stuff and took quite a bit out of the house, and locked it in there. When you bought the place, Harry and me put a lot of it back in the house. The agent didn't know what was there or nothing, but everything as Mr Bertram left, we took care of. We'd a lot of time for Mr Bertram, but them boys – his cousins – they was always greedy young buggers.'

Reggie was losing the thread slightly. He shook his head. 'Albert, are you telling me there *was* a matching pair of those tables in the house, and one was taken by Rupert Cheney-Longville's son?'

'S'right, Mr Reggie.'

Reggie as sitting up now. 'Do you know where he took it?'

Albert shook his head. 'No, I 'aven't got the foggiest.'

'Bloody hell. If I could get my hands on it, I might get out of trouble.'

'That's as I was thinkin' Mr Reggie.'

Reggie had spent all the next day trying to find an address for Jonty Cheney-Longville, without success. He rang to ask for help from Stan Frost, an old friend in London. The hefty former 2nd row forward with the Richmond Heavies Rugby Club did a lot of what he liked to call 'overdue accounts work', which included tracing elusive debtors.

Reggie rang again two days later.

'Sorry, Reg, mate,' Stan said. 'This Jonty bloke seems to have scratched himself from the system. He don't vote, he don't have a mobile – at least not in his own name, and he don't own no drum of his own – or maybe it's in his wife's name, like yours; he hasn't been in trouble with the law, and he don't have a driver's licence.'

Reggie had put the phone down despondently. He'd been building up his hopes of finding the man with the other table – the punter to whom it would be worth most, though Reggie knew that even if he did find him, Jonty could easily have sold the table and lost track of it, or not want to buy the pair, or not be prepared to sell back the one he had for a realistic price.

Chapter Six

On a damp Sunday morning, Reggie was wondering why, with all the other hassles in his life almost overwhelming him, he was sitting on top of a horse with whom he knew he hadn't yet bonded, preparing to ride in what was a highly competitive race in all but name, in which he frankly didn't care if he came last, so long as he survived, even if it was to face his wife demanding to know what had happened to her fifteen grand.

Reggie was a realist, and blamed only himself for the table disaster – even if Evan had planned the whole thing and set him up. Ted Buckton had been absolutely right; no one with any sense would have gone off to an auction after few pints of Floppidick. He vowed to himself that he would never do it again; but that wasn't going to bring back Rosi's fifteen big ones.

He became aware that the shifty Charlie Rafferty was hopping about by his left stirrup. "Ello Reggie. You gonna win?'

'I doubt it.'

Charlie shook his head. 'Listen, Reggie, if you do as I says, you will win, s'long as you don't fall off – and you don't have to do nothing wrong.'

'Why, what are you saying? Why do you want to help?'

Charlie tapped his pimply nose. 'Someone you know has put a good bit of moolah on yer. And so've I.'

Reggie's position was so dire that anything that might bring in a few quid was worth having, but first he asked, 'Who with?'

'One of them bookies from Newtown.'

'Not Crobin, then?'

'No way,' Charlie said emphatically.

'That's all right then. How much d'you stand to win?' Reggie asked.

'Bout a grand,' Charlie admitted.

'If I win, you owe me half,' Reggie said. 'Otherwise, it's not going to happen.'

Charlie had been expecting to come to some sort of a deal, which was fine by him, if it guaranteed a win.

'Done!' he said. 'So, this is all you gotta do… hang about a long way at the back of the field as you move off, until you lose the rest ahead of you, going round the first bend into the woods. Then, when you gets into the wood and comes to a bit of a fork in the track, I'll be there, and I'll show you which way to go. Then you kick on, and about a mile and a half farther, the rest of the field-'ll be coming up a good bit behind you. You just kick hard, and even on this fat 'oss, unless you comes to a grindin' halt, you should reach the post first.'

Reggie wasn't convinced. 'Charlie, why will they be behind me?'

Charlie smirked. 'I'll see to it so's they go the wrong way at the first fork – that'll add 'bout three parts of a mile afore they gets back on the right track – and that'll give you all the help you need.'

'Sounds good to me,' Reggie nodded, feeling he deserved all the advantages he could get at that moment. Besides, there was still a competitive streak in him. 'This 'orse can motor when he feels like it. If that's all it takes, we might have a result then. Just make sure you don't forget our deal…' Reggie narrowed his eyes into fierce slits and thrust out his jaw, like he had as a young hustler in the markets when he wanted to be sure of getting paid for a deal.

Charlie took it in. 'That's a'right. Yer on, Reggie; you'll get yer money.'

Reggie pushed his other problems to the back of his mind and, now that he'd been offered an inside track, concentrated on the job in hand. He looked around at the other runners and riders with renewed interest; most of them were regular hunters who'd been doing it since they were kids. As far as he knew the only other total novice was Jason de Chateauneuf who had trotted in on Gladstone, now transformed into a snorting war-horse as a result of Ted's feeding and exercise regime. Although Jason's knuckles showed white where he gripped his reins, from the way he was bouncing quite securely in the saddle – a small racing saddle, Reggie noted – he appeared far more confident and a lot less incompetent than he had a few weeks before, when he'd come to buy the horse. Jason saw Reggie and manoeuvred his horse through the others to end up with his mount jiggling on its toes right beside Bob the Cob. Jason had evidently been to some smart riding outfitters and had bought all the best tack – racing boots, with a smart yellow silk over his hard hat, lightweight satin breeches and a little stick.

''Ello, Jason. Where've you been? Haven't seen you for a couple of weeks.'

'When I do summat,' Jason answered with a gritty edge to his Geordie vowels. 'I like to do it prop'ly, so I've been to jockey school for a week's intensive trainin'. Which is just as well – this animal's like a new horse since Ted Buckton's had it.'

'He does look on his toes,' Reggie observed.

'He's reet fit, and raring to go,' Jason agreed. 'I don't suppose you'll be troubling the judge, though, will you?' he added with a disparaging sneer, before moving off to talk to those he perceived to be more worthy opponents.

Reggie leaned down to whisper to his mount. 'Listen, you fat bugger, you'd better get your arse into gear, once we're on our own. I'm not going to be beaten by that jumped-up Geordie pipsqueak.'

As he straightened himself, trying to calm the flock of starlings filling his guts, a badly distorting Tannoy system burst into life through a pair of battered aluminium horn speakers. 'The Montgomery & West Salop Hunt Ride will commence in about five minutes,' Ted Buckton's suave, measured tones echoed across the field and off the edge of the oak wood behind them. 'The runners and riders are as follows: 'Jack the Hack, ridden by Lady Nellie Slim, Gladstone, ridden by Mr Jason de Chatternerve...' and so on, until all twenty riders and their horses had been identified.

As the runners milled around in a disorderly way, with their riders twisting this way and that to see the starter on top of a wooden step-ladder, preparing to drop a large white handkerchief to set them off, Reggie consciously kept Bob the Cob at the back of the pack so he wouldn't find himself in the middle of everyone when the hankie came down. He almost had to pinch himself to be sure that he, Reggie ffinch-Leigh, at the age of 61, was about to ride in his first race (even if it wasn't supposed to be a race) when he'd only ridden a horse for the first time less than a year before. At least, he thought, Ted had taught him enough to stay on, given that there was no jumping involved and his apparently reliable mount had no particular interest in unseating him.

The retired major who'd volunteered for the job of 'Starter' spent a few minutes cursing the riders for not organising their unruly mounts in a line, as if he were starting the Grand National. Finally he let them go, when, luckily, Reggie and Bob were facing backwards and missed the start completely. By the time they'd turned, the nearest runner was already ten lengths away.

Reggie managed to settle his horse into a slow, lumbering canter, allowing the others to pull away as they rounded the corner of the wood and were out of his sight, When he reached the bend, there was no sign of them, and Reggie followed the track into the wood, where the hoofprints of the other nineteen horses were clearly visible.

He was aware of Ted Buckton's voice booming from the Tannoy, '... and the last into the woods is Reggie Finchley on Bob the Cob, and we won't see them again until they come out on the far side of Gypsy Dingle.'

Reggie hustled Bob along a broad, leafy track and soon came to a point where it divided. Charlie Rafferty, as he'd promised, was standing in the middle of the right hand fork, where the trail of hoofprints led, and vigorously waved Reggie to the left where the track continued, unmarked by other horses.

'OK, Reggie,' Charlie yelled, 'don't hang about!'

The initial fear Reggie had felt had evaporated and he was having the time of his life. Bob the Cob was giving him an exhilarating, easy ride and going on autopilot now. Reggie shortened his reins, as Ted had shown him, and gave Bob a couple of sharp nudges in the sides with his heels. The horse seemed to be enjoying himself too; he stretched his neck willingly and lengthened his stride until they were flying, and Reggie laughed out loud. 'Way-hay! Come on my son!' he yelled.

Through a tall tunnel of emerald green springtime foliage, on a level grassy track – not too firm, not too soft – they flew for another mile. From the corner of his eye, Reggie spotted a few spectators watching with astonishment as he approached. He reached the edge of the woods and as they burst out into the open, he could hear a note of relief in Ted Buckton's voice as it boomed over the Tannoy, 'Well here's a surprise – the first to show out of Gypsy Dingle is Mr Reginald ffinch-Leigh on Bob the Cob.'

Reggie laughed out loud again. He'd had a lovely ride through the woods, and now, it seemed, he was in the lead. He had no idea what Charlie had done with the rest of the field, but now Reggie had been given a chance to win, he wasn't going to waste it. After the two or three miles he'd ridden, more or less at full tilt so far as he and Bob the Cob were concerned, Reggie was thankful for all the exercise he'd had while learning to ride. He gave his horse a reminder with his heels and leaned forward in his saddle in a way he'd seen in countless western movies which he loved, and slapped the reins on Bob's neck to keep the horse focussed and going on.

Bob responded to the urgency he sensed through Reggie's backside and renewed his efforts. They were travelling over a stretch of beautiful, sheep grazed turf, and the crowds around the winning post were coming into sight. He was already a good furlong from the woods when he heard Ted announce that the next out was Mr de Chateauneuf on Gladstone, who was gaining on Bob the Cob.

'Bloody hell, Bob! You can't let them get to us!'

But he could hear the thundering progress of the revitalised Gladstone closing on him, with more runners coming up behind. He and Bob swung round a long right-handed curve towards the finish where the thick end of a fallen oak marked the edge of the course.

As Reggie heard his pursuer getting ever closer, he steered his galloping cob over to the right so he would pass as near as he could to the end of the tree. He was closing on it when he heard Gladstone's hooves and breath just over his right shoulder. Now, with a chance of winning in his sights, Reggie gritted his teeth, determined to squeeze every inch of speed out of the willing old cob.

With his whole life suddenly turned belly up by the pin-stripe tea-leaves who'd conned him out of every pound he possessed, he knew he had no business to be out racing horses, as if he hadn't a care in the world; but he was damned if he was going to let Chatternerve, the arrogant little tin-pot tycoon, beat him, even in this tuppeny-ha'penny rustic event.

He turned to snatch a look and saw a sudden look of panic on Jason's face as he realised he wasn't going to get past Reggie before they reached the tree.

The next thing Reggie knew, Gladstone had taken off, putting in a mighty leap to clear the obstacle, and as the horse descended to the ground on the far side, his jockey carried on over his left shoulder and hit the ground with a thud, while the horse gathered itself, galloped past Bob and started pulling away.

Bob the Cob was in no mood to concede to this temporary fellow inmate of his stables, and kept on chasing the riderless horse.

Reggie wasn't sure where the finish was. There wasn't any obvious finishing post that he could see, so he gave Bob a final kick in the ribs, and thundered on to a puzzled cheer. He didn't slow down until he was sure he'd won.

Bob, quite knackered now, slowed to a canter, then a trot, and Reggie wheeled him round to walk back to where the rest of the runners were coming home, well strung out as they passed the finish.

Behind them, was Jason de Chateauneuf hobbling across the turf towards the finish with his white breeches smeared grass green and earth brown, his helmet straps dangling and a broken stick in his hand. His small, normally neat little face was twisted into a thunderous scowl.

Ted Buckton on the Tannoy, was sounding very excited. 'So our winner is Mr Reggie ffinch-Leigh on Bob the Cob; Mr de Chatternerve was a faller, taking a tree trunk just before the finish, so second was Lady Nellie Slim on Jack the Hack. I'm now told that all the field except Bob the Cob took the wrong course and it'll be up to the judges to decide if they're disqualified.'

Jason reached Reggie on Bob. 'I'll get you for that, Finchley – trying to ride me off.'

'I never stopped you. If you'd stuck to the saddle, you'd have gone past me and won.'

'You bloody cheated,' Jason snarled, 'you dodgy old barrow boy!'

Reggie laughed to see the Geordie so riled. 'I was the only one who took the right course; the rest of you cheated.'

De Chateauneuf glared back at him, but said nothing, before walking off to find his horse.

News of Reggie's success spread though the local country in hours, it seemed, helped by the story that the Welsh bookie tried to welsh on bets placed by Charlie and another punter, but had to go home two thousand quid lighter, or he would have been lynched. Charlie had coughed up Reggie's half of his winnings without a murmur, and Reggie felt that, for once, his luck had taken a positive turn that day.

When he went into the village next morning to see Lady Wynyates, she'd heard all about it. 'Sounds like a great coup!' she boomed at Reggie, her round rubbery visage quivering with excitement. 'Well done! And you put that nasty little Chatternerve in his place, I heard.'

'I done my best. But now I want to show you a little dog cart that'll suit your ponies.' He had it on his trailer outside the gates.

Told to bring it in, he watched while Lady Wynyates studied it minutely, no doubt thinking of ways to beat him down.

'There's a bit of the old worm *de bois*, down here,' she said, stabbing a finger towards the bottom of the door.

'That's not worm, Lady W; that's just where it got hit by some stray shot when they were shooting across Gnarley's last winter.'

'Rubbish Reggie, but good try. Looks like there's some worm in the wheel-spokes, too, but I can deal with that. Anyway, it's a handsome little thing. How much do you want for it?'

Reggie wanted two thousand pounds – a thousand for Foxy, and another for himself. 'Three thousand,' he answered.

'Fifteen hundred,' the ex-diplomat's wife came back in a breath.

'Come on Lady W. You know I can't drop that much. Two six.'

'Seventeen hundred,' she replied.

'Two four,' Reggie offered with a note of despair.

'Two thousand,' Lady Wynyates declared, 'and that really is my best bid.'

'Done!' Reggie held out a hand to which she applied a painful slap.

'At least now I've got something to drive in the pageant on Saturday. It may not be a war chariot, but it's close enough.'

'I don't suppose the lady warrior went to war behind a pair of Shetlands in ancient times,' Reggie remarked.

'Possibly not, but she is on Saturday.'

Reggie drove back to Mortimer Towers, pleased to know that he hadn't completely lost his old negotiating skills.

Rosi greeted him, still wearing the frosty aura she'd shown when he'd first told her about the table debacle. 'What you doing, Reggie?'

'I just sold a lovely dog cart to Lady Wynyates.' He sat down at the table in the breakfast room that overlooked the front drive to the house.

'She going to be pulled by dogs?' Rosita asked in astonishment. 'She is a big woman. They must be big dogs.'

'No, the Shetland ponies will pull it.'

'Then why is called dog cart?'

'I wish I knew, my little buttercup. Anyway, she's driving it at the fête '

Reggie woke in the morning to find a bright June day and felt ready to take on whatever the village fête and Mortimer Towers' first public engagement could throw at him.

He was encouraged by a light breeze that rippled the poplars beside the house with a soft hiss and gently waved the tops of the beeches, a hundred feet tall on the far side of the lake. The grass was dotted with small tents and gazebos, white and multi-hued, to house the tombola bottle stall, Gypsy Rose Lee, whack-the-rat and the Guess-My-Weight stand, which was to be occupied by Sue's giant mother, Gladys.

Crobin at the pub had already opened a book and was doing good business on the eventual declaration of Gladys' avoirdupois, sufficiently fascinating to have attracted bets from throughout the village and beyond. Twenty-six stone currently stood at the shortest odds of 11/10.

Also scattered across the gently sloping green sward were lurid signs for the punch bag and the 'village stocks'.

Rosita was already up and scuttling about and from the bedroom window, Reggie saw Lara arrive; she had come to give Rosita whatever support she needed and, Reggie guessed, to have a good laugh. He dressed himself in a pink shirt and a pair of lemon chinos and went down to have breakfast on the terrace. Lara was there before him, pouring herself a cup of coffee.

'Hi, Reggie. Are you dressed like a cupcake to match these tasteful entertainments? It's all looking so kitsch and quaint, the carousing rustics will think they're in heaven and have a ball.'

'Now then,' Reggie wagged a finger at her. 'Don't you disparage our locals. They may not look so chic, but they're the salt of the wassaname, and a load cannier than you might think. You enter the spirit of it and you'll have a great time. Also, if you feel like a bit of a punt, there'll be betting on the terrier and ferret racing, and on Gladys Price's body weight, unclothed, which is a startling thought – probably about 'alf a ton; she's built like a concrete karzy. Then if you want a cheap drink, buy a fistful of tombola tickets – specially if you like British sherry. It was fantastic value last year; I reckon people had given them about three hundred quid's worth of booze, and they sold tickets for about £150 to get rid of it all. You'd think they'd have done better just taking the money and not the bottles.'

Lara laughed. 'But that wouldn't be so much fun, and anyway the bottles are usually very dodgy potions people have bought while in a drunken stupor in Magaluf, or been given by someone else.'

'You're right there,' Reggie chortled. 'I gave 'em a bottle I bought in Bogota off one of Rosi's dodgy cousins, and that tasted like it was meant for cleaning the loo. Never mind – you could always get plastered sampling the trifle competition entries.'

'I'll remember that. And what's happening on the lake? Where's all the weed gone?'

'Rosi got Harry Huggins to clear it all so that Terry Cotter, the village potter can show off his skills in coracle handling. He should draw a crowd – mostly ghouls waiting to see him fall in.'

'And what happens in the stocks?'

'Basically, that's a venue for what you might call political and religious debate. First the vicar goes in, then Susanna Taylor-Jones, who's our local county councillor. The punters pay 50p for three tomatoes so squishy they're too far gone even for the car boot sale. They can ask them a question, and when they've answered, pelt them with the tomatoes. It was very popular last year; the MP got in and ended up in the *Daily Mail* with bits of rotten veg trickling down his collar.'

'And the large, knackered army tent? What goes on in there?'

'You steer clear of that, m'girl. By this afternoon, that will be a kind of Hades, full of uncontrolled lust and other urges. That is the Beer Tent, where there is an unofficial competition among the youth of our community – male *and* female, I'm ashamed to say – to see who can drink the most pints and still remain standing.'

Between the stalls, a course had been marked out with orange binder twine for the 'family fun' races – three-legged, wheelbarrow, upside down sack (i.e. blindfolded), dog & child, terrier & rabbit, the musical potties competition and, controversially, the finale – the Strong Ale & Giant Bale Race.

In the middle of the lawn, resting across a series of small hay bales, were four long grey drainpipes, with small sections cut at intervals along the top. From the end of each drainpipe was a string attached to the tyreless rim of the rear wheel of a bicycle set on its back. At the end of the string, and to be placed at the start of the pipes were four felt rats. This, Reggie realised was, was being set up for the ferret racing, for which he'd been persuaded to provide a commentary. He hadn't done anything like it before, but had been practising alone in his dressing-room, aiming at something between Peter O'Sullevan and Jeremy Clarkson.

There was a roped off arena where the judging would take place after an entrance and procession through the stable archway of Best Pony, Lurchers (all types), Best Dog and – Reggie's own particular contribution – the Dog-Whose-Owner-I-Would-Most-Like-To-Take-Home competition – which Rosita predicted would be a source of inevitable conflict.

A few hours later, the fête was in full swing, and Reggie made his way up to the dog-show ring. The terrier racing and lurcher show had attracted a large gathering of shifty backwoods men not often seen in the village or in the grounds of Mortimer Towers. Listening to the owners of the dogs mustered around the ring as the lurcher competition was going on, Reggie gathered that the judging of long dogs was a very arbitrary process.

In front of him, a dark little man with a hairless scalp and a body covered in tattoos of unseemly fantasies was clutching the lead of his rough-coated wolfhound lurcher. Speaking to the man beside him, he waved his free hand towards the unfortunate competition judge. "E's goin' for all them saluki types... That's it for us; we never does no good if it's a saluki bloke – *or* if he likes 'em too grey'oundy.'

His companion, a grimy, dread-locked individual, smelling strongly of horse manure, was holding onto a large wire-haired brindle hound; he nodded in agreement. 'They should say, shouldn't they – "Judge only likes grey'ounds" or wha'ever. It'd save the trouble of coming then – for us as likes a real man's dog.'

Reggie, wondering at the finer points of lurcher-rearing, moved on towards the terrier race track, where a loosely stuffed rabbit skin was to be dragged by the bicycle winch a few yards ahead of the improvised hay bale starting gate for the fifty yard dash. The village butcher, Jones the Beef, was MC of this event and handed Reggie a battered old microphone connected to the crackly PA speakers around the show.

'Here you are, Reggie. Your wife says you're doing the commentary, and I'm sure you'll do a lovely job.'

'Am I? I thought I was just doing the ferret racing. But what the hell - if it makes Rosi happy.'

He found the sleeve of his pristine linen jacket being tugged by Dougy Swallow, owner of the village hardware stores and a very old, mischievous man, now in his nineties, with a reputation still for a wandering eye, and a long-suffering wife. He also had a Jack Russell terrier which never left his side.

'Hey Reggie, look, if mine – that's 'im, Ginger, goin' in trap two – if he don't come out clean, you gotta stop the race. He gets in the box and starts doin' circles and then if he's facing the wrong way when they lifts the gate, he gets left behind – and that's not fair.'

'Come off it, Dougy. They all do that. It's the luck of the draw. Anyway, that dog of yours is about a hundred and two, and he's got legs shorter than that Del Boy off the telly; he's never going to win.'

'But Reggie, I've been entering him for years and he's never won before; I'd like him to have a last chance afore he dies.'

'You'll die first, Dougy.'

'Bloody 'ell, no! I just got a new lover,' he cackled, as he pottered off to give his dog a pep-talk.

'And I know who that lover is,' said a voice from behind Reggie.

Reggie turned to find himself looking into the sly, ruddy features of Foxy Warren.

'Don't tell me, mate. I don't want to even think about it.'

'I won't then, though Crobin's probably takin' bets on it. I just come to race my terrier. Are you doing the entries?'

'No, I'm bloody not. I'm just the official commentator. Is this the dog?' Reggie glanced down at a sleepy-looking fox terrier Foxy had on a length of cord.

Foxy nodded proudly. 'That's Rocket. He'll take some beating, I can tell you.'

Reggie looked doubtfully at the dog. 'He doesn't look much. Just 'cos he's called 'Rocket' doesn't make him quick. He looks like he just wants a good kip.' He sniffed and curled a nostril in disgust.

'And bloody 'ell! He certainly whiffs a bit!'

'Oh, sorry 'bout that; he always gets a bit flatuous before a race.'

'Yeah, well... Don't we all,' Reggie sighed.

'Right,' Reggie announced in a voice that was carried all around his grounds and into the fields beyond, 'all the runners and riders are installed for the first of the terrier races. We have a magnificent field for this opening event. In trap one, Foxy Warren's Rocket, in trap two, Dougy Swallow's Ginger, in trap three, Chris Humperdich's One-Eyed Python, in trap four, Dave Dulas's imaginatively monickered, Spot, in lane five, Dorothy Bromfield's Mange Too. What?'

Mrs Bromfield was mouthing at him. 'It's *French!*'

'I'm very sorry, Dotty. Apparently this is a French name, should be pronounced, *Marnge Tout* – which means he eats everything, in French. And in lane six, Mr J Crobin's Last of the Mohicans, which might explain his haircut – the dog's, not Mr J Crobin's. For anyone who wants to have a bit of money on him, unfortunately there are no licensed bookmakers on the course... If you want to have a bet with an unlicensed bookie, the fête committee will bear no responsibility for the consequences, but Mr Crobin can be found around the start of the terrier racing, the ferret racing, the lurcher competition and the Guess My Weight stand. Now, they're under starter's orders, they're off!

'Last of the Mohicans is out of the gate like an arrow; Ginger and Rocket have ceased running and are doing a bit of mouth to mouth combat. Spot is chasing a miniature dachshund by the tombola; One Eyed Python has just caught Last of the Mohicans by the ankle, and... Bloody hell, he's brought him down, leaving Dotty Bromfield's Marnge Tout to come through and take this first race. Well done, Dotty. Ginger and Rocket are still fighting, and for anyone who's interested, I would say that Rocket is getting the better of it. Spot is a non-finisher.'

Reggie was congratulating himself after commentating a few more terrier races and the scarcely visible progress of the racing ferrets, when he found himself face to face with the diminutive

Sir Compton Wynyates, unconvincingly garbed as a very small Viking chieftain, wearing a WWII air raid warden's helmet with two small cow-horns attached to either side.

'Ah, Reggie. Boadicea and her blood-thirsty warriors are mustering in your stable yard, e'en as we speak. Cecilia would like you to use this script to announce their approach in about five minutes, when she will lead out her hordes in her smart new dog cart, on which I shall be riding pillion.' Leaving this fascinating vision hanging in the air, Her Majesty's former plenipotentiary in Montevideo handed Reggie a card covered in neat, tiny handwriting, turned on his heel and marched off with his thonged rawhide leggings brushing against one another and his horned helmet at a jaunty tilt.

After a suitable pause, Reggie turned the microphone back on and his voice boomed once more across the noisy throng. 'Ladies and Gentlemen,' he began in his best 'barker' delivery. 'For your delight and edification, Boadicea will shortly lead out the village *Pageant of Ancient Britons*, which is intended to reflect the Celtic Iron Age and Neolithic origins of our local population. They will enter from the stable gate. Please make space for her chariot and entourage to pass through you.'

The crowd of punters, most of them by now well-loosened with beer and the consumption of illicit Floppidick cider, swayed and lurched apart as the first of Boadicea's warriors appeared.

The village football team jogged in, flexing their muscles, stripped down to their briefs and smeared with 'woad' – a bright blue concoction of theatrical make-up produced – and applied, Reggie was told afterwards – by Lady Wynyates.

Next to appear through the stable arch was Boadicea herself, in the dog cart she had bought from Reggie, drawn by a pair of Shetland ponies caparisoned in floating scarlet sheets, with bridles sprayed in gold glitter paint. Lady Wynyates, with some kind of historical confusion, despite her expertise in the mediæval, appeared as a fair approximation of Elizabeth Taylor playing *Cleopatra* in a badly-fitting 'Sandy Shaw' wig. Perched precariously on the foot plate behind her in his Viking outfit was Sir Compton.

'And now,' Reggie read from the script Sir Compton had given him, 'to reflect the strong local tradition that King Arthur had his Camelot very close to where we are now and that he was in fact the leader of a squadron of mounted former foreign auxiliaries of the Roman army, we present a cohort of Ancient British cavalry.'

Four anxious-looking women on shaggy-hoofed coloured cobs with red ribbons in their plaited manes rode into view. The warriors were wearing helmets of inverted colanders with strips of scarlet polythene floor brush pinned lengthways along the top, and crenellated cotton tunics with leather-thonged sandals stuck into wooden stirrups.

Reggie recognised one of the mounted warriors as the young woman who manned the desk in the Mobile Library. Library Linda, as the village youths called her, although undoubtedly well-proportioned, was notoriously shy, and could scarcely be cajoled into a 'good morning' or 'hello' while on duty, but now she'd apparently morphed into a homicidal Amazon. As they reached the thick of the crowd, responding to Lady Wynyates' urging, the cavalry let loose a cacophony of extraordinary, blood curdling banshee wails, which took all the spectators by surprise and prompted nervous toddlers into answering howls. As they kicked their horses into a lumbering trot, they unsheathed and brandished grey plastic pirates' cutlasses.

Even the swaying punters hanging around in front of the beer tent were aware that this was the kind of unexpected event which could make their day, and they started cheering loudly.

Foxy Warren was among them, drinking away his disappointment at his dog's disgrace and failure in the terrier race and didn't notice when Rocket's lead slipped from his grasp. The fox-terrier still had scores to settle with Ginger, Dougy Swallow's Jack Russell. He soon scented out his earlier opponent and confronted him with a raucous snarl. Ginger wasn't in the mood to stand his ground, and despite his advanced years, took off as if someone had put a firework up his rear end.

Rocket kept very close behind and caught up with his quarry as they emerged directly between the blue, semi-naked foot soldiers, and Boadicea's chariot ponies, who'd just broken into a trot, with the cavalry coming up fast on either side of the chariot.

The dogs were now in full fight mode, up on their hind legs, snarling furiously and snapping their teeth right under the ponies' noses. The ponies knew from their own bitter experience that you don't get in the way of two terriers engaged in a dispute. Together, they reared up, tipping the chariot backwards, catapulting Boadicea over her husband's head.

'Compton, jump!' Lady Wynyates bellowed as she flew over him and, with an alarming sound of splintering old wood, the wheels disintegrated and the trap turned upside down on top of Sir Compton Wynyates, while the ponies, finding they could tear themselves loose, took off with the stampeding cavalry.

The mounted warriors, still screaming – now from sheer terror – cut a broad swathe through the crowd, heading for the open grass beside the lake, and taking the ponies with them.

Hard on their heels, racing as fast as her short, stiff legs would carry her, Boadicea was distraught about losing her ponies, and furious that her moment of glory had been hijacked. With her long black wig flying behind her, she didn't give a backward glance at her crumpled dog cart, or her husband trapped beneath it.

The cavalry charged headlong into the lake where Terry Cotter had just started trying to show off his manoeuvres in the coracle, which tended, in any case, to behave unpredictably. Foolishly, with his usual bravado, he had positioned himself at the end of the lake where it prepared to revert to the stream it was when it came in at the other end.

The first of the hefty pied cobs thundered into the lake and swam straight into the fragile cow-hide craft, sending it into an uncontrollable spin towards the rim of the lake where the natural water flow spilt over the edge in a six foot drop before the stream continued its journey down a coomb to the River Teme. The small craft and the potter disappeared with a loud cry and a splintering crash as they hit the rocky bed of the stream below.

The mobile librarian, who'd abandoned all pretence of not being terrified, fell off the back of her mount, over its substantial rump, and floundered desperately in the water until Harry Huggins plunged in to lifesave her. He dragged her back onto the grassy bank by the lake where he proceeded, quite unnecessarily as it turned out, to give her mouth to mouth resuscitation, while the drunk hoodlums from the beer tent bellowed 'IN, OUT, IN, OUT,' with loud, raucous cheers.

The two Shetland ponies, having galloped headlong into the water, paddled a few yards before realising that they didn't like it, and turned around to scramble back up the bank. Somewhere in the lake they had lost their scarlet drapery and they started to shake themselves vigorously, giving Lady Wynyates a good soaking as she arrived to fling her arms around them. Taking hold of what remained of their golden bridles, she led them back up the slope, with her Egyptian black wig hanging loosely down one side of her face. Reggie was waiting at the top of the bank to console her.

'Cecilia, thank God you caught 'em before they got into trouble.'

'They're fine,' Lady Wynyates snapped unexpectedly. 'But what about that fucking dog?'

Reggie who had never heard Lady Wynyates use raw expletives, almost backed away in astonishment. 'The dogs? Yeh, well,' he yammered. 'I've had words with Foxy. Dougy Swallow's distraught that his old dog was so upset, though he seems to be all right now, and Ginger...'

'I don't give a damn about Dougy's old pooch; he's harmless enough. But that dog of Foxy's should be put down. He's always getting into scraps, and he tried to roger my Staffy outside the Post Office.'

'Funnily enough, he looked half asleep when Foxy brought him up for the terrier races, then started fighting as soon as they were out of the traps.' Reggie thought about what he could offer to console Lady Wynyates. 'We'll certainly bar him from all future races.'

Lady Wynyates grunted her lack of satisfaction. They were approaching the remains of the dog cart. 'They managed to get Sir Compton out from under the chariot,' Reggie said encouragingly. 'He wasn't too badly hurt, though I don't think he'll be able to wear that helmet again; another dog's gone off with one of the horns.'

'I told him to jump, silly little bugger. Still, I'm glad he's out.'

'And of course,' Reggie took a deep breath and spoke in a strangled voice, 'I'll refund that two grand you gave me for the dog cart.'

'Don't insult me Reggie. I could see those wheel spokes were dodgy. But you were selling it so bloody cheap, I was just going to have them replaced. The trouble was I was frantic to get this pageant ready and I didn't have much time...'

They had reached the scene of the crash. Lady Wynyates looked forlornly at the wreck of Boadicea's conveyance for a moment, then with visible determination, drew herself upright, pulled off the displaced wig, and laughed. 'At least there weren't any photographers here – after that bloody awful picture of my legs waving in the air appeared in the *Clarion*.'

'Oh, Gawd,' Reggie groaned. 'I'm sorry about that.'

'It didn't really matter, I got quite a bit of fan mail as a result,' Lady Wynyates chortled. 'Anyway, we may as well get a drink, eh Reggie?' She spotted her husband sitting humped on a straw bale intended for spectators of the pageant. 'Compton certainly looks as if he needs one.'

Reggie hadn't been expecting the Gladys Price Guess-My-Weight event to be particularly contentious, but he was glad he'd had a couple with Lady Wynyates when, soon afterwards, he had to announce the result.

'Ladies and gentleman,' Reggie began, still enjoying his role as ringmaster. 'It is my pleasure to bring to you the result of this year's Guess-My-Weight competition, which attracted a record-breaking two hundred entries, at a quid a go, half to the church fund, and half to the astute punter who's guessed it right. What might have gone on in the betting exchanges and in any illicit bookmakers' accounts is of no concern to the Church Fund Committee, but if any operators have made a fat profit on all the events today, they will naturally want to bung a bit at the church fund – even if they have to do it anonymously... Mr Crobin. Now let's hear that all important figure which, I'm sorry to say to all you illiterate youngsters, is in old-fashioned avoirdupois, and the name of the clever not to say lucky beggar that guessed it.' Reggie held up a large envelope from which he pulled a slip of paper bearing the results. 'Gladys' recorded weight – wait for it!' he admonished an indignant rustle of impatience, 'was – Bloody Hell! – sorry ladies and gents – eighteen stone, four ounces.'

At this point, as planned, Gladys joined him on his temporary podium of two straw bales and a wooden pallet. There was a gasp as she stepped up. At her most recent public appearance at the Fox & Ferret, when Crobin had first officially opened his book, she had been her customary size – that of a sumo wrestler who'd won a few contests and had a weakness for doughnuts. Now she looked like a sumo wrestler who'd recently contracted anorexia – still large but nothing like as alarmingly bulky as she had been.

'It's a bloody stitch-up!' an angry voice from the crowd bellowed, soon to be joined by others.

'She's chuffin' cheated.'

'Her must of padded herself in the tent!'

Reggie, shaken himself by the transformation in Gladys's weight and the public mood, held up a hand. 'Now then ladies and gents... The vicar weighed her himself. I'm sure he stands by the result. And here he is.'

The vicar who by then was expecting at least some dissent, if not an out-and-out riot, skipped nimbly onto the podium and waved gleefully at a crowd that was swelling as the whiff of scandal grew. 'Hello, everyone. Thanks so much for you support today.'

'Never mind that,' a solid looking rustic with a head like a large red spud growled uncompromisingly. 'Gladys has taken us all for a ride.'

'Yeh, she's gone on a diet and then disguised 'erself,' said his stern-looking mate.

'All's fair in love and guessing games,' crowed the vicar, who prided himself on his use of wordplay. 'A game that's too easy is no fun to play. And I can confirm Mr ffinch-Leigh's figure – Gladys weighed in at a healthy eighteen stone, four ounces.'

The crowd murmured sceptically.

Reggie glanced down at the paper in his hand. 'And the clever punter who guessed her weight and takes home the hundred pound prize is... Oh my Gawd!' he groaned, '...Charlie Rafferty.'

There was an enraged howl from the assembled villagers and shouts of 'Cheat', 'Stitch-up', 'Bloody swindle!'

Reggie turned to the vicar, who shrugged. He'd played no part in identifying the winner.

'Well, there it is,' Reggie told his restless audience. 'Charlie entered a weight of eighteen stone, ten ounces, and he was the nearest by three stone.'

'Should be a steward's inquiry,' the potato head bellowed. 'It's a bloody rip-off! At Crobin's weigh-in last month she was more'n twenty-four stone.'

'Now,' said the vicar, who had known about Gladys's spectacular downsizing but had underestimated the reaction, 'I think we should extend our congratulations to Gladys for achieving such terrific weight loss in such a short space of time.'

Gladys, who had stood without uttering a word during this very public debate about her personal mass, took it as a cue to go on the rampage. She stepped forward and grabbed the microphone from Reggie's hand. 'Listen you lot,' she shouted, 'you've been laughing at me for years, I know, and it serves you bloody right if you've lost.'

A voice from the back of the crowd, but unmistakably Foxy Warren's, yelled, 'How much is Charlie giving you, then?'

Gladys immediately burst into tears, dropped the microphone and scrambled down from the podium to a general murmur of sympathy. The vicar, looking baffled and forlorn, watched her go, while Reggie sighed again and shook his head. He'd grown up used to seeing a dissatisfied rabble around the stalls of dodgy market traders, but if he'd known what a bear garden a competition at a village fête could become, he would never have volunteered his services. Leaving the vicar to deal with any more flak, he followed Gladys from the podium and took her off to the beer tent.

Chapter Seven

Despite moments of turmoil and unplanned drama, the sun set on the fête with an air of great success. The villagers had loved the chaos of the pageant and the fracas following the Guess-My-Weight results, and most went home feeling they'd had their money's worth from all the mishaps, while more money than ever had been raised for the church, which was the main beneficiary of the event. Rosita's efforts and energy had been applauded and she'd been warmly thanked by everyone. The committee had already begged her to let the fête happen at the Towers the following year, to which she had happily agreed.

Lady Wynyates, recognising all that Reggie and Rosita had done, had fully recovered her sense of humour even before Reggie, who understood the value of flattery, had judged her Staffordshire bull-terrier winner of the Dog-Whose-Owner-I'd-Most-Like-to-Take-Home competition.

Terry Cotter, the Demon Potter, had conceded that he could blame no one but himself for taking his coracle too close to the small cateract at the end of the lake before the Ancient British cavalry had charged in and nudged him over the edge.

And, in the absence of conclusive proof, Charlie Rafferty had been exonerated from accusations of collusion with Gladys Price in the Guess-My-Weight event, and was announced the winner, although Crobin refused to pay out the big bet Charlie had had with him.

As the last punters straggled away from the fête, Reggie was sitting with Rosi on the terrace in the still warm sun, and pouring his first glass of claret.

'Rosi, my clever little beauty, you really pulled it off.'

'Oh Reggie, we both did. Everyone say what a marvellous emcee you are, and how funny your commenting ..'

'Commentating?'

'You know what I mean...and how you look after poor Gladys.'

As she spoke, Reggie's mobile tootled.

He answered, to hear for a few moments only the ambient

sounds of the country and domestic fowls at the other end.

'Misser Finchley?'

'Who is it?'

'Misser Finchley, is it?'

'Yeh.'

'It's Owen, the mole.'

Reggie's head shot up with excitement. He'd been growing anxious to hear back from the man who held the key to his deal with Emmet Rafferty.

'Great. What's the news?'

'I got some.'

'What?'

'Moles'

'Already?'

'Aye.'

'How many?'

'I've got about a hundred for you – for starters.'

'Brilliant! When can you bring them?'

'I ain't deliverin'. You've to come and get 'em.'

'OK. I'll be over tomorrow.'

'With the money, mind.'

Reggie winced. 'Of course,' he said, with a certainty he didn't feel. 'I'll see you then.'

Reggie had thought Owen would just bring them when he had them all, and he hadn't expected him to have so many so soon. He would have to talk about the money to Rosita, which he'd been hoping to avoid. While he'd been talking to the mole catcher on the phone, she'd got up to go inside, to the room next to the kitchen which she'd taken over for herself.

She had switched on her new computer and was already yelling lustily at it. *'Cojones! Ojete!'* Lara had tried to teach her how to use it and usually, somehow, Rosita managed to extract what she wanted from the machine, making no effort to understand it, and abusing it like a half-witted servant.

Despite one of these regular outbursts, Reggie's wife was ccstatic at the success of the fête and about having the new wedding reception project. Reggie found her sitting at the table in what she called her 'beez'ness office', sensed her continuing euphoria and came straight to the point. 'Rosi, my little Latino lover, we need to take out a bit of wonga.'

'Oh, Reggie... You didn't go to have a gamble on Sue's mum?'

'No, course not; I knew it would be a stitch up. I've got to pick up a hundred moles tomorrow.'

'Moles? *Moles? Topos!* Why the earth you are getting one hun'red moles?

Reggie sighed. He always remembered too late that it was much less risky to discuss these things with his wife before they happened, rather than after, but he was always badly swayed by his own natural optimism that things would just work out smoothly on their own somehow. 'I've got an order for 'em,' he answered evasively.

'For Gossake! Who from?'

'Rosi, trust me, all right? This is a good deal, there should be a good eight or ten grand in it.'

'What about the table? Fifteen thousan' that cost.'

'Rosi, there's a punter out there for it, trust me – now I *know* there's a pair. I just have to find out what happened to it.'

'If you find this Johnny person...'

'I'll find him, don't you worry my Colombian beauty. And his name is *Jonty.*'

'Whatever. That lill scruff pot, Evan Poo – he make a monkey out of you.'

'He didn't know I was going to buy it. It was Ted Buckton's fault for filling me up with that Floppidick cider before the sale.'

'You couldn't say 'No' to the cider?'

'Of course not, Rosi; you know I don't like to hurt people's feelings.'

'I think you crazy. Moles! *Topos!* For Gossake!' She shook her head. 'OK, I get the money. But where you are going to put them?'

Reggie hadn't yet given this much thought but, relieved that Rosi was going to play ball, he came back fast. 'In the cellars, of course, and I'll get Harry Huggins to dig up a few hundred worms to feed them.'

Rosita looked doubtful, but added nothing. 'OK,' she said. 'How much of wonga you need?'

'Just two gorillas.'

Reggie set off next morning with two thousand pounds inside his jacket pocket to pay Owen the Mole. He'd agreed a price per live mole at double the going rate for a dead one, and was feeling quite pleased with himself, helped by Rosita agreeing to get the money without raising more objections, despite the hiccups in passing on the table. Reggie pushed to the back of his busy mind the guilt he felt at her continuing belief in his business prowess. He certainly wasn't as confident as he pretended that he'd come out of his table purchase without taking a loss, and he knew he'd been lucky that she was still glowing from the thrill of showing off her garden and grounds at the fête.

He was also relieved that no one seemed to think it unusual or odd that they were going to open up Mortimer Towers and its grounds as a wedding venue. It seemed that people found it quite normal for any of the statelier homes in the county to open up their doors for paying events. Reggie had heard Dougy Swallow talking about it to Jones the Beef. 'Now all the toffs are trying to make a few quid out of their big houses, just to pay the bloody heating bills.'

He'd never thought when he moved to the country and took up residence in his

Shropshire mansion that he would end up in the matrimonial business, but it was giving Rosi such a buzz, he couldn't complain, especially if she made a few quid towards their winter fuel costs.

Nor, the next day, would he have guessed that he would be driving west, past the furthest corner of Shropshire to the Kerry Hills to organise picking up a consignment of live moles. Before he'd left, he'd baffled Huggins with his instruction to erect a pen made of sturdy scaffold boards on the stone floor of the Mortimer Towers cellars.

Reggie parked his old Landrover a short way down the lane from the path up to Owen's house. The brand new Landrover Defender he'd seen last time was parked in the same place. Once again, Reggie peered into the back, but there was nothing to be seen. Wondering once again how a man as humbly employed as Owen the Mole could afford such a motor, he headed on up the hill. He was expected, and he had no doubt that his arrival had been noted.

Reggie sensed that Owen the Mole had relaxed a little since their first meeting, perhaps because he was a paying punter now. The small, leather-tanned old man, with his antique tweed jacket tied at the waist with a piece of old sisal, beckoned him through the door as he had last time, and waved him at one of the rickety elm chairs by the empty fireplace. The tiny dwelling reminded him of *Ratty's* home in the illustrated *Wind in the Willows*, which had been the first book his mother gave him to read.

'You'll have a drop of applejack?' Owen croaked, reaching for a bottle on the dresser without waiting for an answer.

Reggie, recognising the need for these rituals and, anyway, ready for a drink, nodded happily. Owen poured a large slug of the pale amber spirit into two small lead crystal glasses and handed one to Reggie.

Owen put his small head to one side, and gave Reggie a quizzical look. 'You got the dosh?'

Reggie grinned and pulled a grubby envelope from his pocket – an envelope he'd specially chosen for its pre-used appearance. He'd taken the bank's paper bands off the wads of used notes, to give the impression that he had his own stash on hand at home. He took them out and put them on the table in front of Owen.

Once the old man was satisfied all the money was there and had tucked it into one of the many pockets in his jacket, he topped up Reggie's glass with cider brandy. 'You going to tell me where they're going, then?'

Reggie grinned. 'Course not. No more'n you'll tell me where you caught 'em.'

'There ain't much secret about that. There's moles everywhere in this country, millions of 'em, they say, and no sign of coming down.' Owen took a sharp slug of his own applejack. 'It's not the 'where', but the 'how' you should be asking.'

'But you won't tell that, will you?'

Owen, who enjoyed the possession of his rare and special knowledge, chuckled. 'No I bloody won't.'

Reggie had spent some time puzzling over what he'd seen in the back of the Landrover the last time he'd turned up, when Owen wasn't expecting anyone. He was sure the few bits of tack he'd seen were connected to Owen's rare trade, but he guessed the old mole catcher was a long way from being ready to talk to him about it.

'Where's my moles, then?'

'I got 'em in ten wood crates, ten in each. You wants to loose 'em out o'there quick as you can. You make sure you puts 'em somewhere secure, 'cos I ain't catching extras for no charge. And they eats 'alf their own weight every day so make sure you got plenty of fresh worms for 'em to eat. Then you come back with another bundle, and I'll have maybe another lot for you.'

Reggie, wondering if the younger Huggins would be able to get enough worms, helped the old man to carry ten heavy crates lined with wire mesh down to his old Landrover. He set off well pleased with the bit of business he'd just done and buzzing with the excitement of getting another deal underway.

While Reggie was doing his business with Owen the Oont up near Beguildy, Lara and Rosita were taking a break from clearing up after the fête. Lara was full of ideas for the first wedding party to be held at Mortimer Towers.

Rosita was fizzing with excitement and full of thanks to Lara. 'It's fantastic – your idea for the weddings. I have so many enquiries. People love the idea to have their reception here. Look the view,' she said waving her arm at the spectacular panorama of the Shropshire Hills from the terrace at the back of the house.

'Yes, it's wonderful,' Lara agreed unequivocally, 'and to be here in this lovely sunshine!' she added, for Shropshire was basking under an unusually blue sky. 'I couldn't spend another minute in

London when it's like this.'

'How is it in London?' Rosita asked, not really missing the metropolis herself.

'Busy, as always. Getting ready for the Paris shows and a few previews. Then my novel's being launched next month. Some arse who wants to get me into bed has told me he can make it into a movie; he's set up a few meetings which'll probably come to nothing.'

'What about the book you say you do with the striptease artiste I introduce to you?' Rosita asked.

'Oh, that?' Lara laughed. '*Thong Without End?* That's been great; she had loads of amazing stories – half of them libellous – but what's left is still terrific. The publishers are thrilled, and they didn't even try to change the name.'

'Any good parties?' Rosita wanted to know.

'There's been a few new club openings, new places for Prince Harry's mates to spend their parents' money on nasty cocktails and throw up. Same as usual, really.'

'I used to like all that, but... ' Rosita shrugged her small shoulders. 'I happy in the country now.'

'I envy you Rosi. You're very lucky. This place is wonderful, so clever and stylish, the way you've made so much of the Victorian kitsch... '

'The way *you* have done it... ' Rosita insisted. 'The peoples around here, they cannot believe it; they thought was a kind of joke before – now they are *amazed.*'

Lara nodded in happy agreement. 'It has worked, and I'm really glad you gave me the chance. It was a challenge, but then it always had tons of character, and it's in a perfect spot. *You* were so clever to see the potential in high Victoriana. And Reggie's great too – honest, thoughtful and so charismatic. You don't know it, because you're foreign, but there aren't many people who could carry off what he's done, turning up in one of England's most old-fashioned counties, an out-and-out, unreconstructed market trader like him, buying a place that looks like this, seeing what could be made of it when no one else round here could, and bringing out an enchanting kind of fantasy, then making friends with most of the nobs in the county.'

'Oh, I *can* see that – I see they confused when first they talk to him, and then when they know him, is like it doesn't matter that he is different, and we are very happy here. I just need to have a thing to keep me busy. And thanks to you, I got it now. Already the magazines – the *County Monthly*, things like that – they want to come and take photos, and when the article you have done is out, there will be more. And I love that. But, Lara, what about you? You got new lover?'

'There's a few candidates, but no successful applicants. I find them all just too predictable and manageable.'

Rosita nodded. 'You need strong man, but not bully. My Reggie like that. Is hard for him, now all the wonga goes. But he will be fine. He just warming up and needs to get his focus, then his instinks will show him where is a deal.'

Lara nodded. 'Of course. He's a natural – someone people like to do deals with.'

'Sometimes strange deals, too. Right now he is buying live *topos* – what you call... *moles*.'

'Moles?!' Lara shrieked. 'What the bloody hell is he going to do with live moles?'

Rosita shrugged both shoulders. 'God knows, but I 'ave to truss him. He's a man with pride.'

'You're right. I'm sure he knows what he's doing.'

'Maybe; maybe no,' Rosita grinned. 'But he's a big boy.'

'He sure is,' Lara grinned and stood up. 'It's so hot. Shall we have a swim?'

'You know we don't have no pool. Reggie say pools are for noovo-rich.'

Lara laughed. 'I know what he means! Anyway, you don't need one. I meant let's swim in the lake – like the village potter yesterday!'

A little later, they'd changed into bikinis and were cavorting gleefully in the calm cool waters of the lake where, the day before, Terry Cotter had spun in his coracle before disappearing over the edge.

They were still there, with their laughter echoing off the trees and shrubs around the lake, when Jason de Chateauneuf arrived.

Rosita hadn't been expecting him, but now she smiled to herself that he had turned up while Lara was looking as good as ever in a Pucci bikini.

'Oh look, here is Mr Chatternerve,' she shrieked.

Jason was walking down towards the lake, as if drawn by some irresistible force. He couldn't believe his eyes.

Ever since he'd first seen her, Lara had become for him the most exciting, tantalising woman he'd ever met – the kind of girl he'd dreamed of when he was a young acne-spotted kid, rattling away on his computer in a bedroom of his family's terraced house by the Lower Tyne, while his mates were busy chanting with the Toon Army up at St James's Park.

Since those days, it had taken him just ten years to make his first million in computer software. He'd left all his Geordie schoolmates behind and adopted the name of his native town (in French, to reflect his cosmopolitanism) and he'd set himself a mission of two major challenges – to acquire a large country estate and to find a sophisticated, beautiful wife to put in it – the kind of woman who would never have even noticed the little working-class nerd he'd once been.

Now he'd bought his estate and, out of the blue, right up here in the depths of the Marches, he had found exactly the girl who'd always featured in his fantasies.

This discovery had been a problem for Jason. Since he'd first come across Reggie ffinch-Leigh and his exotic wife, he'd resented them for the obvious success they'd made of their new lives in the country, and their ability to fit in somehow, despite Reggie making no secret of his origins as a London street market trader.

So far the only times Jason was able to see Lara was when she was on one of her sporadic visits to Shropshire, where she seemed to spend most of her time with the ffinch-Leighs at Mortimer Towers.

Even as he approached her down by the lake, he could feel his confidence wilt. There was something extraordinary in the way she could look at a man as if she might really fancy him, and at the same, see right through him, as if he were an ingenuous twelve year-old.

He knew she was playing with him, as he guessed she did with most of the men who fancied her, and he was determined to show her she couldn't do it with him.

She was walking up the grassy slope now, through the remnants of the fête, wearing only her bikini, carrying her espadrilles and a towel. Her toenails gleamed geranium red on her tanned feet. Her breasts, hidden behind tiny triangles of scarlet cotton were perfect in shape, size and, Jason guessed, texture. He gazed, tantalised, at her bikini bottom, which was tied together loosely on either side of her slender hips.

'Hi, Lara,' he called. 'Good morning Rosi.'

'Hyello, Jason,' Rosi said. 'You didn't come to the fête.'

'You know... I'm very busy at the moment. But I've come now.'

'You want tea?'

'Yes, please,' Jason nodded as he watched the two women approach. He wanted to kiss Lara, easily, like he'd seen Peregrine Rokesay do it, but he didn't trust himself not to mess it up. He kissed Rosi instead; he had to admit that old Reggie's missus was a good-looking woman, too, in an unsubtle, earthy sort of way.

He merely nodded at Lara. 'Actually,' he said, 'I came round to see if Lara would like to come up and look at my place some time – you know, while she's up here... or come out?'

'Out? Where?' Lara asked.

'Oh, I don't know. Dinner? Maybe? I've got the chopper here. We could go to Paris, or Deauville?'

'I didn't come up here to go off somewhere else in some beastly little helicopter. I hate them – they're so cramped and noisy.'

When Reggie pulled up in his Landrover with his load of moles, outside the *porte cochere* at Mortimer Towers, he noticed a new Ferrari parked between his sedate old Bentley and Lara Lydbury's silver DB5 with its hood down.

'Chatternerve,' he chuckled to himself, '...and the lovely Lara. No doubt these things are connected.' Rosita had been planning to get them together again, mostly – Reggie thought – out of a sense of mischief. She loved Lara's way of deflating egotistical men, especially very rich young men like Jason de Chateauneuf who thought they could have whoever they liked. Reggie chuckled to himself as he clambered out of his battered old vehicle.

Rosi was out on the stone terrace with Lara and the young Geordie tycoon. Reggie walked round to join them, kissed Rosita before he glanced at her two guests. He turned to Lara, kissed her, not warmly enough to upset to his wife, but enough to annoy Jason, before turning to him. 'Ah, Chatternerve, I wonder if you can give me a hand. I've got a few crates of moles to unload down into my cellar.'

Jason bridled indignantly. 'I haven't come over here to fetch and carry for you, and mess up my clothes.' He tweaked up a fold of his Italian designer trousers. 'Anyway, what the hell are you doing with crates of moles?'

Reggie grinned. 'Just an honest bit of country trading.'

Lara, glad of the chance to put Jason down, leaped to her feet. 'That's OK, Reggie. I'll do it with you.'

Jason flushed. 'Don't bother, Lara, you don't have to do it.'

'I wasn't offering because I have to. I'd just like to help my old friend Reggie, and I'd hate to see you doing any unnecessary fetching and carrying that might be beneath your enormous dignity or damage your *Giorgio Armani* trousers.'

De Chateauneuf winced and hovered uncertainly. Reggie laughed. 'You sit down Lara. Chatternerve can do it... if your back's better after that nasty fall the other week?' Reggie added provocatively.

Jason's eyes narrowed. 'Just don't go there. You know bloody well I'd have beaten you if you hadn't ridden me into that tree.'

'Maybe if you'd had a few jumping lessons as well at that expensive jockeys' school you went to, you'd have been able to get over it, and win the race.'

'Shudduppa you two,' Rosita interjected. 'You both bloody

useless. Neither of you deserve to win.'

'Too right!' Reggie chortled. 'And it looks like Jason needn't worry about soiling his *Armani* trousers after all; here's Huggins.'

The Towers' tireless gardener had appeared around the side of the house from the walled garden. Rosita had been keeping him going full-time since she'd got all fired up about opening the gardens for the fête and her first wedding party. Huggins was delighted; he loved working up at Mortimer Towers, especially now that it was a functioning house and garden again.

Huggins had made the pen Reggie had asked for, as a holding place for his moles in the basement. In the end, Jason, Huggins, Lara and Reggie all helped to unload the hundred moles into the pen in the cellar of the house, which was far older than the edifice above it, and part of the original 15th-century mansion that Victorian Cheney-Longvilles had pulled down and replaced.

Reggie looked at it. 'Is it mole proof?'

Huggins drew himself up indignantly. 'Course it is – unless they can burrow through stone.'

'And you've sorted them out a bit of nosh?'

'I filled a sack of worms. I'll tip them in the pen.'

Jason stood back and looked at the sea of moles, heaving themselves around the stone floor in confusion, waggling their long slender noses as they scented their lunch. He shook his head as if he were witnessing some kind of madness. 'What sort of scam are you up to now, Reggie? What would you want with a load of live moles? Don't let them anywhere near my place. I had masses of them appear out of nowhere up there, and I've just had a hundred or so cleared off at twenty quid a mole.'

'Twenty quid, sir?' Huggins gasped. 'That's a hell of a price for such a lot of 'em. Who's done them for you?'

'A little Welshman – Owen Preece from Beguildy.'

Reggie had to stop himself bursting with laughter. 'Where did you find him, then?'

'He came round soon after I moved in to see if I needed any vermin control, and left me his card. He was real efficient doing the job. But Reggie, what the bloody hell are you going to do with these moles?'

Reggie returned an enigmatic smile. 'I can't explain to you, Jason; when you've lived in the sticks a bit longer, you'll understand.'

Back on the terrace outside the house, Lara turned to de Chateuneuf. 'So, where are you taking me to dinner?'

Jason didn't let himself be caught out this time. 'It's a surprise. I'll pick you up here at half past seven.'

'No you won't. I'll be at my dad's. I'll introduce you; he likes a good laugh. And no helicopters, mind.'

When De Chateauneuf left, Reggie, Rosita and Lara stayed on the terrace. They still heard his Ferrari fire up and roar away from the house.

Reggie turned to Lara. 'You're having a laugh aren't you – going out with Chatternerve?'

'What do you think? But my pa's just as keen as you to stop him putting up all those wind turbines so I thought I might do a bit of espionage. I'm going to try to find out what his plans are so we know what we're dealing with.'

Reggie chuckled. 'Good girl! I almost feel sorry for him. Here, have another glug before you go off and get into your glad rags.'

'Thanks, Reggie.' She took a sip and looked quizzically at him. 'Are you going to tell me why on earth you're buying all these bloody moles?'

'To fulfil an order, of course.'

'Yes, but what for?'

'I'll be honest with you, Lara. I don't bloody know. I wish I did, but one of my local contacts came to me, knowing that Reggie ffinch-Leigh has the reputation for doing the impossible... He's got a punter who wants them delivered to the Welsh coast – to go to Ireland for some reason.'

'To *Ireland?*' Lara repeated. 'That's weird, Reggie – you know there's no moles in Ireland?'

'What? Aren't there? I never knew that. Bloody hell! I wonder what they want them for? But Lara, how do you know a thing like that?'

Lara picked up the latest edition of the fashion & gossip maga-zine she wrote for. 'I've got a piece about the little Talpidae in here. Of course, it's mainly about their lovely pelts, and the history of their use in fashion. What you might call the unique selling point of mole fur is that it has no knap; it falls either way, so the little fel-lows can move backwards or forwards in comfort along their un-derground tunnels.'

'What made you write about that, then?'

'Is about the famous Paris designer,' Rosita couldn't help join-ing in. 'You know – the one who was drunk, insulting everyone? – Lara say he is doing the big Moleskin story this autumn – isn't it, Lara?'

Lara nodded. 'It sounds bizarre, but we got a strong leak from inside his studio that he's going to show little boleros and tops trimmed with what they call *taupe* – little slivers of moleskin. He's bloody eccentric and his collections are always risky, but this may take off – and it's a little less contentious than other furs, be-cause most countries treat moles as pests that have to be got rid of.'

Rosita pointed with a small, sharp finger at the open page of the magazine. 'There's what Lara has written – there – about where the skins come from, how they get them ready – everything.'

'That's amazing. My punter said nothing about wanting them for their skins, but who knows? Maybe these Paddies are on to it too, building up stocks, to be ready for the rush when it takes off – it's like that with fashion fads. Come to think of it, I used to know some big fashion boys in Ireland. I once sold 'em a pile of army-surplus cavalry nose-bags; they told me they were going to dye them purple and sell 'em as shoulder bags for the dolly birds. I said to them, "You're having a laugh, aren't you? There's three ruddy great holes in the bottom so the nags could breathe while they were noshing – all the girls' tack'll fall through 'em." The Pad-dies just shrugged their shoulders and laughed. "Ah well; what the hell," they said. "The birds is so darned t'ick, they won't think of that till they've got 'em home.".' Reggie chuckled. 'They could still get caught on this mole thing, mind, even if it does take off for a bit. I can remember when there was a massive craze for big plastic hoops – hoola hoops they called them – back in the '60s. Every bird from Billericay to Billingsgate was standing around, waggling their arse all over the place – it was a sight, I can tell you. Then Uncle Arthur told me – he had tears in his eyes – he'd just bought twenty thousand bleedin' hoola hoops from Hong Kong and by the time they arrived at the docks in Wapping, the craze was gone – you couldn't give 'em away! I think he managed to get rid of them years later when they came back into fashion again for about five minutes.' Reggie chuckled. 'Still, that's not my problem. I've got a simple order to fill. I need to get my two hundred moles together and take 'em over to Aberdovey in the next couple of weeks.'

Lara was still grinning at the thought of Arthur's hoola hoops. 'Well, best of luck Reggie. I hope you don't get stuck with your moles.'

Lara climbed into her Aston Martin and slithered up the drive spitting gravel behind her. Reggie and Rosita watched her go. They were both grinning.

'She'll give that little Chatternerve a run for his money,' Reggie observed.

'Hope so,' Rosita giggled. 'That's why I ask him to stay for tea; I wanted to see her play with him and torment him.'

'You like to watch combat, don't you. You'd have loved those gladiator shows like old Caesar used to put on at the Colosseum for the Roman riff-raff.'

'Maybe,' Rosita laughed, 'though I don't really want her to kill him! Anyway, she say she will call me now an' again, to give progress report of dinner.'

Lancelot Lydbury looked at his daughter, raised a bushy brow and gave her a big hug. 'You're a very clever girl! Though I don't know where you got it from. I never passed an exam at school, and your mother – God bless her – was as thick as a donkey's doodah.'

Lara laughed; she loved it that she was still so close to her father, especially since her mother had died ten years before. '*You're* not thick, Pa – you're just barking mad, and a wily old bastard.'

'I hope I'm wily enough to see off that beastly little Chatternerve and his horrid scheme to wreck the landscape with windmills. I know what these young tycoons are like who've worked their way up from the honest *Sun*-reading classes.'

'You mean like Reggie?'

'You know perfectly well I don't. Reggie's scarcely young, and no tycoon; he's the salt of the earth – a fella who got lucky and knows how to make the most of it without being untrue to himself. I admire Reggie Finchley. But that squirt Chatternerve, he's a stubborn little shit who'll hold out on this windmill thing, just to prove he can. He must have a hide like a Nile croc to fend off all the flak he's getting over this preposterous, crooked, totally impractical wind turbine racket. He doesn't need the money; he's just doing it because, in theory, he can – and bugger everyone else!' Lancelot shook his head. 'I don't understand why he should want to live surrounded by people who hate him. Perhaps that's what turns him on, as they say. Anyway, where's he taking you this evening? I can't imagine it'll be for a pint of cider at the Fox & Ferret.'

'I wish it were, but God knows where he'll think of. I'm afraid I detect a pretty desperate air about him, and he'll try and come on strong.'

'My dear Lara, don't do this...'

'Don't be silly, Pa. I can look after myself. Remember Wet-Hands Willy?'

'The one you pushed out of the car while he was driving?'

'That's the one. Pity he ended up in the A&E in Slough Hospital, but he never groped me again.'

'I'm not surprised; he broke his wrist, didn't he?'

Lara nodded with a grin. 'But anyway, if Jumpy Jason tries anything like that, he'll regret it. And I'll be in touch with Rosi all the time. I'll be fine. Now let's have a cup of tea, and tell me all the news.' She always loved hearing her father's version of local events

'News? Up here? That's a laugh. The most sensational thing

that's happened is that Mrs Diddlebury, who plays the organ in St Ken's, has got so darned fat she finds it too difficult to reach the upper notes, and has taken to adapting the music to suit, which means more bum notes than ever and sometimes entirely different hymns.' Lancelot looked at his daughter's bored face. 'Sorry, I told you nothing ever happened.'

'Nonsense, Pa. That's fascinating.'

'Ah, but I forgot about Thurleigh the gardener. He's taken to urinating at random around the garden; as a result he's killed off several important plants, especially if he's been on the toot the night before on that poisonous Floppidick cider. He denied it, of course, but one afternoon when I was snoozing in the folly, I woke up and saw him heading for the delphiniums just outside, unbuttoning as he went. He didn't see me inside, so I managed to film him on my phone camera and when he came in for his tea later, I made him watch it on the TV in the kitchen. He started crying, until I congratulated him on the size of his member, of which, by chance I'd got a good close up shot with my zoom lens.'

'Pa, you can't go round filming the gardener's willy. Is it legal, even?'

'I don't see why not, but that reminds me – Ivor the cowman up at Prossers' was found in the stables with his trousers around his ankles, on the point of entering Sally Prosser's champion Grade A Welsh pony. They felt they had to fire him, though I'm not quite sure why.'

'Pa, no! You're making this up! It must be because you're so bored out here on your own. You must come and stay with me in London for a while, to get a grip on reality.'

Lancelot sat up haughtily. 'Fine, if you don't like hearing about the sordid reality of bucolic existence, I'll just shut up.'

'Has anything happened up here that doesn't involve indiscreet bodily functions?'

Lancelot leaned back again in his chair and stared at the ceiling for a moment. 'Not that I can think of... though, there have been a few sightings of the albino badger, and a gang of chaps in tatty jeans came up from the BBC in Bristol to film it. I said the only

way they could do it was if they were blindfolded and driven up
there in the back of Foxy Warren's van so they couldn't see where
they were going. They complained a bit about the stink... And I
got a couple of hundred quid out of them.' Lancelot chuckled. He
was a very rich man, but he was always glad to get one over the
BBC, whom he deeply distrusted ever since he'd had a picture
stolen soon after a programme about his house had been shown
on TV. 'Which reminds me – I've had the big trebuchet remod-
elled to increase its range by about two hundred yards, and I've
turned it around so that, instead of facing across the valley, it's
facing Pant-y-Groes and my boundary with Chatternerve. The
smaller one still faces across the valley, and we'll be chucking
something across it – not sure what yet. With the big one I can
just about fling a ton over the conifer belt onto his land, just where
he's planning to put the first of those bloody windmills on the
Panty-Hose bog.'

Lancelot's trebuchet, a reconstructed mediæval weapon of war
which was something like an enormous catapult – the missile
launcher of the middle ages – was one of his proudest posses-
sions, and had also been featured on local TV programmes. The
vast oak and iron structure, instead of being on giant wooden
wheels as it would have been in a mediæval siege, was now set
deep into the earth towards the edge of his land.

'Pa, I think you should rely on public objections and the planning process before you bring your siege engine into play. It could
bugger up your own campaign.'

Lancelot sniffed. 'I don't see why, and your friend Reggie would-
n't be so chicken-hearted about it. He's as angry about Chatternerve's wind farm as I am.'

Lara laughed. 'And so is Rosita – absolutely livid that he should
be messing up her precious view. In fact it was Rosi who put me
up to giving Jason the big come on – though frankly, I don't know
what I can do that will help.'

'You'll think of something,' her father said proudly. 'See if you
can get him plastered so he'll open up a bit, or let something slip,
and have a good poke around at his place if you get the chance.

Anyway, you keep your eyes open after the shindig on Saturday night.'

Lancelot had amazed the local community early in the year by announcing that, quite uncharacteristically, he was agreeable to the annual Montgomery & West Salop hunt ball being held in his famously beautiful and historic grounds. A large marquee had already been put up on the vast lawn which swept down from the house to the banks of the River Clun.

Lara sighed. 'I thought my days of dreary hunt balls were well behind me, but I suppose I'll have to come, as it's here. Reggie's got a big table, and Perry Rokesay will have a good crowd.'

'It'll be eventful, I can tell you. As Chatternerve's chucked the travellers off the mill lane, I've let them come up with their bow tops to graze their ponies on the long acre outside the gates.'

'Oh Pa, you've done that just to make the hunt ball punters nervous, haven't you?'

'Partly, but I've got a few plans up my sleeve to let Jason de bloody Chatternerve know where he stands with broad public opinion round here regarding his blasted wind turbines. I want to see him made to look a complete fool and a laughing stock, because I believe that's the only way he'll be made to feel vulnerable. I've always found the travellers very reliable for that sort of thing. Obviously, I've given them strict instructions not to pinch anything from the guests' cars. They understand.'

'Go on then – tell me what you're going to do to Chatternerve.'

'No, I don't want to spoil your fun; but I will tell you that he's under the impression that the Midnight Steeplechase is ridden on horses.' Lancelot gave a short, good-natured grunt that was the closest he ever got to laughing.

Before Jason turned up to collect her from her father's house, Lara was looking forward to seeing what he would come up with to impress her as she'd rejected the idea of flying to Deauville or wherever. So far she didn't have much faith in his taste or judgement, but she didn't underestimate his resourcefulness.

When he came, she wasn't remotely prepared for his arrival in a perfectly restored early Victorian gig with enormous yellow wheels, drawn by a matching pair of handsome Cleveland Bays harnessed side-by-side, which he was driving with a groom sitting on a dickey seat behind his leather-buttoned bench.

As the high stepping horses clipped neatly down the long avenue to the house, Lara and her father stood watching from a tall window, half way down the stairs.

'Good God!' Lancelot gasped. 'He's really pushing the boat out, isn't he? And just look at him!'

When the gig was drawing up, the groom skipped off his perch and ran round to take the horses' heads, while Jason de Chateauneuf stowed his reins and stepped down carefully to the gravelled drive, just outside the great oak porch of the house. His normally neat black hair was tousled and raffish; he wore a loose cream silk shirt with baggy sleeves and a contour-hugging pair of fawn breeches tucked into brown knee-high boots. 'Good grief! I say! Now he thinks he's Mr Bloody Darcy!' Lancelot chuckled. 'Cunning bastard. If I didn't know what a little rat he was, I'd be impressed.' He turned to his daughter to gauge her reaction. 'Ah, I see you're *not* taken in, but you must admit, he's worked hard on the project. Just putting that turnout together must have taken some organising. It looks a though he might be a more formidable opponent than we've given him credit for.'

'Pa, he's a ridiculous little man, and I'm looking forward to putting him back in his box.'

'Of course, you must have your fun, and I dare say in that somewhat come-hither, floaty frock you'll have the whip hand. But be careful; don't underestimate him; he's obviously a very determined sort of chap.'

'Look, Pa. He's come up here, to one of the remoter, most old-fashioned corners of England, thinking he can simply buy his way into some kind of local standing in the naive belief that's all it takes.'

'That *is* all it took in the middle ages – loads of dosh and an ability to bump off your rivals without a second thought. That's what your ancestors did.'

'Maybe, but civilisation has moved on a bit since then – serf-dom and *droit de seigneur* aren't really acceptable these days...'

'I don't know about that,' her father interrupted, 'though I'll grant you, they're no longer legal.'

'You know what I mean. Anyway, there he is knocking on the door. Will you let him in?'

'I'll ask him what his intentions are,' Lancelot said with a wicked grin.

Lara thought she knew what de Chateauneuf's intentions were, but she had to give him points for not pressing them too hard. He handed her up into the gig in a way that would have had a Barbara Cartland heroine throbbing with unsuitable thoughts. She merely smiled to herself at the thought of her climbing into such an elegant 19th century conveyance in the flimsy short dress she'd decided to wear for the date.

Despite her animosity towards de Chateauneuf, Lara wasn't a naturally rude woman, unless it was plainly justified. She'd also grown up with horses and had never lost her enjoyment of them and, like her father, she loved the animals for aesthetic reasons as much as for the excitement and affection that being around them could bring.

Lara was fascinated by Jason's apparent enthusiasm for horses as he steered them competently back down the avenue of horn-beams that led from her father's house to the outside world. 'How come a Geordie lad like you has ended up so keen on horses?' she asked.

He turned to her, pleased she'd asked.

'When I was kid,' he began reflectively, 'living in Newcastle, horses were never part of my world; I only ever saw them on the telly, mostly when my dad was watching the racing, and I used to love the way they moved. But I really liked it when they showed the Royal Coaches – like at Charles and Di's wedding. I wasn't ten by then, but I was knocked out by it, and I always thought if I could make some money, that's what I'd do – and now I can, I have,' he added with a smugness that spoilt it. 'I've been learning how to drive horses for a long time, but I never thought of taking up riding until I decided to join the hunt.'

'I thought that was just to help your application for the wind farm,' Lara said pointedly.

De Chateauneuf stiffened. Lara thought she'd got to him, but after a deep breath he went on. 'Look Lara, as squire of Pant-y-Groes...'

'Squire of Pant-y-Groes?' Lara exclaimed. 'You?' She sighed. 'All right, I suppose you are.'

'As squire, I've got a few obligations: one is to make the most of the estate economically... and the other is to become involved in the activities that take place across my land. I've told the hunt they can go anywhere they like on my land; I think I should be around to see it when they do.'

'And that's when you bought the horse you rode in the hunt ride?'

'Ted Buckton sold that horse, which I heard afterwards had been bought by your friend Reggie – by mistake or something. As it happens, Ted knows what he's doing and he really sorted it out, so I took myself off, and learned to ride so I could do the race, and now I've been back to Newmarket to learn to jump – and d'you know what? – I've bloody cracked it.'

Lara didn't hide her scepticism. 'Are you going point-to-pointing then? You've got to be bloody good, or a bloody fool to do that, and most people start in their teens, not at forty-five.'

'I'm only forty-four. And I'm bloody good. There's a race coming up I might do.'

'What race?' Lara asked, knowing there were no point-to-point races for another six months.

'You'll see,' Jason said.

Reggie and Rosita were sitting on their terrace with the last of Reggie's bottles of vintage champagne on a table between them. They were contentedly watching the sun fill the sky with pink and golden streaks above the Shropshire hills, when Rosita's mobile blurted an Argentinean tango to signal a call.

It was Lara.

'How's it go?' Rosita cackled.

'Not good. I haven't wound him up at all yet. And listen to this! He turned up to collect me in a gig with huge yellow wheels drawn by a pair of beautiful horses.'

'Oh my *God*!' Rosita shrieked. 'Jus' like in *Sense & Sensibility*! The crafty bastar! He suss you out, no? '

'It'd take more than a few *Mills & Boon* moments to bring me round. We drove up to the old hill fort at Caractacus Mount and half way up we were met by one of his Polish blokes with two grumpy Welsh ponies. We climbed on them and they took us up to where dinner was laid on a table with a white cloth, silver, crystal glasses and candles in storm glasses – all set right at the centre of the fort and lit up by the sun in the west.'

'The bastar!' Rosita hissed again.

'It's all right,' Lara grinned. 'I'm immune. We've finished dinner now.'

'What was the food?'

'Absurdly good.'

Rosita grappled with this contradiction. 'Was absurd, or was good?'

'Both,' Lara said in an ambiguous English way which Rosita still didn't understand. 'We finished with a sublime chocolate Nemesis.'

'Ooh,' Rosita gasped with envy.

'Now the lads who served it and were helping with the horses seem to have disappeared – I think he must have told them to go, but he's gone off to have a pee behind a gorse bush. I hope he catches himself on it.'

Rosita tittered. 'But has he tol' you anything 'bout his plans?'

'Not for the windmills. He told me how having dinner like this had been something he'd always wanted to do, and how much it had cost, and then banged on about a massive bankrupt web company he's going to take over and revive, and make himself billions. It's very boring, and there's not a single thing about him that turns me on.'

'Never mind that. You just lead him on, to tell you about his willmills at the Panty-Hose.'

'Oops, here he comes back. I'll come over tomorrow and tell you what happens... bye.'

Rosita grinned at Reggie as she put her phone back on the table. 'Chatternerve is doing an offensive charm, but she resists,' she reportedly proudly.

At that moment, Reggie's Nokia tone struck up.

''Ello? Reginald ffinch-Leigh... I can hardly hear you... Oh, it's you. What's the noise? Sounds like you're in a whore-house, with all that shrieking and laughing... Good heavens! What're you doing there?... Oh, have you?... What's that? You are? Great! Look forward to it.'

Reggie put the phone down and looked at his wife. His face suggested anxiety mingled with pleasant anticipation. 'Oh Gawd! My cousin Porky's coming to stay!' he laughed nervously. 'He wants to stop for a week which means we'll have to take him to the hunt ball! That'll probably be a disaster... and a good laugh.' Reggie chuckled uncertainly. He'd found by now that the locals would forgive him pretty much any social misdemeanour or *faux pas*, but he wasn't so sure they were ready for Porky Bacon.

'Where did he ring with all the racket?' Rosita asked.

'He was in a boutique in the West End; sounded like he was in the changing rooms with all the shriekin' going on.'

'He probably was,' Rosi said with a fond smile.

Up on the highest point of the Iron Age hill-fort of Caractacus Mount, as the sun was sinking towards the mid-Wales hills, Jason de Chateauneuf walked from behind the yellow-bloomed bushes, where he'd been relieving himself, and caught his breath.

Lara Lydbury was standing silhouetted against the evening sun with her flimsy chiffon frock rippled by an evening zephyr.

Jason's hands started to tremble, his pulse raced. He had never got so close to realising one of his most precious fantasies.

So far this evening, he told himself, he hadn't put a foot wrong; she was obviously impressed by what he'd done to give her an extraordinary and unique evening. Taking a deep breath, he strutted across the springy sheep-grazed turf to where she stood beside the small round table at which they'd eaten dinner. They'd had scallops, roast quail and chocolate Nemesis, washed down with Dom Perignon champagne, a bottle of Petrus '98, which he'd been told was the best claret in the world, followed by a bottle of Chateau d'Yquem to go with the chocolate Nemesis.

To achieve this within a matter of hours, he'd commissioned one of the best-known French chefs in London to prepare the meal and had it choppered straight to the remote hilltop where two of his best Polish staff had prepared the setting and the table.

As the light began to fade, the candles in their storm glasses flickered slightly in the breeze.

Lara didn't turn to him until he was beside her.

'Oh, hello?' she said. 'Had a nice pee?'

If he heard the frosty sarcasm in her tone, he ignored it as he reached down to grasp her left hand. He pulled her towards him so eagerly that she lost her footing and toppled towards him. For a brief second, he thought she was falling into his arms.

'Ouch!' she squealed. 'You clumsy arse!'

He bounced backwards in confusion and remorse. 'God, I'm sorry, Lara. Are you OK?'

'Twisted my ankle,' she answered, through clenched teeth.

Jason dropped to one knee and started to massage her left ankle. After a few moments he glanced up, pretending not to see the laughter in her eyes. 'Is that better?' he asked, his Geordie more pronounced under pressure.

'It was the other ankle,' Lara said, 'which is OK now, thanks.'

Jason, deprived of a reason to fondle her other ankle, looked confused and hurt.

Lara laughed and took a step back. 'I think I'd like to go now,' she said.

Chapter Eight

'Porky' Bacon heaved himself and a small 'tigerskin' hold-all off the train at Ludlow Station and stood on the platform for a moment to catch his breath. He was a bulky man wearing a skilfully tailored, grey silk suit and an open-necked pink floral shirt. His large, hot feet were stuffed into loafers of white woven leather. A naked midday sun blazed in a clear sky, bringing out the sparkle of a large diamond ring on Porky's chubby little finger, while the heat quietly shimmered up from the road outside the station.

'Phwoar!' gasped Porky, a regular reader of the *Sun* newspaper, 'You could grill a kipper on that!' He looked around for transport and waved gratefully at an old Rover labelled *Tommy's Taxis*. The driver, as large as Porky, heaved himself out of his seat and hobbled up to take the tigerskin case and stow it in the boot. He opened the rear door of the car, and Porky slid in gratefully.

'Where you wanna go?' the driver asked over his shoulder, having reinstalled himself in his seat.

'Fing is,' Porky replied, 'I come up to see me cousin, Reggie Bottoms, as was; now calls 'isself Finchley. 'E lives in a gaff called Mortimer Towers, out in the sticks somewhere – even more out in the sticks than this place.'

'I know where Mr ffinch-Leigh lives. I've took plenty of folk out there since he come.'

'Oh, you know Reggie do you?'

'I wouldn't say I 'knows' him, but he's what you might call a big cheese since he took over old Mortimer Towers. He's a bit different, like, but they likes him out there.'

Porky chuckled. It was what he would have expected of his cousin, Reggie. 'What about his missus?' he asked mischievously. 'What do they think of her?'

The driver laughed. 'Her's a laugh, they say – foreign, sort of Spanishy, a bit barmy, like, but her's all right. My sister lives in the village, and they 'ad the fate up at the Towers last week. It were like a mad 'ouse, they say, but Mrs F were 'appy as a lark, and give all as'd helped a good drink after. '

'I tell you what, Tommy – you are Tommy, ain'cher?'

'Hell, aye.'

'I want to stop at a good boozer and 'ave a drink before we heads out into the wilderness.'

'A'right,' the driver agreed happily, and drove the car up to the top of the town.

Porky walked into the Castle Inn and liked what he saw. 'This looks like an 'andsome rub-a-dub,' he said approvingly to Tommy.

The pimento-faced man behind the bar looked at him suspiciously. Shiny silk suits were rare in his pub. 'What can I get you... sir,' he asked doubtfully.

'It's that bleedin' 'ot, before I have anything else, I think I'll have a big glass of ice-cold Janet Street.'

The barman was baffled.

'Janet Street?'

'Janet Street Porter,' Porky explained.

'Oh, porter. Bit hot for that, but if it's what you want...' the barman nodded. He unhooked a glass tankard and started filling it with thick creamy black beer from one of the hand pumps.'

Porky looked on in amazement. 'What the 'ell's that? I didn't ask for Guinness.'

'It's porter, sir, like you ordered. It's from our local brewery.'

'Nah, nah. I didn't want that. I told yer – Janet Street Porter – *Water!*'

'I don't do no foreign tongues,' the barman muttered surlily as he turned away to fill a sleever with tap water.

Porky relented. 'I tell you what, laughing boy, I'll 'ave the black stuff after, to save you chucking it away. And give my friend here whatever he wants.'

'Aye up, Tommy!' the barman said. 'You can't have nothing to drink if you're driving.'

'Just give me one of them big tomato juices, and slip a couple of vodkas in it, so no one sees.'

Porky regretted buying Tommy two more Bloody Marys as they set off from the old town and headed across the hills towards Mortimer Towers. Tommy had become more relaxed and evidently relished the chance to gather a little fresh gossip about one of the more colourful residents in the district. 'So, how come you're related to Mr ffinch-Leigh?'

'I'll tell yer. My mum was born Muriel Bottoms and she had two brothers, my Uncle Arthur and my Uncle Sid.' Porky leaned back in his seat, happy to spiel on for a bit. 'Sid married Reggie's mum just before he was born, then he had to go in the army and went off to fight in Korea. But they don't know what happened to him; he was reported missing, presumed dead; they never did find a body. That was a few years before I was born so I never knew Sid, but Uncle Arthur was a clever bloke, a t'rific dealer; he'd have a dabble in just about anything – always kosher, mind. He hated the idea of doing a bit of stir. He used to say "Nothing's worth being buggered in the slammer for." He taught Reggie a lot, and passed most of the business on to him. He didn't have kids, and Reggie didn't have a dad, see, and Arthur didn't get on with mine; truth is, my dad was a bit of a layabout; he always said he was related to that potty painter, but he weren't. That didn't stop him mouthing off like he was, and buying and selling a few Sexton Blakes off the back of it, though he never managed to palm off a dodgy Bacon.'

Porky yawned; so did his driver, who didn't know what he was talking about and was beginning to nod off after three double vodkas. But a firm thump as the old car hit a solid bank woke Tommy up a little. He grinned apologetically in the mirror at his punter. 'But you look like you done all right.'

'Yeh, well, it's in the genes, innit? I always 'ad an eye for a deal, better'n Reggie if the truth be told.'

'Well, your cousin maybe what we call a bit of a cockney up here, but he's a real gent. Always got a joke and a drink for you, they says.'

Twenty minutes after they'd left the Castle Inn, Tommy steered the puffing Rover, with a few bits of vegetation gathered from passing hedgerows, in through the gates of Mortimer Towers.

Porky sat up. 'Bloody 'ell!' he said. 'I knew Reggie'd bought his-self a big drum, but I didn't know it was the size of Buck 'Ouse.'

His wonder grew as the car drew up beneath the grand arches of the stone porch and Tommy released him onto the first of the steps that led up to a manorial oak door. As he huffed up the steps, followed by Tommy carrying his case, and hoping for a glimpse of the inside of the fabled mansion, the door opened to reveal Reggie, beaming a welcome with his arms held wide.

The cousins wrapped each other in a big man hug.

'At last, Porky,' Reggie said. 'I never thought you'd venture so far from London.'

'Wotcha mean, Reggie? I go to Marbella a couple of times every year.'

'Whitechapel-del-Mar? Doesn't count. Anyway, welcome to the magic of the Marches and what my mate, Lord Rokesay calls the Spirit of Camelot, where men are men and ghosts are ghosts. Come on in. You come in too, Tommy, and have a cup of tea – you look like you need one. Ah, here's my little helpmeet,' he added as Rosita bustled up.

"Ello, Rosi, my love.' Porky released his grip on Reggie and wrapped his arms around Rosi's tiny waist. 'How's my big cousin been treating you?'

'Crazy, like always. More crazy – he been doin' some trading.'

Porky released her and took a step back, looking more keenly at Reggie. 'Workin' Reggie? Just for fun, I presume?'

'Mostly,' Reggie replied. 'I miss a bit of wheeling and dealing.' Then, deciding that honesty with Porky was the best policy. He confided, 'And the firm I put my money in hasn't been divvying up quite as regular as it used to.'

'You wasn't in that little venture set up by that poncey kid you knew, that dodgy posh boy used to come down your club?'

Reggie shot a glance at Tommy who was still lurking unobtrusively. 'Tommy, d'you want to go through to the kitchen and get our Sue to give you a cup of Rosie Lee?'

Tommy ambled off slowly, sorry to be missing out on what might have made a great yarn back at the Castle Inn, where Reggie's antics were a regular subject of speculation.

Porky was looking agitated. 'Was it that? That GlobWebLink, 'cos if it was, of course they're not divvying up. Didn't you know, they've gone belly up – wiped out! It was a bleeding Ponzi, wasn't it!' In his agitation, Porky had turned a dangerous shade of red. 'My poor old mate; please tell me it wasn't them? Everyone knew they was dodgy. I 'ope you ain't done yer bollocks.'

Reggie tried to calm his cousin. 'It's all right, Porky. Don't get so aereated. Of course, I know, but I'm OK. There's plenty of deals around.'

'What?! Up here? In yokel land? What do you know about rustic stuff... and they say these farmers are pretty sharp.'

'Well, I haven't completely lost me touch.'

'You think?' said Rosi.

'Now then, my beautiful muse, you're supposed to be on my side.'

'I am Reggie, but...' she turned to Porky. 'You know what he's like; he always count his chickens before he catch them. He got a hun'red moles downstairs in the cellar, all eating their head off with all the worms Huggins can dig.'

'What's this, Reggie?' Porky asked, shaking his head in acute disbelief. 'Moles? *Moles!!* What the hell are you going to do with them?'

'I've got a punter for two hundred of the little fellas. An Irish bloke, in the fashion trade.'

'In the *fashion* trade? I got an interest in the fashion trade,' Porky said. 'And we've never had no call for *moles*.

'Porky,' Rosita cackled, 'you got interest in every bloody trade – and mos' of them dodgy.'

'As it 'appens, this is a big set-up, run by a couple of Bubble brothers, Aristos and Stavros Crappalotapou – well, that's what I call 'em, anyway, 'cos they're full of it. They do what you might call *oat cooture interpretation*.'

'You mean ripping off the Paris fashions,' Reggie observed cynically.

'Somethin' like that. Anyway, if your Paddy punter's in the rag trade why the hell does he want *live* moles?'

Reggie didn't know the answer to this. He raised a hand. 'Porky, I could tell you, but I've promised not to, all right?'

'Oh yeah?' Porky muttered cynically, but at that moment, before he could extract more information from Reggie, Lara came rushing up the front steps and burst into the hall where they were still standing.

''Ello, Lara.' Reggie greeted her with an extravagant hug. 'Do you know my cousin, Porky?'

'Hi,' said Lara, offering a slender hand, and wondering how this stout, hideously attired individual could be related to the tall and dapper Reggie.

Porky, on the other hand, was impressed. He recognised Lara immediately from photos in the gossip pages of the glossy magazines, where she seemed to be at most of the events they covered, as well as from the headshot that sat at the top of the fashion pieces she wrote, in which, now he was in the business, he'd been taking an interest.

''Ello, darlin'. Love your page in the *Sunday Doodah*. I just got involved in the fashion business. I'm a major shareholder in an Oat Cooture company. Here, 'ave a card.' He handed her a small business card bearing the improbable legend, *Bubble & Chic*. 'The name was my idea,' Porky added proudly.

Lara glanced at the card. 'Super,' she said. 'You never know.' She shoved it in the back pocket of her jeans. Porky gaped with excitement.

Rosita grinned; she loved the effect Lara had on men. 'Come... let's go to the drawer room,' she urged Lara and the two men. 'I tell Sue to bring tea, and Lara mus' tell us about what happens with Chatternerve.'

In the high-ceilinged drawing room which Lara had designed and had photographed for her magazine, Rosita, Reggie and Porky sank into the deep, squishy sofas. Lara was too excited to sit as she started to tell them what had happened on Caractacus Mount the night before.

They loved her description of de Chateauneuf's mind-numbing efforts to impress her, and his pathetic attempt to follow it through.

'What did he do when you told him you wanted to go home?' Porky asked, almost feeling sorry for the Geordie mega-million-aire.

Lara grinned. She was enjoying herself.

'After he'd let go of my ankle,' she said, 'he staggered to his feet, as sheepish as any of the old ewes grazing up there. I thought he was going to start blubbing, but he got a grip on himself and started shouting for the men who'd set it all up to come and help.

'His voice was echoing off the ramparts and up the valley, but no one came. The two Polish guys seemed to have disappeared; any-way, when they didn't turn up after about five minutes, he was getting pretty shirty. Presumably the dinner table had to be cleared up and taken away, and we had to get back down to the gig to go home before it got completely dark.

' "Right," he said, "we'd better get back on the ponies. I don't know what the hell's happened to the Poles. They never seem to understand what the hell I'm talkin' about."

'That doesn't surprise me, I thought.

'We walked over the top earth rampart, and found the ponies grazing away quite happily, but they can't have been tethered be-cause as soon as we got near them they looked up, put their ears back and shot off down the hill like Usain Bolt. We watched them go and when they got to where the two carriage horses were wait-ing, they clearly weren't tethered either, and they shot off with the ponies, careering down the hill.'

'Why weren't they tied up?' Reggie asked.

'God knows! But this morning, Pa's daily told me Jason had be-haved really crassly with one of the lads, and there'd been a big showdown and a lot of resentment; I don't suppose *he'll* be turn-ing up for work again. Anyway, it completely wrecked Chattern-erve's plans and I guess he *loathes* not having everything under control. He completely panicked after that; totally lost his cool, grabbed my wrist and started dragging me down the hill.

'I yelled at him to let go of me, which he did, but then he tripped and fell flat on his face in a pool where a spring comes out of the hillside. I was right behind him, and I fell on top of him.

'We lay there for a few moments like a couple of Anabaptists taking the plunge and getting totally soaked. When we got up and staggered out we were covered in mud and green slime and my dress was virtually see-through. He was almost berserk by then, yammering like a madman – if he weren't such a little shit, I'd have felt sorry for him, and then he screamed that he'd dropped his Blackberry in the pool.'

Reggie and Porky were looking at her, listening to her with tears of laughter in their eyes. 'You're 'avin' us on!' Porky spluttered.

'No, no,' Lara protested. 'It sounds funny now, but it was a bloody nightmare at the time. My little Pucci bag had gone right in the water too. We sort of slithered down the rest of the hillside to where the gig was still standing, and we could see the horses but they'd galloped about half a mile up to the far end of a long water meadow.

'Chatternerve turned to me, "You know about horses – you catch 'em?"

'I told him to forget it; we'd have a hell of job now they were all hyped up. But I knew there was a pub just around the corner at the bottom of the hill. I said, 'I don't know what you're going to do but I'm going for help at the Rat & Raven.'

Reggie laughed. 'That's a rough old boozer.'

Lara nodded.

'The place was packed but it all went deadly quiet when I walked in – until they realised I was soaked through with pretty much everything showing; then they started braying like a pack of hyenas. When Chatternerve walked in behind me, he was still soaking in his floppy silk shirt and tight breeches. One of the knobbly old soaks by the bar yelled, "Just got out the lake, Mr Darcy?" and they all howled with laughter. He went as stiff as a corpse and started trying to give orders. Of course, they knew who he was but they obviously weren't going to lift a finger. The only person I knew in there was Foxy Warren, who wouldn't be a lot of help at the best of times.'

'Not unless you was to cross his palm with silver,' Reggie laughed.

'We sort of knew that, but Jason started looking for his wallet, and remembered he hadn't brought it because he'd thought he wouldn't need money. He asked the landlord if he could lend him some. They all just laughed at him. Talk about getting his come-uppance. But he was going mad by then. "Isn't there anyone in this shit-house who'll drive us back to Pant-y-Groes; I can pay when I get there."

'One of the old poachers who's been taking game off Pant-y-Groes for years was sitting behind Jason. He cackled like a loony. "They doesn't give no credit in this pub – not to no Johnny New-comers. It's cash up front or no deal." And the rest of them all howled. They loved seeing Chatternerve at their mercy.'

'I'm bloody sure they did,' Reggie chuckled. 'He's been a total plonker with them, ever since he's come here. He's as tight as a cat's arse and brought in all them Polish people to work on the estate 'cos they're cheaper and work harder, he says. I bet the one that sabotaged your ride home was the one who wanted to bring his girl over from Poland, and Chatternerve wasn't having it – our Sue told us about it. Apparently he refused to find a job for her or let the lad have somewhere they could live together.'

Lara nodded. 'That was the groom Chatternerve relies on to han-dle the horses.'

'That'll teach the little bastard. But how the hell did you get away?'

'While Chatternerve was haranguing the landlord,' Lara went on, 'and anyone else who chose to join in, I had a quiet word with Foxy. I said I'd make sure there was fifty quid in it if he took us home.

'He said he'd take me, but not Jason – I suppose he didn't want to toady in front of all his mates. Of course, after a little persua-sion, he agreed to take us both for a hundred quid, but only if he went out first, and we walked up the lane to his van so no one would see us getting in.

'I thought of leaving Jason behind, but then I wanted to get into his house to have a look around – that was the whole point of coming on his ridiculous fantasy date and I wasn't going to get another chance unless I went through another God-awful evening with him.'

'The things you do for your old mates,' Reggie said gratefully.

'And for my old Pa, too, don't, forget,' Lara added. 'So, Foxy slips out without anyone seeing him, and a few minutes later, I say to Jason, "Come on, let's leave it. I'm going now," and I headed for the door, hoping he'd follow – which he did.

'We found Foxy's van up the lane. I got in the passenger seat and Chatternerve had to climb in the back and sit on top of Foxy's rat traps and poisons and stuff. And the van pongs like a dead sheep, until Foxy lights up a joint the size of a medium sized carrot and sets off for Pant-y-Groes.'

'Have you been to there before?' Rosita asked.

'Loads of times when I was a kid, but not in the last ten years and certainly not since Chatternerve took it over. It's a whopping place, and pretty nice in parts, but he's stripped everything out – someone must have told him minimalism was all the rage, because there's a whole series of white empty rooms with a few pictures you'd have to be mad to buy, and a kitchen that looks like the control room of the Starship Enterprise.

'Anyway Foxy drops us and follows us in. I'm a bit stoned just from passive smoking Foxy's joint, and I'm feeling very brave. Chatternerve's got a face like thunder and says he's going to have a shower and change, and do I want clean clothes. Actually, I did, but I was more or less dry by then and I thought if he was out of the way for bit, I might be able to have a quick poke around. But first I tell him to pay Foxy the hundred quid. "Don't be daft," he says. "I'm not being held to ransom by some little rat catcher."

'Well, I'm not a great fan of Foxy's either, but I'd given him my word, and he was the only guy who would take us home when we didn't feel like walking five miles in soggy clothes, so I was bloody angry. I said, "Chatternerve, just give him his hundred quid – you ridiculous, tight-arsed little worm." '

Reggie laughed. 'Marvellous! Did it work?'

'It did,' Lara giggled. 'He shot off and was back in about thirty seconds waving a couple of fifties. Foxy grabbed them, gave me a wink, and scuttled out, while Jason went off in a huff to have his shower – yelling over his shoulder that I should get myself a bloody drink.

'But I didn't waste any time; I sort of guessed where his office might be, and I was right. Luckily it wasn't locked and I went straight to this massive desk he's got, thinking I only had about ten minutes. Of course, all the drawers were locked but there were some letters and stuff in a tray – that day's stuff from the dates on it.

'I took it all out and looked through it – most of it was just boring stuff about the estate, but at the bottom of the stack was a letter he's going to wish he'd filed and locked away as soon as he'd read it. I had a quick read, and it looked like potential dynamite to me. I wanted to take a shot of it with my phone, but of course it had got soaked in my bag when I fell in the spring, and didn't work, but I spotted a scanner on a side table by the desk. I switched it on and photocopied the sheet. I'd just finished when I heard Jason coming back downstairs. I managed to turn off the copier, put everything back and the copy of the letter in my bag. By the time he walked in, I was flopped on a horrible, hard sofa in the main drawing-room, pretending to be fast asleep.

'He must have been convinced because he crept out of the room and clattered around in the kitchen, then came back with a bottle of champagne and two glasses. "Lara?" he sort of whispered.

'I didn't move. "Lara? Are you asleep?" he says.

"I was," I murmur.

"Oh, well – there's a drink here for you."

'I sat up and pretended to rub my eyes. "I don't want a drink. I've had a bloody awful evening and I want to go home! Can you please arrange it?"

'He looked crestfallen. "All my staff's fucked off! I can't find anyone."

"That's not my problem. Either you drive me home, or call a

taxi."

"But there's never any taxis that'll come out here, even during the day."

"Then you'll have to drive me," I said, "right now."

'I stood up. He looked as if he was about to explode, but he caught the look in my eye, and changed his mind.'

Lara grinned and shrugged a shoulder. 'So he took me home in the Ferrari, and dropped me off.'

'Didn't he try to come in?' Rosita asked.

'Yes, but I told him to piss off. He slunk away shaking his head, and got back into his car.'

Reggie laughed. 'I can just see it; I bet he just couldn't get his head round the idea that the great romantic scenario he'd dreamed up had gone so totally belly up on him.'

Porky was chuckling too. 'It must have cost him a bloody fortune to put it all together. What a woman!'

'Where is the letter?' asked Rosita, ever practical.

'It's in Pa's safe, but he says if you need it, to let him know.'

Although Reggie would happily have wriggled out of his pledge to take a table for ten at the Monty & West Salop Hunt Ball, especially coming so soon after the Charity Race Day (and his unintended acquisition of Lady Watkins' awful daubs), he felt some compensation from the fact that it was being held at Lydbury Manor. And, in any case, Rosita was keen to go.

Reggie didn't know Lara's father well, but what he knew, he liked. While his friend Peregrine Rokesay was pleasantly eccentric, Lancelot Lydbury was an out-and-out maverick and, in most people's eyes, barking mad. This appealed to Reggie and he was looking forward to meeting the potty old baronet again, and seeing at close quarters his famously unspoilt Tudor manor house.

He and Rosita had invited their guests to come for a drink at Mortimer Towers before the ball, so they could all go on from there together. It was a motley crowd that set off from the Towers in the village minibus, with Harry Huggins at the wheel.

With Reggie and Rosi were Porky and Lara, Ted and Belinda

Buckton; Sir Compton Wynyates dressed for no clear reason in a kilt. 'No, he's about as Scottish as a Cornish pasty,' his wife answered to enquiries; she herself was wearing an emerald tiara given to her by a Colombian cocaine baron. Reggie's final guests were the landlord of the Fox & Ferret, Rufus Crobin, who was a keen supporter of the hunt because it often gave him the chance to take bets on local events over whose outcomes he could usually exert some influence, and Doris, his square-jawed, taciturn wife.

When they reached their table in a cavernous marquee which covered half an acre of Lancelot's lawn, Rosita gazed at their immediate neighbours with dismay.

'Who has done this? Putting our table next to Chatternerve?'

'Why? Is it a problem?' asked Porky, highly visible in a white tuxedo with silver trimming.

'He and Reggie never get on,' Rosita explained, 'and after Reggie win the hunt race, Chatternerve hate him, because he make him look like a fool.'

'But you said he was round the other day, when he asked Lara out.'

'Only to see Lara, and when Reggie ask for help to move the moles, he refuse.'

Porky shook his head in bewilderment. 'What *is* Reggie doing with those bloody moles?'

'If he no tell you, I can't,' Rosita said firmly.

Porky didn't pursue this paradox for the moment. 'Is that your mate, Chatternerve, then?' he asked, nodding towards the software millionaire, who had dressed for the ball like the ringmaster of a prosperous Italian circus.

'That's him. And now, we have Lara on our table. She make him look stupid too.'

'He won't mind about that, so long as no one saw it. Some people are like that – it's not what happens that matters, it's how many people get to see it. Crikey! 'Ere comes his guests.'

De Chateauneuf was welcoming his guests, a gang of uncompromising metropolitans out to have a look at rustic England at play, and who looked too rich to give a damn about anything.

'That's all dot.com merchants and city spivs,' Porky muttered disparagingly. 'What the 'ell are they doing here?'

Lara, arriving at the table, overheard Porky's assessment. 'They've got as much right to be here as you, Porky.'

'You're windin' me up, aincher, you naughty bit of crumpet! I'm family, inn'I? And Reggie's a *geezer* round 'ere – he won the bloody hunt race, didn't 'e?' He broke off suddenly to gaze, transfixed, at a gaggle of half a dozen uniformly blond young women in Jordan make-up with plump lips and implausible breasts, hovering around Jason's table and giggling loudly. 'Bloody 'ell!' he gasped. 'Look at that lot; I bet they don't know much about huntin' – well not about huntin' foxes,' he laughed.

Lara tried to keep a straight face. She knew Chatternerve had seen her; he was casting uncertain glances in her direction. She wondered, unconcerned, if he would even dare approach her, when Reggie arrived to organise his party. He seated them carefully, putting Lara with her back to Jason's table.

'Okay,' he announced once they were all sitting. 'There's two races being held after, and we have to nominate a couple for each of them. The main one is...' he looked down to consult a printed programme '...the Midnight Steeplechase.'

'What the 'ell's that?' Porky asked. 'Some mad bucolic frolic?'

Reggie nodded. 'That's about right, Porky. They've laid a course around the grounds, over the river, through the woods and back across the lawns with hay bales every now and again. A man carrying his partner piggy-back has to run round the course, jumping over all the bales.' Reggie looked up. 'Rosi? You and me?'

'NO *WAY*!' Rosita shrieked.

'I'm sorry to hear that,' Reggie went on. 'She'd have enjoyed it.' He fixed his eye on Ted who was leaning back in his chair, quietly shaking his head.

'I have to do the commentary,' he said.

Reggie turned to Her Majesty's former plenipotentiary in Montevideo. 'Sir Compton?'

The ex-ambassador also shook his head. 'No, but Cecilia and I will happily enter the first race – the Chariot Race.'

Reggie consulted the programme. 'That's what I'd call the Wheelbarrer Race,' he explained to Porky. 'It's more of a sprint, down a straight course. So, you'll be wheeling Lady Wynyates?' he asked, doubtfully, thinking of the terrifying sight Lady Wynyates had presented as Boadicea in the village pageant, and he guessed she was at least half as heavy again as her husband.

'No,' Sir Compton said indignantly, 'she'll be wheeling me.'

'That's settled then,' Reggie agreed. 'And it looks like our steeplechase entry will be Porky carrying Lara.'

Porky was trembling with agitation. 'Reggie, I wish I could, but I couldn't jump them bales if I was carrying nothing, never mind this lovely creature.'

'Porky!' Rosita squealed. 'She weigh *nothing!*'

'I'd still hate to drop her.'

Rosita turned to her husband. 'Reggie, you must carry Lara!'

At another nearby table, Lord Rokesay's party was addressing the same question. His daughter, Lady Nellie, was the only keen hunter among the Slims, and she was determined to ride in the race for the honour of the family. She was haranguing all the men on their table who didn't want to carry her. 'You're a bunch of wimps! But don't worry,' she bellowed, in a voice that could carry a holler three miles across a Shropshire vale. 'I'll find my own mount!'

A lot of guests were still looking for their tables or waiting around to be told where they should sit, when a gang of chubby teenage girls in short shiny black frocks burst from the kitchen tent into the marquee, trying to balance on their arms three or four trays containing the first course.

Ted Buckton looked at a plate which, having survived the journey, had just been plonked in front of him. 'What do you think Reggie? Special antique-coloured poylyfilla, or a sample of mediæval render that Lancelot's been using on his house?'

'And mind your 'ampsteads on this toast,' Porky advised.

'Good heavens is that toast?' Sir Compton asked. 'I thought it was a sample of a carefully distressed roof shingle.'

'Can't help you,' Reggie said, and looked at the menu. 'It says here it's country paté; round here that could be anything.'

The guests were used to ambiguous food being dished up by hunt ball caterers; generally they tried not to notice the food and compensated for it by laying into the wine, a choice of red or white from the local agricultural merchant's stock, now being poured and drunk as fast as the waiting staff could replace the empty bottles while the guests tried to deactivate their gastronomic senses in time for the main course – two leathery slabs of overcooked silverside and gloopy gravy with boiled potatoes, followed by a dayglow rubber trifle.

Reggie sat back to watch his guests and admire the resilience of the rural English, compared to the young, urban financial thrusters and their pea-brained girlfriends on the next table, where none of the food had been touched and de Chateauneuf had provided his guests with a supply of Chateau Petrus from his own cellars.

As piles of half-full plates were gathered up by the stout youngsters, the diners moved purposefully outside into the warm night to smoke cigars, cigarettes and, in Ted Buckton's case, a pipe of aromatic shag mixed with home-grown weed.

The imminent start of the races was announced, followed by a commotion as a horse in full racing tack was led up to the entrance of the marquee, where Jason de Chateauneuf seemed to be expecting it.

There was a babble of confusion as most of the guests who were familiar with the event wondered what the horse was doing there and why Chatternerve had brought it. This turned into loud, disbelieving laughter as they realised he was intending to ride it.

Mrs Leinthall-Starkes, omnipotent chairman of the Monty & West Salop Hunt, was incensed, striding up to de Chateauneuf in a full length, shimmering aquamarine ball gown. 'What on earth do you think you're doing with this horse?' she demanded.

'It's for the steeplechase, of course."

'My dear man, are you under the impression that the Montgomery & West Salop Hunt Midnight Steeplechase is ridden on horses?'

'What the hell else would you ride in a hunt steeplechase – bi-cycles?'

The ball guests, with the travellers whom Lancelot had allowed to camp in a field by the lane in return for helping out at the event, were all gathered round now to watch the showdown. Most were howling with drink-enhanced laughter at the sight of Chattern-erve, dressed in his bright red tail coat and white baggy breeches with a gleaming black silk top-hat, being chastised by the formi-dable Mrs Leinthall-Starkes. He looked utterly bemused, stand-ing beside the perfectly turned-out, strapping racehorse, a former big race winner he was rumoured to have bought very recently.

'We don't ride horses in this one, Mr de Chateauneuf.'

'But it doesn't say that in the programme – it just says "Steeple-chase".'

'Now listen, Chatternerve, if you'd taken the trouble to acquaint yourself with our traditions and tried to learn something of the history of this very long established hunt, instead of turning up and waving your cheque book around...'

Jason spluttered indignantly. 'I haven't written a cheque for years...'

'Mr de Chateauneuf, you are a jumped up nincompoop and we don't care how you throw your money around, but please have your horse removed at once so that we can get on with our tradi-tional hunt ball race.

De Chateauneuf's whole body sagged as he cast a few desperate glances at his own guests. Reggie, watching with Rosita and Lara, guessed he'd been boasting to them about his equestrian skills.

'What a dopey plonker,' he said to Rosita, and chuckled as he caught Lara's eye, while Jason's party, who'd thought they were going to see an impressive result from their host and friend in his new persona as sporting country squire, began to see the joke and joined in the laughter with the rest of the crowd.

Lancelot, in an act of apparent kindness, called over to Mickey Rafferty, standing handily by. 'Take this horse away, please, and put it somewhere safe for the time-being so we can get on with the races.'

Once the distraction of de Chateauneuf's gaff had passed, some of the other travelling lads carried on setting up the courses for the two races.

The flood-lit track lay across a stretch of pristine turf, with the winning post for both events by an open-fronted tent that was there to house a rock'n'roll band, the Turnips, who would play there after the races.

Crobin stood nearby, exercising his phenomenal memory in running a book on the races – heats and finals.

'How's it going?' Reggie asked.

'OK on the steeplechase, wagers coming in across the board...' Crobin told him, '...but shite on the chariot race. They're only betting on Lady Wynyates, and she creamed it last year.'

Reggie nodded. 'Yeh; I 'ad a big punt on them, remember?' He turned to look at all the runners who were beginning to gather up at the start, two hundred yards away. After a few moments he turned back to Crobin. 'Don't you worry too much about that. There's an easterly wind picking up; I think the Wynyates might run into trouble this year,' he said. 'What price will you give me on Archie Pemberton?'

'That dopey wazzock? Ten to one.'

'I'll have a fifty on 'im, then.'

Crobin shot him a sharp glance, before nodding. 'You got it, squire.'

Porky loomed up behind Reggie. 'I earwigged that,' he said without apology. 'Which one is Archie P, then?'

Reggie nodded at the long-legged, empty-headed Archie. 'Last year he drove that same little bird – his sister, I think, and he just picked up her legs, tucked them over his elbows, so her fingers 'ardly touched the floor, and pissed off like a rocket.'

'Then why d'you get 'im at tens? Didn't he win?'

'No, he was in front but he took the wrong course just before the finish, and went off down the steeplechase.' Reggie laughed. 'He's not too bright, that Archie, so people don't rate him, but I saw him walking the course with his sister earlier; she'll make sure he keeps on track this year.'

All the guests who weren't taking part in the races were clustering around the winning post. Most of those who hadn't yet picked a runner were now throwing caution to the wind and having a bet to give a little edge to this annual fiasco and were already hooting drunkenly at their chosen runners.

As Reggie watched, the punters' choice, Lady Wynyates, was filling her lungs with large breaths, while Sir Compton crouched down, ready to present a pair of spindly white legs that protruded from his kilt to his wife, and Crobin had to stop taking money on the pair. 'Betting now without Sir Compton and Lady Wynyates,' he bellowed to anyone who might still be interested.

Reggie smiled confidently. He had noted that the gentle breeze that had wafted down the course earlier had become a following wind. His wife joined him.

'Did you bet this race?'

'I did.' Reggie nodded.

'I 'ope you put on Sir Cum'ton.'

'Nope.'

'You crazy? They the form 'orse!'

'I don't think this wind will help them.'

Rosita shook her head. 'Reggie, always you just want to do difference from everyone else.'

'We'll see, my little Latin chrysanthemum, we'll see.'

The runners were lining up now across the start, the pairs all driven by men, bar the Wynyates.

The slightly slurred voice of Ted Buckton, coerced as usual into the role of commentator, boomed through a loudspeaker just above Crobin's head. 'They're under starter's orders; they're off!'

The field surged forwards and immediately spread like the Nile delta, but Archie had sensibly placed himself and his chariot in the middle of the field, and a shrill voice could be heard from the chariot shrieking at her brother to jig to the left or the right as he sprinted a wavy line down the course.

'Archie Pemberton looks to be just in the lead,' Ted Buckton yelled manically, as if he were commentating on the Grand National. 'Also showing on the near side at this halfway stage in the race is the formidable Wynyates combination.'

Reggie found it hard from that distance to judge but as they drew nearer, with Sir Compton's little hands covering the fine turf in a blur, it looked as if Lady Wynyates was sure to head a wandering Archie Pemberton, but the wind gusting strongly behind them caught up Sir Compton's kilt, lifting it right up and over his back, revealing every part of his unclad nether anatomy to the gaping crowd.

There was a great cheer, and Lady Wynyates faltered in her stride as she weighed up the shame of not winning against the ignominy of continuing to display to every member of the Marches Woodland Hunt and their guests her husband's bare backside and dangling manhood.

Her mental tussle continued for a few more strides, until modesty won, and Reggie heaved a great sigh of relief as Lady Wynyates came to an abrupt halt, dropped her husband face down on the grass track and leaned forward to pull his kilt back over his nakedness. Archie Pemberton, ably steered by his sister, passed the winning post at a sprint.

Reggie turned to the self-appointed bookmaker. 'Result, eh Crobin?'

'It was for me. Yours was the only bet I took on Archie Arfwit ,' Crobin said, smiling as he counted out Reggie's money.

Well pleased with this first bet, Reggie went off to research the runners in the next race.

As the crowd that had clustered around the finish of the chariot race began to disperse – some going back to their tables in the marquee to hunt for more wine, others fading into the dark of the shrubberies around the lawns to canoodle, Reggie saw Rosita at the centre of a circle of the women from Jason's table and left her to it, while he went in search of Nellie Slim. He knew her well enough to know that she was highly competitive and would be sure to recruit the most useful mount she could find, using whatever methods it took.

After fifteen minutes of frustrating searching, Reggie spotted Nellie in a quiet corner of Lancelot's stable yard, talking with Lara and a tall, broad-shouldered young man, wearing jeans and a sheepskin waistcoat.

He judged it unhelpful to intrude and waited until the conversation was over, and Lara started walking back in his direction.

'Lara?' he called in a whisper.

'Hiya, Reggie,' she said.

'Was that Nellie sorting out a mount?'

'Yes. She asked me to introduce her to Lofty – Pa's new gamekeeper.'

Reggie was impressed. 'He looks what you might call a promising specimen. Is he going to take her in the race?'

'Yup,' Lara grinned. 'He is, as it were, her chosen mount, and I dare say if they win, she'll be his afterwards. So I'd get your money on now, before word gets out. They'll beat us by miles, even if we were going to try, which, by the way, I presume we're not. In fact, are you sure about carrying me at all? After all, Reggie, this is a young man's sport and I'd hate anything to happen to you, especially as you're Rosi's husband. She'd never forgive me if you ruptured yourself and were off-games...'

''Ere, that's enough of that! 'Course I'm going to take you. I'd be totally gutted if you didn't have me as your chosen mount.'

'Careful, Reggie,' Lara warned with a grin. 'If I didn't know you, I'd think you were coming on to me.'

'As if I would, with my lovely Rosi to come back to every night. Now, I'd better go and get my money on, while Crobin'll still give me 'alf-way decent odds on Nellie.'

The straw bales were laid in pairs across the course, end on end, making the jumps only wide enough for three runners abreast. As a result, the steeplechase was run in heats of three, with the first of each taking part in the final. The young bloods in the hunt taking part in the Midnight Steeplechase had dressed themselves in granddad night-shirts and long-johns, with their female jockeys clad in nightdresses or flimsy negligees. Reggie and Lara hadn't bothered.

Lancelot presided over a draw for the names of the runners in each heat.

Ted Buckton announced the runners of the first heat. 'Mr Reginald ffinch-Leigh, carrying Miss Lara Lydbury; Mr Jim 'Lofty' Loftus carrying Lady Nellie Slim and Mr Jason de Chateauneuf carrying Miss...' Ted paused, to give the name its full impact, '... Madonna McQueen.'

As soon as the draw had been announced, Lancelot arrived quietly by Reggie's side.

'Now, are you sure you should be carrying my daughter, Reggie, old man – I mean, old man? You could do yourself damage. Still as long as you are, you must have an advantage – at least over Chatternerve. Obviously Nellie and Lofty will win your heat but first, Chatternerve needs more shame to befall him. Didn't you love his face when he realised the steeplechase was a pedestrian affair? I'm afraid I rather encouraged him – at least I didn't put him right about it when I had the chance. Now this is what I've done – I've sent Mickey Rafferty down to move the second set of bales in the woods back by about five yards. Where they were, there is a well concealed elephant trap, which is now fully operational.'

'What the hell's that?'

'I've had a pit dug, six feet long, three feet wide, and six feet deep, slap in the middle of the track and covered with slender braches, a few thin turfs and leaves. No one will see it in the dark. There's plenty of room beside it for you and Lofty to skirt round. I've told Lofty, but of course I haven't told Chatternerve; you play it how you think best. OK, old man?'

Reggie and Lara, with Rosi and Porky for support, walked up to the start.

Rosi was worried now. 'Reggie, maybe you don't do this? Why not I get young Huggins to carry Lara – I mean the Lofty man is to carry Nellie – no?'

'I'll be all right, Rosi; I'm not a bleeding octogenarian. If I get tired, I'll stop, sit down and have a little swig of applejack. And look, Lara's about the size of a greyhound puppy; I'd have more chance of rupturing myself carrying Dougy Swallow's terrier.'

Rosi tugged his arm. 'Look, here come Chatternerve with his jockey. That girl Madonna she is called; she say she is a 'fren' of Chatternerve,' Rosi snorted. 'When I hear she is riding him, I give her plenty to drink – I don't think she hold on too well.'

'Smart thinking, Rosi, but I think Lancelot's already got everything fixed. Shouldn't be too hard to beat him.'

'I no so sure. Be careful, my big loco man.'

Reggie, Jason de Chateauneuf and Lofty lined up at the start of the quarter of a mile they were to race, leaning forward like athletes starting the ten thousand metres until the loudspeaker behind them burst into life with Ted Buckton's voice. 'They're under starter's orders; they're off,'

To a ragged cheer from revellers all over the lawns, the field of three set off.

It took just a few strides for Reggie to admit to himself that he wasn't as fit as he'd thought he was after the first glass of wine, when they were selecting their runners, and anyone who'd suggested he wasn't up to the task of steeplechasing, even over twelve inch bales, was right.

He watched hopelessly as Lofty strode away from him with Lady Nellie on his back, kicking his buttocks vigorously as they approached the first 'fence'. In Lofty's slipstream, Jason de Chateauneuf, twenty years younger than Reggie, was also pulling away.

As he trotted away from the start with only Lara's negligible weight on his back, he heard Rosita's shrieks of encouragement behind him. He gritted his teeth and lengthened his stride a fraction.

Lara was more realistic. 'Just pull up if you want Reggie,' she shouted in his ear.

'Not till I'm out of sight,' Reggie muttered thickly. 'I've still got some pride, you know.'

He lumbered on towards the woods, managing to clear two bales on the way, simply by stepping up onto them with both feet and stepping down the other side. As soon as they'd jumped the bale going into the wood, Reggie pulled up. 'Sorry darling, quick sharpener required.'

He pulled his small flask from a pocket of his black dinner trousers, unscrewed the top and put it to his lips for a long pull.

'Phwoar,' he gasped. 'That's better!'

Lara gave him a gentle jab in the hips with her bare heels. 'Come on then, let's go. I can't even hear the others.'

The next bale loomed. Reggie stepped up, tottered for a moment on top, and jumped off gently on the other side, peering ahead into the gloom. 'Right.' He huffed, 'we gotta to be careful after the next jump... OOF!'

Reggie knew his mistake even as he tumbled headlong into the pit that seemed to have opened up at his feet. In the small part of a second it took to fall, he prepared himself for a hard landing on the earth at the bottom of the pit.

It took another moment for him to register that he'd landed on another human body, a small, soft, wriggling, angry presence.

'What are you doin', you bloody great idiot,' a shrill female London voice squawked.

Reggie realised he'd landed on top of Miss Madonna McQueen, and as he had landed, Lara fell on top of him.

'Sorry Reggie,' Lara grunted. 'Pa said it was five yards after the *second* jump.'

'Yeh,' Reggie said. 'He must have counted the one into the woods.'

From beneath them in the depths of what they now knew was some kind of midden pit, there was sudden, strangled roar. 'You numpties! You bloody bastards! You set this up!' Jason de Chateauneuf was underneath Madonna McQueen, and not taking it well.

Lara had managed to get to her feet and was already scrambling up the earth sides of the hole. 'Oh, hello Mickey. What are you doing here?'

''Ello, Lara. You wasn't s'pposed to be down the 'ole. 'Ere – catch on to this rope.'

Reggie had managed to half turn on his side, sticking an elbow into the squealing Miss McQueen as he did. He looked up to see Lara's shapely legs disappear over the edge of the pit, and Mickey Rafferty's face appear, and beside it a length of thick hemp rope. 'Oo's that?'

'It's me – Reggie of course.'

'You wasn't s'pposed to be down there either.'

'Yeh, well – there's a couple more underneath me,' Reggie said, catching hold of the rope and allowing himself to be heaved up by Mickey.

'Thank Gawd,' Madonna McQueen groaned as Reggie's weight was removed from her.

Once Reggie had scrambled out of the hole, he stood up in the dark woodland track and tried to peer into the depths of Lancelot's 'elephant trap'. He couldn't see anything but became aware of Ted Buckton's voice booming from the loudspeakers on the lawns:

'We have a winner in the first heat of the steeplechase: Lady Nellie Slim on Lofty Loftus. However...' Ted paused for dramatic effect, '...there is, so far, no sign of the rest of the field – Miss Lara Lydbury and Miss Madonna McQueen, and their respective mounts. I am assured that a search party has been dispatched.'

Mickey had dropped his rope back into the pit and was hauling out the tiny, flimsily clad figure of Jason de Chateauneuf's jockey.

'Gawd, bloody 'ell!' she gasped as she popped out of the hole. 'That's the last time I come on one of Jason Chatternerve's bleeding country weekends with his so-called Shropshire county set. Do you want to know what's in the bottom of that bloody pit?' she asked no one in particular.

Reggie could guess; he was begging to register the unmistakable aroma of farmyard dung.

'Bloody hell, Lara! What's your father done now?'

De Chateauneuf's voice sounded hollowly from the depths of the pit. 'It's mingin' like a cows' khazi down here! I'm lying in six inches of slurry! I'll do the pompous, effing toffee-nosed bastard for this! Now drop that rope and haul me up, you bloody little chavva!'

If Mickey was offended by the term, he didn't show it. 'I'm very sorry Mr Chatternerve,' he said cheerfully. 'Mr Finchley had it, and he's just walked off with it. I'll go and see if I can get it back from him.'

De Chateauneuf's voice echoed from the depths of the pit and bounced between the oak and ash trees of the old woodland, as a large crowd drifted down to find out what the commotion was about. More of the travellers had turned up too, carrying lanterns and torches to light up the scene, giving the Hunt Ball guests a clear view of Jason de Chateauneuf, so ridiculously resplendent earlier in the evening, being hauled up, with his front covered from top to toe in fresh slurry. His hair, his face, his magnificent red tail coat and baggy white breeches had been turned a slimy *eau-de-nil*.

From the darkness of the woods, a voice called out: 'Three cheers for Squire Chatternerve!'

And the crowd, drunk and happy, all encouraged the travellers with shouts of '*Heave, Heave, Heave,*' until de Chateauneuf was standing beside the hole, forlorn, filthy, and humiliated. The guests he'd invited up from London, transported at great expense in his own helicopter, were nowhere to be seen.

After he'd been invited by Lancelot to clean himself up a little inside the house, Reggie and his supporters went back to their table in the marquee to celebrate his safe return with Lara.

Sir Compton was solicitous. 'Now, are you sure you're all right, my dear fellow? If you'd been a horse and broken your leg falling into Lancelot's trap, you'd have been shot, you know. It was a close thing.'

'But I didn't break me leg, and I'm not an 'orse,' Reggie replied. 'And at least I didn't end up wallowing in cow-shit like our Geordie billionaire.' He glanced at the neighbouring table, now empty of Jason's metropolitan party. 'Where's he gone, anyway?'

Lara laughed. 'He limped off with his tail between his legs, looking a complete arse, and banging on about how his horse had been pinched.'

Sir Compton put his head on one side as if considering a weighty piece of British foreign policy. 'As I understand it, that rather brash young man joined the hunt, learned to ride and took part in the annual cross country event and tonight's races as part of some misguided PR campaign to win support for his application to fill four miles of Marches skyline with monstrous wind turbines which will contribute next to nothing to the nation's sustainable energy requirements. I can only say that, in terms of improving his popularity and general standing within with the local community, it has been a campaign of singular failure.'

'Yeh,' nodded Porky. 'He's totally fucked it up, ain't 'e?

Sir Compton turned to him. 'You put it more succinctly, if, perhaps, a little less elegantly, than I did.'

'*And*,' Porky went on, 'I shouldn't think 'e's done a whole lot for 'is reputation down the smoke, either. Them city flash boys won't be shy to tell the story of Jason de Chatternerve, Squire of Pant-y-Hose, turning up with an 'orse for a grown-up piggy-back race, then being dropped in the shite – in some order!'

Ted Buckton had wandered into the tent and poured himself a large glass of farmers' Argentinean claret. He was taking a break from commentating after two more heats had been run and while hunt officials tried to round up the runners for the final.

'We seem to have lost two of our finalists. The last heat was won by the redoubtable Mickey Rafferty carrying that shy but rather attractive girl who does the mobile library.'

'Library Lindy, they call her,' Reggie said.

Rosita snorted. 'I hear in the shop – now the village boys have found about her, they call her Lindy Looseknickers.'

'They may be right,' Ted mused. 'Since Mickey carried her across the finishing line in triumph, they've disappeared, nowhere to be found. He was lucky, of course, because the early leader had set off at a good crack, despite being what Sir Compton might call more than slightly inebriated, but halfway through the course, up by the big badger sett, he must have caught sight of the albino badger in the moonlight, because he dropped his jockey and rushed off screaming that he'd seen a badger's ghost and it was a warning against the cull. Mickey was then well placed to take up the running.'

Cecilia Wynyates, who also liked to feel she was on top of recent social developments, had more to add. 'I hear that Lady Nellie and Mr Jim 'Lofty' Loftus are also missing.'

Porky laughed. 'That's fair enough. He didn't 'alf earn a bonus; he come home in the first heat like shit off a shovel.'

Lady Wynyates nodded. 'I saw that, while I was waiting – vainly, as it turned out – for Reggie and Lara to complete the course. Unfortunately I was unaware of the arrangement between Lancelot's gamekeeper and Lady Nellie, so I'd backed you, Reggie.'

Reggie shook his head. 'No wonder Crobin makes so much moolah.'

'I must say,' Lady Wynyates went on. 'Nellie did come in looking very fresh-faced and exuberant.'

From outside, on their makeshift stage in the tent by the winning post and without warning, the Turnips burst into action and further conversation within a hundred yards was unsustainable. The marquee emptied instantly; the younger half of the crowd headed for the stage where five men of late middle age with beer-raddled visage, sporting ponytails and bushy sideburns, hammered like smiths at their anvils on three well-worn guitars, an extensive, battered drum kit and a much-abused keyboard. The sound they made was incoherent, unmelodic and deafening, but it evoked in its audience an instant response and a display of dancing, largely devoid of rhythm or beauty.

The older guests almost ran for the comparative tranquillity of the stone-flagged terrace in front of the house at the far end of the lawn, where it was possible to converse without shouting.

Sir Compton, proud of his eclectic grasp on modern culture, turned to his host. 'These chaps seem to have placed themselves musically somewhere between Iron Maiden and Black Sabbath, wouldn't you say?'

'Wherever they've placed themselves, they should have been put out their misery years ago,' Reggie replied. 'This isn't Heavy Metal

– it's more like heavy agricultural machinery and about as bloody tuneful. I don't know why they bother; they must all be drawing their pensions by now.'

Porky Bacon, beside him, snorted. 'Reggie – you're a boring, wrinkled old pillock! I'm goin' down to tell 'em to turn it up a bit. Come on Lara – let's 'ave a bop!'

Lara, who couldn't resist a challenge, set off back across the lawn with Porky's silver trimmings glittering in the disco lights that had been turned on.

Sir Compton was shaking his head in admiration. 'A boring wrinkled old pillock, indeed! I must say, Reggie, your cousin Porky has a real gift for the telling phrase.'

Rosita, for whom parties only added to her natural radiance, was also keen to dance. 'Reggie, you are old poop! I go look for Lor' Rokesay to give him a lesson to dance the tango!'

Sir Compton watched her go. 'She is a marvellous creature, your wife, Reggie – such vitality, such presence. I fear, though, that a tango would be outside the Turnips' standard repertoire, don't you think?'

'All I can tell you is, if Rosi wants a tango, she'll get a tango.'

And at the end of the next track, the Turnips' front man, who performed under the name of Ozzy Ozbarn, announced somewhat sheepishly that, as Lord Rokesay, president of the hunt, had asked for a tango, they would do their best to play one.

When they started playing something approximately Latin in flavour, Sir Compton pursed his lips and sucked noisily through them. 'Oh dear!' he gasped.

Reggie chortled. 'I think I'd better go and watch.'

'Me, too,' said Sir Compton, eagerly.

Archie Pemberton was a young landowner who, in the twenty-five years of his life so far, had won very few prizes. Since winning the Hunt Annual Chariot Race with his sister that evening, it was inevitable that he would be celebrating vigorously. By the time the Turnips had taken to the stage, Archie's spirits, with the help of regular slurps of illicit applejack, had reached a high point where he felt some kind of dramatic gesture was called for.

Ever since his brief and hastily terminated career in a cavalry regiment not known for its demanding intellectual standards, he'd hung on to an illicit store of firecrackers and emergency flares, with a Very pistol to launch them. Letting off a few of these comparatively harmless items of military equipment had become his way of expressing jubilation.

He placed himself and a couple of willing cronies in a dark corner by the woods, a few hundred yards from the house. He opened his celebratory salvo by setting off half a dozen firecrackers, following up the bangs and flashes with three bright pink emergency flares launched in quick succession.

The fiery balls shot in a broad arc well beyond the marquee to bellows of amusement from the drunken majority, who were used to enjoying Archie's little exhibitions, and, from the rest of the gathering, gasps of concern that the flares might have landed too near the kitchen tent behind the marquee.

A quick inspection around both tents revealed that it had passed over them, to come to earth, presumably, in the field beyond the high hedge and out of sight of the party.

It was during a short, merciful break in the Turnips' relentless thundering clamour that a long, anguished cry was heard from the far side of the hedge, soon joined by the harsh crackling of a vigorous fire, and a faint growing halo of light in the sky above.

Through a gap in the hedge appeared an angry, tousled and naked figure, howling like a dog. 'What feckin' idiot set the van on fire?!'

The more alert among the spectators recognised Mickey Rafferty, and saw that he'd been followed through the hedge, with less of a flourish, by Library Lindy, also naked. When she saw the crowd of watchers she stopped to cross her legs and place her small hands over her unclothed pudenda.

Reggie, although no great fan of Mickey's, was sympathetic. 'Oh, no! That's a terrible thing to happen to any young geezer caught *in flagrante delicto*.'

'Ahhh – look the poor little Lindy!' Rosita cried with compassion too. 'She will die of freezing.'

'I expect she's quite embarrassed as well,' Reggie said.

Above the hedge, big healthy flames were visible now, licking up into the summer night sky; it was clear that whatever the flare had landed on was readily combustible.

'Bloody hell,' Reggie exclaimed. 'It must be one of the wooden hoop tops to go up like that. What a shame – they're museum pieces, those wagons. Mind you, Mickey and his dad usually live in a tin one. He'll be in trouble.'

'Why? He didn't put fire to it. That stupid hombre, Archie Arfwit, he fire the rockets; he should be in trouble.'

Reggie chuckled. 'You're right; and he will be. Serve him right for making me buy them Race Day tickets.'

Sir Compton Wynyates was standing beside Reggie, as fascinated as anyone by the sight of a domestic conflagration. 'Do you know why Lancelot has the travellers camping so close to his house and stables?' he asked.

'He likes 'em, Lara says, and because he trusts them, they don't give him any trouble. And he's often up to tricks that aren't strictly kosher, and they help him out. He's a maverick, that Lancelot,' Reggie chuckled. 'He always wants to do the opposite of what everyone else does and, sometimes, I know how he feels.'

'And because Chatternerve chuck them off his place,' Rosita said. 'Lancelot say them to come to – what you say? – snook a cock?'

'That's an interesting concept,' the former ambassador said thoughtfully.

The sun had just nudged up over the hills to the northeast when the remaining gang of black-frocked serving girls who were still standing began to lay up breakfast in the marquee, while a team of noisy women, who had just arrived, bustled in to cook breakfast for the four hundred revellers. The Turnips had left the stage with great reluctance after three continuous hours of very heavy metal – apart from their disastrous tango – when the singer, Ozzy Ozbarn, who had maintained an outstanding level of screaming for the whole set, had finally lost his voice.

The fire brigade turned up, but only in time to watch the very last remnants of the burnt out caravan collapse to the ground in a heap of twisted iron hoops and brackets. Mickey's grandmother, Maeve, whose caravan it was, sat weeping on an upturned brightly painted bucket which had escaped the fire. Even the least tolerant members of the generally intolerant hunt were inclined to be sympathetic, and the old woman had received several offers of temporary housing, including one from Rosita.

Reggie and his friends, having survived the ravages of the Hunt Ball and the conflagration, sat down to large plates of kedgeree, or eggs and bacon, or, in Reggie's case, both, with mugs of builders' strength tea.

'Right, I think home beckons; I'll go and get Huggins up; he's been kipping in the minibus. He should be sober by now.'

Lara arrived after a quick nap in her old bedroom in the house. 'You can't go now. Pa's about to launch a fresh attack on Chatternerve.'

'But the little coward slunk away hours ago.'

'This is more by way of an arm's length artillery attack.'

'Ah!' Sir Compton perked up, trying to extricate himself from his wife's substantial sleeping form which had become draped over him. 'Time for the trebuchets!'

Chapter Nine

Hundreds of spectators had gathered on the top of a ridge which was the border between England and Wales. The hunt ball revellers, mostly awake and expectant now, had been joined by fresh-faced locals who had got up early to see the launch, and busy looking people in purple and turquoise anoraks toting cameras and video kit.

The sun behind them had started its rise over the Clee Hills, while casting an oblique light on two engines of war of a design at least a millennium old. The huge timber structure of Lancelot's larger trebuchet stood like a vast predatory monster. It had not yet been cocked, and the weighted beam lay on the ground with the empty bucket high above the pivotal frame.

It was clear that its trajectory would cast its load directly to the south, over a narrow belt of conifers that crossed the ridge at right angles.

The smaller machine was set to throw to the west, across the valley on that side of the ridge, where sheep grazed a steep slope of scanty turf among patches of outcropping rock. The weapon was already loaded with a small, quite elderly and abused Japanese car, to reflect Lancelot's strong disapproval of products from that country.

At the opposite end of the huge timber beam, which had been cranked high into the air, a two ton weight had been attached.

Mr Lydbury, in the combined role of general and artillery commander, stood by, quivering with excitement, as his team of travellers prepared to draw the peg which would release the beam.

'Fire!' he bellowed. The command echoed back from the far side of the valley, as the top of the beam plummeted earthwards, flicking up the bucket and projectile as if it were a fly. At the top of its arc, the car left the bucket and continued on its journey at an impressive speed, travelling horizontally for twenty yards before it started to drop, and continued on over the sloping valley side in a shallow curve, until gravity took control and drew it plummeting to the ground.

The sheep on the hillside in its line of fire hadn't connected the launch at the top of the hill with the imminent arrival of a small, rusty Japanese car on their patch. When it entered their foggy brains at the last moment that this object was heading straight for them, they scattered at a gallop in disarray with a cacophony of bleating, as the car hit the rocky earth with a hard crash of rending metal.

A great cheer from the onlookers greeted this hilarious but pointless achievement, and Lancelot was able to announce that no sheep had been killed in his little demonstration.

'Where they may safely graze – *not!*' giggled Sir Compton, tingling with excitement, as he prepared himself for the big one.

Emmet Rafferty, his cousins and friends were enjoying their role in these semi-sanctioned acts of vandalism. They happily started to crank the weighted end of the large engine's beam to the top in its upright position. While they were doing this, a small grey tractor was crawling up the ridge towards them, tugging an ancient, mucky trailer.

As it approached, the group gathered around the gaunt mediæval weapon, Porky grunted with approval. 'Looks like a ton of horse crap!' He was finding country pursuits very much to his taste.

'Smell like it, too,' Rosita confirmed.

'Goodness!' gasped Sir Compton. 'Is this to be the projectile for the second launch?'

Reggie, stirring himself from a temporary bout of exhaustion, gurgled with laughter. 'He's an old devil, Lancelot. He's going to chuck it right over those trees; that's the boundary between his land and Chatternerve's – and it looks like he's got the press out to see it – TV an' all!'

Lydbury's helpers started to shovel the contents of the trailer into the capacious bucket of the monster trebuchet, and a buzz of excitement grew as the reek of the well-matured manure filled the air.

Ted Buckton looked on quizzically. 'Over in the Cotswolds, Lancelot could get a fiver a bag for that stuff. Do you think he'll invoice Chatternerve for it after he's dumped it on his land?'

'I wouldn't put it past him,' Lara said.

Once the bucket was full to the brim and overflowing, the travellers got ready to release the massive weighted beam.

On Lydbury's command, it thundered down, propelling the bucket like a rocket to the top, where it released its load and a large, one ton blob of ordure shot over the band of conifers before dropping out of sight on the far side. The spectators cheered, and rushed towards the trees, to see how much mess had been made on the other side.

Some photographers and the TV cameramen had already positioned themselves at the edge of the wood, others were perched strategically on stepladders so they could track the complete trajectory of the airborne dung heap.

Reggie was impressed by the operation. As they hurried towards the trees, he turned to Lara. 'I bet some of those snappers are paparazzi selling their stuff to the national papers! Whether we like it or not, Jason de Chateauneuf is definitely a 'celebrity'.'

'Yes,' she agreed, 'just for being so bloody rich, and the kind of celeb the tabloids love to trash when they get the chance. The headline writers will have a ball! Good old Pa —never does things by halves! Let's go and see how Chatternerve's taking it.'

'Will he be there?' spluttered a breathless Porky, straining to keep up.

'I expect so,' Lara said. 'Pa phoned him just before we set off.'

'Bloody 'ell! What did Chummy say?' Porky wanted to know.

'Actually, I think it was quite a short conversation.'

Beside them, Rosita shrieked. 'AAAgh. There he is!'

They had reached the far side of the belt of trees and had a good view of the ridge on de Chateauneuf's side. Like Lydbury's, the land was a boggy terrain of undrained peat, with a few patches of scanty grazing and clumps of yellow flowering gorse. But on this side, along the ridge in a straight line was a series of excavations which were the preliminary inspection work for the insertion of the concrete bases for the string of wind turbines de Chateauneuf had applied to put up.

Standing by one of them a hundred yards away, beside a brand new, silver Range Rover all liberally spattered with manure, were two Polish farm hands and the squire of Pant-y-Croes.

Sir Compton Wynyates had brought his binoculars. He lifted them to his eyes and chortled happily. 'My goodness; he looks a bit grumpy – actually, very grumpy indeed!'

As he spoke the photographers had broken cover and were running towards the angry young billionaire, snapping shots as they ran.

'GE' THE FOOK OFF OF MY LAND,' de Chateauneuf howled at them in his native Geordie, completely undisguised in his fury.

Lancelot Lydbury had emerged from the belt of trees; he bellowed back. 'A little present for you, Mr Chatternerve. It's top quality shit, like you, but I won't charge you for it.'

'Wheya, stook oop fookin' bastard! I'll sue the crap ou' o' yer...'

The video cameramen chortled, praying that their mics were picking it all up. There were going to be rich pickings from the sale of clips to the networks.

'That won't stop you being the most unpopular man in the Marches!' Lydbury bellowed back. 'As long as you carry on trying to destroy this unique and precious landscape, we'll carry on flinging shit at you.'

With his mean features twisted in rage, Jason de Chateauneuf turned around and, without looking back, clambered into the Range Rover with his two men and slithered at great speed across the boggy ground to drive back down the ridge. As he went, the crowd behind Lancelot Lydbury cheered, whistled and bellowed abuse at the disappearing vehicle.

On Monday morning, Lara drove from her father's to Mortimer Towers where she joined Rosita, Reggie and Porky for a late, leisurely breakfast. She'd brought with her copies of all the tabloids, which she and Rosita spread out on the breakfast table to see what they'd made of Lancelot's attack on de Chateauneuf.

WHEN THE SH*T HIT THE FAN, BEFORE IT WENT UP! one of them put it on their front page, with their usual hypocritical decorousness.

WELL OUT OF ORDURE! trumpeted another.

The general mood was antagonistic towards the young billionaire trying to profit from the government's efforts to be green, and sympathetic to the eccentric landowner whose family had lived on their land since the Norman conquest, and who felt that it was his duty to protect the ancient landscape from such abuse.

'That's tellin' him,' Porky said.

'You should see on YouTube,' Rosita exclaimed. 'Is fantastic to see the horses' pooh fly through the air and falling down all round Chatternerve and his shiny car.'

'He won't like that,' Reggie laughed.

'Serve him right,' Porky said. 'Trouble is, he's the sort of geezer, the more you try and stop him, the more 'e'll want to do it – nothing to do with the wonga. A bloke like that who's come from a council house in the arse end of Geordieland, hasn't got where he has by backing down. You could say it's a sort of habit.'

'It's vanity,' Lara said. 'But he can try what he likes, and I hope he spends a bundle on it, because in the end, he'll lose.'

'You seem bloody confident,' Porky said.

Lara touched the side of her nose like she'd seen old French peasants do. 'I know what I know.'

'Well, best of luck, darling. You deserve it and your dad's a proper gent.' He started getting to his feet. 'Now, I've got to get back down the smoke; me lungs are beginning to get the gyp with all this fresh air.'

Rosita got up too, and flung her arms around him. 'Porky! It was so lovely to see you here. You must come again soon.'

'Don't you worry about that, Rosi. You and Cousin Reggie have been fantastic; I almost like the sticks, now. And you let me know how you get on with them moles,' he laughed. 'I never heard of such a potty deal; and you tell me who your punter is, next time I see yer.'

'We will Porky, we will,' Reggie agreed.

Porky was pulling his blackberry from a pocket in his trousers. 'I'll get old Tommy's Taxis round to take me to the station.'

'That's alright Porky, I'll take you in the Bentley – it could do with the exercise.'

'Don't be silly,' Lara said. 'I'm driving back to London now; Porky can come with me.'

'What? In James Bond's Austin Martin with a beautiful gell? I must have died and gone to 'eaven.'

After Reggie and Rosita had waved their friends away on the steps of the porch, a lorry arrived with four men and a marquee, which they were going to erect for Rosita's first wedding event, due to happen on the following Saturday.

For a moment, Rosita looked uncertain. 'I wish Lara could have stayed to help me.'

'Come on, Rosi; she's got her own life to lead. Besides, you've got me.'

'Reggie, what you know about flowers and wedding decorations?'

'You trust your instincts, my creative little flower, and you'll be fine. And now you've got old Maeve staying in the stable flat, I'm sure she'll give you a hand; she's very grateful to you for giving her a roof over her head.'

'She prefer her caravan; anyway I don't want it like a Big Fat Gypsy Wedding!'

'At least she could knock you up a few corn dollies. Now, I've got to go, my cherub; Owen's got the rest of the moles for me, and I've got to pick them up this morning.'

Reggie had had twelve hours' good sleep after the excesses and deprivations of the hunt ball/trebuchet launch, and was feeling quite perky as he rattled his old Landrover through the lanes to Owen Preece's isolated cottage in the Kerry Hills.

When he got there, he parked beside the old man's much newer vehicle and trudged up the path to the house for his third visit. He was looking forward to another session with the enigmatic old twister. He hadn't quite reached the door when he heard a voice behind him.

''Ello, Mizzer Finchley,' Owen croaked.

Reggie spun round to find the old man carrying two moleskins, suspended from the thumb and forefinger of each of his hands.

'Wotcher, Owen. Did you do them yourself?'

'You mean, skin 'em?'

'Yes.'

'No, though I have done, in the past. I had these skinned by one of them old traveller women. Theym's good at skinning oonts, and martens and squirrels an' all sorts; they does it tidy like, not to damage the hide or the fur. I just been curing 'em.'

'What do you want the skins for?'

Owen gave Reggie a squiggly look. 'I'm not tellin' you,' he answered, like it was a silly question.

Inside, though, he seemed to relent. He offered Reggie some applejack. Reggie nodded his appreciation as Owen reached up for a dusty bottle.

'I'll tell you why I got the skins. There's a woman who stuffs animals comes up from Hay and takes a few off me from time to time. Once in a while I can find her a red squirrel or a pine marten, which is hard to come by, and that brings her back.'

Owen's mention of traveller women made him think of Maeve, Rosi's new tenant in the stable.

'It was a traveller who ordered these moles off me,' Reggie said.

Owen, in the act of pouring applejack into a glass for Reggie, rotated his wrist and stopped pouring. He turned his head to deliver a penetrating stare. 'You never told me that.'

'Like you, I never usually tell anyone who my customers are, but... I reckoned it's a one off, and he won't be needing more.'

'Which traveller is it?'

'Emmet Rafferty,' Reggie answered.

Owen's features gave nothing away. 'Emmet Rafferty, eh? 'E's using you on account of he knows I won't do no business with travellers, not any more. Did he tell you to come and see me?'

'No,' Reggie admitted. 'He aimed me at a little rat catcher called Foxy Warren; it was Foxy told me about you.'

'Emmet knowed I don't do business with travellers – not after one of them tried to rob me a score years ago. But there's no one but me in fifty miles an' more as can catch live moles, and he knows that, too.'

'Why didn't he tell me to come straight to you, then?'

'He'd have thought you'd smell a rat – thinking why wouldn't he come to me hisself. He's a crafty bugger.' Owen looked at Reggie for a moment, giving nothing away. 'D'you know why he wants them?'

'He won't tell me, but I reckon they're going to Ireland.'

Owen stiffened. 'There's no moles there. It must be for some sort of mischief.'

'I thought maybe it's something to do with the fashion trade?'

'You reckon?' Owen looked doubtful. 'I don't know nothing 'bout the fashions. Anyways, you give me the money we agreed and take this lot, but if you wants more... Well, we'll see. And, here, I got a present for you.' From the cluttered sideboard he picked up and *R. Whites Lemonade* bottle, containing a liquid, clearly not lemonade, the colour of pale barley. 'I gives a drop of applejack to all my best customers.'

Reggie drove straight home to Mortimer Towers with his crates of moles. He was sorry to find that he'd been to some extent set up by Emmet, although the Irish traveller had offered him a straight-forward deal, and as long as he got paid, it ought to be worth doing, and he didn't think Emmet would set out to welsh on him; he hoped not, anyway. Now he didn't have much choice but to go through with it.

He phoned ahead and told Huggins to be ready to help him un-load and install the little mammals in a second scaffold board and earth pen that he'd asked him to make.

As far as Reggie could see, the earlier arrivals were thriving in their pen, although they were chomping their way through bucket-loads of earth worms at an alarming rate. Reggie had to admit to himself that in doing the deal with Emmet, he hadn't taken into account the cost of housing and feeding the merchandise; Huggins had to be paid and he was spending half his day digging for worms.

Once the moles were installed in their new home, Reggie got back into the Landrover and drove off to find Emmet Rafferty.

Emmet was in his caravan, watching the cricket.

'Sorry to interrupt,' Reggie said with a hint of sarcasm which Emmet picked up at once.

'What's the trouble, Reggie? You got all the moles yet?'

'Yes, I have. And you know where I got them, don't you?'

'Maybe,' Emmet said, sensing that denial wouldn't work.

''Ere, you set me up, you monkey! You've been pulling my plonker!'

'Come on, Reggie; I wouldn't do that. Sit down; have a glass of this beautiful port.'

Reggie sat, and took a sip from the glass Emmet filled for him. 'This is a bit good, Emmet. Where did it come from?'

'Mr Lydbury give it to me after we slung all the horse shite at Chatternerve's place.'

'He's a fair man is Lancelot,' Reggie chuckled, '*and* a man of very good judgement in the matter of booze.'

'Now, let's sort this out, Reggie. I don't want to fall out wit' you.'

Reggie nodded. 'OK.'

'I told you what I wanted, and we agreed a price; I knew if I sent you to Foxy, he'd tell you where to go. What else could I do? Owen Preece is an old bigot, but he's the only man I ever heard of who can catch live moles. He's been doing it for years, planting them in potential punters' fields and gardens. What difference does it make to you?'

'It would help if you told me why you want them alive.'

Emmet winced. 'I wish I could tell you; I *will* – nearer delivery – I promise, because you're going to have to talk to the punter.'

'But Emmet, if Owen's the only man who can catch live moles for miles around here, where the hell did you get yours?'

Emmet shook his head. 'I didn't.'

'Didn't what?'

'Get any.'

'What?!' Reggie roared. 'Why didn't you tell me?'

Emmet shrugged a shoulder. 'It was better if you thought we were in this together; I only said I was getting some to convince you to do the deal.'

Reggie sighed. He hated being led up garden paths.

'Come on,' Emmet cajoled. 'There's no harm done; you've still done a good deal...'

'Not yet, I haven't – not till I've got the lolly in my arse pocket. I've got a lot of costs to cover, and I had to pay over the odds to Owen.'

'Not really, and you're still going to make a good turn on it.'

'And so are you, I should think – you're not a charitable organisation, are you - provided your punter shows up and coughs up. What about paying me some of my money, now I've got the little fellows, all eating their heads off?'

'I can't pay you; I've not had any money myself. But trust me; the punter will pay you as soon as you deliver.'

'Where to?'

'I told you; we have to leave from Aberdovey. We'll be going to Ireland.'

'I had worked that out,' Reggie snorted.

'I've got some instructions, but no final delivery date.'

'It had better be bloody soon. You can't get a geezer to dig up worms all day for nothing.'

'It will be soon,' Emmet said, in a way in which Reggie detected some nervousness. 'This is what you've to do. Drive down to Aberdovey with the moles; when you get there, find a man with a boat who can take you with the goods over to Ireland. I don't know exactly where yet, but it'll be somewhere near Wexford. Before you go, you have to wait in Aberdovey until you get a call on your mobile with final instructions.'

'They're your punters; why don't they call you?'

'There's no need for me to come,' Emmet said carefully.

'What?! Listen, mate, you're coming too – and that's that. I'm not delivering two hundred bloody moles to some dodgy Paddy, on my own in the middle of the Irish Sea. If I wanted that much excitement, I'd have joined the bloody SAS!'

Emmet put his hands up. 'All right, all right! I'll come and hold your hand.'

'Bloody right, you will. Then when do I get my money?'

'Same time as me. It's cash on delivery – twelve grand: sixty pound for every live oont. They won't let me down – sooner or later they'll need me again. '

'But you said we were charging *fifty* quid an oont.'

'The tenner's for me.'

'So you're getting two grand for nothing?'

'It's called commission, Reggie. It's quite normal, and you're going to get just what we agreed.'

Reggie sighed. 'It's my own bloody fault; I'm too trusting, that's my trouble.'

'Reggie, my friend, nobody's ripped you off.'

'Not yet they haven't.'

'Just relax. If we can pull this off, I may have a few other deals for you.'

'Hgh,' Reggie grunted.

'I've one now.'

'Oh, yeh? What's that?'

'You know Chatternerve, don't you?'

'You know bloody well we can't stand the sight of each other, especially me.'

'You don't have to like him to go and tell him you might be able to find his missing precious racehorse.'

'Why would I do that? For one thing, why should I want to do him any favours; and for another, I don't know where his bloody horse is.'

'You tell him you want a finder's fee, and I'll find out where the horse is.'

'I expect some member of your very extended family has it hidden away somewhere, and, basically, you're saying I go round to Chatternerve and ask for a ransom. That's not my style, Emmet. I thought you knew that; I may have been a street trader once, and I'll buy and sell anything legal, but I'm not a bloody crook.'

'Never mind,' Emmet said philosophically. 'Have another drop o' port. And I tell you what, I do know where the horse is. And Chatternerve's already had the police round there looking for it.'

'Where's that, then?'

'At Mr Lydbury's.'

'But it wasn't there?'

'I didn't say that. It's there all right, but they didn't recognise it. They were looking for a micro-chipped, dark bay thoroughbred horse, about 16.2 hands. All they found was an unchipped chestnut.' Emmet chuckled. 'It took fifteen bottles of a hair colour – Autumn Leaves, it was called – to dye the horse.'

'Autumn Leaves,' Reggie chuckled. 'I like that. Let's have another drop of that lovely port.'

Emmet happily topped up their glasses with Lancelot Lydbury's port. He leaned back in his chair and looked at Reggie knowingly.

'By the way, Reggie, I know that things isn't so good for you at the moment.'

Reggie gave him a sharp glance. 'What're you talking about?'

Emmet raised a placating hand. 'Don't get twitchy. Everyone who does a few deals has troubles from time to time; it's how you get out of 'em shows what kind of a man you are.'

'What are you trying to tell me, you nosy tinker?'

Emmet didn't take offence. He knew he was treading on sensitive ground. 'Don't you worry – it won't go no further – I've made bloody sure of that.'

'What won't?' Reggie was getting more agitated.

'My nephew, Mickey told me he was leaning over your wall a couple of weeks ago, when your Sue comes runnin' out to tell your missus that the bailiffs was there – with a lorry an' all.'

Reggie blinked, closed his eyes and grasped his forehead with one hand. 'Bugger!'

'Reggie, me old mate, it's OK. No one else will know – I told Mickey what'll happen to him if he tells anyone else. We're doin' business, you and me, and I ain't gonna let you down.'

Reggie produced a wry smile. 'Yeh, well... I did have a little visit.'

'Mickey says your missus went back in and saw them off pretty damn quick.'

Reggie managed to raise a laugh now. 'She did; she got rid of 'em all right. She showed 'em the deeds to the house, which is in her name, as a sort of a business precaution, like, and she told them everything in the house was hers, too, and they'd have to come back with proof that it wasn't before they took so much as a spoon.' Reggie grunted with pleasure at the thought. 'I don't think they'll be back.'

'Great!' Emmet chuckled. 'Don't you worry, Reggie. Your secret is safe with me. OK?'

Reggie looked back at him, glad in a way that at least someone else knew what dire straights he was in. He raised his glass of port. 'Then let's hope this bloody deal comes off, then. Here's to the moles!'

The next morning, just three days before the first wedding reception was to be held in the house and grounds of Mortimer Towers, Reggie was woken by a sudden, piercing scream and a long wail of anguish. His brain, badly impaired by the enormous quantity of port he'd drunk with Emmet Rafferty, struggled to remind him where he was, who he was and what might be making the excruciating noise ripping through his scrambled head.

He opened his mouth and tried to cough out the small, incontinent rodent that seemed to have crawled into it and made a nest there overnight. Each cough triggered the insertion of white hot blades in both temples.

But slowly, painfully, as he lay supine and immobile, a sort of consciousness re-established itself in his head. The wailing had translated itself into words. *Topos, bastar' topos!*

Reggie tried to extract some meaning from the words.

He was aware now that it was his wife, his beloved former dancer of the finest burlesque, who was creating this painful racket. He managed to raise his head a few inches from the pillows supporting it.

'What is it, my little cherub?' he croaked. 'Has the 'orrible computer gone doolally on you again?'

'No!' The twin laser beams of his wife's angry chocolate brown eyes seemed to pin Reggie down. 'Your bloody moles! They have excape!'

Reggie was by now alert enough to know that this could be a disaster on more than one front.

'Oh, shit!' he groaned and let his head flop back, and was momentarily grateful that Rosita had insisted on having only pillows stuffed with a thousand feathers from the breasts of pampered young eider ducks.

'REGGIE! Oh My God! You must do something... *please!*'

It was the 'please' that told Reggie the situation, whatever had caused it, was catastrophic.

With a grunt and a sharp pain in his back, he swung his legs over the side of the bed and staggered to his feet.

Walking was less easy.

Rosita wasn't sympathetic. 'Come, you old crock! Come look at my lawn!'

Reggie hobbled across the room towards the view he loved to drink in each morning – the lawns sweeping down to the lake, the great beeches swaying against a cerulean sky and the misty lilac hills beyond.

This time, his eyes got no further than the lawns; the normally pristine green sweep, already disfigured by a large pink marquee, looked as if it had also caught a nasty rash. As far as Reggie's eyes could see, it was covered with large brown pimples.

He gulped; he wanted to scream; he wished someone would inject him, there and then, with a powerful anaesthetic, leaving him unconscious for the next twenty-four hours.

But he knew it was his duty, as head of the Mortimer Towers household, to handle this multiple crisis. He took a few deep breaths, while cursing the depravity of the Spaniard who had invented port. He turned around to face his wife.

'Right, my little rosebud, let's go down and inspect the damage; I'll give young Huggins a ring on the way.'

Harry Huggins, accustomed by now to the excesses and dramas that tended to crop up in a household that contained Rosita, rose to the challenge of disposing of the mole hills with enthusiasm; he too, loved the lawns, and he recognised a situation in which Mr ffinch-Leigh was likely to be generous in his appreciation. He attached a trailer to the sit-on mower and filled it several times with the oonti-tump spoil, including that from a number that had sprouted beneath the sisal carpeting inside the marquee.

Reggie's major concern wasn't the havoc the moles had wrought, but their immediate recapture and return to their earth-filled pens in the basement. Down in the ancient undercroft, it was clear that some renegade moles, no doubt in a natural quest for new territory to colonise, had got themselves over the scaffold board edges of the earth pits. Once on the stone floor and investigating further, they'd evidently found a soft spot where they could burrow beneath a course of bricks where an old opening appeared to have been filled in.

Once Harry Huggins had removed all the tumps, Reggie and he dug out the pens. They placed the moles they found still there in the empty crates Owen had given him to transport them, counting the indignant, writhing animals as they did it.

'Right,' Reggie said, panting with the effort and the trauma of it. 'That's about a hundred and thirty, so around seventy of them's gone awol. No bloody wonder the lawn looks like the battlefields of the Somme!'

He stood up, straightening his back. 'While I sort out how the hell I'm going to catch 'em, can you have a look where they went after they got out through that little hole there at the bottom of the wall?'

'Right you are, Mr Reggie. I'll get Dad to give me a hand.'

Reggie went outside to phone Owen Preece on his mobile.

''Ello? 'Oo is it?' Owen answered.

'It's Reggie here – Reggie ffinch-Leigh.'

'What do you want?'

'Seventy of the moles have escaped; I need to get them back, before they've dispersed all over the county.'

'Oh, ah? What you goin' to do about it?'

'I'm asking you,' Reggie said plainly.

He heard a noisy intake of breath. 'I dunno,' Owen said doubtfully.

Reggie thought the old geezer could have won prizes for acting. 'Can I come and talk about it?'

'All right, if you want. I'm down in Clun. I'll be in the Buffalo in about half an hour.'

For the second time in two days, Reggie headed west across the hills, glad that at least he didn't have to traipse all the way to Owen's cottage.

Reggie hadn't met Owen away from his own ground; he wondered how he would be in a public place like the Buffalo.

He found the old boy wearing the grubbiest flat cap he'd ever seen and sitting on a pew in the front bar of the pub, apparently well at ease, supping a glass of cider.

Reggie sat down beside him.

Owen nodded at him. 'Get yourself a half-pint o' cider, and I'll add a drop of my applejack.'

When Reggie came back with his cider, Owen quite brazenly topped it up from one of his own small bottles and sat back, ready to talk.

'What's the problem?'

'I told you – about seventy of the little buggers have broken out...'

'Did you put chicken wire over the top of your pens?'

'No.'

'Then o' course some of 'em's got out; I'm surprised they all didn't – unless they still had some food left.'

'You never said anything about putting wire over the top.'

Owen shrugged a shoulder. 'That's just common sense. Anyway, what do you want me to do?'

'What the hell d'you think I want you to do,' Reggie said, immediately regretting his display of anger.

'I ain't catching 'em again for free, but as there's a good cluster of 'em, I won't charge you full price. I'll see how long it takes. And I can't promise to get 'em all back.'

'But you will come over?'

'Aye.'

Reggie had thought it would have taken longer to persuade Owen to come; now he was overwhelmed with gratitude at the old man's swift agreement. 'Can I get you a drink?'

'You save your money,' Owen growled. 'You're going to need it. I'll be over tonight, about an hour before sunset.'

Back at Mortimer Towers, Reggie went straight back down to the cellars to find two sledgehammers lying on the floor and a neat pile of bricks which the Hugginses had removed from the old filled-in doorway. It was now opened up enough for a man to pass through and there was no sign of father or son.

'What the hell's going on?' Reggie thundered

''Ere!' Albert Huggins called from the other side, 'Come and have a look!'

Reggie stepped through the gap into damp, musty space. The Hugginses had fixed a clip-light onto an old rusty iron hook set in the stone wall. It lit the immediate area – a narrow stone-walled room with an earth floor.

'I didn't ask you to knock the whole bloody wall down!' Reggie fumed.

'You said to have a look where the oonts went after they got through that little hole at the bottom.'

From the pile of freshly dug earth at the far end of the chamber, it was clear how the moles had made their escape. Reggie reckoned they must have had to burrow fifteen feet or more – no doubt with a few failed attempts at surfacing – to get beyond the stone-flagged terrace outside and out beneath the lawn.

'Did you know this funny little room was here?' Reggie asked Albert Huggins.

The older Huggins nodded. 'Aye. Till around thirty year ago, there was an old oak door; 'twas always locked though, and I never saw on the other side. Then one day, old Mr Bertram says to me to take the door off, get some old bricks together, make up some mortar, and just fill it in over the old timber threshold. That's what

I done, but o' course, in time the timber's rotted and I s'pose a few rats has been in and out, and them moles, once they was sniffin' about, they found a way through it, and off they went.' The old boy cackled.

'Yeh,' Reggie nodded, less amused by the flight of his moles, but intrigued by a narrow flight of wooden stairs running up one side of the space. 'Where do these stairs go?' he asked.

'We ain't been up yet,' Harry Huggins said. 'But Dad reckons it must be behind the fireplace in the library. We can take this light and go up and have a look, if you want.'

'Yeh,' Reggie nodded. 'Of course I want. You lead the way with the light.'

The stairs felt surprisingly solid. Reggie guessed they'd been made at least within the last fifty years. At the top of them was a simple plank door, closed with a bolt and padlock.

Reggie turned to Albert Huggins coming up behind him. 'You'd better go and find the bolt cutters.'

'Maybe not,' the old boy croaked. 'There's a key hanging here, a bit hid behind this stanchion.'

Harry Huggins inserted the key, undid the padlock and drew back the bolt; the door swung open with a loud squeak.

Beyond it was another narrow chamber, about eight feet wide, with brick walls on all sides. To the left was the back of a chimney breast, which, Reggie agreed with old Huggins, must have been the library fireplace. To the right was a plain wall, which would be the end wall of the dining room.

Harry Huggins couldn't find anywhere to clip the light, and taking a step to one side in the room stood holding it as high as he could.

Reggie gaped at what it revealed. Stacked against the walls on both sides, on dry, surprisingly clean oak floor boards were a couple of dozen gilt frames, facing inwards.

'I wonder what the hell these are?' He lifted one – about two feet by three feet – and turned it round to face them. 'Give us a bit of light,' he ordered.

Harry swung the lamp round to shine full on a painted canvas.

'God almighty! What have we got here?' Reggie gasped.

He was looking at what appeared to be a classic 18th or 19th century painting of a race-horse being held by a liveried groom. In the background was a large, vaguely familiar Georgian mansion.

'Jesus! That looks very good! Hell! I wish I knew more about pictures! But that could be a Stubbs, or maybe a Herring?'

'Could be a cod fillet, for all I knows,' Albert Huggins chuckled.

'Thank you, Albert,' Reggie said. 'But seriously, do you have any idea what they would be doing here?'

Albert shook his grizzled head. 'I don't know. Mr Bertram used to buy and sell a few pictures, I knows that. He was for ever going off to the sales, but why these should be here – I got no idea.'

'All right,' Reggie made his mind up. 'We've got too much going on to do anything about them now. For a start, I've got to get my moles back in here and, thank God, Owen Preece is coming tonight. We'll just lock this door up again, and I'll put the key in the safe. We'll come and get them out and have a proper look at them after this bloody wedding party's been and gone.'

Owen Preece's shiny brand new Landrover pulled up outside Mortimer Towers later that evening. Reggie had been waiting impatiently for Owen for the past two hours. The driver's door opened and in sharp contrast to the pristine vehicle, the little old mole catcher, still wearing his grimy cap, with a stained and shredded tweed jacket and much worn cord trousers climbed down.

Reggie went out to meet him.

'I 'asn't been 'ere for *years*,' Owen said.

'But you've been here before, have you?'

'Oh yeh, when the old boy was here. He used to let me catch the moles without killing 'em. He was a canny old bugger; he knew why I wanted them live, so I did him a special price. He would laugh to know I was back.'

'Would he?' said Reggie. 'I'm not finding it too funny. For one thing, my wife's putting on a wedding reception here in two days' time, and the moles are pushing up tumps almost as fast as we can clear them, and for another, I've got to deliver my two hundred any day now.'

'All right, don't you get yourself in a lather. I said I'd be here, and here I am. I'll get to work, and allus I catch, I'll charge you half price.'

Reggie groaned. If Owen caught all the fugitive moles – which was what he wanted – he was about to spend another seven hundred quid.

Owen sensed Reggie's grief. 'Mr Finchley, you wanted two hundred live moles, and that's what you got; you're lucky to be getting these extras at cut price.'

'But they're the ones you already caught!'

'It weren't my fault they escaped.'

'All right, all right,' Reggie conceded. 'Just try and get them all – or my wife will go doolally.'

'I'm going to get started now, afore it gets too dark. So you better send your Hugginses home and, if you're going to watch me work, you got to give me your word you'll never do it yourself, nor tell another living soul how I done it. OK?'

'Fair enough,' Reggie said, wondering if he had sufficient discretion to keep his word.

'You better, 'cause if you don't, you'll feel the full force of the curse of Mefanwy, the Witch of Cefn Llys.'

'In that case, I definitely won't,' Reggie said emphatically.

Although not by nature a superstitious man, Reggie could easily believe that this strange little man was capable of calling down some malediction on him.

Owen had come prepared for a major campaign. He produced not one, but eight deep enamel basins like the one Reggie had seen in the back of the Landrover on his first visit. They were each about fourteen inches across, with steep sides, and about nine inches in depth.

With these he also took out the same number of umbrella like contraptions, which had a stand that could be placed in the middle of each bowl.

He walked the lawn thoroughly, from end to end, prodding the ground every so often using a straight wooden broom handle with

187

a long iron tine attached to the end. Every so often he would in-sert a thin bamboo wand to mark a spot – none of them in the immediate vicinity of the remains of the mole tumps Harry Hug-gins had cleared up.

'What are you doing?' Reggie asked.

'Just marking some runs.'

When he had a dozen or so markers in place, Owen pulled on a pair of thick rubber gloves. 'If they do get my scent, they'll run backwards down their burrow,' he explained.

Using a small spade, he dug a circular hole, just big enough to accommodate one of the enamel bowls, first carefully removing the turf on top in four quarters, then depositing the earth in a tump beside the hole, to be put back later. Into each hole, he placed a bowl so that the top lip was in line with the bottom of one of the runs the moles had made.

When all eight bowls were in place, Owen pottered off back to his Landrover and came back carrying several big plastic sand-wich boxes. When he opened them Reggie saw that they were stuffed full of a wriggling, squiggling mass of grubs and crane fly larvae, which the farmers called leatherjackets. 'Can you let us have a few dozen worms, too?' he asked.

While Reggie was fetching these from the Hugginses' store, Owen dropped a few of the mole delicacies he'd brought into each of the basins before adding the worms that Reggie had brought back. He then placed an umbrella cover over each bowl, and cov-ered that with the four triangles of turf he'd cut, filling in any gaps with spare earth. 'If they senses any light coming through, they won't think about heading this way,' he told Reggie.

When he had prepared all the traps strategically around the lawn, he straightened himself and pulled his gloves off.

'There you are Mr Finchley – all ready to go. We'll see what we've got in the morning. Now, they say you keeps some very fine malmsey here.'

'Do they now? Well they're bloody right. Come up and have a drop.'

It was well after sunset by now, but a mild night, and by the light of a storm lamp, Reggie and Owen sat down at the table on the terrace to drink a glass or two of the famous malmsey.

'Do you want to stay here the night, Owen, so you can get up at sparrow fart to check the traps? You can stay above the stable, if you won't mind being next to old Maeve Rafferty.'

'That's all right. I knows Maeve, but I allus bed down in my own wagon.'

'If that's what you want,' Reggie shrugged, 'That's fine. Now,' he went on, carefully casual, 'tell me how these traps of yours work.'

'What'll happen is this. Those oonts will be buried somewhere in a great tangle of tunnels goin' all this way and that, and they gets around a lot, always following their noses which are 'ighly efficient pieces of olfactory equipment. They'll smell them worms and leatherjackets, and they'll come snuffling along, just following their pointy noses, until suddenly, afore they know it, they're at the edge of a shiny bowl, and slithering down the side. They'll try and get out, o' course, but they can't. They'll just be trying to swim up the side with their great big paws, and getting nowhere; they'll get themselves into some kind of a distress, and start shrieking their heads off, then what'll happen is the rest of them that's not already blundered into a bowl will follow the noise - because moles has got good 'earing – and they'll end up in my bowls likewise. Tomorrow morning, we'll go round and have a look at each of the bowls, and see what they got.'

During the night, Reggie was woken from a fine malmsey slumber by a sharp jab in his side from his wife's elbow.

'Reggie, Reggie – wake up!'

'What is it, my little lovebird?'

'Ou'side! There is terrible screaming, and shrieking, like two cats make love.'

Reggie tried to focus and listen. After a few moments, he smiled with satisfaction that Owen hadn't just been spinning him a load of twaddle. 'That, my darling is all my moles coming to order,' he said. 'Relax. I told you I'd sort it out, and I have. Now you put your earplugs in and go back to sleep.'

Reggie himself sat up and wondered what time it was. The first light of dawn was seeping over the tops of the heavy curtains that were closed over the view of their garden. He got out of bed, tiptoed to the window and tweaked the curtains apart, enough to see that the sun was getting close to poking its head over the hills in the north east. A movement on the lawn below caught his eye and he spotted Owen Preece flitting through the shadows towards the lowest of his trap markers.

Reggie didn't want to miss out on this crucial activity and hauled himself into a pair of red cords and a Fair Isle sweater which Rosita, at Lara's suggestion, had given him for Christmas.

'Bloody 'ell!' Owen said when he saw what Reggie was wearing. 'That's a bit bright; you might scare the oonts.'

I thought they were blind.'

'They're not *that* blind.'

From the small grass mound which covered the first trap they could hear squeaking, and occasional shrieks, with the sound of strong little paws scrabbling on slippery metal

'Get on with it,' Reggie said with a laugh.

'Fetch me over one of them crates,' Owen said, nodding at where he'd stacked several of them.

As Reggie carried them over, Owen pulled on his gloves and started to remove the quartered turfs. He put them aside and lifted the strange umbrella cover he had made, to reveal nine fidgety moles looking dazed and confused, and still complaining from time to time. The grubs and worms had gone – replaced by a heap of droppings.

'They're all alive and they look OK,' Owen said with satisfaction. He dipped in a hand and picked one up to inspect it. 'He's a bit messy, but he'll clean himself up.' He placed it, quite gently, Reggie noticed, in the crate.

'Well that's one...'

An hour or so later, Owen picked up the last of the moles in the eighth trap. That makes sixty-six,' he said with satisfaction. 'You owe me six hundred and sixty pounds.'

Even though he'd known this was coming, Reggie felt queasy, in the way he always did when a deal was going pear-shaped. His profit on this mole malarkey was being steadily whittled away by a number of costs he'd overlooked or hadn't planned for. Why did he still do this kind of thing – he asked himself – getting involved in things he knew nothing about?

In theory, when Emmet had put it to him, it looked fine, but now, hanging over all the uncertainties that already plagued the deal, was the unattractive possibility that, despite Emmet's show of confidence, even after he'd successfully got his live moles to Ireland or wherever they were supposed to go, there'd be no money for him.

In his former existence as a general trader around the London markets, this hadn't happened – not often, anyway – because he was on his own home ground, and everyone knew who he was. Inevitably, though, from time to time, he'd had to ask his old chum, and overdue accounts agent, Stan Frost, to visit a reluctant payer.

Stan, although built along the lines of the alpha male in a family unit of Ugandan mountain gorillas, handled these situations with touching delicacy and tact. He would start the conversation with the reluctant payer along philosophical lines. 'Different fings are important in life, aren't they?' he would venture. 'Money's important, fr'instance, in'it?'

The debtor would usually find themselves agreeing with this self-evident truth, while Stan would start punching the broad palm of his left hand with his substantial right fist, 'But then, 'elf's important too. You can't enjoy yer money, if you 'aven't got yer 'elf. Know wha' I mean?'

This practice had the advantage of being legal, at least up until that point in the proceedings, and it nearly always worked; it had also served as a discouragement to other potential non-payers, but now Reggie was doubtful that a useful resource like Stan Frost could operate effectively among the less than respectable sections of the Irish business community.

But that was too bad; he was committed now. He'd already paid

Owen a lot of money, and he couldn't possibly back out.

Bloody, hell, he said to himself as he took out the bundle which he'd had to squeeze from Rosita, even at your age, you still haven't learned to curb your optimism. Out loud he said, 'Here you are, Owen, my man. Not many people would guess it, but you're a very clever fellow.'

Owen tucked the bundle of notes somewhere close to his unwashed body, and gave Reggie a grin. 'That's the way I like it,' he said. 'And don't forget – you say nothing about my secret methods or the old witch of Cefn Llys will be down to haunt you.' He emphasised his words with a piercing glare. 'And don't lose any more of your oonts.'

Chapter Ten

After a night filled with surreal, Kafkaesque dreams, featuring moles, traps and witches, Reggie's head was still spinning next morning. It was the day before the wedding; the house and garden were bunged up with scurrying cleaners and caterers while a steady flow of traffic pulled up in front of the house to deliver floral artistes, men with posh Portaloos, and others bringing sound systems and large discs of MDF that would be disguised as smart round tables. A DJ arrived to set up his kit, and a couple of Turnips turned up to check the layout.

When he saw them, Reggie groaned to his wife. "Oh Gawd! Not Iron Yokel again?'

'I booked them,' said Rosita proudly. 'Is just what the bride want, and I get commission.'

'Who's the DJ then? He looks like he lay down in front of a steam roller to protest about something, and it didn't bother to stop.'

Rosita dismissed his objection with the flip of a hand. 'You don't have to be fat to play records. And maybe nex' time he protest against Chatternerve's willmills.'

Reggie shook his head. 'What on earth are you talking about, Rosi.'

'Never mind, if you don' understand. Righ' now, I want you to get rid of the rest of your bloody moles – look, five new mole hills already this morning. You say Owen catch them all.'

'All except a few,' Reggie corrected her.

'You get rid of them before tomorrow. If bride turn up to find like a plough field, she want her money back, and I say to her – Get from him.' Rosita prodded Reggie in the chest to make her point.

'All right, my little Celtic Witch,' Reggie replied, still thinking about Owen's threat of a curse. 'Don't get your thong in a tangle. I'll talk to Huggins.'

Even if he had been prepared to run the risk of the witch's spell, Reggie didn't think he had time to gather the necessary tack to do what Owen had done. Besides, he wasn't at all sure it was as easy as Owen had made it look.

Old Albert Huggins was helpful – up to a point. 'Oh, yes,' he said, 'I got traps all right – half a dozen of 'em. You're welcome to 'em.'

'Thanks, Albert, but would you mind setting them for me? Do you know how to do it?'

'I knows all right, and I knows how to find the runs, but I ain't doin' it.'

Reggie had never known Albert Huggins to mutiny before. 'Why on earth not?' he asked.

''Cos last time I killed a mole, my Betty started havin' her funny turns, so I ain't doin' it no more.'

Reggie wondered how the two events could be connected. He shook his head in bewilderment, but knew better than to challenge the old fellow's reasons.

'OK, Albert, but will you show me how to set one?'

'Sorry, Mr Reggie; that'd be like settin' 'em myself.'

Reggie remembered he had a book in his library, published about a hundred years before, called *Good Riddance to Vermin* and Albert Huggins' traps appeared to belong to the same era. Following the instructions of the Edwardian pest controller who had written the book, he inserted half a dozen of the rusty old scissor traps, and had just finished when he heard Evan Pugh's ugly voice over his shoulder.

'Trappin' moles, Reggie?'

'No, looking for truffles,' Reggie answered irritably.

'You'll not find any out here in the lawn. I can tell you where to look, if you want?'

Reggie sighed. 'No, it's all right, Evan. What can I do for you?'

'That table I bought from you, and you bought back at the auction...'

Reggie had, for the time being, shoved the whole disastrous business of the Chippendale table to the back of his mind, until he would have more time to devote to searching for the missing pair. He raised a cynical eyebrow. 'What about it?'

'I'll buy it back from you, for what I gave you first time round.'

Reggie was about to tell Evan not to take him for a complete novice when he started wondering why the shifty little dealer wanted it back.

'Why do you want to do that? If you send it to Lennon's again, I'm not going to buy it again, am I?'

'No, Reggie, of course not; but now you know you made a mistake, I thought you might like to cut your losses.'

'That's very thoughtful of you, Evan. I'm deeply touched, but I think I can do a bit better than that.'

'Oh, but the trade for those things is terrible at the moment; I'm not going to make much out of it, I can assure you.'

'That's very kind of you, Evan. What's the very best you could go to, to help me out of a spot?'

Evan's thin, ferret face twisted as if he were in pain. 'Six?' he managed to squeeze from the back of his throat.

Reggie wanted to hit him; instead he nodded thoughtfully. 'That's very decent of you Evan. I'll think about it.

Evan Pugh carried on shifting from foot to foot, as he tried to persuade himself to raise his offer, now he had Reggie on the hook. 'I tell you what, meet me at the trotting races, Saturday; I've got a runner, and I can give you a good tip. We can talk about the table after.'

'All right, I'd like that. In the meantime, I'll think about your offer. And see you there.'

He watched Evan slink off. He was sure now that the dodgy little dealer knew where the pair to the table was, which meant that there was a lot further to go on his.

Samantha, the stylist who worked at Rosita's hairdressers in Shrewsbury was marrying her boyfriend, an agricultural contractor, at the Registry Office in Ludlow.

Rosita had persuaded Reggie that he should drive them in his Bentley from the unlovely surroundings of the council offices, over to Mortimer Towers for their dream reception.

'Bloody hell!' Reggie had attempted to object. 'I'm not going to start being a chauffeur at my time of life. What if one of my friends saw me?'

'Reggie, they don't give damn; is why they like you - because you not pretend nothing.'

'But they'll think I'm on the skids, and you don't want them thinking that.'

'They know you do anything to help me. I take all the blame!'

Reggie submitted, but he drew the line at wearing a peaked cap with a thistle on the front.

Before he left to collect the newly married couple, his day started badly.

An early morning inspection had revealed a fresh crop of mole-hills, but at least all the traps had been sprung, so there wouldn't be any more hills after that.

Excited and proud of himself for achieving such a result, Reggie started pulling them out.

A quarter of an hour later, he was looking at them all lined up on the terrace without a single mole, dead or alive, to show for his efforts.

Lady Wynyates, who often walked her dogs across their garden (on the grounds that she'd been doing it for years, and her dogs were used to it) was striding up the lawn toward him. 'Lovely day for a wedding,' she trumpeted.

Reggie grunted. 'Rosita won't think so with all these bloody oonti-tumps popping up everywhere.'

'Ah! Was it you who set those traps?'

Reggie nodded ruefully. 'Yeh, but they didn't work – all sprung, but they all got away.'

'They didn't get away,' Lady Wynyates said emphatically. 'I sprung the traps yesterday evening when I was walking Othello. I don't believe in the use of scissor traps to kill small innocent mammals.'

'Innocent?' Reggie spluttered. 'Look at the mess they've made!'

As he spoke, Rosita walked out onto the terrace. 'Reggie, don't eat yourself up about it!' she said. 'Some little bumps are not dis-aster. Huggins can clear them, no?'

Reggie buried his head in his hands, and for a brief moment

wanted to howl.

Samantha and her tractor driver arrived at Mortimer Towers in the Bentley for their wedding reception. Reggie released them from the back of the car with an extravagant flourish and they were greeted with loud halloos from a joyful, unsophisticated crowd of guests.

His only function performed, such were his other preoccupations, Reggie couldn't enjoy the wedding; he was chuffed, of course, for Rosita that it all seemed to be going well, but he couldn't wait for it to end, so he could go to bed.

The enormous quantities of food that Rosi had organised from the catering company run by Jones the Beef and his wife, had disappeared within minutes of its appearance, while the girls serving the Lambrusco which the bride had chosen (and Reggie wouldn't touch) were working like bees in May to keep all the glasses topped up.

A colleague of the groom, another tractor driver, was his best man. When the time came for speeches, this man, having successfully fulfilled his duties with the rings, had been lapping up Lambrusco like a marathon runner in a heat wave. He staggered to his feet, as red as a pomegranate, opened his mouth, failed to speak, failed to close his mouth again, and began to drool a little. Samantha, the bride, incensed by the shame this brought on her and her family, shoved her new husband to one side and pummelled the best man in his ample gut with such force that he collapsed and sank beneath the table where he remained for some time.

Watching from the back of the marquee, Reggie lifted a weary eyebrow, and turned away.

Later in the evening, he was happy to have remained sober and detached from the event; he was there, but he wasn't part of it. However, he could see that despite the bride walloping the best man (which, in any case, some guests had considered a highlight) the event had been a great success in the eyes of Rosita's clients and, in her own extraordinary style, she'd made the whole party work at just the level the punters wanted. The bride's mother recognised Reggie as Rosita's husband and came over to speak to him where he was sitting at a table by the entrance to the marquee.

The Turnips had just started to play at a volume which precluded most discussion, but the proud mother managed to make herself heard above the din.

'Your wife's done a lovely job,' she shouted.

Reggie nodded.

'And the Turnips are playing like this is the best audience they ever had,' she went on, as if Rosita were responsible for that, too.

Reggie nodded. 'They always do,' he said. 'That's their charm.'

The bride's mother, apparently satisfied, drifted away.

Reggie was going to go to the trotting races next day, and was thinking about slipping away to bed when he noticed a large individual who was reeling dangerously between the tables towards him; it was Jones the Beef, whose company had done the catering.

'Reggie...'

'Yes, hello Jonesy.'

'R..Reggie,' Jones the Beef slurred again. 'Your wife has laid on a f..f...fantastic party.'

'Thank you, Jonesy,' Reggie said. 'She was always good at throwing parties for herself, so I guess it wasn't too hard to do it for someone else. And the food you supplied was pretty good, too. When those little birds brought it in and put it on the tables, I was reminded of a film I once saw about Vultures in the African savannah when a buffalo died...'

'I know what you mean,' Jones attempted a chuckle. 'But what I wanted to... talk to you about was my new emp... emporium... Have you heard about it?'

Everyone for miles around knew that Jones the Beef was opening a monster farm shop, based on his successful butchery business.

'Of course I've heard about it, Jonesy.'

Jones nodded with a happy grin. '*MeatWorld*, it's going to be called.'

Reggie winced. He hadn't heard that, but he judged that Jones was not in a condition to deal with any criticism. 'It's not exactly subtle, is it? But at least the punters won't be in any doubt about what you're selling, will they. Although, don't you think it might put the vegetarians off a bit?' he ventured.

'Bugger the veggies,' Jones said dismissively. 'The point is... the point is to tell people we sells *meat*, and to make sure they get the message, I want to put up on the wall... above the main counter... that bloody great bull's head of yours.'

Reggie felt at once as if a weight was being lifted from his back; he felt like flying.

This, he thought, was an omen!

Maybe all the bloody stupid things he'd done – like buying the table, and the bull's head at the auction, and the moles, and half a dozen other idiotic purchases and decisions he'd made over the past few weeks – might at last be starting to come right.

But he didn't let his euphoria show, and allowed himself to slip into dealer mode.

'Oh, what a pity! I think it's sold.'

'What?!' Jones's big rubbery features collapsed like a mudslide in a storm. 'Reggie, you can't have sold it! I've had my heart... my heart set on it since... since...'

'Since this afternoon,' his wife Daisy said, coming up and taking her husband's elbow in a proprietorial way. 'He's wanted it since he sneaked into your toilet in the house - I told him he shouldn't – not after Rosi's spent so much on those smart mobile toilets. But he came back banging on and on about the bloody bull's head.'

Jones turned to her. 'Daisy, I *feel* like I've always wanted it.' He turned back to Reggie. 'Come on, Reggie, old man, you haven't sold it yet, have you? How much were you going to get for it?

'Five thousand,' Reggie said, off the top of his head, remembering, in the way he often did of auction prices, that he'd given £500 for it.

'S'all right. I'll give you six grand.'

'Oh no, you won't,' his wife said firmly, and tried yank him away.

Reggie felt suddenly sorry for Jones the Beef.

'I tell you what, Jonesy. I won't let it go till next Tuesday. Then if you really want it, give me a ring.' He turned to Daisy. 'It's all right darling. I'd never take advantage of a man who wasn't in the best condition for bargaining.'

'Thanks, Reggie. You're a real gent,' Jones the Beef said, trying to shake Reggie's hand, but missing it.

Unusually, Rosita was still asleep when Reggie awoke next morning. He propped himself up on one elbow and gazed at her peaceful, perfect features – pert nose, slightly pouting lips. He was very proud of what she'd done

How wonderful, he thought, to be married to a woman who looked so spectacular, who could lift his spirits with just a tilt of her chin, and who knew how to turn a tidy profit on a deal... a profit which would go some way towards paying next winter's oil bill.

Without waking her, he climbed out of bed and went down to have breakfast out in the morning sun. He was cracking into his second boiled egg when the phone rang.

He picked it up. 'Hello, Reginald ffinch-Leigh.'

'Hello Reggie. It's Daisy Jones here.'

Reggie guessed she was phoning about payment of the catering bill for the wedding.

'If you want Rosi, I'm afraid she's not back in the land of the living yet.'

'I don't blame her,' Daisy said. 'But it was you I wanted to talk to.'

'I'm all yours,' Reggie said, more lightly than he felt.

'It's about that stuffed bull's head.'

'Don't worry about it,' Reggie said, accepting the disappointment philosophically. 'I know old Jonesy was pissed as a crocodile when he said he'd buy it. I wouldn't hold him to it.'

'No, of course you wouldn't – I know that. And I know you never had another punter for it, either. But I'd like to buy it for him – for his birthday.'

Reggie nearly dropped the phone. 'Good God!' he exclaimed before he could stop himself.

'What we'll do is this: we don't send you a bill for the catering yesterday, which was two and a half thousand, near enough, and then give you the same again.'

That sounded like five grand to Reggie – less than Jonesy had been prepared to pay the night before, but still four and a half more than he'd paid for it at Lennon's that drunken afternoon with Ted Buckton.

'You've got a deal, Mrs Jones!' Reggie said. 'I'll have the old bull dusted off, have his whiskers clipped, give him a good brush and polish his nose. Then you tell me where and when you want him delivered.'

'You get him ready, and I'll be round to pick him up, with the cash, in an hour.'

As he changed gear in the Landrover, nestling by his crotch, deep in the pocket of his salmon pink chinos, Reggie could feel a comforting bundle of grubby twenties, no doubt all passed across the counter of the Jones's butcher's shop.

'What a turn up!' he smiled happily to himself.

He knew exactly what he was going to do with the money. Rosita would be able to keep the two and a half grand she now didn't have to pay Jones the Beef for the catering. He would be able to pay her back the five hundred plus buyer's premium he'd spent on the Hereford bull's head, leaving him nineteen hundred quid to spend on Evan Pugh's tip – for, as it was obviously intended to sway Reggie into selling his table cheap to the little Welsh weasel, he was in no doubt it was a good one.

For a while, as the romantic rolling scenery of the Black Mountians swept across his windscreen, he felt that maybe he was on top of the mole deal. After all, he had all the little buggers safe, secure (with chicken wire stapled across the tops of the pens) and well supplied with fat juicy worms. All he had to do was to cart them to the coast and find a boat to take them a few hours across the Irish Sea, and the deal was done.

So confident did Reggie feel that, with no one to hear him and take offence, he broke into a robust, atonal rendering of Frank Sinatra's *My Way*.

He thought, too about the trotters – harness racing, as it was called officially – a form of horse racing with which he, like ninety nine percent of the population was entirely unfamiliar. No one could tell him why trotting racing, so popular in France and America, in Britain, was mostly to be found along a short stretch of the Welsh Marches.

When Reggie had asked Evan how the races were run, the Welshman had been a little vague. 'It's not what you might call formal type racing – there are rules, like, but not so many as get in the way of the fun of it. That's why we like it.'

Reggie found this encouraging. He liked English racing well enough, and always enjoyed putting on his most extravagant tweeds once a year for the Cheltenham Gold Cup, when Rosita, for whom all racing was Royal Ascot, would turn up as if she were about to take part in a Mardi Gras parade in Rio. But this Welsh racing sounded earthier, and with scope to make use of his natural understanding of the more devious elements of human nature.

'The races is only half the game,' Evan had explained. 'It's the battle between the bookies and the punters that's really what it's about.'

The hills opened up into an area of wide moorland as Reggie approached the village that was to host the trotting meeting. It was being held on a ramshackle race-track, which comprised a run of rickety, covered seating along a hundred-yard stretch on one side of a tight little oval course, set by boggy ground beside a meandering river.

Opposite the 'stands' was a scattering of tents and vans smelling strongly of fried onions, selling beer, sweets and hamburgers, alongside which the bookmakers – resilient, wily men – had set their pitches.

Reggie wandered around for a while, drinking in the atmosphere of the event, wondering again why this activity was restricted to one of the remoter corners of Britain. He was keeping an eye open for Evan Pugh, interested to see how the hard-nosed little antiques dealer fitted into the world of horse and chariot. He found Evan fussing around a nervy, black animal tethered to a battered old horse trailer.

'All right, Evan?' he greeted him.

Evan spun round, evidently pleased to see him. He leaned into him, cupping his hand around his mouth. 'This is him,' he jerked a thumb at the black horse, Highway Express. He's feeling very pleased with hisself. Providing he doesn't bugger hisself earlier, get your money on him to win the Open.'

'A good bet?' Reggie asked, barely moving his lips, like Evan.

'As much as you want. He won't be a helluva good price but we'll do what we can to keep it up.'

Reggie wondered what Evan and his associates could do to affect the odds, and thought, when the time came, he would stand and watch the price for a while before he got his money on. 'Best of luck, then,' he nodded to Evan.

'Sure. I'll see you after the race; you can buy me a drink then, and we can sort out that table,' he added with a nervous grin.

Reggie walked back towards the bookmakers and looked at the list of runners for the first race, billed as a novice event. None of the names meant anything to him; he'd never watched a trotting race in his life and had no idea what to expect. For the time being, until Highway Express was due to run, he thought he'd keep his money firmly in his pocket.

He found a seat on the stand and settled down to try to understand the proceedings, lighting up one of his black Honduran cigars to help. The runners in the first race were appearing on the course. To him they looked like normal racehorses, if a bit sturdier and shorter in the back. They were harnessed to flimsy-looking sulkies, tiny conveyances consisting of two high wheels, an axle, an aluminium frame which held a small driver's seat, and a pair of shafts. Most of the horses had an additional piece of harness in the form of straps linking their upper legs.

This looked like something of a hindrance to Reggie. Wondering what they were for, he turned to a stout man with laboured breath and a head like a mangel-wurzel who had sat down beside him. The man was surveying the scene with an air of familiarity, and showed all the signs of being a regular at the trotters.

'Hello, mate,' Reggie asked. 'D'you know much about this game?'

The man nodded with what Reggie recognised as the slight xenophobia with which a lot of people in this remote part of the country tended to greet those who, from the way they spoke, had obviously come from one of the great metropolises. 'I hope you don't mind my asking,' Reggie added, 'but I'm not from around here.'

'What d'you wanna know?' the stout man asked in an unexpectedly high voice and a Breconshire accent.

'For one thing, why have the horses got those straps around their scotch eggs.'

The man looked blank.

'Sorry mate – around their legs.'

'So's they can only move their legs one side at a time – 'pacing' they call it – let's 'em take a bigger stride than if they was trotting diagonal, like. Also,' he went on, enjoying his superior knowledge, 'them hobbles makes it harder for 'em to 'break' – as they say – that means to break into a canter, like, or a gallop, which they wants to do as they goes faster.'

'But they're not allowed to?'

'Not really; they gotta trot, and if they breaks too often, they'll get disqualified. Anyways, it slows 'em down.'

Reggie nodded, amazed at how much there was to know about this alien sport. 'Thanks, mate,' he said with a friendly nod. 'Would you like a cigar?' He proffered one from his big leather cigar case.

The stout man nodded vigorously. 'Ta,' he said, taking one and examining it excitedly between his thumb and fingers before pulling out a box of matches from a pocket in his shabby tweed jacket.

Reggie watched the first three races from where he sat, with a little help and a commentary from his neighbour, who, he gathered, had already placed his bets. 'Don't like walking around too much – does my knees in,' he'd explained.

Reggie hadn't bought a race card and asked his neighbour if he could borrow his. To his alarm, he saw that Evan's horse, Highway Express, was due to run in the next race.

He stood up. 'I think I'll go and have a bet on the next one,' he announced, 'just to add a bit of interest.'

'You be careful now. It's not easy to pick winners this time of the afternoon.'

Reggie wondered vaguely what he meant, as he set off to the bookies' pitches to survey their boards. As he wandered up and down the line of the dozen who'd come to take on the canny Breconshire farmers, seeing what odds they were offering on the six runners, his heart began to thump a little as he thought about the size of wager he should have on Evan's certainty.

Highway Express was marked as second favourite, at the unspectacular odds of 2/1. Obviously Evan wouldn't be the only one who rated the horse, Reggie thought, feeling somewhat reassured. But the odds meant he'd have to have a big bet to make it worth while. Taking a deep breath, he plunged his hand into his pocket and pulled out a bundle he'd already separated out, and went up to what looked like the most prosperous of the bookmakers.

Speaking quietly, from the side of his mouth, he said, 'I'll have fifteen hundred quid on Highway Express.'

The bookie, tall and wearing a clean brown trilby, did a double take, trying to guess whether or not a foreigner like Reggie could have any real information. 'Sorry friend, maximum five hundred.'

Put out, and wrong-footed, Reggie fumbled twenty-five £20 notes from his bundle and handed them over. The man took the money and thrust it into a leather Gladstone bag hanging from the post beside him, speaking over his shoulder to his busily scribbling clerk. 'Four nine two: Highway – a thousand to five hundred.' He handed Reggie an orange ticket numbered 492.

As the man scrubbed the odds off his board to mark the price down, Reggie was moving down the line a couple of pitches to another bookie before anyone could telegraph the price change up the line. He sorted out another five hundred pounds and got it on again at two to one.

By the time he reached a third bookie, word had passed and the price was already being posted down at 3 to 2. Reggie, chuffed that at least he'd got a second bet on at twos, philosophically took the lower price, seven fifty to five hundred.

Stuffing the three tickets deep into his trouser pocket, feeling as if they'd already been converted into four and a quarter thousand, and the race was just a formality, he made his way buoyantly back to his place on the stand.

His new friend was still there, still sucking happily on the black cigar Reggie had given him.

'D'you get your money on all right?' he asked.

'Yes thanks,' Reggie nodded smugly. He guessed this local didn't have access to the information he had.

'Who've you put it on, then?'

'Highway Express.'

The stout little man looked alarmed. 'I hope you didn't put on too much.'

Reggie blinked, and felt suddenly sick. 'Why?'

'They won't let him win.'

Reggie felt he'd been kneed in the gonads.

All his innards seemed to drop at once; but he fought back. What did this bloke know? He wouldn't know that Evan Pugh was planning some kind of coup.

He took a deep breath, and, as if it didn't matter a damn to him, he gave a light laugh. 'Oh well, we'll see in a few minutes.

The starting gate for the races was provided by a rusty old pick up with a long board fixed across the back, wide enough to fit six horses across it as they grouped themselves in a line behind it. As it gathered speed, they chased it for fifty yards or so half way down the first straight until it suddenly veered sharply to the right and swung off the course, leaving the runners unimpeded to race on towards the first long, one hundred and eighty degree bend.

Highway Express was well drawn on the inside of the track but reached the corner just a fraction later than the team outside it.

There wasn't quite enough room for it to get around the corner on the inside, and Reggie saw the driver take a check. Coming out of the bend, on the straight on the stands side, Highway Express started to slip through again, managing to get to the next bend at the same time as the team coming from the wide outside, which this time left just enough room for Highway to get through.

Reggie who had been vigorously chewing his cigar, heaved a sigh of relief as his horse sped down the far side, keeping abreast of its nearest rival, until they came to the next bend, where the driver seemed to panic and took what, to Reggie, looked like an unnecessary tug, which let the other horse head him and get in front. In the final straight Reggie watched in abject horror as his fifteen hundred quid slipped down the drain in front of his eyes when Highway Express came in third of six, with the other two going away strongly, led by a light bay called Morgan's Fandango.

Reggie wanted to go away somewhere quiet and tear tufts of hair from his head. Instead, he pulled from his jacket pocket his small silver flask of applejack which he'd brought for emergencies like this, and allowed himself a good pull.

The apple spirit slithered down his throat and suffused his whole body with a welcome warmth, restoring the naturally sanguinity of his persona.

His chubby companion nudged him. 'Bad luck,' he said.

Reggie shrugged manfully, 'What the hell,' he said. 'I'm new to this game. Can't expect to pick a winner first time out.'

'The trouble is,' said his mentor, 'you has to know who's trying to do what; they don't always go out to win every race; it depends.'

'On what?' Reggie wondered; he didn't feel like confiding that Highway Express's owner had told him categorically the horse would win, and that it was in the horse's owner's strong interests to give him good information.

'I expect you're right,' Reggie said with what he hoped looked like a philosophical shrug as he slowly tore up his three losing tickets.

For the next few races, Reggie stayed put, trying to get his thoughts in order. Before Daisy Jones' phone call that morning, he'd had zero surplus cash. After the call, he'd found that Rosi could save two and a half thousand pounds, he could pay her the six hundred that he'd paid for the bull's head, and he'd had a losing bet of fifteen hundred quid. He still had four hundred to spare – a lot more than he'd had at nine o'clock that morning.

He would have one more bet before he went.

He turned to his neighbour. I think I might have another bet. Anything you could recommend?'

'There's a good horse in the Open.'

'Hang on,' Reggie interrupted him. 'We've already had the open – my horse lost.'

'That was just the first of two heats for the Open. As they can only run six in a race – you know, for safety, like – they have to shorten the field; so the first three from each heat goes into the final.'

'They have heats?' Reggie gasped. He had no idea that happened in any form of horse racing.

'Oh yes. It opens up a bit of another dimension, you might say.'

'So Highway Express will run again in the final?'

'Of course; he came in third didn't he?'

'Maybe I should back him again.'

His friend sucked in a sharp breath. 'I don't know; to me he looked well beat by the others.'

Reggie nodded. 'Yes, you're right; he did.'

Five minutes later, Reggie was fishing a bundle of four hundred pounds from the pocket of his pink chinos. The bookie who taken his first bet on Highway Express recognised him. 'You can get a better price on Highway this time.'

Reggie had already noted it was being offered at three to one. He shook his head. 'Nope,' he said. 'I'll have four hundred on Morgan's Fandango.'

The bookie nodded. 'Ticket six eight three; Morgan's; six hundred to four hundred.' He handed over the ticket, which Reggie thrust in his pocket once again, though with far less confidence than the last time. He walked back to his seat, needing the companionship of his new advisor.

Reggie tried to reassure himself; there was no doubt that Morgan's Fandango had been going very well and pulling away when it won the heat; and the bookies had all made him favourite for the final. He settled down to watch what he hoped would at least show him a thousand quid, making him only nine hundred pounds down on the day.

Only Nine hundred! he yelled inwardly at himself. He couldn't afford to be nine hundred quid down; he didn't have nine hundred quid – not really. He still owed Rosita the thick end of twenty grand for all his dodgy purchases, as well as two hundred moles, not to mention the recapture of sixty-six of them. And even if everything went right with the moles, that was only going to produce ten grand.

Reggie sighed heavily and leaned back in his seat to watch the race.

It would take about six minutes to run. Highway Express took off behind the start car going well – on the outside this time – and reached the first corner neck and neck with Morgan's Fandango, just inside him. With that advantage, Fandango came into the second straight just ahead. Highway Express' driver, whose body language was entirely different from the earlier race, leaned forward aggressively with his long whip and flicked the animal's backside, prompting the horse to extend its stride in a way that even a novice like Reggie could recognise. It pulled easily past Fandango, and hit the next corner on the tight inside.

From then on it was obvious that Highway Express was going to romp home. With each stride, he pulled away from his rivals, and Reggie's gut seemed to drop another foot.

After Highway Express crossed the line half a dozen lengths clear, Reggie had no desire to see Evan Pugh. He certainly wasn't going to to accept his miserable offer of six grand for the Chippendale table – especially not if the other half of the pair had somehow, as Reggie strongly suspected, come to light.

Evan Pugh, though, did want to see Reggie. He wanted to confirm that Reggie had got a fat bet on the winner of the Open race at a fairly generous three to one. If he had, there was a good chance, he would sell the table to Evan at a price that would allow him a very tidy profit on it.

As it was, Evan had also put five hundred on his own horse, more than he'd ever done before, and he was feeling very pleased with himself.

'Reggie!'

Reggie recognised Evan's voice; and ignored it – probably in vain, he knew – but he just didn't feel like turning round to deal with it.

Evan ran the twenty yards that separated them to catch up with Reggie.

'Reggie...'

Reluctantly, Reggie turned.

Evan couldn't tell from Reggie's inscrutable visage what had happened.

'Did you get your money on Highway all right?' he gasped, concerned and panting from his run.

'Yes,' Reggie answered flatly.

Evan was dumfounded. Why wasn't the man showing more jubilation? 'How much did you put on?' he asked excitedly.

'Fifteen hundred.'

Evan almost jumped in the air with joy at these tidings. 'At three to one! You cleared four and a half thousand. Brilliant!'

'No.' Reggie said, with a rueful shaked of his head. 'I lost it.'

'How...?' Evan began to realise what must have happened. 'Oh my God! You never put it on the heat?!'

'You said he'd win the Open!'

'Bloody hell, man, the Open – the final, not the heats! I told you we were seeing what we could do to keep the odds out. Dave did everything he could to stop that animal coming in the first two of the heat – you could have told that from the whiteness of his bloody knuckles, man – otherwise we wouldn't have got much more than evens for him in the final. I told you!'

'Yeh, well. I didn't know about heats and finals. You said he'd win, so I backed him as soon as I knew he was running.'

Evan sighed. This wasn't going to help his deal, he knew. 'But you must have put something on him in the final, surely?'

'No, I put four hundred on Morgan's Whatever.'

'Bloody Hell! That was never going to win the final; they wanted it to win its heat; that's when they were having their bet! My God, Reggie – what were you thinking? Haven't you ever been to the Trotters before?'

'No.'

'Shit! But you can't say I didn't give you a hell of a tip.'

'I'm not saying you didn't; and I'm not selling you that table, either.'

Reggie struck off at a quick stride towards the Landrover, with Evan trailing behind him, aggrieved and frustrated, already thinking of other ways to get Reggie to part with his table. But even in the tone of the old vehicle's engine as it thundered out of the car park, Evan could sense Reggie's fury.

Sunday evening was quiet and warm. Reggie sat in his library with Rosita and half a bottle of quality claret. The windows were wide open, allowing in the whispering sound of a breeze stirring the aspens beside the walled garden, while the thrushes and black-birds practised their arpeggios and wistful evening airs.

Reggie, despite everything that fate had thrown at him over the past few weeks, was feeling calm, and purged in a way that only full confession could have achieved. He had unburdened himself to his wife, who had reassured him that whatever he had done, however much of an idiot he had been, or how bad his judgement was, she still loved him.

'But,' she said, stroking the back of his hand with a long crimson fingernail, 'if you do it again, I ask Lancelot Ly'bury to put you in his treebucket and chuck you over the top of the Titterstone Hill.

'Thanks, my little foxglove. I'm sure you will.'

'Reggie, things not so bad. I have strong feeling this table person comes closer. You have customer for your moles, for sure, and now, the pictures you find behind the fireplace – they are fan*tas*-tic!'

'I don't know, my *querida*. I've a nasty feeling they're all Sexton

Blakes.'

'Sex'n'blakes? What is this?'

'Fakes, my seraph. Bogus works of art which are not what they purport to be.'

'They aren't purporting nothing. They very *beaut*iful. I put my wall any time.'

'Yeh, I'll grant you they're 'andsome enough, but they may not be worth much.'

'You take tomorrow to auction place in Shoosberry,' Rosita suggested practically. 'See what they say for worth.'

'If I go looking for a valuation, I'll take them somewhere nearer London. I don't want anyone knowing where they've come from.'

'Whatever,' Rosita, went on encouragingly. 'Maybe they save your bacon. Then you must take the *topos*. You make the little dodgy Emmet to come with you, all the way. He get you in this; he make sure you get your money, so he get his, innit?'

'To be honest, I think it's all a bit out of his control; but he's definitely coming with me.' Reggie paused and assumed a calm, sanguine demeanour. 'Now, there is one last thing I haven't told you.'

'Oh, no! Reggie! What is this?'

Reggie raised a calming hand, and took another sip of soothing claret. 'You know you're expecting a bill from Jones the Beef for Friday's wedding catering?'

'Yes, of course - about two and half grand, Daisy say.'

'You don't have to pay it. She's written it off as part of their payment for the bull's head.'

'*Cabeza de Toro!* How much you get for that bloody thing?'

'Five K. Two and a half in cash – which I told you what happened to, apart from £600 I just gave you – and two and a half against their bill to you.'

'Reggie! That is the best thing you tell me, and you leave it to last! You are special man!'

Emmet rang to speak to Reggie on Monday morning.

'I've heard from our punter,' he said. 'He wants the moles to be in Aberdovey by tomorrow evenin'. I give him your mobile number and he'll ring you at eight, OK?'

'Emmet – you're coming too, or I'm going to deliver all these bloody moles to your caravan, and sit there until you pay me for 'em.'

There was a pause and a long sigh. 'How's it going to help you if I'm there or not?'

'It's going to help me to know that if anything happens to me, it'll happen to you too.'

'I'll think about it.'

'Listen, Emmet. I thought you were an honourable geezer; a bloke who keeps his word. I'll keep my word, I can tell you. If you're not up at my place ready to leave by three o'clock tomorrow afternoon – you get the moles, and the bill. And I've never written off a debt in my puff.'

Reggie put the phone down thinking that he wouldn't have been very scared of himself; threatening to dump two hundred moles at Emmet's gaff wasn't the heaviest ultimatum he'd ever delivered.

On the other hand, he still believed that Emmet was fundamentally sound, and a man who could be trusted. He wanted to see his judgement proved right, for once.

Chapter Eleven

Ten minutes after Reggie had finished his phone conversation with Emmet, he was in the Bentley, purring down a motorway towards London. The ridiculous cock-up at the trotters had worried him more than usual. He felt that he'd been so careless, he must be cracking up, or perhaps it was a simple case of old age mashing his bonce, and wrecking his judgement. Old age, he thought ruefully, was irreversible; but, whatever happened, he never wanted to turn gaga on the lovely, dynamic Mrs ffinch-Leigh.

But he took comfort from her instincts over a possible result from the Chippendale table, and her optimism over the pictures, which he had stowed in the capacious boot of his old car.

He arrived with four of them at the prestigious Home Counties auction house that was his destination, in time to catch the staff before they'd gone out for lunch.

Their assessment of his '18th century Sporting Pictures' was about as chilly as the reception he'd had in their front office.

'Mr... er... ffinch... er... Leigh?' The slender young man was looking down a nose as long and curved as a pirate's cutlass and managed to convey that not only would he never have invited Reggie across his own threshold, but also that he didn't believe a word he'd said about how he'd come by the pictures he'd brought in.

'These pictures are so wrong,' said Marcus Dubarry-Ravenscroft, 'that they wouldn't even be able to tell you if they'd been made in China, Bombay or the arse end of Naples. They wouldn't know a badger-hair brush from a plastic spoon; they're about as bogus as Dale Winton's suntan.'

'So, they're not the real thing, then?' Reggie asked mildly. 'In fact, I don't remember asking you if you thought they were real; I have my own views on their authenticity. I simply asked to you tell me what you thought they'd fetch in a sale here.'

'I see; fair enough. You found these 'concealed' in a 'sort of hidden chamber' in your house, and you have no idea where they came from – you say – or how old they are. I can tell you, they can't have been there long; they don't look more than a few years old. However, now you'd like to sell them?' The man sniffed, un-expectedly flaring his nostrils. 'I can't really tell you what we might get – assuming we were to accept them as entries; it would de-pend on the calibre of people attending the sale. From time to time, we do get some naive and very inexperienced buyers – young ignorant people who think that pictures are for covering walls. If two of these came in on the same day, you might expect a bit of an auction, and they might go as high as two or three hun-dred pounds for pictures like these. If only dealers were in, it would be under a hundred.'

Reggie gave a diagonal nod of his head to indicate that he'd heard what had been said. 'Thank you, Mr... er... Mr... er... Dooberry. That's most helpful. I'll let you know if I intend to con-sign the paintings.'

Reggie chuckled as he left. Crass, boorish snobbery never of-fended him. It was no more personal, he thought, than a monkey blowing a raspberry at a punter in the zoo.

The second firm of art auctioneers he took them to were more impressed.

Mr Peacock, a bustling little man in a pink and turquoise bow-tie, inspected them closely through his demilune pince-nez. 'They may be fake, unsigned 'Herrings', but if they are, they're of a very high calibre. The paints are right, the canvas, stretchers, tacks and so on are right. I would be inclined to say that they're 'school-ofs', rather than copies and, as such, worth a few thousand apiece, maybe up to £10,000 for this big landscape with the cattle.'

'Thank you, Mr Peacock,' Reggie said, fairly sure that the man's assessment was wrong, but heartened by his response.

He put the pictures back in his boot, and headed back to the Marches feeling that whatever else these pictures had about them, they had a fair bit of scope.

Shortly before six that evening, he was walking up the stone steps to the front door of Mortimer Towers when it opened in front of him, and Rosita came out to greet him.

'Well?' she asked excitedly as they walked into the drawing-room.

'I don't know what they're worth, but we'll get a few grand apiece for them, which right at the moment is a major turn up.' He stopped by the drinks tray and poured them both a large gin and tonic. 'For the time being, though, let's hang them on the walls in here, and let a few people see them, let them sell themselves, maybe – in a kind of inertia selling.'

'That's a good idea, Reggie. We get a better price that way.'

Reggie nodded. 'That's what we'll do then. I should trust your instincts more.'

'They better than your instinks, thass for sure.'

'So, my lovely *paloma blanca*, has anything else happened here today?'

'Oh, yes. A man ring,' Rosita answered casually. 'He is coming here.'

'What man?' Reggie asked cautiously.

'Maybe the man you look for.'

'What man I look for?'

'Johnny... Johnny Chain and Something.'

Reggie looked at her blankly. 'What's he coming for?'

'About your table, of course...'

'Jonty?' Reggie gasped. 'Cheney-Longville? How come he rang?'

'I don't know,' Rosita protested. 'He say he ring about the table sold at Lennon's. I say, 'You mean the one my husband buy?' And he say 'Yes,' so I tell him, 'You come and see the table'. And he say he come at six o'clock.' She looked at the neat little gold Patek Phillipe that Reggie had given her in better times. 'Is about in ten minutes.'

As she spoke, a car pulled up noisily on the gravel sweep outside the *porte cochère*. 'See,' she said, 'he is early; he mus' be so keen.'

Reggie looked out of the window and saw a very new Volvo estate car parked haphazardly in front of the house. From it was climbing, a tall, good-looking man of about fifty, who looked vaguely familiar to Reggie.

'You're right; I haven't met him before but I'm sure this must be him. You leave him to me.' He set off to open the front door to his visitor, trying to guess what extraordinary miracle had led the man to this place at this point in time.

He opened the door as the man was mounting the stone steps two at a time. He looked at Reggie with interest. 'Hello, I'm Jonty Cheney-Longville. Are you Mr F-f-finch-Leigh?' he stuttered as people often did when first encountering Reggie's name.

'ffinch-Leigh,' Reggie corrected him. 'Yes. What can I do for you?'

'I saw a table in Lennon's catalogue for last month's sale – the mahogany Chippendale demilune with satinwood and maple marquetry inlay?' he said, in crisp, old-Etonian tones.

'You'd better come in,' Reggie said, ushering the man through the double front doors.

Jonty followed him across the hall towards the library.

Rosita came out of the drawing room to greet him too, and Reggie introduced her.

'This is my wife, Rosita. This is Jonty Cheney-Longville,' Reggie explained unnecessarily.

'You like coffee?' Rosita asked.

'That's all right, *querida*,' Reggie said. 'We'll have a drop of the old malmsey.'

He was pleased to see his visitor's eyes light up at the suggestion as he opened the door to the library.

After he'd poured a drink for him, Reggie was able to sit and spend a few moments having a good look at his visitor. Jonty had an air about him of a man who dealt only in the finest things. He was wearing a beautifully cut jacket – Italian, Reggie guessed – in a light Scottish tweed. His shirt, the silk scarf draped around his neck and his shoes had all come from the smartest men's shops in London's Jermyn Street.

His physical likeness to Rupert Cheney-Longville left Reggie in no doubt that Jonty was his son. There was even a hint of his father's voice, from Reggie's hazy memory of the man – a fastidious, patrician voice, though with a warm, likeable timbre to it.

Jonty too was gazing at Reggie. 'Tell me, Mr f...finchley, have we met before?'

'I doubt it.' Reggie shrugged, 'unless you used to be a regular at the Burlington Burlesque Club.'

'No, I wasn't, though I know from googling that you used to own it... and your wife performed there before you were married. But you look somehow rather familiar.'

'Why were you looking me up on Google?'

'Because I saw on line that the table had been up for sale at Lennon's Auctions, and I found out you'd bought it.'

'How?'

'I phoned Lennon's and asked them who'd bought it. Of course, they wouldn't tell me, but they did tell me who'd consigned it – a bloke called Evan Pugh.'

'Yeah,' Reggie said guardedly. 'That's right.'

'I got hold of him easily enough and asked him where he'd got it, and he was very cagey. Then I asked him outright if it had come from this house – in fact, I said I knew it had, because I had the other one of the pair, which had also come from here.'

Reggie's bottom jaw dropped and eyes opened wide in wonder at the way events could sometimes turn. Thank God, he thought, that he hadn't won on that horse two days before, or he'd have felt more or less obliged to sell the table to the little Welsh weasel.

'What did he say to that?' Reggie asked, more than a little curious.

'He didn't deny it; indeed he said he'd arranged to buy it back and would be in a position to sell it to me. Then I found out that this house belonged to a Mrs ffinch-Leigh, got the phone number, and rang.' He shrugged. 'I told her I was ringing about the table sold at Lennon's; she didn't seem at all surprised and she said, yes, you'd bought it and I could come and see it any time.'

Reggie didn't show his gratitude for his wife's lack of caution. 'Yes, well, I suppose you could have a look at it, if you really want to. It's a very handsome piece of furniture, that's for sure.'

'You don't want to sell it then?' Jonty asked.

Reggie's eyes swept the room, before they came back to rest on his visitor's. 'No,' he said, 'I don't think so.'

But he knew he hadn't fooled Jonty, who looked back sceptically. 'But you must have wanted to before. You sold it to the nasty little Pugh, who sent it to the sale, where you bought it back, I imagine for about three times what you'd been paid by him.'

'Yeh, well, after it had gone, I found I missed it – very much. I was a bit pissed when a mate told me it was coming up for sale that day, so I went straight over there and bid for it – more than I should have, no doubt, but I'm very glad I did.'

Jonty, smiling slightly, took a sip of Reggie's fine malmsey. He put his glass down and leaned forward. 'Bollocks, Mr ffinch-Leigh. You thought it was the pair of the one you'd sold Pugh, and you thought if you didn't pay *too* much for it, he'd take it off you for decent profit because the pair would be worth thirty-five to forty thousand.'

'Did he tell you that?' Reggie asked – outraged.

'No, he didn't have to. I've been in this business all my life. It was, as you might say, bleedin' obvious.'

He leaned back and took another sip of malmsey. He nodded at the glass. 'This is really very good. Did you find it in the cellar here?'

'As it happens, I did,' Reggie admitted.

'Do you still want the table to rejoin its partner?'

Reggie didn't speak for a moment, trying to work out the best course to take. He decided, and took the plunge.

'You're right, I bought back a table I'd found here and already sold. I didn't know Evan Pugh had put it in the sale, and yes, I did think it must be the pair. Then Albert Huggins, the old boy who used to work for Bertie Cheney-Longville told me you'd taken the other one, years ago. I've been trying to track you down for the last two weeks without a sniff. I told my wife, and that's why she assumed you wanted to come and see it.'

Jonty nodded affably. 'You wouldn't have found me on any database in the country; I value my privacy too much. I have an entirely different identity for trading purposes. But then, as you say, I do have the pair to your table, and I'd like to reacquaint them.'

'Have you got a punter for them?'

Jonty smiled. 'All I'll say is that I'm prepared to buy yours, for the right money.'

Reggie did his best to disguise the feeling of relief that was beginning to envelope him like a warm bath.

'The fact is, though,' Jonty went on, 'there's some question over title to the items of furniture that were still in the house when old Bertram Cheney-Longville died and the place was sold. My dad came down here, just after he died, and managed to put his hands on a few things...'

Reggie nodded.' Old Albert Huggins told me. That's why I started looking for you.'

'At the time,' Jonty said, 'there was quite a bit of confusion and dithering on the part of my father and uncle, with the result that some of the contents of the house and more particularly, stuff in the barns and outbuildings got included in the sale of the house, which is how you found yourself with what you might call the rump of it – stuff nobody could be bothered to sort out or value. Frankly, it could be legally challenged.'

Reggie had already rehearsed his own position over this, since the Hugginses had told him about the slightly bizarre circumstances in which the place was left. 'Well, of course,' he said lightly, 'anyone can challenge anything, if you don't mind paying lawyers a pile of wonga – probably more than the disputed chattels are worth.'

Jonty smiled. 'It's OK, Reggie – if I may call you that – I've no intention of pouring a lot of spondulicks down some lawyer's gullet. But you know, old Bertram was an inveterate wheeler-dealer and a big hoarder; you must have found quite a bit of interesting stuff around the place.

Reggie chuckled. 'Funny you should say that. Come with me a minute.' He stood up and walked from the room. Jonty followed him, out through the front door and down the steps to where the Bentley was parked. Reggie lifted the lid of the boot, and reached in to lift out the first of the four pictures he'd placed in there that morning. 'Here,' he said to Jonty, 'you grab another and bring it back in.'

They carried two of the large canvases into the drawing room, where Reggie propped one on a sideboard, against the wall. The natural light caught it there, and showed it off well.

Jonty similarly placed the one he'd brought in, and stood back with a smile on his face.

'All right,' Reggie asked. 'What do you know about these, then?'

'I know nothing about them, but I'm guessing you've showed them to me because you found them somewhere in the house – presumably well tucked away?'

Reggie nodded.

'Have you only just found them?' Jonty asked.

'Yeh. Last week. I'd asked the Hugginses to find out how the moles had got out...'

'Moles?' Jonty asked.

'Don't ask,' Reggie groaned, 'not now. Anyway they tore down a bricked-up doorway, which old Albert knew about, though he had no idea about the flight of stairs behind it, which led up to a kind of hidden room between the library and the dining room. That's where I found these pictures.'

'The four in the car?'

'Yes,' Reggie said. Jonty didn't need to know about the other eight. 'Have you gotta clue where they've come from?'

Jonty shook his head. 'Not for sure, but it's possible they were part of the last batch he brought over from Florence – twenty-five, maybe thirty years ago.'

'Batch?' Reggie queried, 'from Italy?'

Jonty shrugged an elegantly attired shoulder. 'From what I gathered from Dad who knew him quite well, he'd found a workshop just outside Florence – some old *castilio* up in the hills, I think, where they'd been producing copies of old masters and what-not for decades – a whole team of really skilled arists who, between them, could paint pretty much anything. They'd been letting these trickle out onto the market all over Europe, generally to order, where there was some kind of provenance to match. There were some big Irish houses, for instance, burned to the ground during the troubles, many of them with a lot of important pictures inside, now assumed destroyed, which started to come to light, with more or less plausible provenance.'

'Bloody hell, those Irish,' Reggie said, half thinking of the wheeler-dealers who had ordered his moles.

'I think these were more likely members of the Anglo-Irish community. Bertie didn't have anything to do with them, though it might have given him the idea. He persuaded the studio to do a lot of 19th century English sporting pictures – hunting, shooting, racing and so on, and he was selling them one or two at a time in salerooms all over the place – a lot in Scotland, I think.'

'Did he get away with it?' Reggie asked. 'I never 'eard of him doing any stir.'

Jonty grinned.'No, old Bertie was pretty careful; he never got his collar felt. But someone had alerted the art squad at the Met who started sniffing around quite heavily. I guess Bertie thought he'd better dispose of whatever he had left before they found their way up here. He obviously couldn't sell them anywhere then, so I suppose that was when he hid them. And then, as it happened, soon after that he died.'

Reggie was nodding his comprehension. That was it; the old boy had been importing top of the range. Dubarry-Ravenscroft had smelt a rat; and Peacock had recognised quality forgery when he saw it.

Reggie assumed an air of innocence. 'I showed them to an auction house today who said they were 'school ofs', and very good quality – worth around ten grand apiece.

Jonty shrugged doubtfully. 'Maybe that big landscape... And if you let them out very slowly, every few years, you might get four or five for the others. They're certainly good, but they're also 'wrong', and most – though by no means all – dealers will recognise that. What are you going to do with them?'

'I thought we might just hang them here; give 'em a little airing and see if anyone shows any interest. I mean, they're good for covering a largish bit of wall, ain't they?'

'Yah,' Jonty nodded vaguely. 'But I tell you what, could I have a look at this table of yours?'

'Sure; it's in the library.'

'Yes. I saw it there,' Jonty said.

They went back into the library, where Reggie topped up their glasses with the venerable malmsey. Jonty walked across to the table, taking out a magnifying glass as he went and knelt down on one knee in front of it.

'It's very good,' he said to Reggie over his shoulder. 'Better than the one I've got. I can sort out that bit of lifting. I'll have it, but Reggie, I want you to bear in mind that, as I've got the pair, I'll obviously pay more for it than anyone else. But, I'm afraid, not *much* more.'

Reggie sighed, as if resigned to the fact that he wasn't going to sell it. 'Go on then; how much would you offer?'

'Eight.'

Reggie winced. 'You know what I'm into it for.'

Jonty spread his hands. 'Yes, but that is, as they say, your problem. I'll tell you what, though – I'll go to ten.'

Reggie shook his head, sadly. 'That's still not enough.'

'All right then, I'll sweeten it for you a little. I'll take the table and those four pictures you've found for fifteen.'

'Twenty?' Reggie came back at once, with a happy lift in his voice.

Jonty wrinkled his nose and thought about it for what seemed to Reggie like half an hour, though, in fact, less than ten seconds, before he smiled and held out a hand. 'Done,' he said.

'Too bloody right I have been.' Reggie shook his hand. 'You've basically got those pictures for nothing. But there it is... a bird in the hand, as they say – or as my cousin Porky Bacon likes to say, "a hand in the bird...".'

Reggie slept well that night, lulled by the knowledge that he had, with a good helping of luck, been able at least to recover his money – and his wife's confidence – by selling the Chippendale table back to a member of the Cheney-Longville dynasty, as well as earning a good bonus from the sale of four pictures, which until three days before, he didn't even know he owned.

Over breakfast that morning, Reggie was waxing optimistic.

'You know something, my little flower, even with all the hassle of transporting these bloody moles to Paddyland hanging over me like the sword of Damo-Wassername, I'm feeling pretty happy. Here's a kite for you for twenty K, which brings me just about back into credit at the Banco Rosita. With a bit of luck and a following wind, I'll be back home by Wednesday night with a ten grand wedge in me arse-pocket. Then we can think about what we're going to do with those other pictures.'

'This Honty fellow,' Rosita said. 'He only buy if he can sell for good profit, no?'

'I should say so,' Reggie agreed emphatically.

'So they are worth much more than he gives you.'

'I reckon,' Reggie chuckled. 'And I reckon young snotty-chops Dubarry-Firkin knew that bloody well too. I wouldn't have been surprised – if he could have tracked me down – if he sent some-body round to make me an offer.'

Still chuckling about the way things had turned out over the table that had been giving him fitful nights ever since he'd bought the thing back at auction, Reggie went off to the library after breakfast to phone Emmet Rafferty. He knew that although the traveller lived in a caravan, he always had a small solar charger to keep his mobile's power topped up.

Emmet answered straight away. 'Don't worry Reggie, I'll be there.'

'Too right, mate, but listen, I'm never going to get all the crates in my Landrover.'

'You'll get 'em into that big green car o' yours, no trouble.'

'What? My Bentley?'

'That's the one.'

'I'm not carting two hundred defecatin' moles in my Bentley, thank you very much. I want you to bring up some kind of trailer – one of those small stock trailers.'

'I haven't got one.'

'Then find one, Emmet or I'll use your cut on this rotten deal to hire one.'

'All right, all right. I'll get one.'

Reggie was relieved when Emmet kept his word and turned up

on time with a surprisingly clean sheep trailer – the type that a farmer might take a dozen lambs to market in.

'Nice one, Emmet,' Reggie greeted him.

'So long as it's back by tomorrow night.'

The Hugginses, still unaware of the purpose or destination of the two hundred moles that had kept them busy over the past week or so, were very happy to help load them in their crates into the trailer.

'One last thing,' Reggie said to Harry Huggins, 'can you dig me another bucket full of fat worms for the little fellas. We don't want them to starve in transit.'

'Right ho, Mr Reggie. I'll put 'em in the Landrover then.'

Reggie and Emmet had an hour or so to kill before they had to leave in order to be at Aberdovey in time for the punter's phone call.

'D'you want to come with me over to Ted Buckton's?' Reggie asked. 'He's got a horse for me to look at.'

'Sure thing.' Emmet was never happier than when looking at horses.

The fact was that Ted Buckton was feeling he had unfairly talked Reggie out of keeping the horse, Gladstone. Reggie had liked the look of the animal from the moment he first saw it, and although it had a few dodges, it had turned out to be at least as good as he'd thought. 'I'm sorry, Reggie,' Ted told him, 'I did such a good job sorting the horse out, the jammy Chatternerve got all the benefit.'

To appease his conscience, Ted had found a similar animal which he thought would suit Reggie, and which he was prepared to sell to him at the price he'd paid.

Since winning the hunt ride, which he considered the sporting highlight of his life, Reggie had let it be known that, all being well, he'd like to go out with the hunt the following autumn.

Emmet agreed that the horse had all the signs of being a good buy, and Reggie left Ted's place having agreed to come back and try it out over a distance, once he'd wrapped up his deal in Ireland.

Ted was, of course, deeply sceptical about the trading of moles with any Irishmen, but wished him the best.

They drove back to Mortimer Towers to get ready to set off for the Welsh coast with their valuable cargo. Reggie had just turned in through the main gates when, with a nasty rattle and a drawn out grating noise, the rear drive shaft split apart and dropped off.

Emmet crawled underneath and confirmed that it was a proper day's job to put it right.

'Then we'll have to use your old Toyota,' Reggie said.

'No way, that's on its last legs. I've to spend a day on it before I can go off on any long jaunts. Have you got a tow bar on your big car?'

Reggie sighed. 'As it happens, I have; we'll just have to bolt it on.'

Ten minutes later, the trailer was hitched to the Bentley, and they were ready to roll.

Rosita came out to see them off. 'Look for yourself, my special man,' she gushed, while Reggie tried to quieten her down in front of Emmet.

'And you look after yourself, my Spanish rose.'

As she leaned through the driver's window and planted a big scarlet 'O' on his right cheek, he fired the six and half-litre engine into life.

Reggie enjoyed the drive across wild, under-populated and open country of mid-Wales, interspersed with stretches of winding, light-dappled wooded coombs by scurrying brooks. The Bentley purred along happily, barely noticing the trailer behind it, and making an incongruous sight.

Emmet was happy too. 'This is the way to travel, Reggie. Would you ever want to sell this ve-hickle?

'I hope not, Emmet, but you'll be the first to know if I do,' Reggie promised, 'and I think, between me and her, I'll be the first to go.'

Emmet knew a good pub in the small Welsh port, where they could stay overnight, if they needed to. Reggie's finer senses rebelled at the thought of sharing with Emmet, but his practical parsimony prevailed, and he booked a twin room, hoping they wouldn't need it.

'Right,' Reggie said. 'I'll go down and find a boat. You're looking a bit dodgy; I'll go on my own.'

Down at the small harbour he asked around and, with the Bentley prominently in the background, he soon found a skipper with a boat – the *Red Herring* – who said he might be willing to take him and Emmet across the Irish sea with a small cargo.

Dai Bebb, who looked a little daunted by the task of handling Reggie, was also worried about taking a cargo. 'It isn't drugs, is it?'

Reggie drew himself up. 'Do I look like a drug merchant? We've just got a small load of moles.'

'What do you say it is?' Dai asked, to make sure he'd heard right.

'We've got two hundred moles.'

'What are you taking them for?'

'It's to do with fashion,' Reggie said airily, 'they're going to a big Dublin couturiers.'

Dai Bebb wasn't sure. 'Hang on; I'll ask the missus; she knows about the law.'

He walked away down the quay, talking into his mobile phone. When he'd finished he came back. 'She can't find no ban on transporting moles. But they haven't got drugs in them, have they?'

'Of course not, for Gawd's sake! How much do you think you could get into a bloody mole.'

'All right, then. I'll take you.'

Reggie negotiated that if they had to go overnight, there was a two hundred pound bonus in it. Dai was happy about that, and Reggie left with his mobile number.

He drove back to the pub and parked the Bentley and the trailer in the car park behind the pub, where Emmet met him.

'We'd better check on the merchandise,' Emmet said.

They opened the trailer and opened up each of the crates. The moles were stirring, and becoming a little noisome. 'They're sounding a little grouchy' Emmet said. 'Maybe you'd better feed the little buggers.'

Reggie nodded. 'Right.' He looked around. 'Where's the worms?'

Emmet held his hands up. 'Don't ask me.'

Reggie smacked his forehead with the broad palm of his right hand. 'Bloody hell! Harry put them in the Landrover, before we went over to Ted's.'

'Oh Jaysus,' Emmet cried out. 'Did you leave them in there?'

Reggie was too busy grinding his teeth in frustration to even attempt to answer, or to blame Emmet.

'They're not going to last another whole night without a feed, not with so many of them together,' Emmet said.

'All right! All right!' Reggie groaned. 'We'll have to see what we can do. Let's get back to the bar.'

They closed and locked the trailer before walking round to the front of the pub to find a corner of the bar to sit down and form a plan.

'We'll need a drink,' Emmet said.

'You get 'em,' Reggie grunted.

Emmet wandered up to the bar where he had to wait for a hen party of girls in traditional Welsh dress and tall pointed hats like witches to order a string of exotic cocktails from a small, spot-covered barman. 'What?!' they were asking him. ''Aven't you ever heard of a Slow Comfortable Screw?'

The young women all shrieked with laughter 'No, of course he hasn't! Jest look at 'im!'

Reggie's mobile rang. He looked at his watch. It was already eight o'clock; his stomach seemed to leap into his mouth.

He answered. ''Allo?'

''Ave you got the merchandise?' The words were spat out sharply in an accent from somewhere in the north west of Ireland.

'Yeh,' Reggie answered hoarsely.

'How many?'

'Two hundred.'

'What you feeding 'em?'

Reggie hesitated, guiltily. 'Worms?'

'Right answer. Good. I'm your customer.'

'Yeh, well. I was expecting your call.'

'Are you all ready to go?'

'Of course,' Reggie said, feeling more confident now. 'What are you going to use 'em for? Are you in the fashion trade?'

'No, we're not in the feckin' fashion trade. We're going to hold the feckin' Irish government to ransom. If they don't release our people, we're going to release the feckin' moles. Simple as that! You make sure we get 'em, and you'll get your money. We don't like to be let down... understand?'

Reggie was quaking. He could barely breathe. 'Yes,' he whispered.

'Get into Wexford Harbour by three in the morning. Don't go into port; just anchor up,' Reggie's customer ordered. 'We'll find you.' He cut off.

Reggie slowly took the phone from his ear and looked at it, shaking his head in shock as he tried to take in the horrible truth of his situation. These men he was dealing with – didn't they kill people who let them down? Losing a bit of wonga was one thing. But ending up brown bread? Rosi would never forgive him!

'What the hell's happened to you?' Emmet asked, plonking two pints on the table in front of Reggie, who looked up and glared at him.

'Emmet, do you know who these punters are?'

Emmet sat down slowly. 'Sort of, but I'm not exactly sure.'

'And do you know why they want the moles?'

'Sort of.'

'They're bloody terrorists of some kind; probably the kind that kill people! What are they going to do? I didn't do the deal to get mixed up in any killing!'

'Listen,' the Irish traveller put a hand on Reggie's arm. 'No one's going to be killed, for God's sake. Otherwise I wouldn't be doing it either. That's the point; this is aimed at the Irish government and the economy. No one gets hurt.'

'What are they going to do, then?'

'Maybe you don't know, but the Global Championships of Golf are about to start in Ireland. Every big hitter in the world will be there to win, and it's played on the four most prestigious golf courses in the country.'

'What the hell has this got to do with us?'

'Reggie, did you know there's no moles in Ireland?'

Reggie nodded slowly. 'Yes, Lara told us when she was up last week.'

'Can you not think what an outbreak of the industrious little pests would do to the greens of those championship courses?'

Reggie remembered the lawns at Mortimer Towers the previous week, and the catastrophe the moles had caused there. 'Cor,' he gasped. 'You're right. That lot,' he nodded in the direction of the car and trailer, 'could do a mountain of damage; the places would look terrible; the whole competition – the whole country would be a bloody laughing stock!'

'That's the point – a whole lot of humiliation, but no deaths. What they're planning probably isn't even a crime.'

Reggie shook his head – this time in admiration. 'That's brilliant! Why didn't I think of that? Me and Rosi thought it was for the fashion trade.'

'The fashion trade? Moles?'

'Yes, there's some big cheese, piss-arse frock maker in Paris who's been using mole skin for trimmings in his so-called collection. There's a few firms that'll want to get in and rip off the 'look', as Lara calls it.'

'Well, these people certainly aren't in the fashion business.'

'No, but surely you must know who we're dealing with?'

'The trouble is, it could be one of two rival groups; it's either the Real Army of Rebels of Eire, who call themselves RARE, or the Provisional Irish Free Army, who're called PIFA. They both used to be the same thing, but they, like, splintered and now they're always at each other's throats. I wouldn't know how to tell the difference between them. But they found their way to me,' Emmet shrugged. 'It was a good deal, but I had to pull you in – you know why. Listen, Reggie, it doesn't matter who the punter is, you've not done a single illegal thing, and you'll be well paid for it.'

Reggie sighed. 'OK, mate. All right. But we've still got to get the little bastards over there and the rate we're going at they'll all starve before we've got across the sea.'

'You needn't worry about that, now,' Emmet nodded. 'While I was up at the bar, fighting through all those teenage witches, I saw a fella I know, and asked him if he knew where we could get a load of worms in a hurry.'

'A fella you know? Here? How come?'

'I used to do a bit of business here, bringing in stuff from Ireland, you know, by night. Look here he is now.'

A skinny man in tight jeans and a Levi denim jacket had ambled over. He had curly black hair, a rosy complexion and long woolly sideboards. Emmet waved a hand at him and turned to Reggie. 'This is my friend, Finbar; he's a wicked spoons player.'

Reggie stuck out a hand. 'That must come in handy,' he said drily. 'I'm Reggie.' They shook hands. 'Would I be right,' Reggie went on, 'in thinking you're from the Emerald Isle?'

'You would,' Finbar replied.

'And what did you used to trade with my friend Mr Rafferty?'

Finbar leaned forward and spoke behind his hand in a guttural whisper. 'Dogs.'

Reggie sat back in his chair, distressed. 'Drugs?' He looked at Emmet. 'Not drugs?'

'No Reggie, you deaf old bugger – DOGS!'

'Dogs?!' Reggie asked. 'What kind of dogs?'

'Greyhounds, of course – racing dogs,' Emmet laughed. 'There's some great breeders over there, and people racing dogs at the old track in the Black Country wanted them – but that's all gone now.'

Reggie, mollified, turned back to Finbar. 'You can get the worms we need?'

'Sure; how soon do you need them?'

Reggie looked at the fob watch he'd pulled from his breast pocket. 'Two hours; no later.'

'I'll get right on to it.' He paused, to make a quick assessment... 'though it'll cost you to get 'em that quick.'

'How much?'

'Two hundred.'

Reggie groaned; he had no choice.

'All right. Be down at the harbour with them – ten o'clock – no later.'

Dai Bebb looked on doubtfully as Reggie and Emmet unloaded twenty small wooden crates from the stock trailer into the saloon of his small leisure fishing boat.

'Look now, make sure they don't piss all over my seating,' he fussed.

He looked even more worried when Finbar arrived in a rusty old corrugated Daihatsu and lugged a big, dirty hessian sack from the back which, after some dispute with Dai Bebb, he dropped into the cockpit of the boat.

Reggie was impatient. 'Come on, we've got to get out of here. Chummy – the punter wants us in Wexford by 3am.'

The *Red Herring's* skipper cast off, and they chugged away from the harbour and down the estuary of the Dovey.

Once they were out in a calm open sea, heading due west at a good steady pace, Reggie opened up the sack of worms that Finbar had delivered, and been paid two hundred pounds for.

He put his hand in and gingerly picked a few out. 'Bloody hell, Emmet, I think they're all dead!'

Emmet came up behind him, opened up the sack and peered in. 'I don't think it matters, so long as they're fresh, and these are.'

'You sure?'

'Sure. Let's divvy them out to the hungry moles.'

He and Reggie, with the captain watching, pursed-lipped, dropped a few handfuls of worms into each crate, and were gratified to see the moles going straight for them.

'Bloody hell,' Reggie observed, 'they're wrapping their laughing gear around the worms like they haven't eaten for a week.'

'Great,' Emmet grinned. 'I'd hate to be delivering dead moles to these fellas, I don't think they'd be at all pleased to see us.'

Reggie watched the Welsh coast fade behind them in the thickening gloom. He wondered if the deal would really be done by the morning. He'd known very few deals that happened exactly as proposed. His Uncle Arthur had always told him, 'Don't forget, Reggie, the deal's not done until you're walking away with a pocketful of kosher readies, or the cheque's cleared.'

Emmet was down below, feeling very sick. 'This is why I didn't want to come,' he moaned at Reggie.

'Shut up and have a slug of this,' Reggie said sympathetically, handing over his silver flask of applejack.

Once Emmet was unconscious, and thus suffering no further discomfort, Reggie clambered up the stairs to the cockpit and wedged his back into a corner of a padded bench. Soon, he too was unconscious.

''Ere, Reggie! Wake up! Wake up!' Emmet had hold of Reggie's left shoulder and was shaking it like an empty ketchup bottle.

From where he'd been flopped onto the padded bench, fast asleep, Reggie jerked upright. The moon, shimmering on the Irish Sea behind them, reminded him where he was – on a small motor cruiser with two hundred moles to be delivered, live and healthy, to another small boat a mile or two off the coast of Wexford in the Irish Republic, before dawn, in return for £10,000 from an unknown man with a voice alarmingly similar, Reggie thought, to the Rev Ian Paisley's.

On the face of it, they weren't doing anything seriously illegal, although Reggie guessed it must be some kind of offence to import any known vermin into the Republic of Ireland. This didn't worry him too much as they were going to transfer the cargo before they landed, unless the terms of the deal got altered at the last minute, the way things did in rummy deals like this; and everything about this venture had smelled iffy right from the start.

Reggie had got very agitated when he first discovered Emmet had been relying on him to get hold of all the moles, because he knew Owen the Oont wouldn't deal with him, and he knew no one else with Owen's secret trick of catching moles alive. And now, here was his unelected business partner, an illiterate, needle-sharp little Irish traveller who, in his experience never lost his cool, with all the blood drained from his face, jabbering and staring at him like he'd just watched a vampire drink a pint of his blood. Emmet struggled a moment to find his voice. 'All the chuffin' moles is dead!' he managed to squeeze through his larynx. 'Every last one of the little boggers!'

Reggie stiffened with shock. That the moles should be alive and well was absolutely vital to this deal. Dead moles were entirely without value to the customer, who, Reggie now knew only too clearly, was certainly not involved in the murky outer fringes of the fashion trade. Moles that were dead didn't throw up large earth tumps, which negated their undoubted capacity to destroy international championship golf courses in a matter of hours, especially in a land where no mole had ever been known to exist in a natural state, and no defences were on hand.

Reggie gulped and blinked, as he woke up, trying to absorb the magnitude of this news. Before he'd fallen asleep, the plan was on course – always with the strong possibility that they might not get their money before they let go of the moles, but at least they'd had the merchandise in a saleable condition.

Now, if what Emmet had told him was true, they had nothing – nothing, at least, that their punter wanted.

And in his experience, punters who didn't get what they wanted could turn nasty, especially ones who were signed up members of the PIFA or RARE.

Reggie turned to the taciturn Welshman at the helm of the *Red Herring*. 'Turn this bloody tub around now,' he bellowed, generating faint echoes off the gently swelling sea. 'If we get there to meet these Paddies with a pile of dead moles, we'll be brown bread!'

Dai Bebb didn't need convincing. He immediately started yanking the wheel through a hundred and eighty degrees, putting the moon in front of them now, which created a kind of flare path across the sea pointing towards Aberdovey and the first glimmerings of a new day.

Reggie was thinking fast. He didn't know how long he could leave it before the moles were too far gone to remove from their one remaining potentially valuable commodity. He pulled his phone out of his pocket. 'Thank God,' he breathed. 'I've got a signal.' He punched his home number on the key pad, and listened apprehensively as it rang. It was a quarter to four; Rosita liked her sleep, and could react alarmingly when woken from it, provided, of course, that the bedside phone woke her at all, which it didn't always.

But after a few rings, a sleepy voice answered. 'Hyello?'

Reggie thought warmly of her blinking open her dazzling eyes, and stretching her golden arms. 'G'morning, Rosi, my little domestic deity.'

'Wha'?'

'It's yer man – 'alf way across the Irish Briny.'

'Reggie…?'

'Yeh, 'course, it's me. Listen, I've been thinking we might do better to sell my moles as skins, not as a team of earth-moving navvies.'

'Reggie – what the fox you talk about?'

'You remember Lara told us there'd be a big demand for mole pelts early this autumn?'

'You mean for the moley-skin bolero things of the Paris guy?'

'Yeh, that's it. Can you get onto her and tell her we've got a couple of hundred fresh pelts for sale, and see if she can come up with a punter for 'em?'

Rosita didn't answer for a few moments, although Reggie could hear her rousing her sleepy body. 'For fox sake, Reggie! Is four o'clock!'

'Yeh, I know. Don't ring her now, leave it till seven, but make sure you do. Soon as we're back in Wales we've got to find someone who can skin 'em and get the furs ready.'

'You goin' to kill all those little creeters?'

'No, they're already brown bread – every single one of 'em.'

'Wha?! How they do that?'

'I dunno. Emmet's only just told me.'

'I *know* you can't truss that slippy bugger! Where are you?'

'I told you – in the middle of the bloody Irish Sea, heading back to Wales.'

'Bloody 'ell, Reggie – you *crazy*! I tell you is crazy deal, with mad Irish crooks, and that dodgy Emmet. When you gonna learn?'

'Listen my little guardian angel, what happened, happened. I didn't kill the little pests, and obviously I'm very sad about 'em, but there it is.'

He heard a long sigh over the phone. 'OK, Reggie - I call Lara.'

Reggie banged his head on the door frame over the stairs down to the saloon of the boat. He and Emmet had stowed their twenty plastic crates, each holding ten moles, on large sheets of polythene to catch the natural detritus that might have been generated. When they'd set off, there had been sounds of movement and the occasional alarming squeal from their wriggling cargo. Now there wasn't a sign of life in a single one of the crates Reggie inspected with Emmet.

'I told yer,' Emmet said. 'They're all goners – every one.'

Reggie groaned. 'Two hundred dead oonts! After Owen had managed to catch 'em, and all the hassle of keeping them alive. All those bloody worms! And why haven't they eaten all the ones we gave them before we left? I paid good money to the fellow that brought them.'

Most of the substantial meal that Reggie had laid on for his cargo's journey across the sea seemed to have been ignored, or only partially consumed.

'They didn't die of starvation, that's for sure. Bloody 'ell!' Reggie was struck abruptly by the thought that he hadn't allowed for every possibility, like you should with any complicated deal. 'I should have checked on Rosi's internet Google whassit if moles get seasick. I'll bet you a pound to a penny that's what happened. My God!' he groaned remorsefully. 'I should have known that – I should have checked. Owen could probably have told me – he knows everything about 'em, and he'll be well pissed off if all the live moles he caught have croaked!'

'He won't give a Leprechaun's bollock – you paid the old hustler, and that's all he was after. Anyways, it's not your fault. I don't know if they get seasick, but this lot was definitely poisoned. The old mole catchers used to use fresh worms soaked in strychnine until it was banned by the health and safety people, and I reckon these were strychnine worms. I reckon it was Finbar. It was a bit too much of a bloody coincidence, him turning up like that. I reckon he's workin' for one of those bloody 'armies' – on the other side to the lot we're working for – and they've had a tip off and told him to sabotage the mole scam – you know – nip it in the bud, like.'

'But if they wanted to stop us, why didn't they just shoot us, or blow up the boat?'

'Too messy. They don't want to be callin' out the bobbies. I reckon they just wanted to get rid of the little critters before they could ever be loosed on the golf courses to do their damage. No one's ever going to go looking for who poisoned a few moles, are they – even if you did go mad and report it – which you ain't gonna do, I'm thinking.'

'Bloody hell, Emmet! You may be right. I should've smelled a king rat when we were talkin' to that bloke in the pub – I mean – how the hell did he know where he could get a sack of worms so fast. He's not going to be there in Aberdovey when we get back.'

'No way! Anyways, it wouldn't be healthy for us to catch up with him.

'No, I suppose you're right,' Reggie sighed. 'We don't want him and his mates banging us up and force-feeding us strychnine worms.

Chapter Twelve

As soon as Dai Bebb had secured the *Red Herring* to the small quay in Aberdovey, Reggie backed the Bentley with the trailer right up to the edge. He and Emmet unloaded the twenty plastic crates of dead moles from the saloon of the boat into the trailer. They removed the remains of strychnine-treated worms in the hessian sack and put them in the Bentley's boot, to be disposed of later. Reggie banged the lid down and went back to pay off Dai Bebb. 'And here's an extra fifty to clear up the mess.'

By that time, the skipper had been so certain he wasn't going to be paid at all, he was overcome with gratitude.

Reggie brushed aside his fulsome thanks. 'That's all right mate, you done what we asked.' He'd found over the years that settling up fast and well for services provided meant you always got people again when you needed them – and usually on better terms.

He climbed into the Bentley and headed back into town. He turned to his colleague, crouching in the big leather seat beside him. 'What a total balls-up, eh, Emmet? This is your deal, so how the hell do you think we're going to get out of it? I'm already five grand out of pocket.'

'In the name o' Jaysus, Reggie, I'm sorry. I should have known Finbar was trouble.'

'Yeh,' Reggie sighed. 'But listen, I might find a way out of this and, if I do, how much d'you think I'll owe you?'

Emmet was smart, and he was a realist. 'Nothin', of course, but I'll do what I can to help.'

Reggie smiled his approval. 'Well done, Emmet; I'm glad we understand each other. But we've got to cover our own arses too, haven't we? The first thing is to make sure our punters don't turn up and find we're not there. We need a call box.'

'What's wrong with your mobile?'

'I'm going to ring the Irish Garda; I don't want them tracing the call to my bloody phone. There's one,' he said jubilantly, stopping the car in the deserted main street of the town, getting out and crossing to the phone box.

A few minutes later, he climbed back in with a smile on his face. 'Within the next few minutes, Wexford harbour will be crawling with Garda. They won't really know what they're looking for, but they'll be looking for a mole – maybe more than one – in the PIFA or the RARE. Our punters, whichever the hell they are, won't be looking to take delivery of *their* two hundred moles, not in the middle of the harbour in full view of the shore.'

Emmet who'd been worrying himself sick about what form of retribution his aggrieved punters would take, looked suddenly relieved. 'That should do it!' he said. 'I'll call my man in a bit and tell him we got into Wexford harbour but had turn back because we saw police all over the place, and we had to scupper the moles in case we got hauled in and searched!'

'Nice one, Emmet! 'Ere, 'ave a cigar.' Reggie waved his battered leather cigar case at Emmet.

'Jaysus, you're not going to smoke one o' they stinkin' things, are you?'

'Well, don't have one if you don't want,' Reggie said between teeth that were already clutching one of his black torpedoes. He lit it, took a long pull of its pungent smoke, and smiled with pleasure.

Before he started up the car, he pulled out his phone and looked at the time. 'Half past three. I wonder if Owen the Oont's at home?'

He prodded the mole catcher's number and listened to it ring for a while before it was answered. ''Ello?'

'Owen?'

'Yes. Is that Misser Finchley?' Owen sounded completely awake and alert. Reggie couldn't really imagine him sleeping anyway – it would mean taking his eye off the ball for too long.

'Yes. Sorry to call at this hour, but I've got a bit of an urgent problem.'

'Bloody hell,' Owen groaned. 'They hasn't escaped again has they?'

'No. They got nobbled. They're all dead.'

'Oh, no,' Owen sounded momentarily upset. 'What did you do to them?'

'I did nothing. They ate some poisoned worms.'

'Who gave 'em to 'em, then?'

'Well, I did, but I didn't realise.'

'I told you – only live worms!' He sounded angry. 'Anyway what do you want me to do about it?'

'I need to have them skinned. How long have I got?'

'You needs to get 'em off inside o' half a day.'

'Do you know someone who could do it – and tan them so they're soft enough to be used for clothing?'

'Course I do. I told you.'

'Could you tell me how to get hold of them?'

'Go round and knock on the door of that flat you got – above your stables.'

'You mean old Maeve Rafferty – Emmet's mother?'

'Yeh, I told you some o' they traveller women are good at it. But I doubt she'll do it for you.'

'Why wouldn't she?'

''Cause you're not one o' them.'

'But nor are you.'

'No, but I knowed her a very long time.'

Reggie thought for a moment, and looked at Emmet. 'OK, Owen, thanks for telling me; I'll see what I can do.' He clicked his phone off. 'Emmet, there is something you can do for me, and you might be able to salvage something from the deal for yourself.'

Emmet had been listening to Reggie's half of the conversation. 'You want me to ask Mum to skin all the oonts?'

'Correct. Can she do that?'

'Oh, yes.'

Reggie laughed out loud with relief. 'I don't bloody believe it! I think with a bit of luck, we'll get out of this '

'But Reggie, who are you going to sell two hundred moleskins to?'

'I'll let you know. In the meantime, we'd better get home and wake up your mum.'

They were only a mile from Mortimer Towers when Reggie's mobile rang.

'Reggie?'

'Porky?' Reggie exclaimed. He looked at his watch; it was just after six. 'What are you doing up at this time of the morning – or haven't you gone to bed yet?'

'Course I have,' Porky grunted. 'I'm not a bleedin' hedgehog.'

'I was just thinking about you.'

'And I can guess why.'

'Why?'

'I just had a call from the lovely Lara – what a pleasure to wake up to her dulcet tones.'

'Never mind the bloody poetry, Porky. What did she want?'

'She's had a call from your missus, asking her if she knows anyone who might pay good money for two hundred moleskins...'

'Blimey, I didn't think she was going to call Lara till seven!'

'But she's the best, your missus; she doesn't like to let the grass grow, especially when it comes to wrenching you out of the shite.'

'But why did Lara ring you?

'Because she knows I have access to quality couture production at *Bubble & Chic*, and she says if I get the right garments made and trimmed in this genuine mole fur, she knows someone who'll buy them – it's going to be all the rage this autumn, she says, and there'll be lots after it – especially from whoever's first past post.'

Reggie was almost weak with relief, and the excitement of crawling out from under the deal.

'So, when can I come and get them?' Porky was asking.

'Hang on Porky – I've got to get them skinned.'

'Reggie, it's the early bird that gets the worm, innit?'

'Don't talk to me about bloody worms!'

'What...'

'Don't ask; I'll tell you another time. And Porky, we got to agree a price.'

'Reggie! Me old cuz, blood is thicker than wonga!'

Emmet's mother, Maeve, like mothers everywhere, was always

ready to help a son out of trouble. She called in two old cronies to help her and commandeered the tack room in the stable block.

'Now, Emmet,' she ordered her son like a small boy. 'You get off into town and get me a sack of potato flour, some coarse salt and a big jar of what the chemists call aluminium sulphur, or somethin' like that – it's for to cure the skins nice and soft if it's for garments you want them.'

Reggie and the Hugginses carried the crates of deceased moles into the place where Maeve was going to skin and tan them. He watched for a few minutes as the three women slit the moles' bellies and pealed the loose skin off the tiny bodies.

'Cor, I can't handle this,' he muttered squeamishly.

On the way back to the house, he found Harry Huggins and told him to take the sack of dead worms from the back of the Bentley and get rid of them.

'I'll put 'em in the compost, shall I?'

Reggie thought for a moment. 'No 'Arry, I don't think so. You take them straight to the landfill, and make sure you wash your hands after.'

He could see Harry wanted to know why.

'Don't ask, Harry; it's a long story.'

Reggie carried on back to the house where he found Rosita in the kitchen, simultaneously talking to Lara on the phone and telling Sue what to do. She also found time to turn and greet her husband.

'Reggie, you go for sleep, but to the shower first – you stinks like a dead rat. Lara is bringing Porky tonight.'

It was a long time since Reggie had stayed up all night, and he was more than happy to lie in bed, feeling clean and listening through the open windows to the morning sounds in the garden he loved.

Untroubled for the first time in weeks, he was soon asleep and dreaming of riding his new horse across the hilltops, while Jason de Chateauneuf was being swallowed up in a bog of horse manure, with Lancelot Lydbury dancing a jig nearby.

He was woken by Rosita shaking his shoulder.

'OK, Reggie – you sleep enough. Some geezer comes, wants to talk about paintings.'

Reggie smiled; just the thought of his small stash of lovely big, handsomely framed canvases made him feel that the heavens were smiling on him.

'Bung him a cup of tea in the library and tell Harry Huggins to take all the pictures from the secret room up to the drawing room.'

'You sure? He look too rough; I chuck him out!'

'Here, Rosi, don't be a snob,' Reggie admonished gently. 'Some of the best punters come in the most unlikely guises.'

When Reggie saw this potential buyer, though, he thought his wife was right. The man had mean little eyes that wouldn't make contact with Reggie's; he was wearing a cheap suit that hung off him like a dishcloth, and he stood with one shoulder dropped, as if he were ready to take off at very short notice.

''Ello,' Reggie said cautiously. 'What can I do for you?'

'Morning, Mr Finchley. Sorry to pitch up without warning, but I heard you had a few nice pictures for sale and I was anxious to see them, if you haven't already shifted them.'

'How were they described to you?'

'Nineteenth century sporting scenes and horses, maybe one of the Herrings?'

'I don't know about Herrings. None of them's signed.' Reggie watched the man sharply as he went on. 'I showed 'em to a bloke, Marcus Dubarry-Ravenscroft, maybe you know him?' Reggie saw the man flinch infinitesimally as he shook his head. 'According to him, they were rubbish, Sextons – know what I mean? I don't think they'd be of any interest to a discerning punter such as yourself, Mr... errr?'

'Smith?' the man suggested. 'I'd still like to see them.'

Reggie shrugged an indifferent shoulder. 'I've got a few in the drawing-room.'

He led the man across the hall to the room where young Huggins had propped the paintings against the wall on pieces of furniture. As they walked in, Reggie noticed, 'Smith' was having trouble controlling his excitement. He stood for a minute or two in the middle of the room, gazing in turn at each of the eight large and impressive canvases.

'Oh, dear,' he said at last. 'You were right. I can see, just from here, they're all wrong. What a shame. But then, of course,' he went on quickly, 'I'm sure I could do *some*thing with them... at the right price?'

'Which is?' Reggie asked bluntly.

The punter sniffed and dithered while he decided where to pitch his offer. 'Well, I'd be paying more than I would in a sale, of course, but I could go to four or five hundred each? Say thee grand for the eight pictures?'

'No,' Reggie said drily. 'I don't think we'll say that – or anywhere near it.' He turned towards the door to show the man out.

'Hang on; I could go up...'

Reggie interrupted him with a cutting gesture. 'You've had your bid, Mr Smith. And you can tell Mr Dubarry-Ravenscroft that next time he sends someone out after cheap pictures, he should choose someone a little more... convincing. There's the door. Please don't come back.'

'But Mr Finchley...'

'Goodbye, Mr Smith,' Reggie said with a big phoney grin.

He walked back to the drawing room, now with a real smile on his face, and watched the man slink down the steps and get into an old Jaguar.

Rosita came bustling in. 'What horrible little man, eh?'

'Yeh, you were right. But that says to me these pictures are worth a bloody sight more than I thought. That Dubarry bloke must have thought he had a chance of getting his hands on these pictures for peanuts. He'd have clocked my car number and traced me through some bent individual in the DVLA and sent that little rodent round – what a plonker! You know what, my little muse, I reckon Mister bloody Jonty's really had it away. And I'll tell you what I'm going to do, I'm taking one into Lennon's. We might do better to sell them quietly out here, one by one. They'll put them up on their web-thingy, which brings in punters from all over. I've got a feeling in me water that there's a much healthier market than people like to admit for top quality Sexton Blakes.'

'Sex'n'blakes, again? What you are talking about?'

Reggie sighed, and placed a large hand gently on his wife's shapely behind. 'I'm going to have to send you off to English lessons, aren't I? But I can tell you, with Porky taking the moleskins off my hands, and these lovely pictures, things are seriously looking up. Ah,' he went on, looking out of the window again. 'Here's Emmet. Let's hope he's got all the doings for 'is Mum to turn those smelly little corpses into desirable ladies' wear trimmings.'

He went out to meet Emmet on the steps.

'Reggie – I got something to tell you.'

'Something good, by the look on your happy boat race.'

'Yeh. Yer man's been back to me. He said sorry about the feck-up in Wexford. We couldn't have handed over the merchandise, for sure, but they still want to go ahead. They'll take two hundred in a couple of months' time, ready for the next big golf tourney.'

'That's good is it, Emmet?'

'Listen, at least they're not coming looking for us, but they might, if we don't deliver next time.'

Reggie sighed. Happiness, he knew, never came completely un-alloyed.

Lara Lydbury's convertible DB5 roared up to the house in the late afternoon and delivered the unlikely combination of her and Porky Bacon.

'We come bearing gifts,' Lara called as she climbed out.

'Like a pair of bubbles,' said Porky, wielding a magnum of Dom Perignon.

On the terrace outside, Porky filled glasses from his bottle of champagne and Lara presented Reggie with a large envelope.

'What's that? A kite for the moleskins?'

'No, Porky's got readies for them.'

'Yeh, Reggie, as agreed, enough to cover your costs. Is that OK?'

'Course it is, Porky. At two o'clock this morning, when I saw every one of the poor little critters were goners, I thought I was facing a total write-off.'

'Glad to be of service, me old mate and cuz.'

'So, what's in the envelope?' Reggie asked Lara.

'It's a photocopy of what I found the night Chatternerve tried to romance me – the memo I found in his office. It'll come in very useful, though you won't need it for now. In fact, you may never need it because, for the time being at least, Chatternerve has backed off his plans to deface our beautiful hills with his ugly, fatuous wind farm. He was so humiliated in front of everyone and all his London 'chums' by everything that happened over the hunt ball weekend – ending up in the midden pit, the missing horse, the flung dung, even the fracas and the farce in the pub when he took me up Caractacus Mount – it must have totally put him off his game. Basically, he's withdrawn his planning application.'

'Fan*tas*tico,' Rosita crowed.

'And I think it's brilliant news, too!' chuckled Porky. 'I'm really beginning to appreciate all this rural idyll stuff.' He stood up. 'This calls for another bottle of the Dom; I'll fetch one from the motor.'

Reggie shook his head with pleasure. 'That is amazing! But what happened about that 'orse – the posh one he brought to ride in the midnight steeplechase? Emmet told me they took it off and had it dyed, so when the police came round, they never found it.

'Pa had it sent back,' Lara said.

'Why, because he felt sorry for him?'

'No, of course not,' Lara grinned. 'The trouble was Charlie Rafferty as usual overstepped the mark. Pa just told him to hide the horse for a while, to get Chatternerve's gander up for a bit, then Charlie goes off and dyes it, but of course he didn't even do that properly. They used some vegetable dye that's not too permanent, then they put the animal out in a field to graze with their carthorses. There was an almighty storm in the night, and it so happened that Chatternerve was prowling around next morning in his Range Rover and spotted a sort of ginger-bay striped horse, where the dye was washing off.'

'Chatternerve was banging on about what a good runner it was.' Reggie was already laughing. 'Autumn Leaves, Emmet said the hair dye was called. I suppose Chatternerve smelt a mighty rat?'

'Too right, he did. He rang Pa in a fury, and said he was sending the police round. But they'd already been on one wild goose so they didn't turn up until the next day. By then Pa had got the vet to slip the chip back in, they rinsed the rest of the Autumn Leaves off the horse and put it in one of Chatternerve's paddocks.'

'And the police didn't do anything?'

'Nothing. Jason couldn't even prove it had been taken.'

'That's brilliant, and it's great that he's given up on the windmills; so why are you giving this document you nicked to me?'

'Because Pa reckons Chatternerve will try again, once he's got over his embarrassment and regrouped. He thinks you'd be the best person to present it to the appropriate individual, when the time comes. But of course, it all depends on how thick-skinned Chatternerve is; maybe it'll never happen.'

Mr Russell was a fussy little man who'd been the picture specialist dealing in agricultural paintings at Lennon's salerooms for forty years. He was reputed to know more about pictures of Hereford bulls and Ryeland rams than anyone else in the Marches, and probably well beyond.

Reggie had wrapped the big painting of a country horse fair in the 1860s in brown paper, to protect it in transit and also to add to the drama of revealing it for the first time to this renowned expert.

When Reggie unveiled the picture, Mr Russell stood looking at it for several minutes before he walked up to it and turned it around to examine the back.

After a while he took a pace back. 'Look Mr Finchley. This is a fine picture; it's not absolutely top drawer; if it were it would be worth hundreds of thousands. Also, frankly, there are a few question marks over it. But it's very well executed and it's very desirable. What were you hoping it might fetch?'

Reggie composed himself. 'I was thinking of a reserve of around twenty thousand pounds,' he said.

'Hmm,' Mr Russell considered. 'Yes, I think that would be about right.'

Reggie drove back to Mortimer Towers through the heat of a July afternoon. He felt as buoyed as he'd ever been by the way things had turned around for him. That and his incurable optimism had led him to believe that if there had once been a studio, some thirty or so years before, where pictures were produced, painted and aged so well that most professionals were prepared to minimise any doubts over their authenticity, that studio, or somewhere very like it, could surely still be found.

'Rosi!' Reggie called as he opened the front door to his house. There was no reply. He walked round to the terrace behind the house which still lay in warm sunshine.

From the lake below it, he watched Rosita emerge, wearing her newest, smallest bikini. She was wet, tanned and tousled.

'My cup runneth over,' Reggie thought, as he broke into a trot down the slope of the freshly mown lawn until he reached his wife coming towards him. He lifted her off the ground, wet as she was, and swung her round a couple of times, before putting her back on her feet, leaning down and giving her an unequivocal kiss on her lips.

'Mrs ffinch-Leigh, I've got a new plan. How would you like a little holiday? We can have a look at Botty Whassername's *Venus*, we can stroll across *Ponte Vecchio*, we can have a look at that Michael Angelo's *David*...'

Rosita clapped her hands. 'Ohh! I *always* want to see him close up.'

'You don't want to look *too* close, my little flower. His head's too big, and his other bits are too small.'

'Of course,' Rosita said with a grin. 'He is a man!'

Reggie chuckled. 'That's my Rosi! Listen, you know you wanted me to deal in pictures – not 'orses – or moles, come to that? Well, we're going to go and buy a load of lovely old pictures and bring 'em back for me to sell. And while we're there, we'll have time for a bit of culture and romance.'

'Why, where we are going?' She gazed up at him with eyes wide and sparkling.

Reggie raised an affectionate brow.

'For Gawd's sake Rosi, where d'you think? We're going to Florence!'

The End